Bantam Books by Amanda Quick
Ask your bookseller for
the books you have missed

Mystique

Mystique

Amanda Quick

BANTAM BOOKS

NEW YORK   TORONTO   LONDON   SYDNEY   AUCKLAND

MYSTIQUE
A Bantam Book/July 1995

Book design by Donna Sinisgalli

Library of Congress Cataloging-in-Publication Data
Quick, Amanda.
    Mystique / Amanda Quick.
        p.   cm.
    ISBN 0-553-09698-2
    1. Great Britain—History—Norman period,
1066–1154—Fiction.
    I. Title.
    PS3561.R44M97   1995
    813'.54—dc20   95-2248
                                                     CIP

Published simultaneously in the United States and Canada

Bantam Books are published by Bantam Books, a division of Bantam Doubleday Dell Publishing Group, Inc. Its trademark, consist-
ing of the words "Bantam Books" and the portrayal of a rooster, is
Registered in U.S. Patent and Trademark Office and in other coun-
tries. Marca Registrada. Bantam Books, 1540 Broadway, New York,
New York 10036.

PRINTED IN THE UNITED STATES OF AMERICA
BVG   0   9   8   7   6   5   4   3   2   1

For my brother

James Castle

with love

Mystique

Chapter 1

Alice prided herself on being well schooled in logic and possessed of intelligence. She was a lady who had never put much credence in legends. But, then, she had never needed the assistance of one until quite recently.

Tonight she was very willing to believe in a legend, and as it happened, there was one seated at the head table in the hall of Lingwood Manor.

The dark knight known as Hugh the Relentless dined on leek pottage and pork sausage just as though he were an ordinary man. Alice supposed that even a legend had to eat.

She drew courage from that practical thought as she descended the tower stairs. She was dressed in her best gown for the momentous occasion. It was fashioned of dark green velvet and trimmed with silk ribbon. Her hair was bound in a fine net of gold threads that had belonged to her mother and secured with a delicate circlet of gold-colored metal. She wore a pair of soft green leather slippers on her feet.

Alice knew that she was as ready as she would ever be to greet a legend.

Nevertheless, the scene that she encountered at the bottom of the staircase gave her pause.

Hugh the Relentless might well dine in the manner of an ordinary man, but there the resemblance ceased. A small shiver that was part dread and part anticipation went through Alice. All legends were dangerous and Sir Hugh was no exception.

She paused on the last step, the skirts of her gown clutched in her hands, and gazed uneasily into the crowded hall. A sensation of unreality seized her. For a disquieting moment she wondered if she had stumbled into a sorcerer's workroom.

Although it was filled with people, an ominous stillness shrouded the chamber. The air was heavy, as though weighted with awful portent and somber warning. No one, not even a servant, moved.

The troubadour's harp had fallen silent. The dogs huddled together under the long tables, ignoring the bones that had been tossed down to them. The knights and men-at-arms who occupied the benches sat as though hewn from stone.

The flames on the central hearth lapped futilely at the shadows that seemed to seethe and roil in the chamber.

It was as if a spell had been cast over the once familiar hall, rendering it strange and unnatural. She ought not to have been surprised, Alice thought. Hugh the Relentless was reputed to be infinitely more fearsome than any magician.

This was the man, after all, who carried a sword said to be inscribed with the words *Bringer of Storms.*

Alice looked down the length of the hall, straight into Hugh's shadowed features, and knew three things with great certainty. The first was that the most dangerous tempests were those that raged inside this man, not those attributed to his blade. The second was that the bleak winds howling deep within him were contained and controlled by the force of an unyielding will and a steely determination.

The third thing she learned in a single glance was that Hugh knew how to use his legendary reputation to his own advantage. Ostensibly a guest, he nevertheless dominated the hall and everyone within it.

"You are Lady Alice?" Hugh spoke from the heart of the oppressive shadows. His voice sounded as though it came from the bottom of a very deep pool inside a very dark cave.

The rumors that had preceded him had not exaggerated. The dark knight was dressed entirely in unadorned, unembroidered, unrelenting black. Tunic, sword belt, boots—all were the color of a starless midnight.

"I am Alice, my lord." She deliberately sank into a very low, very deep curtsy on the assumption that good manners never hurt one's cause. When she raised her head she found Hugh watching her as though he were quite fascinated. "You sent for me, sir?"

"Aye, lady, I did. Pray, come closer so that we may speak." It was not a request. "I understand you have something in your possession that belongs to me."

This was the moment for which Alice had been waiting. She rose slowly from the graceful obeisance. She started forward between the rows of long dining tables, trying to recall everything she had learned about Hugh during the past three days.

Her information was scanty at best and based primarily on gossip and legend. She did not possess nearly enough knowledge to satisfy her. She wished she knew more because so much depended upon how she dealt with this mysterious man during the next few minutes.

But time had run out for her. She would have to make do with the bits and pieces of information she had managed to glean from the whispers that had swirled through the village and her uncle's hall.

The soft rustle of her skirts on the floor rushes and the crackle of the fire were the only sounds in the great chamber. An air of terror and excitement hung over the scene.

Alice glanced briefly at her uncle, Sir Ralf, who sat next to his dangerous guest. There was a sheen of sweat on Ralf's bald head. His plump figure, garbed in a pumpkin-colored tunic that had the unfortunate effect of emphasizing his gourd-shaped frame, was all but lost in the shadows that seemed to emanate from Hugh. One of Ralf's pudgy, beringed hands was clamped around a tankard of ale but he did not drink from the vessel.

Alice knew that for all his loud, blustering ways, tonight Ralf was anxious to the point of raw fear. Her burly cousins, Gervase and William, were equally alarmed. They sat stiffly at one of the lower tables, their eyes on Alice. She could feel their desperation and understood what inspired it. Facing them sat Hugh's grim-faced, battle-hardened men. The hilts of their swords gleamed in the firelight.

It was up to Alice to placate Hugh. Whether or not blood flowed tonight was in her hands.

All knew why Hugh the Relentless had come to Lingwood Hall. Only the occupants were aware that what he sought was not here. It was his probable reaction to that unhappy news that had everyone trembling at the knees.

It had been decided that it would be up to Alice to explain the situation to Hugh. For the past three days, ever since word had come that the grim knight was to be expected, Ralf had complained loudly to one and all that the impending disaster was entirely Alice's fault.

Ralf had insisted that she must bear the burden of attempting to convince Hugh that he should not wreak vengeance on the manor. Alice knew that her uncle was furious with her. She also knew that he was very frightened. He had good reason.

Lingwood Manor had a small, motley contingent of household knights and men-at-arms but they were farmers at heart, not warriors. They lacked experience and proper training. It was no secret that the manor could not possibly withstand an assault by the legendary Hugh the Relentless. He and his men would turn the entire place into a most unpleasant mincemeat pie in less time than it took to snap one's fingers.

No one thought it strange that Ralf expected his niece to assume the responsibility of soothing Hugh. Indeed, most would have thought it unusual if he had not done so. Everyone on the manor knew that Alice was not easily intimidated by anyone, not even by a legend.

At three and twenty years of age she was a woman with a mind of her own and she rarely hesitated to let others know it. Alice was well aware that her uncle grumbled about her decisive ways. She knew full well that he called her shrew behind her back, although not when he wanted one of her potions to ease his painful joints.

Alice considered herself resolute but she was no fool. She was aware of the dangers of the moment. But she also knew that a golden opportunity had arrived tonight along with Hugh. She must seize it or else she and her brother would be trapped forever here at Lingwood Manor.

She came to a halt in front of the head table and looked at the man who brooded in the hall's best carved oak chair. It was said that Hugh the Relentless was not the most comely of men in the best of light, but tonight the combination of flame and shadow rendered his features as forbidding as those of the devil himself.

His hair was darker than black chalcedony and brushed back from a peak above his forehead. His eyes, a strange shade of golden amber, were brilliant with a remorseless intelligence.

It was plain to see how he had won the appellation of *Relentless*. Alice knew at once that this man would stop at nothing to obtain what he wanted.

A chill went through her but her resolve did not waver.

"I was disappointed that you chose not to join us for the meal, Lady Alice," Hugh said slowly. "I am told that you supervised its preparation."

"Aye, my lord." She gave him her most winning smile. One of the small facts she had managed to discover about Hugh was that he valued well-prepared, finely seasoned dishes. She was confident that the food had been above reproach. "I trust you enjoyed it?"

"An interesting question." Hugh contemplated the matter for a moment as though it were a problem in philosophy or logic. "I found no fault with the flavor or with the variety of the dishes. I confess I have eaten my fill."

Alice's smile dimmed. His measured words and obvious lack of appreciation annoyed her. She had spent hours in the kitchens today overseeing the banquet preparations.

"I am pleased to hear that you could find no obvious fault with the dishes, my lord," she said. Out of the corner of her eye, she saw her uncle wince at her tart tone.

"Nay, there was nothing wrong with the meal," Hugh conceded. "But I must admit that one always wonders about the possibility of poison when one learns that the person who oversaw the preparation of the food elects not to eat it herself."

"*Poison.*" Alice was outraged.

"The very thought adds spice to a meal, does it not?"

Ralf flinched as though Hugh had just drawn his sword. A collective gasp of horror came from the nearby servants. The men-at-arms stirred uneasily on the benches. Some of the knights rested their hands on the hilts of their swords. Gervase and William looked as though they were about to be ill.

"Nay, my lord," Ralf babbled quickly, "I assure you, there is absolutely no cause to suspect my niece of having poisoned you. I swear, sir, on my honor, she would not do such a thing."

"As I am still sitting here, none the worse for having dined well, I am inclined to agree with you," Hugh said. "But you cannot blame me for being wary under the circumstances."

"And just what circumstances would those be, my lord?" Alice demanded.

She saw Ralf squeeze his eyes closed in despair as her tone went from tart to downright rude. It was not her fault that the conversation was not beginning on an auspicious note. Hugh the Relentless had injected the antagonistic element, not she.

Poison, indeed. As if she would even think of doing such a thing.

She would have considered using one of her mother's more noxious recipes only as a last resort and then only if her sources had informed her that Hugh was a stupid, cruel, brutish sort who lacked intelligence. And even under those conditions, she thought, growing more irate by the moment, she would not have set out to kill him.

She would merely have used some harmless concoction that would have rendered him and his men so sleepy or so nauseated that they would have been unable to murder the household in cold blood.

Hugh studied Alice. And then, as though he had read her thoughts, his hard mouth curved faintly at one corner. The smile contained no hint of warmth, merely an icy amusement.

"Do you blame me for being cautious, lady? I have recently learned that you are a student of the ancient texts. 'Tis well known that the ancients were very adept with poisons. In addition, I hear that your own mother was an expert with strange and unusual herbs."

"How dare you, sir?" Alice was furious now. All thought of handling this man with care and circumspection had flown out the window. "I am a scholar, not a poisoner. I study matters of natural philosophy, not the dark arts. My mother was, indeed, an expert herbalist and a great healer. But she would never have used her skills to hurt anyone."

"I am, of course, relieved to learn that."

"I have no interest in murdering people, either," Alice continued rashly. "Not even rude, ungrateful guests, such as you, my lord."

Ralf's ale mug jerked in his hand. "Alice, for the love of God, be silent."

Alice ignored him. She narrowed her eyes at Hugh. "Be assured that I have never killed anyone in my life, sir. And that, moreover, is a claim that you, I'll wager, cannot make for yourself."

The dreadful stillness that overlaid the crowd was broken by choked-off exclamations of horror from several of the listeners. Ralf moaned and dropped his head into his hands. Gervase and William looked stupefied.

Hugh was the only one in the hall who appeared unperturbed. He gazed at Alice with a thoughtful expression. "I fear you are correct, lady," he said very softly. "I cannot make such a claim."

The shocking simplicity of the admission had the same effect on Alice as running straight into a brick wall. She came to an abrupt halt.

She blinked and recovered her balance. "Aye, well, there you are, then."

Hugh's amber eyes lit with brilliant curiosity. "Where, precisely, are we, madam?"

Ralf valiantly attempted to stop the downward spiral of the conversation. He raised his head, wiped his forehead on the sleeve of his tunic, and looked at Hugh with a pleading expression. "Sir, I pray you will understand that my foolish niece meant no offense."

Hugh's expression was doubtful. "Nay?"

"Of course not," Ralf sputtered. "There is no call to be

suspicious of her merely because she did not choose to dine with us. In truth, Alice never dines here in the main hall with the rest of the household."

"Strange," Hugh murmured.

Alice tapped the toe of her slipper. "We are wasting time, my lords."

Hugh glanced at Ralf.

"She claims that she, uh, prefers the solitude of her own chambers," Ralf explained hurriedly.

"And why is that?" Hugh returned his attention to Alice.

Ralf grunted. "She says she finds the level of the, uh, *intellectual discourse,* as she terms it, here in this hall too low for her taste."

"I see," Hugh said.

Ralf shot Alice a belligerent glare as he warmed to an old and familiar complaint. "Apparently the mealtime conversation of honest, stout-hearted men-at-arms is not sufficiently elevated to suit my lady's high standards."

Hugh's brows rose. "What is this? Lady Alice does not care to hear the details of a man's morning practice at the quintain or learn of his success in the hunt?"

Ralf sighed. "Nay, my lord, I regret to say that she shows no interest in such matters. My niece is a perfect example of the foolishness of educating females, if you ask me. Makes them headstrong. Causes them to believe that they should wear the braies. Worst of all, it breeds ingratitude and disrespect for the poor, hapless men who are charged with their protection and whose sad lot it is to have to feed and shelter them."

Goaded, Alice gave Ralf a fulminating glance. "That is nonsense, Uncle. You know perfectly well that I have been suitably grateful for the protection that you have extended to me and my brother. Where would we be without you?"

Ralf flushed. "Now, see here, Alice, that is quite enough out of you."

"I'll tell you where Benedict and I would be if it had not been for your generous protection. We would be sitting in our own hall, dining at our own table."

"Blood of the Saints, Alice. Have you gone mad?" Ralf stared at her in mounting horror. "This is no time to bring up that matter."

"Very well." She smiled grimly. "Let us change the topic. Would you prefer to discuss how you managed to spend what little of my inheritance I managed to preserve after you gave my father's manor to your son?"

"Damnation, woman, you are not exactly inexpensive in your habits." Ralf's anxiety about Hugh's presence gave way briefly before the long list of grievances he felt toward Alice. "That last book you insisted I purchase for you cost more than a good hound."

"It was a very important lapidary written by Bishop Marbode of Rennes," Alice retorted. "Indeed, it sets out all the properties of gems and stones and it was a wonderful bargain."

"Is that so?" Ralf snarled. "Well, let me tell you how that money could have been better spent."

"*Enough.*" Hugh reached for his wine cup with one large, well-shaped hand.

The movement was a small one, but coming as it did from the depths of the vast pool of stillness that enveloped Hugh, it startled Alice. She took an involuntary step back.

Ralf quickly swallowed whatever further accusations he had intended to make against her.

Alice flushed, annoyed and embarrassed by the stupid argument. As if there were not more important matters at hand, she thought. Her fiery temper was the bane of her existence.

She wondered briefly and with some envy how Hugh had achieved such great mastery over his own temper. For there was no doubt he kept it in an iron grip. It was one of the things that made him so dangerous.

Hugh's eyes reflected the flames on the hearth as he contemplated her. "Let us dispense with what is obviously a long-standing family quarrel. I do not have the time or the patience to settle it. Do you know why I have come here tonight, Lady Alice?"

"Aye, my lord." Alice decided there was no point in dancing around the subject. "You seek the green stone."

"I have been on the trail of that damned crystal for more than a sennight, lady. In Clydemere I learned that it had been purchased by a young knight from Lingwood Hall."

"As a matter of fact, it was, my lord," Alice said briskly. She was as eager to get down to business as he.

"For you?"

"That is correct. My cousin Gervase discovered it for sale by a peddler at the Summer Fair in Clydemere." Alice saw Gervase start visibly at the mention of his name. "He knew I would find the stone extremely interesting and he very kindly procured it for me."

"Did he tell you that the peddler was later found with his throat slit?" Hugh asked very casually.

Alice's mouth went dry. "Nay, he did not, my lord. Obviously Gervase was not aware of the tragedy."

"So it would seem." Hugh glanced at Gervase with predatory interest.

Gervase's mouth opened and closed twice before he managed to find his tongue. "I swear I did not realize that the crystal was dangerous, sir. It was not very expensive and I thought it would amuse Alice. She is very fond of unusual stones and such."

"There is nothing particularly amusing about the green crystal." Hugh leaned forward just far enough to alter the pattern of light and shadows on his harsh features. His face became more demonic. "In truth, the longer I chase it, the less amused I am by it."

Alice frowned as a thought occurred to her. "Are you quite certain that the death of the peddler was linked to the crystal, my lord?"

Hugh looked at her as if she had just asked if the sun would likely rise on the morrow. "Do you doubt my word?"

"Nay, of course not." Alice stifled a small, inward groan. Men were so ridiculously touchy about their powers of logic. " 'Tis merely that I do not see any connection between the green stone and the murder of a peddler."

"Is that so?"

"Aye. The green stone is not particularly attractive or valuable so far as I could discern. Indeed, it is rather ugly as crystals go."

"Your expert opinion, is, of course, appreciated."

Alice paid no attention to the sarcasm in his words. Her mind was leaping forward, pursuing the logic of the interesting problem. "I will concede that a vicious robber might have killed to obtain the stone if he was under the mistaken impression that it had value. But in truth, it was quite cheap, else Gervase would never have bought it. And why would anyone murder the poor peddler after he had already sold the crystal? It makes no sense."

"Murder is eminently logical in such a situation if one is attempting to cover a trail," Hugh said, far too gently. "I promise you that men have killed and been killed for far less reason."

"Aye, mayhap." Alice braced her elbow on her hand and tapped her fingertip against her jaw. "By the eyes of the Saints, I vow that men are certainly extremely keen on doing a great deal of stupid, unnecessary violence."

"It does happen," Hugh conceded.

"Nevertheless, unless you have some objective evidence that indicates a clear connection between the murder of the peddler and the green crystal, sir, I do not see how you can conclude with any certainty that there is a link." She nodded once, satisfied with her own reasoning. "The peddler might very well have been killed for some other, unrelated reason."

Hugh said nothing. He regarded her with a chilling curiosity, as if she were some strange, heretofore unknown creature that had materialized in front of him. For the first time, he appeared somewhat bemused, as though he did not know quite what to make of her.

Ralf groaned in obvious misery. "Alice, in the name of the Rood, pray do not argue with Sir Hugh. This is no time to practice your skills in rhetoric and debate."

Alice took umbrage at the grossly unfair accusation. "I am not being ill-mannered, Uncle. I am merely attempting to point out to Sir Hugh that one cannot deduce something as serious as a motive for murder without solid evidence."

"You must take my word on this matter, Lady Alice," Hugh said. "The peddler is dead because of that damned crystal. I think we can both agree that it would be best if no one else died because of it, can we not?"

"Aye, my lord. I trust you do not think me lacking in proper manners, 'tis merely that I question—"

"Everything, apparently," he finished flatly.

She scowled at him. "My lord?"

"You appear to question everything, Lady Alice. At another time I might find the habit mildly entertaining but tonight I am in no mood for such distraction. I am here for only one purpose. I want the green crystal."

Alice steeled herself. "I mean no offense, my lord, but I would like to point out that my cousin purchased that stone for me. In actual fact it is now my property."

"Damnation, Alice," Ralf wailed.

"For God's sake, Alice, must you quarrel with him?" Gervase hissed.

"We are doomed," William muttered.

Hugh ignored them all, his full attention on Alice. "The green crystal is the last of the Stones of Scarcliffe, lady. I am the new lord of Scarcliffe. The crystal belongs to me."

Alice cleared her throat and chose her words cautiously. "I realize that the stone may have once belonged to you, my lord. But I believe one could argue that, strictly speaking, it is no longer yours."

"Is that so? Are you trained in the law as well as in matters of natural philosophy, then?"

She glared at him. "That stone was procured by Gervase in a perfectly legal transaction. It was then passed on to me as a gift. I do not see how you can possibly lay claim to it."

The unnatural silence that gripped the chamber was shattered by another collective intake of breath. Somewhere a tankard crashed to the floor. The harsh clang of metal on stone echoed through the hall. A dog whined.

Ralf made a small, croaking noise. He stared at Alice with bulging eyes. "Alice, what do you think you are doing?"

"Merely establishing my claim to the green crystal, Uncle." Alice met Hugh's eyes. "I have heard it said that Hugh the Relentless is a hard man, but a just and honorable one. Is that not true, my lord?"

"Hugh the Relentless," Hugh said in ominous tones, "is a man who knows how to hold on to that which is his. Be assured, lady, that I consider the stone mine."

"Sir, that crystal is very important to my investigations. I am presently studying various stones and their properties and I find the green crystal most interesting."

"I believe you described it as ugly."

"Aye, my lord. But it has been my experience that objects that lack superficial charm and attraction often conceal secrets of great intellectual interest."

"Does your theory apply to people as well?"

She was confused. "My lord?"

"Few would call me charming or attractive, madam. I merely wondered if you found me interesting."

"Oh."

"In an intellectual sense, that is."

Alice touched the tip of her tongue to her lips. "Ah, well, as to that, aye, my lord, one could certainly describe you as interesting. Most assuredly." Fascinating would be a more accurate description, she thought.

"I'm flattered. You will no doubt be even more *interested* to know that I did not come by my name by accident. I am called Relentless because of my habit of always pursuing a quest until I am successful."

"I do not doubt that for a moment, sir, but I really cannot allow you to claim my green stone." Alice smiled brightly. "Mayhap in the future I could loan it to you."

"Go and fetch the stone," Hugh said in a terrifyingly calm voice. "Now."

"My lord, you do not comprehend."

"Nay, lady, 'tis you who do not comprehend. I am done with this game you seem to delight in playing. Bring the stone to me now or suffer the consequences."

"Alice," Ralf shrieked. "Do something."

"Aye," Hugh said. "Do something, Lady Alice. Bring the green crystal to me at once."

Alice drew herself up and prepared to deliver the bad news. "I fear I cannot do that, my lord."

"Cannot or will not?" Hugh asked softly.

Alice shrugged. "Cannot. You see, I have recently suffered the same fate as yourself."

"What in the name of the devil are you talking about now?" Hugh asked.

"The green crystal was stolen from me only a few days ago, my lord."

"God's teeth," Hugh whispered. "If you seek to provoke

me to anger with a maze of falsehoods and misleading words, you are close to success, madam. I warn you, however, that you may not care for the result."

"Nay, my lord," Alice said hastily. "I speak the plain truth. The stone disappeared from my workroom less than a sennight past."

Hugh shot a cold, questioning glance at Ralf, who nodded morosely. Hugh switched his disturbing gaze back to Alice, pinning her ruthlessly with it.

"If this is a true fact," he said icily, "why was I not informed of it at once when I arrived here this evening?"

Alice cleared her throat again. "It was my uncle's opinion that, as the stone is my property, I should be the one to tell you of its loss."

"And present your claim to it at the same time?" Hugh's smile bore a strong resemblance to the edge of a finely crafted sword blade.

There was no point in denying the obvious. "Aye, my lord."

"I'll wager that it was your decision to delay informing me of the loss of the stone until after I had dined well," Hugh murmured.

"Aye, my lord. My mother always claimed men were more reasonable after a good meal. Now, then, I am pleased to be able to tell you that I have a plan to recover the stone."

Hugh did not appear to have heard her. Instead he seemed lost in some private musings. "I do not believe I have ever encountered a woman such as yourself, Lady Alice."

She was momentarily distracted. A glow of unexpected pleasure warmed her insides. "Do you find me interesting, my lord?" She hardly dared add the rest. "In an intellectual sense?"

"Aye, madam. Most interesting."

Alice blushed. She had never had a man pay her such a compliment. She had never had a man pay her *any* compliment. It gave her a thrilling feeling of excitement. The fact that Hugh found her as interesting as she found him was almost overwhelming. She forced herself to set the unfamiliar sensation aside and return to practical matters.

"Thank you, my lord," she said with what she felt was commendable composure under the circumstances. "Now, as I was saying, when I learned that you were to pay us a visit, I conceived a scheme whereby we might recover the crystal together."

Ralf stared at her. "Alice, what are you talking about?"

"I shall explain everything soon enough, Uncle." Alice beamed at Hugh. "I'm sure you'll be interested to hear the details, my lord."

"A few, very few, men have, at various times in the past, attempted to deceive me," Hugh said.

Alice frowned. "Deceive you, my lord? No one here attempted to deceive you."

"Those men are now dead."

"Sir, I believe we should return to the subject at hand," Alice said crisply. "Now, as we both have an interest in the green stone, the logical thing to do is to join forces."

"There have also, I regret to say, been one or two women who played dangerous games with me." Hugh paused. "But I doubt that you would wish to learn of their fates."

"My lord, we digress from the topic."

Hugh stroked the stem of his wine goblet. "But now that I think back on those few females who tried my patience with silly games, I believe I can say with some certainty that they were not at all similar to yourself."

"Of course not." Alice began to grow annoyed again. "I am not playing a game with you, sir. Just the opposite. It is to our mutual advantage to combine my wits with your knightly skills so that we may recover the stone together."

"That would be difficult to do, Lady Alice, given that I have seen no evidence that you possess any wits." Hugh turned the goblet between his fingers. "At least none that have not been addled."

Alice was incensed. "My lord, you insult me most grievously."

"Alice, you will be the death of us all," Ralf whispered in despair.

Hugh paid his host no heed. He continued to study Alice. "I do not insult you, lady, I merely point out an indisputable fact. Your wits must have flown if you believe that you can toy with me in this manner. A truly clever woman would have realized long ago that she trod on very thin ice."

"My lord, I have had enough of this nonsense," Alice said.

"So have I."

"Do you wish to be reasonable and listen to my plan or not?"

"Where is the green stone?"

Alice reached the end of her patience. "I told you, it was stolen," she said very loudly. "I believe I know the identity of the thief and I am willing to help you discover his whereabouts. In return, I wish to strike a bargain with you."

"A bargain? With me?" Hugh's eyes held infinite danger. "Surely you jest, lady."

"Nay, I am quite serious."

"I do not think you would like the terms of any bargain you might strike with me."

Alice considered him warily. "Why not? What would your terms involve?"

"Your very soul, most likely," Hugh said.

Chapter 2

"You have the look of an alchemist gazing into his crucible, my lord." Dunstan indulged in his old habit of spitting over the edge of the nearest obstacle. In this instance it was the old wall that surrounded the bailey of Lingwood Manor. "I like it not. In my experience the expression bodes ill for my aging bones."

"Your bones have survived worse than an unpleasant frown or two." Hugh rested his forearms on the top of the wall and gazed out over the dawn-lit landscape.

He had risen half an hour ago, prodded from sleep by a familiar restlessness. He knew the mood well. The storms that abided deep within him were stirring. They shifted and swirled in new patterns. It was always like this on those occasions when his life was about to take a new turn.

The first time Hugh had experienced the sensation had been when he was eight years old. That was the day he had been summoned to his grandfather's deathbed and told that he was to be sent to live in the keep of Erasmus of Thornewood.

"Sir Erasmus is my liege lord." Thomas's pale eyes had

burned in his thin, haggard face. "He has agreed to take you into his household. He will see that you are raised and trained as a knight. Do you understand?"

"Aye, Grandfather." Hugh had stood, subdued and anxious, by the side of the bed. He had stared in silent awe at his grandfather, unable to believe that this frail old man who lay at death's door was the same fierce, embittered knight who had raised him since the death of his parents.

"Erasmus is young, but strong. A fine, skilled warrior. He went on Crusade two years ago. Now he has returned with much glory and wealth." Thomas had paused, his words briefly severed by another racking cough. "He will teach you the things you will need to know in order to achieve our vengeance against the house of Rivenhall. Do you comprehend me, boy?"

"Aye, Grandfather."

"Study well. Learn all that you can while you are in Erasmus's care. When you become a man, you will know what to do and how to do it. Remember everything that I have told you about the past."

"I will remember, Grandfather."

"Whatever happens, you must do your duty by your mother's memory. You are the only one left, boy. The last of your line, even though you were born a bastard."

"I understand."

"You must not rest until you have found a way to wreak vengeance upon that house from whence sprang the viper who seduced my innocent Margaret."

To young Hugh, it had not seemed altogether right to seek vengeance on his father's house, in spite of what he had been taught about the evil nature of the Rivenhall clan. His father, after all, was dead, just as his mother was. Surely justice had been done.

But that justice had not satisfied Hugh's grandfather. Nothing could satisfy Sir Thomas.

Eight-year-old Hugh had dutifully brushed aside his moment of uncertainty. Honor was at stake and nothing was
more important than his honor and that of his grandfather.
That much he fully comprehended. He had been steeped in
the importance of honor since the moment of his birth. It was
all a bastard had, as Sir Thomas had frequently pointed out.

"I will not rest, Grandfather," Hugh had promised with
the fervent intensity only a boy of eight could muster.

"See that you don't. Never forget, honor and vengeance
are all."

Hugh had not been surprised when his grandfather had
died with no words of love or a farewell blessing for his only
grandchild. There had never been much in the way of affection
or warmth from Thomas. The brooding anger that had resulted
from the untimely seduction, betrayal, and death of his beloved
daughter had tainted all of the old man's emotions.

It was not that Thomas had not cared for his grandson.
Hugh had always known that he was vitally important to his
grandfather, but only because he was Thomas's sole means of
vengeance.

Thomas had died with his daughter's name on his parched
lips. "Margaret. My beautiful Margaret. Your bastard son will
avenge you."

Fortunately for Margaret's bastard son, Erasmus of
Thornewood had made up for much of what Thomas had
been unable to give Hugh. Perceptive, intelligent, and possessed of a gruff kindness, Erasmus had been in his early twen-
ties when Hugh had gone to live with him. Fresh from his
triumphs in the Holy Lands, he had played the part of father
in Hugh's life. As a boy, Hugh had given his mentor his
respect and youthful admiration.

As a man, Hugh now gave his liege lord absolute and
unswerving loyalty. It was a rare and much-prized spice in the
world in which Erasmus moved.

Dunstan wrapped the edges of his gray wool cloak more

securely around his stocky frame and studied Hugh out of the corner of his eye. Hugh knew what he was thinking. Dunstan did not approve of this business of chasing after the green crystal. He considered it a waste of time.

Hugh had tried to explain that it was not the crystal itself that was valuable, rather what it represented. It was the surest way to secure his grip on Scarcliffe. But Dunstan was impatient with such notions. In his opinion good steel and a stout band of men-at-arms were the keys to holding Scarcliffe.

He was fifteen years Hugh's senior, a battle-scarred veteran of the same Crusade that Erasmus had taken. His tough, weathered features reflected the harshness of that time. Unlike Erasmus, Dunstan had returned from the quest with neither glory nor gold to show for his troubles.

Dunstan's skills as a warrior had been useful to Erasmus but everyone, most especially Erasmus, knew that it was Hugh's uncanny ability to plot stratagems that had made Erasmus a quietly powerful man. Erasmus had recently rewarded his loyal man with Scarcliffe, a manor that had at one time belonged to Hugh's mother's family. Dunstan had chosen to go with Hugh to his new estate.

"No offense, Hugh, but your frowns are not as other men's scowls." Dunstan grinned briefly, exposing the gaps between his stained teeth. "They convey a remarkably oppressive air of doom. Even I am struck by it on occasion. Mayhap you have perfected your legend as a dark and dangerous knight a bit too well."

"You are wrong." Hugh smiled faintly. "I have obviously not perfected my legend well enough if I am to judge by Lady Alice's reaction last night."

"Aye." Dunstan's expression turned glum. "She certainly did not shrink and cower as she ought to have done. Mayhap the lady does not have very keen eyesight."

"She was too busy attempting to bargain with me to notice that my patience was stretched thin."

Dunstan's mouth curved sourly. "I vow, that particular lady would not back down from the devil himself."

"A most unusual female."

"It has been my experience that women with red hair are invariably trouble. I met a red-haired wench once in a London tavern. She plied me with ale until I fell into her bed. When I awoke both she and my purse were gone."

"I'll try to remember to keep an eye on my money."

"See that you do."

Hugh smiled but said nothing. They both knew that watching over his money and accounts would pose no undue hardship. Hugh had a talent for business affairs. Few of his acquaintances could be bothered with such mundane matters. They spent lavishly and depended upon the usual sources— ransoms, jousts, and, for those fortunate enough to possess land, income from poorly managed estates—to replenish their treasuries. Hugh preferred a more certain approach to securing his income.

Dunstan shook his head sadly. " 'Tis a pity that the trail of the green crystal has led to one such as this Lady Alice. No good will come of it."

"I'll grant that matters might have been simpler if she were more easily intimidated, but I am not yet certain that this is an unfortunate twist of events," Hugh said slowly. "I have been thinking on this for the better part of the night. I see possibilities here, Dunstan. Interesting possibilities."

"Then we are likely doomed," Dunstan said philosophically. "Trouble always finds us when you do too much thinking on a problem."

"You will note that her eyes are green."

"Are they?" Dunstan scowled. "I cannot say that I happened to notice the color of her eyes. The red hair seemed an ill enough omen to me."

"A very distinctive shade of green."

"Like those of a cat, do you mean?"

"Or those of a fey, elfin princess."

"Worse and worse. Elves practice a very slippery sort of magic." Dunstan grimaced. "I do not envy you having to deal with a flame-haired, green-eyed little shrew."

"As it happens, I have recently discovered that I like red hair and green eyes."

"Bah. You've always preferred dark-haired, dark-eyed women. Lady Alice is not even particularly beautiful, in my opinion. You're taken with her rare boldness, that's all. You're amused by the courage she showed in challenging you."

Hugh shrugged.

" 'Tis nothing more than a passing novelty, my lord," Dunstan assured him. " 'Twill soon pass, just as does the sore head one gets from drinking too much wine."

"She knows how to manage a household," Hugh continued thoughtfully. "That banquet she arranged last night would have done credit to a great baron's wife. It could have been served in any noble hall. I have need of someone who can organize a household with such skill."

Dunstan began to look alarmed. "What the devil are you saying? Think of her tongue, my lord. 'Twas as sharp as my dagger."

"Her manners, when she chose to display them, were those of a great lady. Seldom have I witnessed a more graceful curtsy. A man would be proud to have her entertain his guests."

"From what I saw last night and from all the gossip I have heard since we got here, I have the impression that she does not choose to display those pretty manners very often," Dunstan said quickly.

"She is old enough to know what she is doing. I am not dealing with some dewy-eyed innocent who must be protected and cosseted."

Dunstan's head snapped around, his eyes widening in surprise. "By Saint Osyth's teeth, you cannot be serious."

"Why not? After I recover the green crystal, I am going to be extremely busy. There is a great deal of work to be done on Scarcliffe. Not only must I see to the problems of my new lands, but the old keep must be set to rights."

"Nay, my lord." Dunstan looked as though he were strangling on a bite of meat pie. "If you are about to suggest what I think you are about to suggest, I beg you to reconsider."

"She is obviously well trained in the art of household management. You know that I have always abided by the basic principle that it pays to employ skilled experts, Dunstan."

"That principle may have served you well when it came to selecting stewards, blacksmiths, and weavers, my lord, but you are talking about a *wife* here."

"So? Blood of the devil, Dunstan, I'm a knight by trade. I do not have any notion of how to organize a household and neither do you. I have never even stepped foot inside a kitchen. I am not entirely certain what goes on in such a place."

"What has that got to do with anything?"

"A great deal, if I am to eat well. And I do enjoy good food."

"Aye, that's a fact. No offense, sir, but to my mind you're too choosy by far when it comes to your fodder. Don't know why you cannot be satisfied with plain roast mutton and good ale."

"Because a diet of roast mutton and ale grows boring after a time," Hugh said impatiently. "In addition to the business of good meals, there are other matters of import involved in a household. A thousand of them. Halls and chambers must be cleaned. Garderobes must be washed. Bedding must be aired. Servants must be supervised. And how does one go about getting a fine, fresh scent in one's clothing?"

"I am seldom concerned with that particular problem, myself."

Hugh ignored him. "In short, I want Scarcliffe Keep to be

properly managed and that means I require an expert, just as I do in my various business affairs. I require a lady who has been properly trained to manage a large household."

A vision of his future danced before Hugh's eyes. He wanted a comfortable hall of his own. He wanted to be able to sit at the head table under his own canopy and dine on well-seasoned dishes. He wanted to sleep in clean sheets and bathe in scented water. Most of all, he wished to entertain his liege lord, Erasmus of Thornewood, in a manner befitting his station.

That last thought dimmed the luster of the vision. Erasmus had not looked at all well six weeks ago when Hugh had been summoned into his audience chamber to receive the fief of Scarcliffe. It was clear that Erasmus had lost weight. There was a tense, pinched look about his features and a melancholic expression in his eyes. Erasmus had started at every small sound. Hugh had been greatly alarmed. He had asked Erasmus if he was ill. Erasmus had refused to discuss the subject.

On his way out of Erasmus's keep, Hugh had heard the rumors. He learned that doctors had been summoned and had left muttering about an illness of the pulse and heart. Hugh had no faith in doctors, but in this instance he was worried.

"My lord, I am certain that you can find another lady far more suited to the task of being your wife than this one," Dunstan said desperately.

"Mayhap, but I do not have the time to spare to search for her. I will not have an opportunity to hunt for another wife until next spring. I do not wish to make camp in Scarcliffe Keep in its present condition for the entire winter. I want a proper hall."

"Aye, but—"

" 'Twill be so efficient and convenient, Dunstan. Think of it. I have explained to you that recovering the crystal will go a long way toward reassuring the people of Scarcliffe that I am their rightful lord. Pray consider how much more I might impress them if I actually return to my new lands with a wife."

"Only think of what you are saying, my lord."

Hugh smiled with satisfaction. " 'Twill win them all to me for certain. They will see at once that I plan a future among them. 'Twill give them confidence in their own future. 'Tis their hearts and their confidence I must have if I am to make Scarcliffe plump and prosperous, Dunstan."

"I'll not deny it, but you would do well to find some other female. I do not like the look of this one and that is the honest truth."

"I will admit that, at first glance, Lady Alice does not appear to be the most amenable and tractable of females."

"I am pleased that you noticed that much," Dunstan muttered.

"Nevertheless," Hugh continued, "she possesses intelligence and she is well past that frivolous stage that seems to overtake all young ladies."

"Aye, and she is no doubt well past a few other things also."

Hugh narrowed his eyes. "Are you implying that she is no longer a virgin?"

"I would only remind you that Lady Alice is of a decidedly bold nature," Dunstan mumbled. "Not exactly the shy, blushing, unopened rosebud, my lord."

"Aye." Hugh frowned.

"Red hair and green eyes indicate strong passions, sir. You witnessed her temper last night. She has no doubt indulged other strong emotions from time to time. She is three and twenty, after all."

"Hmm." Hugh considered Dunstan's words. "She is clearly of an intellectual nature. No doubt she has known some curiosity about such matters. She would have been discreet, however."

"One can only hope."

Hugh shook off any reservations Dunstan had given him. "I feel certain that she and I will deal well enough together."

Dunstan groaned. "What in the name of the devil gives you that impression?"

"I told you, she is an intelligent woman."

"A surplus of intelligence and learning only serves to make females more difficult, if you ask me."

"I believe she and I can come to terms," Hugh said. "Being intelligent, she will learn quickly."

"And, pray, just what will she learn?" Dunstan demanded.

"That I possess some wit myself." Hugh smiled fleetingly. "And doubtless a good deal more will and determination than she can possibly command."

"If you would deal with Lady Alice, I'd advise you first to demonstrate to her that you are vastly more dangerous than she presently believes you to be."

"I shall use whatever stratagem seems most appropriate."

"I do not like this, my lord."

"I am aware of that."

Dunstan spat over the edge of the wall again. "I can see there is no point trying to reason with you. This business of securing your new lands is turning out to be somewhat more difficult than you had anticipated, is it not?"

"Aye," Hugh agreed. "But that state of affairs seems to be my lot in life. I have grown accustomed to it."

"True enough. Nothing seems to come easy, does it? You'd think the Saints would take pity on us once in a while."

"I will do whatever I must to hold on to Scarcliffe, Dunstan."

"I do not doubt that. All I ask, my lord, is that you use some caution in your dealings with Lady Alice. Something tells me that even the stoutest of knights could easily come to a bad end around her."

Hugh nodded to indicate that he had taken heed of the

warning but he silently consigned it to the nether regions. This morning he would strike his bargain with the mysterious and unpredictable Lady Alice. He fully intended that the lady, for all her clever ways and proud airs, would discover that she had gotten more than she had expected.

Last night, sensing that he might be up against a more wily adversary than he had first anticipated, Hugh had announced to the crowded hall that he did not do business in public. He had told Alice that he would discuss the bargain alone with her today.

In truth he had postponed the negotiations because he had wanted time to contemplate this new knot in what had become an exceedingly tangled skein.

Hugh reflected that he had received several dire warnings during the course of this venture. But no one had warned him about Alice.

The first clue to her nature had come early in the evening when her uncle had heaved a long-suffering sigh at the mention of her name. The lady, it seemed, was a great trial to Ralf.

Based on what little he had learned, Hugh had expected to find himself dealing with a bitter, petulant spinster possessed of a tongue that could flay a man alive. The only part of the description that proved to be accurate was the bit about her tongue. It was clear that Alice did not hesitate to speak her mind.

Her bold speech aside, the woman who had confronted him in the hall last night had been quite different from the one Ralf had described.

Alice was not bitter, Hugh realized at once. She was determined. He recognized the difference immediately. She was not petulant, she was strong-minded and no doubt a good deal more intelligent than those around her. A difficult woman, mayhap, but definitely an interesting one.

From Ralf's description of his niece, Hugh had expected to

find himself confronting a towering creature constructed along the same lines as his war-horse.

He had been in for a surprise.

Lady Alice was very slender and elegantly graceful. There was naught about her to remind him of his war-horse. Her long green gown had skimmed the curves of her supple body, hinting at breasts the size of ripe peaches, a tiny waist, and lushly rounded hips.

Dunstan was correct on one count, Hugh acknowledged. There was certainly sufficient fire in Alice to burn any man and it started with her hair. The flame-colored tresses had been bound in a sparkling gold net that had gleamed in the glow of the hearth.

Her face was fine-boned with a firm nose, a forceful little jaw, and an expressive mouth. Her eyes were huge. They tilted slightly upward at the corners. Delicate red brows arched provocatively above them. Pride and spirit were evident in the set of her shoulders and the angle of her chin. She was a woman who drew a man's gaze not because she was beautiful, although she was far from plain, but because she compelled attention.

Alice was not a woman to be ignored.

If she was embittered at finding herself unwed at the age of three and twenty as Ralf had indicated, Hugh saw no evidence of it. Indeed, he had a strong suspicion that she enjoyed not having to answer to a husband, a fact that might pose a small problem for him. But Hugh considered himself adept at solving problems.

"Lady Alice wishes to bargain with you," Dunstan said. "What do you think she seeks in exchange for helping you find the green stone?"

"Mayhap some books," Hugh said absently. "According to her uncle, she is very fond of them."

Dunstan grunted. "Will you give her one or two of yours, then?"

Hugh smiled. "I may allow her to borrow them from time to time."

He returned to his contemplation of the morning. The air was crisp. The farms and fields of Lingwood Manor lay quiet and still beneath a leaden sky. It was early fall. The harvest was partially complete and much of the land lay stripped and bare, awaiting the fast-approaching chill of winter. He wanted to get home to Scarcliffe as quickly as possible. There was so much to be done.

Lady Alice was the key. Hugh could feel it in his bones. With her, he could find the damned green stone and unlock his future. He had come too far, waited too long, hungered too deeply, to stop now.

He was thirty years old but on cold mornings such as this one he felt closer to forty. The storms inside him blew fiercely, filling him with a great restlessness, an inchoate need that he did not fully comprehend.

He was always aware of the tempests that shrouded his soul but only in the deepest hours of the night or in the gray mists of dawn could he sometimes actually perceive the dark winds that drove him. He avoided such opportunities when he could. He did not care to peer too deeply into the heart of the storm.

He concentrated now on the task that lay ahead of him. He had land of his own. All he had to do was hold on to it. That was proving difficult.

During the past few weeks Hugh had begun to discover why the lands of Scarcliffe had passed through so many hands in recent years.

It was a fact that in recent memory no man had success-fully held Scarcliffe for more than a short span of time before losing it through death or misfortune. Some said Scarcliffe was haunted by ill omens, bad luck, and an old curse.

He who would discover the Stones and hold fast
these lands

*must guard the green crystal with a
warrior's hands.*

Hugh did not believe in the power of ancient curses. He
trusted in little else other than his own skills as a knight and
the determined will that had brought him this far. But he had
a healthy respect for the power such foolish nonsense often
wielded over the minds of other people.

Regardless of his own opinion of the irritating prophecy,
he knew that the disheartened folk of Scarcliffe believed in the
old legend. Their new lord must prove himself by guarding the
green crystal.

Since arriving to take possession of the manor less than a
month earlier, Hugh had found the inhabitants who now
called him lord surprisingly sullen. The good people of Scarcliffe obeyed him out of fear but they saw no hope for the
future in him. Their gloominess showed in everything they
did, from the lackluster way they milled flour to the halfhearted manner in which they worked the fields.

Hugh was accustomed to command. He had been trained
to it. He had been a natural leader of men for most of his
adult life. He knew he could coerce a minimal level of cooperation from those he governed but he also knew that was not
sufficient. He needed willing loyalty from his people in order
to make Scarcliffe thrive for all their sakes.

The real problem was that the inhabitants of the manor
did not expect Hugh to last long in his position as lord. None
of the other lords had survived more than a year or two.

Within hours of his arrival, Hugh had heard muttered
omens of impending disaster. Crops had been trampled by a
band of renegade knights. A freakish lightning storm had done
considerable damage to the church. A wandering monk who
preached doom and destruction had appeared in the vicinity.

To the people of Scarcliffe, the theft of the green crystal

from the vault of the local convent had been an event of cataclysmic proportions. It had also been the last straw. Hugh knew that in their eyes it was proof positive that he was not their true lord.

Hugh had realized immediately that the fastest way to gain the trust of his people was to recover the green stone. He intended to do just that.

"Have a care, my lord," Dunstan advised. "Lady Alice is no anxious maiden to be awed by your reputation. She will no doubt try to bargain as though she were a London shopkeeper."

"It should prove an interesting experience."

"Do not forget that last night she appeared more than willing to trade her soul for whatever it is she expects to have from you."

"Aye." Hugh almost smiled. "Mayhap her soul is just what I shall require."

"Try not to barter away your own in the deal," Dunstan advised dryly.

"You are assuming that I have one to lose."

Benedict's twisted leg prevented him from actually storming through the door of Alice's study chamber. Nevertheless, he managed to convey his anger and outrage with a flushed face and fierce green eyes.

"Alice, this is madness." He came to a halt in front of her desk and tucked his staff under one arm. "Surely you cannot mean to bargain with Hugh the Relentless."

"His name is Hugh of Scarcliffe now," Alice said.

"From what I have heard, *Relentless* suits him all too well. What do you think you are doing? He is a most dangerous man from all accounts."

"But an honest one apparently. 'Tis said that if he strikes a bargain, he will keep it."

"I vow that any bargain made with Sir Hugh will be on his terms," Benedict retorted. "Alice, he is said to be very clever and keen on plotting stratagems."

"So? I am rather clever myself."

"I know you think that you can manage him as you do our uncle. But men such as Hugh are not easily managed by anyone, especially not by a woman."

Alice put down her quill pen and contemplated her brother. Benedict was sixteen years old and she had had the sole responsibility for him since their parents had died. She was well aware that she had failed in her duty by him. She intended to do what she could to make up for the fact that she had allowed his inheritance to slip into Ralf's hands.

Her mother, Helen, had died three years earlier. Her father, Sir Bernard, had been murdered by a street thief outside a London brothel two years past.

Ralf had followed fast on the heels of the news of Bernard's death. Alice had soon found herself deeply embroiled in a hopeless legal battle to hold on to the small manor that was to have been Benedict's inheritance. She had done her best to retain control of the tiny fief, but on that score Ralf, for all his ox-brained wit, had outmaneuvered her.

After nearly two full years of argument and persuasion he had convinced Fulbert of Middleton, Alice's liege lord as well as Ralf's, that a trained knight ought to control the manor. Ralf had claimed that, as a woman, Alice was incapable of managing the estates properly and that, with his ruined leg, Benedict could not be trained as a knight. Fulbert had concluded, after much prompting by Ralf, that he needed a proper fighting man in charge of the tiny manor that had belonged to Lord Bernard.

To Alice's rage and disgust, Fulbert had given her father's manor to Ralf. Ralf had, in turn, given the lands to his eldest son, Lloyd.

Alice and Benedict had been obliged to move to Lingwood shortly thereafter. Once safely in possession of the fief, Lloyd had married the daughter of a neighboring knight. Six months ago they had had a son.

Alice was practical-minded enough to realize that no matter how well she argued her brother's claims in the courts, she would likely never regain possession of Benedict's inheritance. The knowledge that she had failed to fulfill her responsibility to Benedict was a source of deep pain for her. She rarely failed at a task, especially not one as important as this had been.

Determined to make up for the disaster in the only way possible, Alice had set out to give Benedict the best possible chance for advancement in the world. She had determined to send him to the great centers of learning in Paris and Bologna, where he would be trained in the law.

Nothing could make up for his lost lands, but Alice intended to do her best. When she was satisfied that Benedict was safely on his way in life, she would fulfill her own dreams. She would enter a convent, one that possessed a fine library. There she would devote herself to the study of natural philosophy.

Only a few days ago both of her objectives had seemed out of reach. But the arrival of Hugh the Relentless had opened a new door. Alice was determined to seize the opportunity.

"Do not alarm yourself, Benedict," she said briskly. "I have every confidence that Sir Hugh will prove to be a reasonable man."

"Reasonable?" Benedict waved his free hand wildly. "Alice, he's a legend. Legends are never reasonable."

"Come now, you cannot know that. He seemed perfectly amenable to rational discourse last night."

"Last night he toyed with you. Alice, listen to me, Erasmus of Thornewood is Sir Hugh's liege lord. Do you know what that means?"

Alice picked up her quill and tapped the tip thoughtfully against her pursed lips. "I have heard of Erasmus. He is reputed to be quite powerful."

"Aye, and that makes his man, Sir Hugh, powerful, too. You must be careful. Do not think that you can bargain with Sir Hugh as though you were a peddler in the village market. That way lies madness."

"Nonsense." Alice smiled reassuringly. "You worry overmuch, Benedict. 'Tis a fault I have begun to notice in you of late."

"I worry for good cause."

"Nay, you do not. Mark my words, Sir Hugh and I shall get on very well together."

A large figure loomed in the doorway, casting a wide, dark shadow across the carpet. It seemed to Alice that there was a sudden chill in the room. She looked toward the opening. Hugh stood there.

"You echo my own thoughts, Lady Alice," he said. "I am pleased to see that we are of similar minds on the matter."

Awareness prickled along the surface of Alice's skin as his deep, resonant voice filled the study chamber. He spoke very softly yet his words seemed to still even the smallest of competing sounds. The bird on the window ledge fell silent. The echoes of horses' hooves down in the bailey faded.

Alice felt her insides tighten in anticipation. She could not stop herself from staring at Hugh for a moment. This was the first time she had seen him since last night's confrontation in the flame-lit hall. She was eager to discover if his presence had the same odd effect on her this morning that it had had on the first occasion.

It did.

Against all reason and the evidence of her own eyes, she found Hugh the Relentless to be the most compelling man she had ever met. He was no more handsome in the morning light than he had been last night yet something about him drew her.

It was almost as if she had developed an extraordinary additional sense, she thought, and that she now employed a level of sensation that went beyond hearing, vision, touch, taste, and smell. All in all, a most intriguing problem in natural philosophy, she decided.

Benedict jerked around to face Hugh. His staff struck Alice's desk. "My lord." His jaw tightened. "My sister and I were having a private conversation. We did not see you standing there."

"I have been told that I am rather difficult to overlook," Hugh said. "You are Benedict?"

"Aye, my lord." Benedict straightened his shoulders. "I am Alice's brother and I do not think that you should meet alone with her. 'Tis not proper."

Alice raised her eyes toward the ceiling. "Benedict, please, this is ridiculous. I am no young maid whose reputation must be protected. Sir Hugh and I merely intend to converse on matters of business."

" 'Tis not right," Benedict insisted.

Hugh leaned one broad shoulder against the doorjamb and crossed his arms over his chest. "What do you think I am going to do to her?"

"I don't know," Benedict muttered. "But I won't allow it."

Alice lost her patience. "Benedict, that is enough. Leave us now. Sir Hugh and I must be about our business."

"But, Alice—"

"I will speak with you later, Benedict."

Benedict flushed darkly. He glowered at Hugh, who merely shrugged, straightened, and got out of the doorway to make room for him to pass.

"Fear not," Hugh said to him quietly. "You have my word

that I'll not ravish your sister during the course of this bargain she wishes to strike."

Benedict turned an even darker hue of red. With one last, angry glance at Alice, he stalked awkwardly past Hugh and disappeared down the hall.

Hugh waited until he was out of earshot. Then he met Alice's eyes. "A young man's pride is a tricky thing. It should be handled with some delicacy."

"Do not concern yourself with my brother, sir. He is my responsibility." Alice indicated a wooden stool with a wave of her hand. "Please be seated. We have much to discuss."

"Aye." Hugh glanced at the stool but he did not sit down on it. Instead he walked to the brazier and held his hands out to the warmth of the glowing coals. "That we do. What is this bargain you would make with me, lady?"

Alice watched him with an eagerness she could not conceal. He seemed quite amenable, she thought. There was no sign that he meant to be difficult. A sensible, reasonable man, just as she had concluded.

"My lord, I shall be blunt."

"By all means. I much prefer directness. It saves a great deal of time, does it not?"

"Aye." Alice clasped her hands together on her desk. "I am prepared to tell you precisely where I believe the thief took my green crystal."

"It is my crystal, Lady Alice. You seem to have a habit of forgetting that fact."

"We can argue the fine points of the matter at another time, my lord."

Hugh looked faintly amused. "There will be no argument."

"Excellent. I am delighted to see that you are a man of reason, sir."

"I make every effort."

Alice smiled approvingly. "Now, then, as I said, I will tell you where I believe the crystal to be at this moment. In addition, I will even agree to accompany you to its present location and point out the thief."

Hugh considered that. "Very helpful."

"I am glad you appreciate it, my lord. But there is even more to my part of this bargain."

"I cannot wait to hear the rest," Hugh said.

"Not only will I help you find the crystal, sir, I will go one step further." Alice leaned forward to emphasize her next words. "I shall agree to relinquish my claim to it."

"A claim that I do not accept."

Alice started to frown. "My lord—"

"And in exchange for this magnanimous offer?" he interrupted calmly. "What is it you would ask of me, Lady Alice?"

Alice braced herself. "In exchange, my lord, I ask two things. The first is that, two years from now, when my brother is old enough, you will arrange for him to go to Paris and, mayhap, Bologna, so that he may attend the lectures given there. I would have him become proficient in the liberal arts and particularly in the law so that he may eventually obtain a position of high rank at court or in the household of some wealthy prince or noble."

"Your brother wishes to pursue a career as a secretary or clerk?"

"It's not as though he has a great deal of choice in the matter, my lord." Alice tightened her fingers. "I was not able to protect his rightful inheritance from our uncle. Therefore, I must do the next best thing for Benedict."

Hugh studied her speculatively. "Very well, that is your affair, I suppose. I am prepared to finance his studies in exchange for getting my hands on the crystal."

Alice relaxed. The worst was over. "Thank you, my lord. I am pleased to hear that."

"What was the second thing you would have of me?"

"A very minor request, my lord, of no real consequence to one in your position," she said smoothly. "Indeed, I daresay you will barely take notice of it."

"What, precisely, is it, lady?"

"I ask that you provide me with a dowry."

Hugh gazed into the brazier coals as though he saw something of great interest there. "A dowry? You wish to be wed?"

Alice chuckled. "By the Saints, whatever gave you that notion, my lord? Of course I do not wish to wed. Why on earth would I want a husband? My goal is to enter a convent."

Hugh turned slowly toward her. His amber eyes gleamed intently. "May I ask why?"

"So that I may continue my studies in natural philosophy, of course. To do so, I shall need a large library, which only a rich convent can provide." Alice cleared her throat delicately. "And to get into a fine religious house, I shall naturally need a respectably large dowry."

"I see." Hugh's expression was that of the hawk that has sighted its prey. "That is unfortunate."

Alice's heart sank. For a moment she simply stared at him in open disappointment. She had been so certain that he would agree to the arrangement.

Desperately she rallied her arguments. "My lord, pray think closely on this matter. The green crystal is obviously very important to you. I can see that you obtain it. Surely that is worth the cost of my dowry."

"You misunderstand me, lady. I am willing to provide a bride price for you."

She brightened. "You will?"

"Aye, but I'll want the bride to go with it."

"*What?*"

"Or at least the promise of one."

Alice was too stunned to think clearly. "I do not comprehend, my lord."

"Nay? 'Tis simple enough. You shall have a portion of what you want of me from this bargain, Lady Alice. But in return I demand that you and I become betrothed before we set out after the green crystal."

Chapter 3

Hugh would not have been surprised to learn that this was the first time in her entire life Alice had been rendered speechless.

He contemplated her wide green eyes, her parted lips, and the stunned amazement on her face with some amusement and not a little satisfaction. He doubted that there were many men gifted with the ability to bring the lady to such an abrupt halt.

He prowled the room as he waited for Alice to find her tongue. What he saw did not astonish him. Unlike most of the rest of Lingwood Hall, this chamber was dusted and well swept. The air was scented by fresh herbs. He had anticipated as much.

Last night, while dining on such delicacies as sturgeon dressed in spicy cold green sauce and finely seasoned leek pie, he had been greatly impressed by Alice's talent for household management. This morning he had quickly learned that whatever magic she had worked for the banquet had not been applied to the rest of Sir Ralf's household, except for the chambers in this wing. Alice had obviously claimed these rooms for herself and her brother.

Here, all was spotless. Signs of efficiency and order were everywhere, from the carefully placed tapestries that hung on the walls to limit drafts to the gleaming floors.

The new light of day had revealed a different scene in the rest of Sir Ralf's hall. Odoriferous garderobes, unswept floors, tattered carpets, and an odor of dampness in many of the chambers made it plain that Alice had not bothered to exert her wizardry outside her own small world.

Here in Alice's study chamber Hugh discovered not only the cleanliness he had expected, but also a variety of interesting items. The chamber was filled with a number of strange and curious things.

Some well-worn handbooks and two fine, leather-bound volumes occupied the place of pride on a nearby shelf.

A collection of dead insects was displayed in a wooden box. Bits and pieces of what appeared to be fish bones and an assortment of shells were arranged on a table. In one corner a metal bowl was secured above an unlit candle. There was a chalky residue in the vessel, evidence of some past experiment.

Hugh was intrigued. The collection bespoke a lively mind and an inquiring nature.

"My lord," Alice finally managed to say, "what in the name of the Cross are you talking about?"

She was not responding well to the notion of marriage, Hugh acknowledged. He determined to pursue a less obvious route to his goal. He was skilled at stratagems. He saw no reason why he could not apply that talent to securing himself a wife.

"You heard me. I have need of a lady whom I can claim as my own."

"But—"

"Temporarily."

"Well, you cannot claim me, sir. Find yourself another lady. I'm certain that there are any number of them scattered about the countryside."

Ah, but none such as yourself, Hugh thought. *I doubt if there is another female such as you in all of Christendom.* "But you are so very convenient, Lady Alice."

She bristled very nicely with outrage. "I am no man's convenience, sir. Pray, inquire of my uncle just how *convenient* I am. I believe that he will disabuse you of that notion. He finds me a great trial."

"No doubt because you have deliberately set out to make yourself one. I am hoping, however, that you and I can do business together as colleagues rather than as adversaries."

"Colleagues," she repeated cautiously.

"Associates," he clarified helpfully.

"Associates."

"Aye, business associates, just as you, yourself, suggested last night when you declared that you wished to strike a bargain with me."

"This was not quite what I had in mind. Mayhap you had best explain precisely what you mean, my lord."

"Mayhap I should do just that." Hugh paused beside a complicated instrument composed of a set of circular brass plates and a siting rule. "Where did you obtain this very beautiful astrolabe? I have not seen the like since I was in Italy."

She scowled. "My father sent it to me. He found it at a London shop a few years ago. You are familiar with such instruments?"

Hugh bent closer to the astrolabe. "It is true that I have made my living with my sword, lady, but it would be a mistake to assume that I am a complete fool." Experimentally he moved the siting rule that angled across the metal plates, shifting the position of the stars in relation to the Earth. "Those who have made that error in the past have generally paid a price."

Alice jumped to her feet and hurried around the edge of the desk. " 'Tis not that I thought you a fool, sir. Quite the opposite." She halted beside the astrolabe, frowning at it. "The thing is, I have been unable to determine the proper workings of this device and I know of no one who has any knowledge of astronomy. Could you teach me how to use it?"

Hugh straightened and looked at her intent face. "Aye. If we seal our bargain today, I shall undertake to teach you the proper use of the astrolabe."

Her eyes lit with a degree of enthusiasm that could have been mistaken for passion in another woman. She blushed. "That is most gracious of you, my lord. I discovered a book in the small library of the local convent that describes the device but there were no instructions for its use. I vow, it has been most frustrating."

"You may consider the instruction a betrothal gift."

The glow faded quickly from her huge eyes. It was promptly replaced by renewed wariness. "About this betrothal, my lord. As I said, I would have you explain yourself."

"Very well." Hugh wandered over to a table holding a large array of stones and crystals. He picked up a chunk of reddish stone and examined it. "I regret to say that I find myself the victim of a most annoying curse, lady."

"That is no doubt your own fault, my lord," she said crisply.

He glanced up from the stone, surprised by the asperity of her tone. "My fault?"

"Aye. My mother always said that diseases of that sort came from frequenting brothels, sir. You will no doubt be obliged to take a dose of theriac and have yourself bled. Mayhap you should undergo a good purge while you're at it. In my opinion, 'tis nothing more than you deserve if you have been hanging about such places."

Hugh cleared his throat. "You are an expert in these matters?"

"My mother was very skilled with herbs. She taught me a great many things concerning their uses in adjusting the balance of the bodily humors." Alice glowered at him. "However, she always said that it was infinitely wiser to avoid certain ailments in the first place rather than to attempt a cure after the damage has been done."

"I do not disagree with that principle." Hugh looked at her. "What happened to your mother?"

A shadow flickered across Alice's face. "She died three years ago."

"My condolences."

Alice heaved a small sigh. "She had just received a shipment of strange and unusual herbs. She was very eager to conduct experiments with them."

"Experiments?"

"Aye, she was forever concocting potions. In any event, she mixed some of the new herbs in a recipe she had recently discovered. It was supposed to be good for treating those who suffered from serious pains of the stomach and bowel. She accidentally drank too much of the concoction. It killed her."

A cold feeling seized Hugh's gut. "Your mother took poison?"

"It was an accident," Alice said hastily, obviously alarmed at his conclusion. "I told you, she was performing an experiment at the time."

"She experimented upon herself?" he asked, incredulous.

"She frequently tried new medicines on herself before she gave them to the sick."

"My own mother died in much the same manner," Hugh heard himself say before he stopped to consider the wisdom of imparting such a confidence. "She drank poison."

Alice's lovely eyes filled with quiet sympathy. "I am very sorry, my lord. Was your mother a student of strange herbs and such?"

"Nay." Hugh tossed aside the reddish stone, angry at his

lack of discretion. He *never* discussed his mother's suicide or the fact that she had deliberately administered the lethal poison to his father before drinking it herself. " 'Tis a long story that I do not care to repeat."

"Aye, my lord. Such matters can be very painful."

Her sympathy irritated him. He was unaccustomed to such sentiment and he had no wish to encourage it. Sympathy implied weakness. "You misunderstood me, lady. When I said that I was the victim of a curse, I was not referring to an illness of the body."

She gave him a quizzical look. "Surely you do not mean a magical curse?"

"Aye."

"But that is utter nonsense," Alice scoffed. "By the Saints, I have no patience with those who believe in magic and curses."

"Nor do I."

Alice seemed not to have heard him. She was already setting sail on a new course. "Mark me, I am well aware that it is quite the thing for learned men to travel to Toledo these days in search of ancient secrets of magic, but I'm certain that they waste their time. There is no such thing as magic."

"I happen to agree with you about the foolishness of magic," Hugh said. "But I am a practical man."

"So?"

"So, in this instance I have concluded that the quickest way to achieve my own ends is to comply with the requirements of an old legend, which is, in part, a curse."

"A legend?"

"Aye." Hugh picked up a bit of clouded pink crystal and held it up to the light. "The good people of Scarcliffe have endured a variety of masters during recent years. None of them have endeared themselves to the local folk. And none of them have lasted long."

"You intend to be the exception, I take it?"

"Aye, lady." Hugh set the pink crystal down, leaned back against the table, and rested one hand on the hilt of his sword. "Scarcliffe is mine and I will hold fast to it while there is breath in my body."

She searched his face. "I do not doubt your intention, my lord. What, exactly, are the stipulations of this legend?"

" 'Tis said that the true lord of Scarcliffe must accomplish two things. First, he must guard the last remaining stone of an ancient treasure. Second, he must discover the location of the rest of the Stones of Scarcliffe."

Alice blinked. "The green crystal is truly valuable then?"

Hugh shrugged. "It is in the eyes of my people. They believe that it is part of what was once a large collection of priceless gems. All but the green stone disappeared a long time ago. The local convent has had the care of the crystal in recent years. But it disappeared a fortnight ago."

"Stolen, you say?"

"Aye. And at a most inauspicious moment."

She eyed him with sharp perception. "Shortly after you arrived to take control of Scarcliffe?"

"Aye." The lady was quick-witted, Hugh thought. "I want it back. 'Twill go far toward quelling the fears and uncertainties of my people."

"I see."

"If I return with the stone and a suitable bride, my people will understand that I mean to be their true lord."

Alice looked distinctly uneasy. "You wish to wed me?"

"I wish to become *betrothed* to you." *One step at a time,* he reminded himself. He did not want to frighten her off at this stage. Now that he had hit upon this scheme, he was convinced it would work. But he needed Alice's cooperation. There was no time to search for another bride. "For a very short period of time."

"But a vow of betrothal is very nearly as binding as a wedding vow," Alice protested. "Indeed, some church scholars

claim that it is equally binding and that there is no real difference between the two."

"You know as well as I do that such scholars are in the
minority. In truth, betrothals are broken readily enough, especially if both parties are agreed on the matter. I see no problem."

"Hmm."

Alice was silent for a long moment, her brows knitted
together in an expression of grave consideration. Hugh could
see that she was turning his proposal over and over in her
mind, checking for pitfalls and traps. He watched her, fascinated.

With a strange jolt of awareness, he realized that she reminded him of himself when he was plotting stratagems. He
knew exactly what she was thinking. It was an odd experience
to study her like this. It was as though he had a fleeting
glimpse into her mind. A sensation of eerie familiarity gripped
him for a moment. He had the strange feeling that he knew
Alice far better than their short acquaintance warranted.

The knowledge that her wits were as sharp as his own and
might very well work in much the same manner left Hugh
feeling disoriented. He was not accustomed to the notion that
he might have something so fundamental in common with
another person, let alone with a woman.

It struck him that he had always considered himself as
being set apart from others, removed from their lives, detached
and distanced from them even as he intermingled with them.
He had spent his life feeling as though he lived on an island
while everyone else in the world existed on the opposite shore.

But for a brief moment in time it seemed as though Alice
shared the island with him.

Alice watched him with a shrewd gaze. "I had intended to
enter a convent as soon as my brother was safely launched in
the world."

Hugh shook off the odd sensation and forced himself back

to the matter at hand. " 'Tis not uncommon for a lady whose betrothal has been broken to enter a convent."

"Aye." Alice offered nothing further. She was clearly engrossed in consideration of the matter.

Hugh abruptly wondered if she would wear such a radiantly fierce expression when she lay beneath a man in bed.

That thought made him reflect upon the matter of whether or not she had ever lain with a man. Alice was three and twenty, after all, and Dunstan was correct. She was not what one would term a shy, unopened rosebud.

On the other hand, she was no flirt, Hugh thought. Judging by the collection of stones, dried beetles, and assorted equipment cluttering her study chamber, it appeared that her passions were more easily inflamed by matters of natural philosophy than thoughts of passion and lust.

Alice folded her arms beneath her breasts and drummed her fingers against her arms. "Precisely how long would this betrothal need to last to suit your purposes, my lord?"

"As to that, I cannot be precise, but I should think a few months would do it."

"*A few months.*"

" 'Tis not such a great length of time," he said smoothly. "By spring I shall have everything under control at Scarcliffe." *By spring I shall have you safely wedded and bedded.* "You have nowhere else to go, do you?"

"Nay, but—"

"You may as well spend the winter at Scarcliffe. Your brother will be welcome there, too, naturally."

"What if you wish to become betrothed to a woman you genuinely desire to wed while I am living under your roof, sir?"

"I shall face that problem if and when it arises."

"I am not certain. This is all so different than what I had planned."

Sensing that he was winning, Hugh pressed his point. "Spring will be here before you know it. If you are not content at Scarcliffe we can consider other solutions to your situation."

Alice swung around. She clasped her hands behind her back and began to pace the chamber. "You would need my uncle's permission to become betrothed to me."

"I doubt that I will have any difficulty in obtaining it."

"Aye." Alice made a face. "He is eager enough to be rid of me."

"I shall ensure his eagerness with a suitable offer of spices."

Alice gave him another keen glance as she turned to start back across the chamber. "You have a store of spices?"

"Aye."

"Are we speaking of valuable spices, my lord, or merely poor quality salt?"

He hid a smile. "Only the best."

"Cinnamon? Saffron? Pepper? Fine white salt?"

"Those and more." Hugh hesitated, debating how much to tell her about his personal finances.

Most successful knights who had not inherited their father's patrimony made their fortunes through ransoms and booty. They gained wealth either by competing in tournaments or by selling their swords to generous lords who rewarded them for their services. Few lowered themselves so far as to engage in trade.

Hugh had taken his share of ransoms, valuable armor, and fine war-horses in various tournaments and he had, indeed, been fortunate in his choice of lords. But the true source of his rapidly growing personal wealth was the spice trade.

Until this moment Hugh had not cared for the opinion of the world in such matters. But he suddenly realized that he did not want Alice to scorn him for the fact that he engaged in trade.

On the other hand, she was a practical-minded woman.

Mayhap she would not care. The knowledge that he had a solid, secure source of income might even serve to reassure her of his intentions.

Hugh swiftly calculated the possibilities and decided to risk the truth.

"I do not generally make it widely known," he said quietly, "but I do not rely solely upon my sword for an income."

She looked at him with surprise. "You deal in spices, sir?"

"Aye. During recent years I have become involved in an extensive trade with several merchants from the East. If and when you choose to enter a convent, I shall be able to provide a dozen respectable dowries for you, lady."

"I see." She looked overwhelmed. "I shall need a plump dowry if I wish to enter a fine convent."

"Naturally. Convents are as choosy as husbands from landed families, are they not?"

"Especially if they are expected to overlook a somewhat sullied reputation," Alice muttered. "And if I go to live with you as your betrothed and we are not eventually wed, my reputation will be in tatters."

Hugh nodded. "It will be assumed that we have lived together as man and wife. But, as you say, a suitable dowry will persuade any fine convent to ignore such petty details."

Alice continued to tap her fingers against her arms. "I'd advise you not to let Sir Ralf know that you are willing to pay a large dowry for me, sir, else he will likely try to cheat you."

A grin tugged at the corners of Hugh's mouth. He controlled it with an effort. "I have no desire to be fleeced, lady. Never fear, I have had a fair amount of experience in the art of bargaining. You have my oath that I shall make it a point not to pay overmuch for you."

She frowned, unconvinced. "Sir Ralf has no scruples in matters of business. He stole my brother's inheritance."

"Mayhap I shall even the score by stealing you from him for a pittance."

Alice fell silent again as she continued to pace. "You would do all this in exchange for my help in recovering the green stone and for our temporary betrothal?"

"Aye. 'Tis the shortest, most convenient route to my goal."

"And therefore, 'tis naturally the path you elect to take," she murmured half under her breath.

"I do not believe in wasting time."

"You are a bold man, sir."

"I sense that we are well matched," Hugh said softly.

Alice came to a halt. Her expressive face was bright with renewed enthusiasm. "Very well, my lord, I shall agree to your terms. I shall spend the winter with you at Scarcliffe as your betrothed. In the spring we shall reassess the situation."

Hugh was startled by the degree of exultation that swept through him. It was a simple business arrangement, he reminded himself. Nothing more than that. He tried to temper the surging satisfaction.

"Excellent," he said simply. "The bargain is struck."

"I foresee a large problem, however."

"What is that?"

Alice paused beside the astrolabe. "It occurs to me that although my uncle will be much pleased at the prospect of ridding himself of my presence in his household, he is unlikely to believe his good fortune."

"Do not concern yourself, Lady Alice." Hugh was impatient to get on with the matter now that he had completed the bargain. "I told you, I shall deal with your uncle."

"But he will be extremely suspicious of your sudden desire to wed me," she insisted.

Hugh frowned. "Why is that?"

"In case it has escaped your notice," she said tartly, "I am somewhat beyond the customary age for a bride."

Hugh smiled slightly. "One of the reasons you are so eminently suited to my needs, Lady Alice, is precisely because you are no longer a young, frivolous innocent."

She wrinkled her nose. "Aye, there is that, isn't there? I can well believe that you would not wish to strike this bargain with a female who is still part child or one who has had no experience of the world."

"You are correct." Hugh wondered again just how much experience of the world Alice had had. "I need a business associate, not a demanding bride who will pout and sulk when I do not have time to entertain her. I require a woman of mature years and practical ways."

A wistful expression passed across Alice's face. "A woman of mature years and practical ways. Aye, that is a very good description of me, my lord."

"Then there is no reason why our arrangement should not go forward."

Alice hesitated. "We come back to the problem of convincing my uncle that you truly wish to contract a marriage with me."

"I told you, you may leave that problem safely in my hands."

"I fear 'twill not be so simple as you seem to believe," she said. "Shortly after Sir Ralf removed my brother and me from our home and brought us here to Lingwood Manor, he made several attempts to marry me off."

"The attempts failed, I see."

"Aye. My uncle got so desperate that he actually offered a small dowry, but even with that none of his neighbors could be convinced to take me off his hands."

"There was not so much as a single offer?" Hugh was surprised. After all, a dowry was a dowry and there were always a few poor men desperately in need of one.

"One or two knights with small fiefs nearby went so far as to pay us a visit to meet me in person. But upon becoming acquainted with me, they quickly lost interest."

"Or were persuaded to lose interest?" Hugh asked dryly.

She turned a shade of pink. "Aye, well, I could not tolerate any of them for more than a few minutes. The thought of actually marrying one was enough to induce hysteria."

"Hysteria? You do not appear the type of female who is prone to hysteria."

Her eyes gleamed. "I assure you, I fell into the most severe fits in front of two of my suitors. There were no others after that."

"You found the prospect of remaining in your uncle's household preferable to marriage?"

Alice shrugged. "Until now it has been the lesser of two evils. So long as I am unwed, I have at least a chance of obtaining my own ends. Once married, I am lost."

"Would marriage be so terrible?"

"Marriage to any of the louts my uncle chose would have been intolerable," Alice said forcefully. "Not only because I would have been unhappy but because none of them would have had any patience with my brother. Men who are trained for war tend to be cruel and unkind to youths who cannot be trained in arms."

"I take your point," Hugh said gently. He realized that her concern for her brother underlaid most of her decisions.

Alice's mouth tightened. "My father had no use for Benedict after my brother fell from his pony and injured his leg. He said Benedict could never be trained as a knight and was therefore quite useless. For the most part he ignored his son after that."

"It is understandable that you do not want to expose Benedict to similar unkindnesses from another lord."

"Aye. My brother suffered enough from being ignored by our father. I did what I could to make up for the poor treatment he received but it was not enough. How does one take the place of a father in a boy's life?"

Hugh thought of Erasmus. "It is not easy, but it can be done."

Alice gave herself a small shake, as though she were mentally casting aside unhappy memories. "Ah, well, 'tis not your problem. I shall see to Benedict."

"Very well. I shall speak to Sir Ralf at once." Hugh turned to leave the study chamber.

He was vastly pleased with the results of the bargaining. True, he had only succeeded in coaxing Alice into a vow of betrothal, but a betrothal was near enough to a wedding. Once he had her under the roof of Scarcliffe Keep he would worry about the details of the arrangements.

Alice raised an imperious hand to hold his attention. "One moment, Sir Hugh."

He paused and turned back politely. "Aye?"

"I warned you that you must not arouse Sir Ralf's suspicions and thereby induce him to demand a king's ransom for my hand. We shall need to concoct a reasonable explanation to explain why you wish to wed me. After all, you have only just met me and I have no dowry to offer."

"I'll think of something."

She gave him a quizzical look. "But what?"

Hugh stared at her for a moment. It occurred to him that in the morning light, her hair was a lovely hue. There was a straightforward, clear-eyed perception in her gaze that drew him. And the curve of her breasts beneath her blue gown was very enticing.

He took a step back toward her. His mouth was suddenly dry and he could feel a distinct tightening in his loins. " 'Tis obvious that, under the circumstances, there is only one reasonable explanation why I would ask for your hand."

"And what is that, sir?"

"Passion."

She stared at him as though he had just spoken in some strange, unknown tongue. "Passion?"

"Aye." He took two more steps toward her, closing the gap between them.

Alice's mouth opened and closed. "Nonsense. You will

never convince my uncle that a legendary knight such as yourself would be so . . . so utterly witless as to get himself betrothed for such a trivial reason, my lord."

He came to a halt and closed his hands around her delicate
shoulders. He was astonished at how very pleasant it was to
touch her. She was fine-boned but sturdy. There was a resilient
feminine strength about her that excited him. She was fiercely
alive under his hands. He was close enough to smell the scent
of herbs in her hair.

"You are wrong, madam." His tongue felt thick in his
mouth. "Witless passion is obviously the only force strong
enough to make a man overcome good sense and sound reason."

Before she could comprehend his intention, Hugh pulled
her against his chest and covered her mouth with his own.

He acknowledged then, for the first time, that the desire to
kiss her had been brewing within him since he had first seen
her in the firelit hall.

She was a creature of shimmering magic. He had never before touched a woman such as this one.

This was madness. No woman could be allowed to affect
him so intensely.

He knew that the easiest way to rid himself of the dangerous sensual curiosity that plagued him was to surrender to the
impulse. But now, as he felt the small shiver that coursed
through Alice, he wondered if he had unleashed a force that
would be far more difficult to control than he had anticipated.

She stood very still beneath his hands, as though uncertain
how to react.

Hugh took advantage of her confusion to indulge himself
in the taste of her.

Her mouth was as warm and moist as figs drenched in
honey and fresh ginger.

He could not get enough of the taste.

Kissing Alice was more intoxicating than walking into a

storehouse full of rare spices. She was everything the dark imaginings of the night had promised. Sweet, soft, and fragrant. There was heat in her, the sort of fire that inflamed all of a man's senses.

Hugh deepened the kiss, searching for a response.

Alice made a tiny, muffled sound. It was neither a protest nor a cry of fear. It seemed to Hugh to be a choked exclamation of pure astonishment.

He eased her more tightly against his body until he could feel the thrust of her soft breasts beneath her gown. Her hips pressed against his thighs. His shaft stirred hungrily.

Alice moaned softly. Then, as though she had been freed of a spell that had bound her in place, she abruptly gripped the sleeves of his tunic. She rose on tiptoe and clung to him, straining against him. Hugh felt her pulse quicken.

And then, to his great satisfaction, Alice parted her lips beneath his. He seized the opportunity to plunder the lusciousness that had been opened to him. He was suddenly mad with a desire to possess all of her, as if she were a seasoning that had no name, exotic beyond description.

Hugh was well aware of the effects the unique spices of women had upon the male senses. He had long ago learned to control and moderate his taste for them. He knew that a man who was not the master of his own appetites was doomed to be mastered by them.

But it was suddenly very difficult to recall his own rules. Alice was a heady mix. The taste and scent of her beckoned him as he had not been beckoned in a very long time. Mayhap in his entire life.

He wanted more. Much more.

"Sir Hugh," Alice finally gasped. She freed her mouth and looked up at him with wide, stunned eyes.

For a moment Hugh could think of nothing else except retaking her mouth. He started to lower his head once more.

Alice put her fingertips on his lips. Her brows snapped

together in a quelling expression. "A moment, if you please, sir."

Hugh forced himself to take a deep, steadying breath. The realization of how close he had come to sacrificing the iron self-mastery that had served him so well all of his life struck him with bruising force.

He shook off the disturbing suspicion that Alice might be able to exert a woman's power over him. It was simply not possible. He had not been vulnerable to feminine wiles since the earliest days of his youth. He certainly had no intention of allowing this particular woman to work her way past the armor of his control.

Every move he made was calculated, he reminded himself. Kissing Alice had merely been one more such maneuver. To judge by the rosy flush on her cheeks, the stratagem had worked. The lady was not immune to passion. That fact would no doubt prove useful.

"As I said," Hugh muttered, "I believe I can convince your uncle that I have been swept away by passion."

"Aye, well, I shall leave the matter in your hands, my lord." Alice's cheeks were very pink. She turned away, not meeting his eyes. "You appear to know what you are about."

"Rest assured that I do." Hugh took a deep breath and went toward the door. "See to your travel preparations and those of your brother. I wish to be on the road by noon."

"Aye, my lord." She glanced at him. Satisfaction and a womanly pleasure gleamed in her vivid eyes.

"There is just one more small detail that must be dealt with before we leave," Hugh said.

Alice gave him a politely inquiring look. "What is that, sir?"

"You have neglected to tell me in which direction we shall be traveling. It is time for you to fulfill your end of the bargain, Alice. Where has the green stone been taken?"

"Oh, the stone." She gave a shaky chuckle. "By the Saints,

what with one thing and another, I very nearly forgot about my part of this arrangement."

"The green stone is what this is all about," Hugh said very coolly.

The glow promptly disappeared from Alice's eyes. "Of course, my lord. I shall lead you to the stone."

Chapter 4

*S*ir Ralf choked on his morning ale. "You wish to betroth yourself to my niece?" His round, heavy features screwed themselves into a grimace as he sputtered and coughed. "Your pardon, sir," he gasped. "But did I hear rightly? You want to wed *Alice*?"

"Your niece suits my requirements in a wife." Hugh helped himself to a wedge of aging bread. The unappetizing breakfast fare that had appeared from the kitchens this morning indicated that Alice had lost interest in culinary matters after she had arranged last night's banquet. The lady had achieved her goal and had promptly ceased working her magic.

Hugh wondered wryly what she herself had dined on this morning in her private chambers. Something more interesting than weak ale and old bread, he suspected.

Ralf stared at him, openmouthed with amazement. "She meets your requirements? You actually believe that Alice will make you a proper wife?"

"Aye."

Hugh did not blame Ralf for his incredulity since his host

had not been the beneficiary of Alice's mastery of household arts.

The great hall was empty this morning except for Hugh and Ralf, who sat at a small table near the fire, and a sullen band of drudges moving about in a desultory fashion. The servants made a halfhearted show of cleaning up after last night's feast but it was plain they took little interest in the task. One took occasional swipes with a cleaning cloth and another made a few idle attempts to scrub the wooden boards. There was little soap and water involved in the process.

The ale-soaked rushes that had covered the stone floor last night were still in place together with the bits and pieces of food that had fallen among them. No amount of scented herbs scattered about could disguise the smell of rotting meat and sour wine. Not that anyone was bothering to toss fragrant herbs onto the moldering pile.

"The wedding will have to be held at some future date in the spring." Hugh eyed the stale bread. He was hungry but not hungry enough to eat another slice. "I cannot spare the time for a proper celebration just now."

"I see."

"And there is the business side of the thing to be considered."

Ralf cleared his throat. "Uh, certainly. The business side."

"I think it would be best if Alice and her brother accompanied me back to Scarcliffe so that I will not be put to the trouble of making another trip to collect my bride at some later date."

"You're going to take her with you today?" Ralf's beady eyes reflected undisguised disbelief.

"Aye. I have instructed her to see that she and young Benedict are packed and ready to leave by noon."

Ralf blinked several times. "I don't comprehend this, sir. Forgive me, I don't mean to pry into your personal affairs, but I cannot help but wonder at this turn of events. Granted, Alice appears young for her years, but you do realize that she is three and twenty?"

" 'Tis no great matter."

"But 'tis well known that a young bride is much easier to train than one of more advanced years. The youthful ones are more docile. Easier to manage. My own wife was fifteen when we wed. I never had a bit of trouble out of her."

Hugh looked at him. "I do not anticipate any difficulty in managing Lady Alice."

Ralf flinched. "Nay, nay, of course not. I'll wager that she would not dare to gainsay you, my lord." He sighed ruefully. "Not the way she does me, in any event. Alice has been a great trial, you know."

"Is that so?"

"Aye. And after all I've done for her and that lame brother of hers." Ralf's heavy jowls shuddered with indignation. "I gave her a roof over her head and food to eat after her father died. And what thanks do I get for doing my Christian duty by my brother's children? Naught but constant quarrels and irksome demands."

Hugh nodded soberly. "Annoying."

"By the Rood, it's damned annoying." Ralf scowled furiously. "I tell you, sir, that, except when it suits her purposes, as it did last night, Alice cannot even be bothered with the management of my hall. You will note, however, that her own chambers are kept clean and perfumed."

"Aye." Hugh smiled to himself. "I did notice."

" 'Tis as if she lived in a different household up there in the east tower. One would never know it was connected to the rest of Lingwood Hall."

"That was plain enough," Hugh said, half under his breath.

"Not only does she dine in the privacy of her own chambers together with young Benedict, she gives her own instructions to the kitchens regarding the food that is served there.

And it's a far cry from what the rest of us eat, I can assure you."

"That does not surprise me."

Ralf seemed not to hear the comment. He was in full sail on the sea of righteous indignation. "Last night was the first decent meal I've had here in my own hall since my wife died seven years ago. I thought things would be different when I brought Alice here. Thought she'd assume her natural female responsibilities. Thought she'd supervise things the way she did when she was in charge of her father's manor."

"But it did not work out that way, I take it?" Hugh suspected that Alice had practiced her own form of revenge against her uncle.

Ralf sighed glumly. "She blames me for taking her and her brother away from their home, but I ask you, what choice did I have? Benedict had but fifteen years at the time. And you've seen him. The boy's crippled. No amount of training will turn him into a proper fighting man. He could not possibly defend his own lands. My liege lord, Fulbert of Middleton, expected me to see to the defense of my brother's lands."

"Which you chose to do by installing your son as lord there," Hugh observed softly.

" 'Twas the only solution, but my shrew of a niece would not acknowledge the fact." Ralf swallowed ale and slammed his mug down on the table. "I did my best to secure her future. Tried to find her a husband."

"After you realized that she was not going to take over the management of your household?" Hugh asked with mild curiosity.

"Was it my fault none of my neighbors would have her as a wife?"

Hugh recalled Alice's description of her very convenient fits of hysteria. "Nay, 'twas most definitely not your fault."

"Not once did she thank me for making the effort. I vow, she did her best to foil my every attempt to do my duty by her.

I have no proof, mark you, but to this day, I remain convinced that she plotted stratagems to discourage her suitors."

Hugh reluctantly decided to risk one more piece of the aged bread. "Your problems are over, Sir Ralf. You need not concern yourself with your niece again."

"Bah. So you say now, but you have not had extensive experience with Alice." Ralf narrowed his eyes. "Aye, no experience whatsoever. You don't know what she can be like, sir."

"I shall take my chances."

"Will you? What if you change your mind about the betrothal? Likely you'll try to return her in a few weeks' time after you've had a taste of her sharp tongue and demanding ways. What am I to do then?"

"I will not change my mind. You have my oath on it."

Ralf looked skeptical. "May I ask why you are so certain that she will suit you?"

"She is intelligent, healthy, and convenient. Although she does not always choose to practice them in this household, 'tis clear that she is well trained in the wifely arts. Furthermore, she possesses the manners of a fine lady. What more does a man need? The whole thing seems very efficient and most practical from my point of view."

In spite of what he had told Alice, Hugh had no intention of using passion as an explanation for forging this hasty match. He and Ralf were both men of the world. They each knew that lust was a ludicrous reason for contracting such an important business arrangement as marriage.

Looking back on the incident in Alice's study chamber, Hugh was not certain why he had even broached the possibility of using passion as an excuse. He frowned, wondering what had put the notion into his head. He never allowed himself to be influenced by passion.

Ralf watched him with a distinctly uneasy expression. "You believe that marrying Alice will be an *efficient* move, my lord?"

Hugh nodded brusquely. "I require a wife to see to my

new household. But I do not wish to invest a great deal of time and effort in the business of securing one. You know how complicated that can become. Negotiation can carry on for months, even years."

"True, nevertheless, Alice is somewhat unusual and not merely because of her advanced age."

"No matter. I feel certain she will do nicely. And I have too many other tasks requiring my immediate attention to be bothered with a long search for another bride."

"I understand, sir. Indeed, I do. A man in your position does not want to be burdened with a lot of fuss and bother over a bride."

"Aye."

"No denying a man does have to acquire one. The sooner the better, I suppose. One has to see to one's heirs and lands."

"Aye," Hugh said. "Heirs and lands."

"So. You find Alice convenient."

"Very."

Ralf fiddled with a chunk of bread. His eyes darted to Hugh's impassive face and quickly slid aside. "Ah, pray forgive me, sir, but I must ask whether or not you have discussed this matter with Alice herself."

Hugh raised one brow. "You are concerned with her feelings on the subject?"

"Nay, nay, 'tis not that," Ralf assured him hastily. " 'Tis merely that in my experience, it is exceedingly difficult to persuade Alice to cooperate in a plan if she is not inclined toward it in the first place, if you see what I mean. That woman always seems to have plans of her own."

"Have no fears on that point. Your niece and I have already agreed on this arrangement."

"You have?" Ralf looked startled by that news.

"Aye."

"And you're certain that she is in agreement with the scheme?"

"Aye."

"Astounding. Most astounding." For the first time a cautious flame of hope appeared in Ralf's eyes.

Hugh gave up chewing on the hard crust. He tossed it aside. "Come, let us get down to the business at hand."

Ralf's expression promptly turned crafty. "Very well. What is your price? I warn you, I cannot afford to give Alice much in the way of a dowry. The harvest was somewhat less than satisfactory this year."

"Was it?"

"Aye. Very poor. And then there were the expenses involved in maintaining Alice and her brother. Admittedly Benedict was not a great problem, but Alice, I regret to say, is rather costly to keep."

"I am prepared to offer a chest of pepper and one of good ginger as a betrothal gift."

"She is always demanding money for her books and her collection of stones and other useless bits—" Ralf broke off, dumbfounded, as Hugh's words sank in. "A chest of pepper and one of ginger?"

"Aye."

"Sir, I do not know what to say."

"Say that you will accept the bride gift so that I may have done with this matter. It grows late."

"*You* wish to give *me* a dowry for Alice?"

" 'Tis customary, is it not?"

"Not when the bride goes to her lord with nothing in hand but the clothes on her back," Ralf retorted. "You do understand that she brings no land with her, sir."

"I have lands of my own."

"Aye, well, so long as you comprehend the situation." Ralf's expression was one of bewilderment. "In truth, sir, I expected you to demand a large dowry from me in return for taking her off my hands."

"I am prepared to take Alice as she is." Hugh allowed an

edge of impatience to underline his words. "Do we have a bargain?"

"Aye," Ralf said quickly. "Most definitely. Alice is yours for the pepper and ginger."

"Summon your village priest to witness the betrothal vows. I wish to be on my way as soon as possible."

"I shall see to the matter at once." Ralf started to heave his bulk out of his chair. He hesitated midway out of his seat. "Ah, your pardon, Sir Hugh, but there is just one more small point I should like to have made plain before we proceed with this betrothal."

"What is it?"

Ralf licked his lips. He glanced around the chamber as though to make certain that none of the servants could overhear. Then he lowered his voice. "Will you be wanting your chests of pepper and ginger returned to you in the event that you decide not to proceed with the wedding?"

"Nay. The pepper and ginger are yours to keep, regardless of the outcome of our bargain."

"I have your oath on that, too?"

"Aye. You have the oath of Hugh the Relentless."

Ralf grinned in relief and rubbed his plump hands together. "Well, then, let us get on with the thing. No point in delaying, is there? I shall send a servant for the priest at once."

He turned and bustled off, more cheerful than he had been at any time since Hugh's arrival.

A movement in the doorway caught Hugh's attention.

Dunstan, his face set in grim lines, strode into the hall. He came to a halt in front of the table where Hugh sat. His eyes were dark with disgust.

"We have a problem, my lord."

Hugh eyed him thoughtfully. "From your expression, 'twould appear we are on the eve of the crack of doom. What is the matter, Dunstan? Are we under siege?"

Dunstan ignored the comment. "A few minutes ago Lady

Alice summoned two of the men to her chambers to carry her belongings to the baggage wagons."

"Excellent. I am pleased that she is not one to dawdle over her packing."

"I don't believe that you will be quite so pleased with her when you learn just what it is she expects to contribute to the baggage train, sir."

"Well? Don't keep me in suspense, Dunstan. What has she packed that annoys you so?"

"Stones, my lord." Dunstan's jaw tightened. "Two chests of them. And not only are we to carry a sufficient quantity of stones to build a garden wall, but she has made it plain we must also take another chest full of books, parchment, pens, and ink."

"I see."

"And a fourth packed with strange alchemical apparatus." Dunstan's face was mottled with outrage. "Then there is the matter of her clothes, shoes, and personal belongings."

"Lady Alice has a large number of tunics and robes?" Hugh asked, mildly surprised.

"Nay, but what she does have apparently requires an additional chest. My lord, you have stated that we are on a mission of grave import. You have said that speed was of the essence. That there was no time to waste."

"That is true."

"Devil's teeth, sir, we are a company of men-at-arms, not a troupe of traveling jongleurs." Dunstan threw up his hands. "I ask you, how are we to make haste about our business if we must be burdened with a baggage train laden with a woman's collection of stones and alchemical apparatus?"

"The lady in question is my future wife," Hugh said evenly. "You will obey her instructions as you would my own."

Dunstan stared at him. "But I thought—"

"See to the travel preparations, Dunstan."

Dunstan's teeth snapped together with an audible click. "Aye, my lord. May I inquire as to our destination?"

"I do not yet know. I will after I take my betrothal vows."

"No offense, but I have an unpleasant suspicion that regardless of the direction in which we set out, we are bound for only one destination."

"And what destination is that?" Hugh asked politely.

"Trouble," Dunstan muttered.

"It is always good to be in familiar territory, is it not?"

Dunstan did not deign to answer. Muttering ominously, he turned on his heel and stalked toward the door.

Hugh glanced around the hall. There was not even a simple water clock or a sand hourglass to mark the time. Apparently Ralf had no interest in such convenient and efficient machines.

Hugh made to rise from his chair with the intention of going outside to check the position of the sun. The clatter of footsteps and the scrape of a wooden staff on the tower stairs made him pause.

Benedict appeared. The young man was clearly anxious but also quite determined. He came toward Hugh with rigid shoulders.

Hugh examined him thoughtfully. With the exception of his sadly damaged left leg, Alice's brother was tall and well formed. The lack of muscular bulk in his shoulders and chest indicated that he had never received training in arms.

Benedict's hair was darker than his sister's glowing tresses, almost a deep brown. His eyes were very nearly the same unusual shade of green as Alice's, however, and were enlivened with a similar degree of intelligence.

"My lord, I must speak with you at once."

Hugh leaned forward, braced his elbows on the table, and loosely linked his fingers. "What is it, Benedict?"

Benedict cast a quick glance about and then moved closer so that he would not be overheard. "I have just had a talk with my sister," he hissed. "She told me of this crazed bargain the two of you have concluded. She says she is to be betrothed to you until the spring and that the betrothal will be broken when it is *convenient* for your purposes."

"She used those words? Convenient for my purposes?"

Benedict shrugged angrily. "She said something close to that, aye. She said that you are a man who values efficiency and convenience."

"Your sister is of a practical nature herself. Let us be clear on one point here, Benedict. It is Lady Alice who spoke of severing the betrothal in the spring."

Benedict scowled. "What does it matter who said the words? 'Tis clear that this is no genuine betrothal if it is to end in a few months."

"I take it that you have some objection to the arrangement?"

"I most certainly do." Benedict's eyes were fierce. "I believe that you seek to take advantage of my sister, sir. You obviously intend to use her for your own ends."

"Ah."

"You think to seduce her and have the conveniences of a wife until spring, do you not? Then you will toss her aside."

"Not likely, given the price I paid for her," Hugh muttered. "I am not one to waste my money."

"Do not make a mockery of this," Benedict raged. "I may be a cripple, but I am no fool. And I am Alice's brother. I have a duty to protect her."

Hugh studied him for a long moment. "If you do not approve of our bargain, there is an alternative."

"What alternative?" Benedict demanded.

"Convince your sister to give me the information I seek without attaching a price to it."

Benedict slammed his fist down onto the table. "Do not think that I haven't tried to persuade her to be sensible."

"Do you know the whereabouts of the stone?"

"Nay, Alice says she only reasoned it out herself a few days ago. She would not tell me because by then we had heard that you were on the trail of it." Benedict's expression turned glum. "Alice immediately began to make her plans."

"Of course."

"She is a great one for making plans, you see. When she heard that you were after the stone she began to concoct a scheme to remove us both from Lingwood Manor."

"That is not all she bargained for," Hugh said. "Did she mention that she made me promise to provide her with a large dowry for the convent of her choice and to send you off to Paris and Bologna to study law?"

"I do not want to study law," Benedict retorted. " 'Tis all her idea."

"But you do wish to be free of your uncle, do you not?"

"Aye, but not at the risk of Alice's reputation."

Hugh took pity on him. "Your sister is safe enough with me."

"No offense," Benedict gritted, "but you are not called Hugh the Relentless for naught. 'Tis said you are very keen on stratagems. I fear that you have some secret plans for Alice. As her brother, I cannot allow you to hurt her."

Hugh was impressed. "There are not many who would challenge me as you have done."

Benedict flushed. "I realize that I am not skilled in arms and that I am no match for you, Sir Hugh. But I cannot stand by and watch you take advantage of my sister."

"Would it relieve your brotherly concerns to know that I have no intention of harming Lady Alice?"

"What is that supposed to mean?"

"It means that I shall honor my vows of betrothal. From the moment Alice puts herself in my keeping, I shall fulfill all of my obligations to her."

"But that would mean marrying her," Benedict protested. "And she does not wish to marry you."

"That is her problem, is it not?"

Benedict looked baffled. "I do not comprehend you, sir. Surely you do not mean that you actually intend to wed her?"

"Your sister is content with the bargain. I fear you must be satisfied with that much for now. All I can offer you is my oath that I will take proper care of her."

"But, my lord—"

"I said, you have my oath on the matter," Hugh repeated softly. " 'Tis generally considered more than an adequate bond."

Benedict's face turned a deeper shade of dull red. "Aye, my lord."

"You will say naught of your suspicions to your uncle, do you comprehend me? 'Twould be of no use. Sir Ralf will not listen to you and Alice will be most upset." Hugh smiled. "To say nothing of my own reaction."

Benedict hesitated. Then his mouth thinned in mute surrender. "Aye, Sir Hugh. I comprehend you very well."

"Try not to be too anxious, Benedict. I am very good at stratagems. This one will work."

"I just wish I knew exactly what your stratagem is," Benedict grumbled.

*T*hree hours later Alice experienced a strange rush of expectancy as Hugh assisted her into the saddle. Her plan had worked. She and Benedict were free of Sir Ralf at last.

Suddenly, for the first time in months, the future seemed fraught with promise. A crisp breeze stirred the folds of her traveling cloak. Her gray palfrey tossed its shaggy head as though eager to begin the journey.

Out of the corner of her eye Alice saw her brother mount his horse. Although hampered by his bad leg and encumbered by the staff, Benedict had taught himself a surprisingly efficient, if somewhat odd, method for getting into the saddle without assistance. Those who knew him had long since learned not to offer a helping hand.

Alice saw Hugh watch with concealed interest as Benedict climbed atop his horse. For a moment she feared Hugh might order one of his men to help her brother. She was relieved when he did not do so.

Hugh glanced at her at that moment and raised his brows slightly as though to say he had comprehended her thoughts. She gave him a grateful smile. He nodded and vaulted lightly into his own saddle.

Hugh understood. The small, silent exchange sent a curious wave of warmth through Alice.

She was only too well aware that Benedict was not happy with the sudden change in their fortunes. He was as eager as she to escape Lingwood Manor but he was convinced that they might very well have leaped from the hot cook pot into the fire.

Alice took a far more optimistic view. Everything was going along quite nicely, she told herself.

All of her worldly possessions, together with Benedict's, were safely stowed in one of Hugh's baggage wagons. There had been a few minutes of concern early on when Sir Dunstan had complained forcefully about her chests of stones and equipment, but that had soon been settled. Alice was not entirely certain why the obstinate Dunstan had ceased railing about her baggage but she was content with the results.

The vows of betrothal had taken mere minutes to repeat in front of the village priest. A strange shiver of sensation had shot through Alice when Ralf had placed her hand in Hugh's, but she attributed the feeling to her excited state and to the fact that she was not accustomed to a man's touch.

Just as she was not accustomed to a man's kiss, she reminded herself. In spite of the coolness of the day, her body heated at the memory of Hugh's embrace.

"Well, lady?" Hugh looked at her as he took up the reins.

The edge of his cloak was thrown back, revealing the hilt of his sword. Sunlight gleamed on his black onyx ring. "The time has come for you to begin to fulfill your part of our bargain. What is our destination?"

Alice took a deep breath. "To Ipstoke, my lord, where a joust and fair are to be held in a day's time."

"Ipstoke?" Hugh frowned. "That is less than two days' ride from here."

"Aye, my lord. A troubadour named Gilbert stole my green crystal. I believe he will attend the fair."

"A troubadour stole the stone? You are certain of this?"

"Aye, sir. Gilbert stayed in my uncle's hall for a time." Alice tightened her lips. "He was a rogue and a fool. While he was here he tried to seduce every female servant he could find. His songs were poor and he could not even play a decent game of chess."

"A poor troubadour, indeed." Hugh studied her with a disturbingly intent gaze.

"Aye. He was also a thief. He made an excuse to visit my study chamber and he saw the green stone. He asked me about it. Shortly after he left Lingwood Manor, I noticed that the stone had disappeared."

"What makes you think he will have taken it to the Ipstoke fair?"

Alice smiled, quite satisfied with the logic of her deduction. "One evening, while deep in his wine, he mumbled something about going to Ipstoke to play his foolish songs for the knights who will have gathered for the jousts."

"I see."

"There is no reason to doubt it. It is a perfectly reasonable thing for a troubadour to do. There will be a number of knights seeking sport at Ipstoke, will there not?"

"Aye," Hugh said quietly. "If a joust is to be held, there will be no shortage of knights and men-at-arms present."

"Precisely." Alice gave him a complacent smile. "And

where there are knights seeking sport and the chance to make money from ransoms on the jousting field, there are troubadours seeking to entertain them. Is that not true?"

"Aye."

"In addition to an opportunity to earn coin for his songs, I suspect that Gilbert plans to sell my crystal at the fair."

Hugh was silent for a moment. Then he nodded. "Your logic is sound, lady. Very well, Ipstoke it is."

" 'Tis likely that Gilbert does not yet know that you are in pursuit of my stone," Alice said. "But if he chances to discover that you are on his trail, he may not remain long at Ipstoke."

"Then we shall take care that he does not learn that I am after it until it is too late for him to flee. There is just one more thing, lady."

"Aye?"

"You seem to have formed the habit of forgetting that I am the true owner of the green stone."

Alice blushed. "That is still a matter of opinion, my lord."

"Nay, madam. 'Tis a matter of fact. The stone is mine. Our bargain is sealed." Hugh lifted his hand in a signal to his men.

Alice glanced back over her shoulder as the company clattered through the gates of Lingwood Hall. She saw Ralf and her cousins standing on the hall steps. She waved at Gervase, the only one for whom she had felt some attachment. He raised a hand to bid her farewell.

As Alice started to turn her head, she noticed that Ralf was smiling. Her uncle appeared vastly pleased with himself. An uneasy suspicion went through her.

"I trust the rumor I heard about my dowry was mere gossip," she said to Hugh as he guided his large black stallion into place beside her palfrey.

"Personally, I do not pay much attention to gossip."

She slanted him an assessing glance. "You will not credit

this, sir, but there was a tale going round the hall to the effect that you actually promised my uncle two chests of spices."

"Two?"

"Aye, one of pepper and one of ginger." Alice chuckled at that outrageous piece of nonsense. "I am well aware that such overblown gossip is clearly false, my lord. Nevertheless, I am concerned that you may have been cheated. What, precisely, did you give Sir Ralf as a dowry?"

"Do not concern yourself with such details, lady. 'Tis of no great import."

"I would not want to think that you were fleeced, my lord."

Hugh's mouth curved faintly at one corner. "Never fear. I am a man of business. I long ago learned to get my money's worth out of every transaction."

Chapter 5

Ipstoke was a crowded, colorful scene. Even Benedict's sullen mood lightened at the sight of the bright banners and striped tents that dotted the grounds outside the old keep walls. Peddlers and pie-sellers of all descriptions mingled with acrobats, jongleurs, knights, men-at-arms, and farmers. Children ran hither and yon, shouting with glee.

Massive war-horses towered over long-eared asses and sturdy dray ponies. Baggage wagons laden with armor lumbered along next to carts filled with vegetables and wool. Troubadours and minstrels wandered through the crowds.

"I vow, I have never seen so many people in one place in my whole life." Benedict gazed about in wonder. "One could well imagine that everyone in the whole of England is here today."

"Not quite," Alice said. She stood with Benedict on the gentle rise of ground where Hugh had decreed that his somber black tent be pitched. Black banners flapped in the air above her head. Hugh's choice of color formed a stark contrast to the vivid reds, yellows, and greens of the neighboring tents and banners. "I expect that when you travel to Paris and Bologna you will encounter far more wonderful sights than this."

Some of the excitement dimmed in Benedict's eyes. "Alice, I wish you would not talk about my going off to Paris and Bologna as though it were a certainty."

"Nonsense." Alice smiled. " 'Tis very much a certainty now. Sir Hugh will see to it. 'Tis part of our bargain and everyone assures me that he always honors his bargains."

"I do not care for this bargain you have made with him. I was not overfond of our uncle but 'tis better to deal with the devil you know than one with a reputation such as that of Hugh the Relentless."

Alice scowled. "His name is Hugh of Scarcliffe now. Do not refer to him as *Relentless.*"

"Why not? 'Tis what his own men call him. I have been talking with Sir Dunstan. He tells me that Hugh is well named. They say he never abandons a quest."

"They also say that his oath is as strong as a chain fashioned of Spanish steel, and that is all that is important to me." Alice brushed the matter aside with a wave of her hand. "Enough of this chatter. I must see to my end of the bargain."

Benedict glanced at her in astonishment. "What do you mean? You have brought Sir Hugh here to Ipstoke and you gave him the name of the troubadour who stole the green crystal. You need do nothing more."

" 'Twill not be quite so simple as all that. You are forgetting that you and I are the only ones who can identify Gilbert the troubadour. No one else in Hugh's company of men-at-arms has ever seen him."

Benedict shrugged. "Sir Hugh will make inquiries. Gilbert will soon be found."

"What if Gilbert is using another name?"

"Why would he do that?" Benedict demanded. "He has no way of knowing that Sir Hugh has come here in search of him."

"We cannot be certain of that." Alice considered the matter for a moment. "Nay, the quickest way to find Gilbert is for me to wander into the crowd and seek him out. He is bound to be here somewhere. I can only hope that he has not yet sold my green stone. That might complicate matters."

Benedict stared at her. "You're going to search for Gilbert by yourself?"

"You can accompany me, if you like."

"That's not the point. Have you discussed this scheme with Sir Hugh?"

"Nay, but I do not see that it matters overmuch." Alice broke off as Dunstan walked across a patch of grass to join them.

She could not help but notice that Dunstan appeared far more cheerful at that moment than she had yet seen him. His normally dour countenance was enlivened with an expression of enthusiasm and anticipation. His stride was jaunty. He was wearing his hauberk and carried a recently polished helm under one arm.

"My lady." Dunstan greeted Alice with brusque formality. It was rapidly becoming clear that he did not like her very much.

"Sir Dunstan," she murmured. "You look as though you are going off to war."

"Nothing so tame. A jousting match."

Alice was surprised. "You are going to participate in a joust? But we are here on a matter of business."

"Plans have changed."

"*Changed!*" Alice stared at him in amazement. "Does Sir Hugh know of this change?"

"Who do you think changed the plans?" Dunstan asked dryly. He turned to Benedict. "We could use some assistance with the armor and horses. Sir Hugh suggested that you give us a hand."

"Me?" Benedict was startled.

Alice frowned. "My brother has not been trained to handle armor and weapons and war-horses."

Dunstan clapped Benedict on the shoulder. "Sir Hugh says 'tis time he is trained in such manly matters."

Benedict staggered and caught his balance with the aid of his staff. "I am not particularly interested in learning about those things."

Dunstan grinned. "I have news for you, young Benedict. You are Sir Hugh's man now and your new lord believes that 'tis not efficient to have men in his household who are not properly trained and who cannot be counted upon in a siege."

"A siege." Alice was horrified. "Now hold a moment here. I will not have my brother exposed to harm."

Benedict glared at her. "I do not need a nurse, Alice."

"Of course you don't, lad." Dunstan grinned at Alice. His expression said he knew that he had won this small contest. "Your brother will be a man soon. 'Tis past time he learned the ways of men."

"But he is to study law," Alice yelped, outraged.

"So? Seems to me that any man who would study the law has a special need to be able to take care of himself. He'll have any number of enemies."

"Now see here," Alice began furiously. "I'll not have—"

Dunstan ignored her. "Let's be off, Benedict. I'll take you to the refuge tents and introduce you to the squires."

Benedict was reluctantly intrigued. "Very well."

"Benedict, you stay right here, do you hear me?" Alice snapped.

Dunstan chuckled evilly. "Who knows, Benedict? Sir Hugh plans to take the field himself shortly. Mayhap he will allow you to help him with his own personal armor."

"Do you really think so?" Benedict asked.

"By the Saints." Alice could not believe her ears. "Do not tell me that Sir Hugh intends to waste time on a silly joust."

Dunstan gave her a sunny smile. "You have as much to

learn as your brother, Lady Alice. Of course Sir Hugh will take the field today. Vincent of Rivenhall is here."

"Who is Vincent of Rivenhall?" Alice demanded. "What has he got to do with this?"

Dunstan's bushy brows rose. "I've no doubt your betrothed lord will soon explain that to you, my lady. 'Tis certainly not my place to do so. Now, pray excuse me. Benedict and I have work to do."

"Hold." Alice was seething now. "I am not at all satisfied with this turn of events."

"You must take up your dissatisfactions and complaints with Sir Hugh," Dunstan murmured. "Come along, Benedict."

"Wait," Alice ordered. "I need Benedict's assistance."

"But, Alice—" Benedict said unhappily.

"You will not need Benedict for anything this afternoon," Dunstan assured Alice.

She glowered at him. "And, pray, just how do you know that, Sir Dunstan?"

"Why, 'tis obvious." Dunstan gave her an absurdly innocent smile. "You will be occupied with very important matters yourself."

"What important matters?" she asked icily.

" 'Tis plain enough. As is the case with any newly betrothed lady, you will surely want to watch your future lord demonstrate his skills on the jousting field."

"I have absolutely no intention of doing any such thing."

"Nonsense," Dunstan said. "The ladies all love to watch the sport."

Before Alice could summon up further wrath, Dunstan quickly dragged Benedict off in the direction of one of the refuge tents. The shelters had been erected at opposite ends of the large field. The knights, squires, and men-at-arms gathered beneath them to prepare for the day's jousting.

Alice was outraged. She could not believe that Hugh had altered his plans to find the green stone merely because of a jousting match. It made no sense.

When Dunstan and Benedict had disappeared into the crowd she whirled about and started toward the black tent. She would search out Hugh and let him know precisely what she thought of this situation. It was ludicrous for him to enter a joust when they had vastly more important matters to see to.

She came to an abrupt halt when she found her path blocked by a massive black war-horse. She recognized the beast at once. There was no mistaking the huge hooves, broad head, muscular shoulders, and sturdy construction of Hugh's prized stallion. The smell of well-oiled steel and leather assailed her nostrils.

Alice blinked at the sight of Hugh's booted foot in the stirrup. It looked very large. Her gaze rose slowly upward. This was the first time she had seen him in his hauberk. The finely linked mail of his battle armor gleamed in the warm afternoon sun. He had his helm tucked beneath one arm.

Hugh was sufficiently intimidating at the best of times, but when he was clad for war, Hugh the Relentless was a truly unnerving sight. She shaded her eyes with her hand as she looked up at him.

"I hear that 'tis a new custom among ladies of fashion to give their favored knights a token to wear into the jousts," Hugh said quietly.

Alice caught her breath and then hastily regrouped her energies. She was, she reminded herself, thoroughly incensed. "Surely you do not intend to participate in the jousts, my lord?"

" 'Twould be remarked upon if I did not. I do not wish to arouse suspicion concerning my true reason for being here at Ipstoke. The stratagem was to mingle with the fair crowds, if you will recall."

"I see no necessity for you to waste a great deal of time playing silly games atop your horse this afternoon when you could be tracking down Gilbert the troubadour."

"Silly games?"

"That is all they are in my opinion."

"I see. There are many ladies who enjoy watching such contests." Hugh paused deliberately. "Especially when their lords are participants."

"Aye, well, I have never had much interest in such sports."

"Will you give me a token?"

Alice eyed him suspiciously. "What sort of token?"

"A scarf or a bit of ribbon or lacing will do."

"There is certainly no accounting for fashionable customs, is there, my lord?" Alice shook her head, amazed. "Imagine giving a man a perfectly good length of clean cloth or a fine silk ribbon to wear while he dashes about in the mud. The token, as you call it, would likely be ruined."

"Mayhap." Hugh gazed down at her with unreadable eyes. "Nevertheless, I think it would be wise if you gave me such a token, Alice."

Alice gazed at him blankly. "Whatever for, sir?"

"It will be expected," Hugh said very evenly. "We are, after all, betrothed."

"You wish to carry my favor into the joust in order to convince everyone that we truly are betrothed?"

"Aye."

"But what about my green stone?"

"All in good time," Hugh said softly.

"I thought the stone was extremely important to you."

"It is and I will have it by the end of the day. But something else has come up. Something that is just as important."

"What is that, pray tell?" Alice demanded.

"Vincent of Rivenhall is here and intends to participate in the joust." Hugh's voice was curiously empty of emotion. The very flatness of his tone was frightening.

"What of it?" Alice asked uneasily. "By the Saints, sir, I should think you would be able to forgo a bit of sport for the sake of the stone."

"I assure you, the opportunity to take the field against Vincent of Rivenhall is almost as important as recovering the stone."

"I would not have thought that you would find it necessary to prove yourself against another knight, my lord," Alice said, disgruntled. "I rather assumed that you were above such things."

"It would be wise for you to refrain from making too many assumptions about me, Alice."

Alice's mouth went dry. She contented herself with a glare. "Very well, my lord. Henceforth, I shall assume nothing."

"Be assured that I will explain the matter of Sir Vincent to you at some other time." Hugh stretched out his hand. "At the moment, I am in a hurry. Your favor, if you please."

"This is really too much." Alice glanced down at her clothing. "I suppose you may take the ribbon that trims my sleeve, if you feel that it is absolutely necessary."

"It is."

"Do try not to soil it, will you? Good ribbon costs money."

"If it is ruined, I shall buy you another. I can afford it."

Alice felt herself grow warm beneath his mocking gaze. They both knew that a new ribbon would be as nothing to him.

"Very well." Alice undid the ribbon from her sleeve.

"Thank you." Hugh reached down to take the strip of green cloth. "You may watch the jousts from beneath the yellow and white tent on the far side of the field. That is where the other ladies will sit."

"I do not intend to watch the jousts, sir," Alice said heatedly. "I, for one, have better things to do."

"Better things?"

"Aye, my lord. I am going to search for Gilbert. There is no point in both of us wasting the afternoon."

Hugh's mailed fist closed very tightly around the green ribbon. "Do not trouble yourself about the troubadour, Alice. He will be found soon enough. In the meantime, you will watch the jousts in the company of the other spectators."

Without waiting for a response, Hugh gave the big warhorse an invisible signal. The beast swung about with astonishing agility and set off eagerly in the direction of the jousting field. His great hooves sent a tremor through the ground.

"But, Sir Hugh, I just told you that I do not wish to watch the jousts—" Alice broke off in disgust when she realized she was speaking to the war-stallion's retreating hindquarters.

For the first time she experienced some qualms about the bargain she had made with Hugh. It was obvious that her new business associate did not fully comprehend the true meaning of what it meant to be equal partners.

Chapter 6

he rosy-cheeked pie-seller handed Alice a crusty pastry stuffed with minced, honeyed chicken. "Aye, there be a number of troubadours about. Don't think I noticed one wearing a yellow and orange tunic, though." The woman took Alice's coin and popped it into her belt pouch. "Now, then, will there be anythin' else, m'lady?"

"Nay."

The pie-seller brushed crumbs from her hands and turned to deal with the next customer. " 'Ere, me good lad, what'll ye have? I've got excellent fruit pies and tasty lamb, too. Take yer choice."

Alice eyed her pie with distaste as she walked away from the stall. It was the fourth one she had bought in the last hour. She was not at all certain that she could manage to eat it.

She had thought to conduct her search for Gilbert in a systematic fashion but the task was proving difficult. Thus far she had covered only a third of the fairgrounds. Finding one particular troubadour in this crowded place was a slow process.

She had attempted to start several casual conversations at

various stalls and tents but she had soon discovered that no one was willing to waste time in idle chatter. Having ascertained that peddlers, pie-sellers, and merchants were far more prone to indulge her carefully worded questions if they thought that she was going to spend good coin, Alice had reluctantly begun to do just that. To her dismay, she had already gone through most of the contents of her purse and had learned nothing. Along the way she had been obliged to consume three pies and two mugs of cider.

She hesitated at the end of a row of brightly striped peddlers' tents, wondering what to do with her newest pie. She hated to throw it aside. Waste of any sort offended her sensibilities.

"Psst. Fine lady. Over here."

Alice glanced up from the pie and saw a youth of about sixteen years hovering in the shadow of a nearby awning. He gave her a grimy-faced grin.

"Excellent bargains, m'lady. Come and see." The young man glanced hurriedly over his shoulder and then whipped a small dagger out from beneath his dirt-stained tunic.

Alice gasped and took a step back. Thieves and pickpockets were a constant threat at fairs. She clutched her skirts and made to run.

"Nay, nay, do not fear, fine lady." The youth's dark eyes filled with alarm. "I mean you no harm. I am called Fulk. I offer this beautiful dagger for sale. See? 'Tis fashioned of the best Spanish steel."

Alice relaxed. "Aye, 'tis a pretty little dagger but I have no use for such."

"Mayhap you could give it to yer lord as a gift?" Fulk suggested with a determined gleam in his eye. "A man can always use a good dagger."

"Sir Hugh has arms enough as it is," Alice retorted. She was still fuming over the fact that Hugh had elected to fritter away the afternoon on the jousting field.

"No man has enough good steel. Come closer, m'lady, and examine the workmanship."

Alice studied the dagger with little interest. "Where did you get this?"

"My father sells daggers and knives in a stall on the other side of the fairgrounds," Fulk said smoothly. "I assist him by mingling with the crowd to search out customers."

"Try another tale, lad."

"Very well." Fulk groaned. "If ye must know the truth, I found it lying by the side of the road. A shame, is it not? I believe it to be the property of some passing traveler. It must have been dropped by accident."

"More likely it was filched from a knife-seller's stall."

"Nay, nay, m'lady. I give ye me oath that I came by this blade in an honest fashion." Fulk turned the dagger to display the inlaid handle. "See how beautiful it is. I'll wager these be rare and valuable gems."

Alice smiled wryly. " 'Tis no use practicing your wiles on me, lad. I have only a few coins left in my purse and I intend to use them to purchase something far more useful than that dagger."

Fulk gave her an angelic smile. "What do ye wish to purchase, fine lady? Just let me know what ye want and I shall fetch it for ye. Then ye can pay me for it. Twill save ye a lot of dashing about amongst these dirty stalls."

Alice eyed him thoughtfully. "Very helpful of you."

He swept her an almost courtly bow. " 'Tis me great privilege to serve ye, m'lady."

It occurred to Alice that he just might be able to assist her. "What I am in need of is some information."

"Information?" Fulk slipped the knife back inside his tunic sleeve with a businesslike flick of his wrist. "That won't be any problem. I frequently sell information. Ye'd be surprised how many people wish to purchase that particular commodity. Now, then, just what sort of information do ye seek?"

Alice plunged into the tale she had concocted for the pie-sellers and peddlers. "I am searching for a handsome troubadour who has long brown hair, a small beard, and pale blue eyes. He favors a yellow and orange tunic. I heard him sing earlier and I wish to listen to some more of his songs but I cannot find him in this crowd. Have you seen him?"

Fulk tilted his head to one side and gave her a shrewd look. "Are ye in love with this troubadour?"

Alice started to utter an indignant protest and then caught herself. She gave what she hoped was a fluttering sigh instead. "He is most comely."

Fulk snorted in disgust. "Ye be not the only lady who thinks so. By the teeth o' Saint Anselm, I don't know what it is about troubadours. They all seem to have pretty ladies swooning at their feet."

Alice stilled. "Then you have seen him?"

"Aye. I've seen yer fancy poet." Fulk lifted one shoulder in a careless shrug. "His tunic is very pretty, just as ye said. Always favored yellow and orange meself."

"Where did you see him?" Alice asked eagerly.

"Last night he entertained a group of knights around one of the campfires. I, uh, happened to be nearby at the time and overheard him."

"Is that when you stumbled upon the lost dagger?" Alice asked politely.

"As it happens, it was." Fulk was not the least chagrined by her deduction. "Knights are a careless lot, especially when they've had too many cups of wine. Always losing daggers and purses and such. Now, then, how much will ye pay me for finding yer handsome troubadour for ye?"

Alice fingered her nearly empty purse. "I have only a couple of coins left. I suppose the information is worth one of them. Mayhap two if you're quick with it."

"Done." Fulk grinned again. "Come with me, m'lady. I know where to find the troubadour."

"How is it you can be so certain of that?"

"I told ye that ye weren't the only female in love with him. Last night I heard him tell a certain blond-haired lady that he would meet her today while her lord takes the field in the jousts."

"By the Saints," Alice muttered. "You are, indeed, a fount of information, Fulk."

"I told ye, information sells as well as anything else and there's not nearly so much risk involved." Fulk turned and set off through the maze of stalls with a jaunty swagger.

Alice tossed aside her uneaten pie and hurried after him.

Fifteen minutes later she found herself on the outskirts of the fairgrounds. She glanced back uneasily as Fulk led the way around the old stone wall that surrounded Ipstoke Keep. They had left the crowd behind. She was alone with Fulk.

She followed him up a gentle slope of rising ground. When she reached the crest she glanced back once more. She discovered that she could see across the tops of the tents and banners all the way to the distant jousting field.

A throng of spectators had gathered to view the melee. Even as Alice watched a great shout went up. The sound of it was carried toward her on the breeze. Two opposing groups of knights charged toward one another from opposite ends of the field.

Alice winced as they slammed together. Several horses and men went down in a fearsome tangle. Armor glinted in the sun and horses flailed. Alice found herself searching for a familiar black banner but it was impossible to identify Hugh or any of his men from this distance.

"This way, m'lady," Fulk whispered. He rounded one of the ramshackle outbuildings. "Hurry."

Alice told herself that Hugh was much too clever and too skilled to get hurt. Knights of his caliber thrived on mock combat. She shuddered. Her father had been no different. Sir Bernard had spent a great deal of his life in northern France seeking the glory and wealth to be had from the endless round of tournaments. Bernard had sought something else as well on those journeys, Alice thought wistfully. Escape from his responsibilities as a husband and father.

She had only scattered memories of her father. Those memories were sprinkled across the years like so many bright beads from a broken strand.

Bernard had been a handsome man with a hearty laugh, a curly red beard, and vivid green eyes. He had been loud and boisterous and full of enthusiasm for the hunt, the joust, and, according to Helen, Alice's mother, London brothels.

Bernard was gone a great deal of the time but his visits to his manor were wonderful events in Alice's childhood. He swooped down upon the household with presents and stories. He scooped Alice up in his arms and carried her through the great hall. While Bernard was home it seemed to Alice that everything, including her mother, glowed and shimmered with happiness.

But all too soon Bernard would set out again for a joust in some distant place or an extended trip to London. Many of Alice's memories from her early years included scenes of her mother crying after one of Bernard's frequent departures.

The family had seen more of Bernard for a time after his son and heir was born. Helen had been radiant during that period. But after Benedict was permanently injured in the fall from his horse Bernard had gone back to his old habits. The trips to London and northern France became frequent and prolonged once more.

As the years passed, Helen responded to her husband's lengthy absences by spending an ever-increasing amount of time at work on her handbook or mixing her herbs and potions. She grew distant from her children, seemingly obsessed by her studies.

In the later years Helen no longer greeted Bernard's brief visits with glowing happiness in her eyes. On the positive side,

Alice thought, her mother no longer cried for hours after Bernard's leave-takings.

As her mother secluded herself for longer and longer periods in her study, Alice gradually took over the myriad responsibilities of managing the household and manor. She also assumed the task of rearing Benedict. She feared she had not been a great success in her efforts to be both mother and father to him. She had been unable to make up for the pain that Bernard's careless rejection had caused. The silent resentment in Benedict's eyes whenever his father was mentioned still made Alice want to weep.

But the knowledge of just how badly she had failed had not struck home until she managed to lose Benedict's inheritance.

"M'lady?"

Alice pushed aside the melancholy memories. "Where are we going, Fulk?"

"Hush." He waved frantically to silence her. "Do ye want them to hear ye?"

"I want to know where you're taking me." She walked around a sagging wooden storage shed and saw him crouched behind a stretch of thick foliage.

"Last night I heard the troubadour tell the blond-haired lady that he would meet her down there in the bushes by the stream."

"You're certain?"

"If he's not there, ye don't need to pay me," Fulk said magnanimously.

"Very well," Alice said. "Lead on."

Fulk plunged into the greenery that hid the stream from view. Alice picked up her skirts and followed cautiously. Her soft leather boots were going to be ruined, she thought.

A moment later a high, keening cry stopped her in her tracks. She grabbed Fulk's arm.

"What was that?" she whispered, horrified.

"The blonde, most likely," Fulk muttered without any show of surprise.

"Someone is attacking her. We must go to her aid."

Fulk blinked and then stared at her as though she were mad. "I don't think she'll be wantin' any help from the likes of us."

"Why not?"

"From the sounds of it, your fancy troubadour is plucking her harp string quite nicely for her."

Another high, feminine scream sounded in the distance.

"Plucking her string? I do not understand. Someone is hurting that woman. We must do something."

Fulk rolled his eyes. "The troubadour is tumblin' her in the tall grass, m'lady."

"Tumbling her? As though she were a ball, do you mean? Why on earth would he do that?"

Fulk groaned softly. "Don't ye comprehend, m'lady? He's makin' love to her."

"Here? In the bushes?" Alice was so shocked that she tripped over a twig and nearly fell flat on her face.

"Where else?" Fulk reached out to steady her. "They can hardly use her lord's tent, now, can they? And the troubadour doesn't have one of his own."

Alice felt herself grow exceedingly warm. It was unsettling to realize that this boy who was no older than Benedict knew a great deal more about such matters than she did.

"I see." She tried to sound casual.

Fulk took pity on her obvious embarrassment. "Do ye want to wait here until they're finished?"

"Well, I suppose so. I certainly don't want to interrupt them."

"As ye wish." Fulk held out his hand. "I've fulfilled me part of the bargain. If ye'll be so kind as to pay me now, I'll be on me way."

Alice frowned. "You're quite certain that it's Gilbert the troubadour who is with that lady?"

"Take a look over there." Fulk nodded toward a bright patch of yellow and orange cloth that lay on the ground beneath the drooping branches of a tree.

Alice followed his gaze. "That does look like Gilbert's outer tunic. And I think I see his lute."

A hoarse, masculine groan reverberated through the greenery just as Alice handed Fulk the last of her coins.

"From the sound of things, yon troubadour is playing his own instrument now. A horn, I believe." Fulk's fingers closed tightly around the coins. "But don't fret, fine lady. I heard him tell the blond-haired lady that he was good for more than one tune."

Alice frowned again. "I don't believe that I comprehend—"

But Fulk had vanished into the shrubbery.

Alice hesitated, not certain how to proceed. She had intended to confront Gilbert when she found him and demand that he surrender her green stone. Now, for the first time she wondered if he would even admit to possessing it. What would she do if he simply denied all knowledge of the stone?

And then there was the awkward business of Gilbert's blond-haired lady. What did one say to a man and a woman who had just finished making love? Alice wondered. Especially when that love was clearly adulterous.

Alice was forced to conclude that Gilbert was far bolder than she had realized. In having dared to seduce a married lady, he risked castration or even death at the hands of the woman's husband. A man who was willing to dare so much for passion would likely laugh at Alice when she asked him to return the green stone.

It occurred to her that things would have been much simpler at this juncture had Hugh accompanied her. He would have had no qualms about challenging Gilbert.

Trust a man to be fooling about on a jousting field when there were more important matters to be dealt with, she thought, irritated.

Another husky groan startled her. This one seemed louder than the last, as though it were approaching some peak or hurdle. It occurred to her that she had no notion of how long it took to make love. Mayhap Gilbert and his lady would emerge from the bushes at any moment. They would see her standing there looking quite foolish.

If she was going to act, it had to be soon.

Alice took a deep, steadying breath and marched determinedly toward the pile of discarded clothing. When she reached it she saw at once that Gilbert had left not only his lute but a small canvas sack next to his tunic.

The sack was just the proper size to carry a large stone.

Alice hesitated once more and then reminded herself that Gilbert had stolen the crystal from her. She had every right to take it back.

Stealthily she opened the flap of the sack. An object approximately the size of the stone lay inside. It was swathed in an old rag.

With trembling fingers Alice lifted the heavy object out of the sack and eased aside a portion of the dirty cloth. The familiar dull sheen of the strange, clouded green crystal winked at her. The crystal's flat, wide facets caught the light but they did not reflect it very strongly.

There was no mistaking her green stone. A surge of satisfaction went through Alice. It was not an attractive chunk of crystal, but she found it fascinating. She had never seen a stone or crystal quite like it. She sensed it contained secrets, although in the short space of time in which it had been in her possession she had been unable to reason out what those secrets were.

A hoarse shout from the vicinity of the bushes made Alice

start. She leaped to her feet, stone in hand. Then she heard Gilbert's voice.

"When I sing to your lord's men at the campfire tonight, my sweet, you will know that the lady in my song is you. Will you blush?"

"Of course, but who will see in the shadows?" The woman laughed. "You are indeed a rogue, Sir Troubadour."

"Thank you, madam." Gilbert chuckled. "I shall sing of your alabaster breasts and milk-white thighs. And of the honey and dew I found between those lovely thighs today. Your lord will be none the wiser."

"You had best pray that my lord does not recognize me in your poem," the lady said dryly, "else you will surely find yourself deprived of your fine lute."

Gilbert laughed uproariously. "There would be no pleasure in the chase if there were no risk involved. Some men prefer to take their sport on the jousting field. I prefer to take mine between the soft thighs of their ladies."

Alice hesitated no longer. Clutching the rag-wrapped stone, she fled. She could only pray that Gilbert would not hear her footsteps on the soft ground.

She had not gone far when she heard his angry shout. She knew that he had just discovered his loss.

Alice ran faster. She did not think that Gilbert had seen her.

She was breathing hard by the time she reached the stone wall of the old keep. She ducked behind a small wooden shed while she paused to catch her breath. In another few minutes she would be safe amid the fair crowds, she told herself. Gilbert would never be able to find her.

She took a deep breath. Pulse racing, she scurried out from behind the poor protection of the shed and dashed across an open field toward the first row of tents.

Two men armed with daggers stepped straight into her

path. One gave her a toothless grin. The second wore a patch over his right eye.

Horrified, Alice stumbled to a halt.

"Well, now, what have we here but a fine lady with an interesting bundle in her hand. Seems the lad sold us sound information, Hubert."

The man wearing the eyepatch chuckled humorlessly. "Aye, so he did. Mayhap we should have paid him for his services, after all."

"Never pay for what ye can get for free, I always say." Toothless glided forward. He beckoned with his free hand. "Give us the stone, lady, and there'll be no trouble."

Alice drew herself up very straight and fixed him with a furious glare. "This stone belongs to me. Step aside at once."

Eyepatch chortled. "Sounds like a fine, proper lady, don't she? Always wanted me one of them."

"You can have her," Toothless muttered. "As soon as we've finished our business."

Alice clutched the stone and opened her mouth to scream for help. She knew with a sense of despair that there was no one around who would come to her aid.

"*H*as Benedict returned?" Hugh studied the far end of the jousting field. He could see Vincent's banners snapping in the breeze. Anticipation coursed through Hugh, icy and invigorating.

I shall not forget, Grandfather.

"Nay, m'lord." Dunstan followed Hugh's gaze. A knowing expression appeared in his eyes. "Well, well, well. I see that Vincent of Rivenhall is finally preparing to take the field."

"Aye, and about time, too." Hugh glanced toward the refuge tents, searching for Benedict. There was no sign of him.

"Blood of the devil, where is that boy? He should have returned by now with news of his sister."

Hugh had sent Benedict off to fetch Alice when it had become apparent that she was not among the spectators. For some reason Hugh had been first disappointed and then thoroughly irritated to realize that Alice was not sitting with the ladies. He told himself that he had a right to be angry. He had, after all, given her specific instructions and she had ignored them. But he had an uneasy feeling that the matter went deeper.

She had doubtless found it convenient to pay him no heed because she did not consider him her rightful lord.

"Mayhap she has no interest in the sport." Dunstan spat on the ground. He surveyed the colorful flock of fluttering ladies who sat beneath the bright yellow awning on one side of the field. " 'Tis a man's game, after all."

"Aye." Hugh searched the crowd at the refuge tent once more, looking for Benedict.

"I remember the days when the ladies couldn't be bothered to come to a joust," Dunstan said. "Now they've turned these affairs into a matter of fashion. It's enough to make a stout knight weep."

"I can wait no longer," Hugh said. "Vincent is nearly ready. Have my horse brought to me."

"Aye, m'lord." Dunstan signaled to the squire who held the reins of Hugh's black war-horse.

Hugh cast one last look at the spectators. There was still no sign of Alice. "God's teeth. The lady has a lot to learn."

A broad-shouldered, heavily bearded man with small, glittering eyes walked out of the refuge tent. "Sir Hugh. I heard you were here. Could not resist the opportunity to unhorse Vincent of Rivenhall, eh?"

Hugh glanced at the newcomer without much enthusiasm. "They tell me that you have done well today, Eduard."

"I took a good war-horse and some armor from Alden of Granthorpe." Eduard chuckled hugely. "Left Sir Alden flopping about in the dirt with a broken leg. An amusing sight. Looked like an overturned turtle."

Hugh said nothing. He did not like Eduard. The man was several years older than himself, a hardened mercenary who sold his sword to anyone who could pay his price. That, in itself, was no great crime. Hugh knew full well that had his own fate not sent him into the household of Erasmus of Thornewood, he would have chosen a similar career.

Hugh's dislike of Eduard was based on other factors. The mercenary was a skilled warrior but he was crude and ill-mannered. Hugh had heard unpleasant rumors concerning the man's violent propensities toward young females, including one that several months ago a twelve-year-old tavern wench had died from Eduard's rough lust. Hugh did not know if the gossip was true, but he did not find it difficult to believe.

"Ready, my lord." The squire steadied the eager stallion.

"Excellent." Hugh turned away from Eduard.

"My lord Hugh." Benedict limped around the corner of the tent just as Hugh set one booted foot into the stirrup. He was panting for breath.

"My lord. I cannot find her."

Hugh paused. "She is not in the tent?"

"Nay, my lord." Benedict came to a halt and braced himself with his staff. "Mayhap she is browsing through the peddlers' stalls. She is not overfond of jousts and such."

"I instructed her to watch the sport in the company of the other ladies."

"I know, my lord." Benedict looked anxious. "You must make allowances for my sister, sir. Alice is not in the habit of following instructions. She prefers to go about matters in her own fashion."

"So it would seem." Hugh settled himself into the saddle and reached down to take the lance from one of his men. He glanced at the frail strip of bright green ribbon that fluttered near the point of the weapon.

"My lord, I pray you will be tolerant of her nature," Benedict pleaded. "She has never taken guidance well. Especially from men."

"Then 'tis time she learned to do so." Hugh glanced down the length of the field. Vincent of Rivenhall was mounting beneath a red banner.

In spite of his irritation with Alice, Hugh was becoming increasingly uneasy. The prickling sensation on the back of his neck was not caused by anticipation of the coming clash with Vincent.

Something was wrong.

He had assumed that Alice had failed to take her place among the onlookers out of sheer pique. Hugh was well aware that she had not cared to be told that she must attend the jousts. He assured himself that she was sulking and determined to deal with the matter later. After he had gone against Vincent of Rivenhall.

Hugh and Vincent were forbidden the satisfaction of open aggression against each other because of their mutual allegiance to Erasmus of Thornewood. Erasmus had no intention of allowing his best knights to expend their energy and squander their incomes warring against each other. The two were obliged to limit their encounters to those rare occasions when they found themselves on the same jousting field. At such times the old feud could be conducted under the guise of sport.

The last time they had engaged in mock combat, Hugh had felled Vincent with a single blow of his lance. As the joust had been a major event sponsored by two great barons, there had been no tame limits on the ransoms. The victorious knights had been free to claim whatever they could get from their victims.

Everyone had fully expected Hugh to set a high price on

Vincent of Rivenhall. At the very least he could have claimed his opponent's expensive war-horse and armor.

Hugh had taken nothing. Instead, he had quit the field, leaving Vincent on the ground as though he were of no account. The insult had been outrageous and unmistakable. Ballads had been sung about it and another tale had been added to the growing legend of Hugh the Relentless.

No one but Hugh and his sole confidant, Dunstan, knew the real truth. There had been no need to strip Vincent of his costly armor and horse. Hugh had plotted a far more subtle and infinitely more effective stratagem against Vincent of Rivenhall, one that would unfold in the fullness of time. Another six months or a year at most.

The final triumph would be complete. Hugh was convinced that it would calm the storm winds that swirled across his soul. He would know peace at last.

In the meantime these occasional meetings on the jousting field served to whet the appetite of the *Bringer of Storms.*

Hugh tucked his helm under his arm and looked down at Benedict. "Take two of the grooms and look for your sister among the peddlers' tents."

"Aye, my lord." Benedict started to turn away. He hesitated. "Sir, I must ask you what you intend to do with Alice when she is found."

"That is Alice's problem, not yours."

"But, my lord—"

"I said, that is between Alice and myself. Go, Benedict. You have a task to fulfill."

"Aye, my lord." Reluctantly, Benedict turned to make his way back through the crowd of men clustered near the refuge tents.

Hugh prepared to address the small company of men who rode beneath his black banner. They faced him eagerly. There was always money to be made when they took the field with Hugh the Relentless.

Hugh had discovered early on that there was a secret to winning tournaments as well as battles. The secret was discipline and a sound stratagem. It never failed to amaze him how few men practiced those arts.

Knights were, by nature, a rash, enthusiastic lot who thundered out onto the jousting field or into actual combat with no thought to anything except individual glory and booty. They were encouraged to do so by their peers who vied for the same honor and loot and by the troubadours who sang songs about their heroism. And then, of course, there were the ladies. They preferred to bestow their favors upon the heroes of the ballads.

Such undisciplined antics made for amusing poems, in Hugh's opinion, but they also made victory in either mock or real combat a haphazard event.

Hugh preferred his victories to be predictable. Discipline and adherence to the stratagem that he had determined before the conflict were the keys to predictability. He had made them the cornerstones of the techniques he used to train his men.

Men-at-arms and knights who put their own lust for glory and plunder before their willingness to follow Hugh's orders did not last long in his employ.

"You will maintain orderly ranks and follow the stratagem that we discussed earlier," Hugh said to his men. "Is that plain?"

Dunstan grinned as he donned his helm. "Aye, m'lord. Never fear, we're ready to follow your plan."

The others grinned acknowledgment.

"Remember," Hugh cautioned. "Vincent of Rivenhall is mine. You will occupy yourselves with his men."

There were sober nods in response. All of Hugh's men knew of the ill feelings that existed between their lord and Vincent of Rivenhall. The feud was no secret.

Satisfied that all was in readiness, Hugh started to mount his war-horse. He would deal with Alice later.

"My lord, wait," Benedict yelled.

Hugh looked back impatiently. He saw raw fear on Benedict's face. "What is it?"

"This boy, Fulk, says he knows where Alice is." Benedict pointed to a dusty youth of about his own age. "He says that two men with daggers have gone in pursuit of her. He says he will tell us where to find her. For a price."

It occurred to Hugh somewhat belatedly that the reason Alice was not sitting with the spectators or sulking in her tent was because she had gone in search of Gilbert the troubadour. *Surely she would not have been so reckless.*

But even as Hugh tried to reassure himself, a cold feeling settled deep inside his guts.

An image of the hapless Clydemere peddler lying, throat slit, in a pool of blood, temporarily clouded his vision.

Hugh looked at the grinning Fulk. "Is this true?"

"Aye, me fine lord." Fulk's grin widened. "I'm a merchant, ye see. I trade in information or anything else that comes me way. I'll be happy to tell ye where the red-haired lady is. But ye best hurry if you're planning to rescue her afore those two footpads catch up with her."

Hugh ruthlessly quashed the rage and fear that threatened to well up within him. He forced all evidence of emotion from his mind and his voice. "Speak."

"Well, now, as to that, me lord, first we must set the price."

"The price," Hugh said softly, "is your life. Speak the truth now or prepare to pay."

Fulk stopped grinning.

Chapter 7

$\mathcal{A}$lice ran for the storage shed. Her only hope was to reach it before the two dagger-wielding thieves caught her. If she could get through the door she might be able to barricade herself inside.

"Stop her," the man with the eyepatch yelled to his companion. "If we lose that damned stone this time we'll never get paid."

"The wench runs like a hart," the other man panted. "But she won't escape."

The frightening *thud-thud-thud* of her pursuers' booted feet behind her was the most terrifying sound Alice had ever heard. The storage shed seemed very far away. She was hampered by the weight of the heavy green stone and by her own skirts.

The two thieves closed on her.

Alice was ten paces away from the small outbuilding when she heard the thunder. It shook the very ground beneath her feet.

Some part of her awareness registered the fact that the sun was still shining. There was no sign of a storm.

The thunder was an ominous drumbeat behind her.

And then she heard one of her pursuers scream.

The horrible cry brought Alice to a stumbling halt. She whirled around in time to see the thief with the toothless grin go down beneath the hooves of a black war-stallion. The beast seemed not to notice the slight obstacle. It surged forward, seeking fresh prey.

Alice recognized the great war-beast and the unhelmed knight astride it. The black manes of horse and rider alike snapped in the wind. Steel flashed in the sun.

Alice clutched the stone and stared at the awesome sight she beheld. She had seen knights and war-horses enough in her life but she had never seen anything so fearsome as this.

Hugh the Relentless and the black juggernaut he rode came forward as one, a great engine of battle that nothing could stop.

The one-eyed man yelled and veered sharply from the chase, seeking refuge in the bushes that bordered the stream. He did not have a hope of outrunning the stallion. Apparently realizing that he was doomed, he turned helplessly to face his fate.

Alice started to close her eyes against the inevitable scene of death and destruction. But at the last instant the highly trained war-horse, obedient to its rider's unseen command, altered course. The huge creature brushed past the thief, leaving the one-eyed man untouched.

The big animal came to a shuddering halt, swung around on its haunches, and paced back to where the one-eyed man cowered. The stallion tossed his head, blew heavily, and stomped one massive hoof as though to protest the end of the chase.

The one-eyed man fell to his knees in terror.

Hugh glanced at Alice. "Are you all right?"

Alice could not find her tongue. Her mouth had gone dry. She nodded quickly.

Satisfied with her response, Hugh turned his attention to the thief. When he spoke his voice was terrifyingly soft. "So, you would hunt the lady as though you were a hound in pursuit of a hare."

"Do not kill me, m'lord," the one-eyed man pleaded. "We meant no harm. We was just frolicking with the lass. Only wanted a good tumble. Where's the harm in that?"

"The lass," Hugh said with exquisite care, "is my betrothed wife."

The thief's eye widened as he saw the ground open beneath his feet. Hell clearly awaited him. He made one more stumbling effort to defend himself.

"But how was we to know that, m'lord? She looks like any other wench. Found her comin' out of the bushes, we did. Naturally, we assumed she was looking for a bit of sport."

"Silence," Hugh commanded. "You are still alive only because I have inquiries to make of you. If you do not watch your tongue I may well decide that I don't need your answers."

The thief shuddered. "Aye, m'lord."

Dunstan came pelting around the corner of the old stone wall. Benedict, moving with the surprising speed he could affect with the aid of his staff, followed close behind him. Both men were out of breath and red in the face.

"Alice," Benedict yelled. "Are you unhurt?"

"Aye." Alice realized that she was trembling. She did not look at the man who had fallen beneath the war-horse's hooves.

Hugh glanced at Dunstan. "See to the one on the ground. He went down beneath Storm's charge and is likely dead."

"Aye, m'lord." Dunstan ambled toward the fallen man. He prodded the still body with the toe of his boot and spat casually into the grass. "I believe you're correct in your assumption, sir." Dunstan bent down to take a closer look at the object that lay beside the fallen man. "He carried a nice little dagger."

" 'Tis yours if you want it," Hugh said as he dismounted. "Along with anything else you can find on him."

"That will not amount to much."

A collective shout went up in the distance. The sounds of the latest clash on the jousting field were borne on the wind. Dunstan and Benedict both looked back in the direction of the tournament grounds.

Alice was conscious of an acute tension.

"I believe Vincent of Rivenhall has taken the field," Hugh said after a moment.

"Aye, sir." Dunstan heaved a sigh of regret. "That he has. 'Twould appear he has gone against Harold of Ardmore. That won't be much of a contest. Vincent will ride straight over the top of young Harold."

Hugh's jaw tightened but his voice remained as calm as though they had all been discussing the latest farming techniques. "I regret that you must content yourself with whatever booty you find on these two thieves today, Dunstan. 'Tis plain that due to certain recent events we will not have the opportunity of taking more lucrative victories in the jousts."

Dunstan shot a hooded glance toward Alice. "Aye, m'lord."

Hugh tossed the reins of the war-horse to Benedict. "Summon the sheriff and tell him that I will wish to question this man later."

"Aye, sir." Benedict seized Storm's reins. The stallion gave him a flat stare.

Hugh looked at Alice with unreadable eyes. "You are certain that you are unhurt?"

"Aye," Alice whispered. For some idiotic reason she felt as if she were about to burst into tears. She had the most ridiculous desire to throw herself into Hugh's arms. "You saved my life, my lord."

"That would not have been necessary had you obeyed my instructions to attend the jousts." Hugh's voice held no inflection.

Alice went cold. Mayhap it was true what they said about him, she thought. Mayhap Hugh the Relentless lacked all the warmer feelings. The weight of the rag-wrapped stone was suddenly very heavy in her hands. Belatedly she remembered that she held it.

"I have discovered the green stone, my lord," she said, hoping that knowledge would break through the invisible steel hauberk he wore over his emotions.

"Is that so?" He gave the object in her hands a cursory glance. "I am not pleased with the price you very nearly paid for it."

"But—"

"I had already made inquiries concerning the whereabouts of Gilbert the troubadour. He was to have entertained certain knights and their ladies this evening. The stone would have been safely in my hands by morning. There was no necessity for you to risk your neck for it."

Alice's precarious emotions underwent a sudden shift. She was outraged. "You should have told me of your scheme before you went off to the jousts, my lord. We are partners, if you will recall. We made a bargain."

"Our bargain, as you term it, has nothing to do with the fact that when I give instructions, I expect them to be obeyed."

"By the Saints, sir, that is most unfair."

"Unfair?" He started toward her. "You think I lack a sense of fairness merely because I object to your taking foolish risks?"

Alice stared at him in amazement. "You are angry."

"Aye, madam."

"I mean truly *angry*," she breathed. "Simply because I put myself in danger."

"I do not consider that such a simple matter, lady."

Hugh's forbidding expression should have deepened Alice's alarm, but for some reason it did not. A tiny flame of hope flared to life within her.

"I believe that you are actually more concerned about me than you are about the green stone, sir."

"You are my betrothed wife," Hugh said evenly. "As such, you are my responsibility."

Alice smiled tremulously. "My lord, I do believe you are something of a fraud. You are not nearly so cold as people claim. Today you saved my life and I will never forget it so long as I live."

She set the cloth-shrouded stone on the ground, straightened, and rushed straight into Hugh's arms.

To her astonishment, they closed around her.

The meshed steel links of Hugh's hauberk were cold and hard but the strength in him was oddly comforting. Alice clung to him.

"We will speak more of this later," Hugh said into her hair.

*H*ugh waited until after the evening meal had been prepared and eaten around the fire before he went to Alice's tent.

It was a very nice tent, he thought wryly as he walked toward it. Large, commodious. Quite comfortable. It even had a partition down the middle inside. It was the only tent that had been brought along on the journey.

It was his tent.

Hugh had assigned it to Alice without bothering to inquire whether or not she would be so gracious as to share its close confines with him. He'd known in advance what her answer would be to such a question.

Last night he had slept near the fire alongside his men. Tonight he had every expectation of doing so again while Alice enjoyed the comparative luxury and privacy of the tent.

Thus far Alice had not only slept alone in the tent, she had taken her meals there, too. As her uncle had sourly noted, she did not appear to have any interest in the conversation of knights and men-at-arms.

Hugh thought of her snuggled into his blankets and had to stifle a groan. A deep, restless need settled into his lower body. He had been too long without a woman. As a man of discipline he refused to be governed by his own lusts but he paid a price.

He knew the gnawing ache of unfulfilled sexual desire all too well. He had experienced it often enough over the years. He cheered himself with the thought that things would be different when he got himself a wife.

That notion naturally led to the all-too-obvious observation that he very nearly did have a wife. For most couples a betrothal was so close to a vow of marriage that few objected if the man and woman chose to consummate the union. In fact, such a consummation virtually ensured that the wedding would take place.

It was Hugh's ill fortune to be betrothed to a lady who considered herself his business partner rather than his future spouse. He wondered what it was going to take to convince Alice that marriage would be an interesting alternative to the convent.

The problem troubled him. It had all seemed so simple at first. Now he was starting to have doubts.

He had many abilities, Hugh thought. He was not without wits. Erasmus of Thornewood had seen to his education and Hugh was well aware that he was far more widely read than most men. But when it came to understanding women, especially a woman such as Alice, Hugh felt his skills to be sadly lacking.

"My lord?" Benedict rose from where he had been sitting near the fire and hurried over to Hugh. "May I have a word with you?"

"Not if it's about your sister," Hugh said.

"But, my lord, I would have you comprehend her better before you go to her. She meant no harm this afternoon."

Hugh paused. "She very nearly got her throat slit this day. Do you wish me to encourage her in such foolishness?"

"Nay, sir, but I'm certain that she will not do anything so rash again. I must point out that you have gotten what you wanted. The green stone is now safely back in your possession. Can you not let matters rest?"

"Nay." Hugh studied Benedict's worried face in the flickering shadows cast by the fire. "Calm yourself, lad. I do not beat women. I will not strike your sister."

Benedict looked unconvinced. "Sir Dunstan has explained that you are angry because you were unable to go against Vincent of Rivenhall in the jousts this afternoon."

"And you fear I shall take out my irritation on Alice?"

"Aye, that is exactly what I fear. Alice has a way of annoying men who seek to order her about, my lord. My uncle was forever losing his temper with her."

Hugh stilled. "Did Sir Ralf ever strike her?"

"Nay." Benedict smiled ruefully. "I do not think he dared do so. He knew she would have her revenge in some fashion that he could not predict."

"Aye." Hugh relaxed. "I gained the impression that Ralf was somewhat intimidated by Alice."

"At times I think he was actually afraid of her," Benedict said quietly. "Alice believed it was because of our mother's reputation."

"Your mother?"

"Aye. She was a great student of herbs, you see. A true mistress of the lore of plants." Benedict hesitated. "She knew the properties of many strange and unusual species, the ones that could heal as well as those that could kill. And she taught Alice about them from a very early age."

An icy sensation chilled the skin of Hugh's arms. "In other words, Sir Ralf feared that Alice might have learned enough from your mother to poison him, is that it?"

"Alice would never do anything so terrible." Benedict was clearly shocked by the notion. "My mother taught her to heal, not to cause harm."

Hugh reached out and gripped Benedict's shoulder. "Look into my face, lad."

Benedict's anxious eyes met his. "Aye, my lord?"

"There are things that must be made plain between Alice and myself. Among them is the fact that as my betrothed wife, she must abide by my instructions. I do not give orders for the sake of whim. I give them for the safety of those in my charge."

"Aye, sir."

"Alice and I may argue over this matter but I give you my oath that I will never strike your sister. You must be satisfied with that."

Benedict searched Hugh's face for a long moment, as though seeking to see clearly through the shadows. Then some of the rigid tension went out of his young shoulders. "Aye, my lord."

Hugh released Benedict. "She will come to understand that while she is in my keeping, she must obey me just as everyone under my command does. Unfortunately, there may be times, such as today, when her very life depends upon her obedience."

Benedict groaned. "I wish you good luck in convincing her of that, my lord."

Hugh smiled slightly. "Thank you. I suspect I shall need it."

He turned and continued toward the black tent. It was a fine night, he reflected. Cool but not cold. Campfires dotted the darkened landscape around Ipstoke. Sounds of drunken revelry, loud laughter, and occasional bits of song drifted on the evening air.

It was a typical evening following a day of jousting. Victorious lords and knights were celebrating their triumphs in ballad and story. The losers were negotiating the generally friendly, but often expensive, ransoms that would be demanded of them.

More than one man would be impoverished by the day's events. Several would be nursing bruises and the occasional broken bone.

But after this fair at Ipstoke was concluded, most of the winners and losers alike would hurry off to the next joust, wherever it was to be held. Such meets were a way of life for many men. The fact that jousting was technically illegal in England did nothing to quell enthusiasm for the sport.

Hugh was one of the few who took little pleasure in the business. For the most part he indulged himself in tournaments only when he wished to provide his men with the training such contests supplied.

Or on those rare occasions when he could ascertain that Vincent of Rivenhall would be his opponent.

The glow from within the black tent told Hugh that Alice had lit a brazier for warmth and a candle for light. He eased aside the flap and stood quietly in the opening. Alice did not hear him enter. She was seated on a small, folding stool, the only one that had been brought on the journey.

Alice had her back to him. The line of her spine was graceful and achingly feminine. Her head was bent intently over an object cradled in her lap.

The dark, burnished copper of her hair was bound up in a net. It glowed more richly than the coals in the brazier. Her skirts flowed in elegant folds around the legs of the stool.

His betrothed wife. Hugh drew in a deep breath as a wave of sharp desire crashed through him. His fingers tightened around the flap of the tent. *He wanted her.*

For a moment all he could think about was his startled reaction earlier that day when Alice had thrown herself into his arms. His emotions at the time had teetered on some unseen brink. He had been torn between rage at the risk she had taken and a gut-wrenching realization that she had almost gotten herself killed. He had very nearly lost her.

The sense of possessiveness that seized him made his hand tremble.

As though she had sensed his presence, Alice suddenly turned her head to gaze at him. She blinked and Hugh could almost see the thoughts in her head shift from one subject to another. Then she smiled at him and Hugh had to close his hand into a fist to keep from reaching for her.

"My lord. I did not hear you come in."

"You were obviously concerned with other matters." Hugh called forth every shred of self-mastery that he could claim. Deliberately he let the tent flap fall closed behind him.

"Aye, my lord."

He walked across the tent carpet and looked down at the object in her lap. "Still studying my crystal, I see."

"I am still studying *my* crystal, sir." She stroked the heavily faceted green stone with her fingertip. "I am attempting to comprehend why Gilbert the troubadour and those two thieves thought it so valuable."

"We won't learn much from the troubadour. Gilbert has vanished." Learning of the troubadour's disappearance had been yet another source of annoyance that day. Nothing seemed to be going right, Hugh thought morosely.

"I'm not surprised," Alice said. "There was something quite oily about Gilbert. I never cared much for him or his songs."

Hugh watched her face in the candlelight. "I'm told that women find him attractive."

Alice gave a ladylike snort. "I certainly did not. He tried to steal a kiss one evening while he was staying in my uncle's hall."

"Did he, indeed?" Hugh asked softly.

"Aye. It was most annoying. I dumped a mug of ale on his head. He did not speak to me after that."

"I see."

Alice looked up. "Did you learn anything from the one-eyed thief?"

"Very little." There was no point searching for a second stool. Hugh sat down on one of the heavy wooden chests that contained Alice's collection of stones. "He talked freely enough, but he knew only that his companion had made a bargain with someone to recover the crystal. I believe that the one-eyed man and his associate killed the peddler in Clyde-mere."

"Oh." Alice's voice sounded a bit unsteady.

"Unfortunately, the man who went down beneath Storm's hooves was the one who actually struck the bargain. He is dead and therefore can tell us nothing."

"I see."

Hugh narrowed his eyes. "Those two men would have murdered you without so much as a second thought."

She gave him a brilliant smile. "But you saved me, sir."

"That is not the point I wish to make."

She grimaced. "I know what point it is you wish to make, my lord. But look at the positive side. One of the murderers is dead and the other is in the sheriff's safekeeping. We are both safe and the stone has been recovered."

"You're forgetting one thing."

"What is that?"

"Whoever hired those two men to find the crystal is still out there somewhere and we have no clue to his identity."

Alice's fingers tightened around the crystal. "But whoever it is must know that his attempts to steal the stone have failed. It is back in your hands now, my lord. No one would dare to try to take it from you."

"I appreciate your confidence," Hugh muttered, "but I don't think we should assume that all potential thieves will have the same faith in my skills."

"Nonsense. My uncle assured me that you are well nigh a legend, sir."

"Alice, I regret to inform you that what constitutes a legend in out-of-the-way places such as Lingwood Manor or Ipstoke amounts to no more than a moderate reputation elsewhere."

"I do not believe that for one moment, sir," she said with a wholly unexpected show of loyalty. "I saw the way you dealt with those thieves today. When that tale gets back to the one who hired them, he will most certainly think twice before making any more attempts to take the stone. I am certain that we have seen the last of his handiwork."

"Alice—"

She tapped the crystal with her forefinger. Her brows snapped together in a contemplative expression. "Do you know, sir, I would very much like to find out why someone stole this stone in the first place."

Hugh's attention was briefly caught by the ugly crystal. " 'Tis possible, I suppose, that someone mistakenly believes it to be a valuable gem. It is, after all, said to be the last of a great treasure."

She eyed the stone with evident skepticism. "To judge by the low price he placed upon it, the peddler who sold it to my cousin Gervase certainly did not think it valuable. He believed it to be merely an unusual object. A trinket of interest only to a student of natural philosophy."

"I suspect that the thief was motivated by a belief that the stone had a far different sort of value."

Alice looked up sharply. "What sort of value is that, sir?"

"I told you that possession of the crystal is linked by a legend and a curse to the lordship of Scarcliffe."

"Aye. What of it?"

Hugh shrugged. "Mayhap there is someone who does not wish me to become the new lord of Scarcliffe."

"Who would that be, sir?"

Hugh absently drummed his fingers on his thigh. "Mayhap 'tis past time that I told you about Vincent of Rivenhall."

"The man you sought to go against in the jousts today? My brother told me that you were most annoyed because you were obliged to miss the contest. Indeed, I am well aware that it was my fault you found it necessary to forgo the joust."

"Aye. It was."

She gave him a dazzling smile. "But in the end you must admit that regaining the stone was the important thing, my lord. And we have done that, have we not? All is well, so we can forget about the unfortunate incidents of the recent past."

Hugh reluctantly decided that it was time to deliver his little lecture on obedience. "It is not my way to forget unfortunate incidents, as you term them, madam. Indeed, it is my belief that one must use such events to teach firm lessons."

"Never fear, sir, I have certainly learned mine," she assured him cheerfully.

"I wish I could believe that," Hugh said. "But something tells me—"

"Hush." Alice held up a hand to silence him. "What is that?"

Hugh scowled. "What is what?"

"Some troubadour is singing a ballad. Listen. I believe it is about you, my lord."

The words of a song sung in a lusty masculine voice floated into the black tent.

"The knight called Relentless was fearless
'tis said.
But I tell you today from Sir Vincent
he fled."

"Aye, 'tis about me," Hugh growled. Vincent had found a way to have his revenge, he thought. Such was the price one paid when one got oneself betrothed to a woman such as Alice.

Alice set down the stone and leaped to her feet. "Some drunken troubadour is slandering you, my lord."

"Which only goes to prove true what I said earlier. What constitutes a pleasant little legend in some parts is naught but a poor jest in others."

"Sir Hugh once caused bold knights
to shudder and quail.
But henceforth let the truth of his
cowardly nature prevail."

"This is outrageous." Alice stalked toward the tent flap. "I shall not stand for it. You missed that silly joust today because you were occupied with the business of being a true hero."

Belatedly, Hugh realized that Alice intended to confront the troubadour. "Uh, Alice, wait. Come back here."

"I shall return in a moment, my lord. First I must correct that troubadour's idiotic verse." Alice slipped through the tent flap. It dropped back into place behind her.

"God's teeth." Hugh rose from the wooden chest and crossed the tent carpet in two strides.

He reached the flap and yanked it open. He saw Alice in

the light of the campfire. She had her skirts clutched in her hands as she went briskly toward the neighboring encampment. Her chin was angled determinedly. His men stared after her in consternation.

The troubadour, heedless of impending trouble, continued with the next verse of his song.

> *"Mayhap his fair lady will search*
> *for another strong knight who can please.*
> *For the Bringer of Storms has gone soft,*
> *now 'tis limp as a midsummer breeze."*

"You, there, sir troubadour," Alice called loudly. "Cease braying that foolish song at once, do you hear me?"

The troubadour, who had been wandering among the encampments, pausing to sing his new ballad wherever he was invited to do so, broke off abruptly.

It seemed to Hugh that the night became suddenly and unnaturally quiet. His own men were not the only ones gazing at Alice in astonishment. She had the attention of all those gathered about the nearby fires.

The troubadour swept Alice a deep bow as she came to a halt directly in front of him.

"My lady, forgive me," he murmured with mocking courtesy, "I regret that my song does not please you. 'Twas composed only this afternoon at the request of a most noble and valiant knight."

"Vincent of Rivenhall, I assume?"

"Aye." The troubadour laughed. " 'Twas indeed Sir Vincent who requested a song to celebrate his great victory on the jousting field. Would you deny him a hero's ballad?"

"Aye, that I would. Especially when he was not the champion today. 'Twas Sir Hugh who played the true and gallant hero."

"By refusing to take the field against Sir Vincent?" The

troubadour grinned. "Forgive me, but that is an odd notion of a hero, madam."

" 'Tis obvious that neither you nor Sir Vincent knows the true facts concerning what happened this afternoon." Alice paused to glower at the circle of listeners she had collected. "Hear me, all of you, and listen well for now I shall tell you what really happened today. Sir Hugh was obliged to miss the joust because he was occupied with a hero's task."

A tall man dressed in a red tunic walked into the circle of firelight. The flames revealed his aquiline features.

Hugh groaned as he recognized the newcomer.

"What heroic task took Sir Hugh from the field of honor, my lady?" the tall man asked politely.

Alice whirled to confront him. "I would have you know that Sir Hugh saved me from two vicious thieves this afternoon while Sir Vincent was playing games. The robbers would have murdered me in cold blood, sir."

"And who are you?" the tall man asked.

"I am Alice, Sir Hugh's betrothed wife."

A ripple of interested murmurs greeted that announcement. Alice paid them no heed.

"Are you, indeed." The tall man examined her in the firelight. "How interesting."

Alice fixed him with a quelling glare. "Surely you will agree that saving my life was a far more heroic deed than engaging in a bit of nonsensical sport."

The tall man's gaze went past Alice to where Hugh stood a short distance behind her. Hugh smiled faintly as he met eyes that he knew were very nearly the same color as his own.

The tall man turned back to Alice. He swept her a sardonic bow. "My apologies, madam. I am sorry if the troubadour's song offended you. And I rejoice to know that you survived your encounter with thieves this afternoon."

"Thank you," Alice said with icy politeness.

"You are obviously something of an innocent, madam."

The tall man stepped back out of the firelight. "It will be amusing to see how long Hugh the Relentless remains a true hero in your eyes."

He did not wait for a response.

Alice glared after him and then turned once more to the troubadour. "Find another song to sing."

"Aye, my lady." The troubadour's expression gleamed with laconic amusement as he swept her another bow.

Alice whirled about and strode back toward Hugh's encampment. She paused when she saw him standing in her path.

"Oh, there you are, my lord. I am pleased to say that I do not believe we shall be troubled again by that ridiculous ballad about Sir Vincent of Rivenhall."

"Thank you, lady." Hugh took her arm to lead her back to the tent. "I appreciate your concern for me."

"Don't be ridiculous. I could not allow that idiot to sing his lies about you, sir. He had no business making a hero out of Sir Vincent of Rivenhall when you were the true hero of the day."

"Troubadours must make their living in whatever way they can. No doubt Sir Vincent paid well for his ballad."

"Aye." Alice's face lit with sudden enthusiasm. "A thought has just occurred to me, sir. We should pay the troubadour to invent a song about you, my lord."

"I'd prefer that we did not do that," Hugh said very distinctly. "I have better things to spend my money on than a ballad featuring myself."

"Very well, if you insist." Alice sighed. "I suppose it would be quite expensive."

"Aye."

"Nevertheless, it would be a very lovely song, I'll wager. Well worth the cost."

"Forget it, Alice."

She made a face. "Do you know the identity of that tall man who came to stand by the fire?"

"Aye," Hugh said. "That was Vincent of Rivenhall."

"Sir Vincent?" Alice came to an abrupt halt. She gazed at Hugh with astonishment. "Do you know, sir, there was something about him that reminded me a little of you."

"He's my cousin," Hugh said. "His uncle, Sir Matthew, was my father."

"Your cousin." Alice looked dumbfounded.

"My father was the heir to Rivenhall." Hugh smiled with the humorless amusement he had long cultivated for this particular topic. "Had Sir Matthew not neglected to marry my mother before he got her with child, I, not Sir Vincent, would have inherited the Rivenhall lands."

Chapter 8

lice was very conscious of the amused gazes of Hugh's men. She went briskly back toward the tent, aware that several of those gathered around the fire were concealing wide grins. Even Benedict was watching her with a strange expression, as though he were having difficulty restraining laughter.

"If my ears do not deceive me," Dunstan remarked in a voice that managed to carry clearly across the fire, " 'twould seem that yon minstrel has found himself a new song to sing."

"Hugh the Relentless may put aside his sword
for he is betrothed to a lady who will defend her lord."

"Aye," someone else said with satisfaction. " 'Tis far more entertaining than the other."

Laughter filled the air.

Alice grimaced and glanced back over her shoulder. The troubadour whom Vincent had paid to sing the nasty ballad about Hugh was indeed strumming a new tune on his lute. He was wandering back through the encampments, regaling one and all with the song.

> *"She has brought him a dowry more priceless than*
>   *lands*
> *Sir Hugh's honor, it seems, is safe in her hands."*

A cheer of approval went up.

Alice blushed furiously. She was the new subject of the poem. She looked uneasily at Hugh to see if he was embarrassed.

"Wilfred is right," Hugh said calmly. "The minstrel's new song is much more entertaining than his last one."

Benedict, Dunstan, and the others howled with laughter.

"Sir Vincent may have been successful in the joust this afternoon," one of the men declared, "but he was roundly defeated tonight."

Alice was profoundly grateful for the shadows that concealed the red banners in her cheeks. She fixed one of the squires with a determined look. "Will you please bring some wine to my tent?"

"Aye, m'lady." The man stifled his laughter and leaped to his feet. He started toward the supply wagon, which stood nearby in the gloom.

"You may fetch a cup of wine for me while you're about it, Thomas," Hugh called. "Bring it to *my* tent."

"Aye, m'lord."

Hugh's grin flashed briefly in the firelight as he lifted the tent flap. " 'Tis not often I have the opportunity to toast one of Sir Vincent's defeats."

"Really, sir, you go too far." Alice hurried through the opening into the comparative privacy of the tent. "I did not defeat Sir Vincent. I merely corrected his misconceptions concerning today's events."

"Nay, madam." Hugh let the flap fall closed. "Make no

mistake. 'Twas a defeat. A very decisive one. And the trouba-dour's new song will ensure that a great many people hear of it. I vow, 'tis almost as satisfying as a victory against him in the joust would have been."

She pivoted to confront him. "That is a very poor jest, sir."

Hugh shrugged. "Mayhap I overstate the case a trifle. Un-horsing my cousin in the joust would have been somewhat more gratifying, I'll grant you. But not by much." His chilled smile came and went. "Not by much."

"M'lord?" Thomas raised the tent flap. "I have the wine for you and my lady." He offered a tray containing two cups and a flagon.

"Excellent." Hugh swept the tray from Thomas's hand. "That will be all for now. Leave us so that I may honor my noble defender in a suitable manner."

"Aye, m'lord." With a last, speculative glance at Alice, Thomas bowed his way out of the tent.

Alice scowled as Hugh filled the cups with wine. "I do wish you would cease amusing yourself with this unpleasant incident, my lord."

"Ah, but you do not know how uniquely entertaining it is." Hugh handed one cup to her and then saluted her with his own.

"Is it so important for you to see Sir Vincent humiliated?"

"A taste of Vincent's humiliation now and again is all that I am allowed by my liege lord."

"I do not comprehend your meaning, sir."

"Erasmus of Thornewood has forbidden Vincent and me to take up arms against each other except in a jousting match. He claims 'twould be a wasteful indulgence that he cannot afford."

"Erasmus of Thornewood sounds a very intelligent man."

"He is that," Hugh admitted. "But his notion of sound economy leaves me hungry. You served me a well-seasoned dish tonight, madam. You must allow me to enjoy it to the fullest. However, your excellent cookery is not what I find so vastly entertaining."

Alice was becoming impatient with his sardonic answers. "What is it that amuses you so, my lord?"

Hugh smiled at her over the wine cup. His amber eyes gleamed like those of a hawk that had recently stuffed itself on a plump pigeon. "I do believe that tonight marks the first time in my entire life when someone else has come to my defense. I thank you, madam."

The wine cup trembled in Alice's fingers. " 'Twas the least I could do. You saved my life this afternoon, sir."

"I would say that our partnership is working rather well, wouldn't you?" Hugh asked with suspicious blandness.

The look in his eyes threatened to destroy Alice's composure. This was ridiculous, she thought. She had been through too much today. That was the problem.

Desperate, she racked her brain for a way to change the subject. She said the first thing that came into her head. "I had heard that you were born a bastard."

A lethal stillness came over Hugh. The wicked amusement died in his eyes. "Aye. 'Tis the truth. Does it trouble you to find yourself betrothed to a bastard, madam?"

Alice wished she had kept her mouth closed. *What a stupid thing to say.* Where were her wits? To say nothing of her manners. "Nay, my lord. I was merely about to remark that I know very little of your family history. You are something of a mystery to me." She paused. "By choice, I suspect."

"I have discovered that the less people know of the truth, the more they are inclined to believe in legends. What is more, they usually prefer the legend to the truth." Hugh sipped his wine with a contemplative air. "Sometimes that is useful. Sometimes, as is the case with that damnable green stone, it is a nuisance."

Alice gripped her wine cup very tightly. "I am a student of

natural philosophy, sir. As such, I seek honest answers. I prefer to know the truth that lies beneath the legend."

"Do you?"

She fortified herself with a tiny sip of the wine. "Tonight I have learned a few more facts about you, but I still feel that there is much that I do not know."

"You have an inquisitive nature. Such a temperament can be dangerous."

"In a woman?" she asked tartly.

"In either man or woman. The world is a simpler and no doubt safer place for those who do not ask too many questions."

"That may be true." Alice grimaced. "Unfortunately, curiosity is my besetting sin."

"Aye, so it would seem." Hugh watched her for a long moment. He appeared to debate some issue with himself. Then he walked to a wooden chest and sat down upon it. He cradled his wine cup in both hands and studied the contents as though it were an alchemist's brew. "What do you wish to know?"

Alice was startled. She had not expected him to volunteer any information. Slowly she sank down onto the folding stool. "You will answer my questions?"

"Some. Not all. Ask your questions and I will decide which ones I choose to answer."

She took a deep breath. "Neither you nor Sir Vincent is responsible for the circumstances of your birth. 'Tis your ill fortune that you were born a bastard and therefore did not inherit the Rivenhall lands."

Hugh shrugged. "Aye."

"But I do not see how you can blame your cousin for that turn of events. And you do not strike me as the sort of man who would bear a grudge against the innocent. So how does it come about that you and Sir Vincent are sworn enemies?"

Hugh was silent for a time. When he eventually spoke his voice was devoid of any nuance of feeling or emotion. It was as though he merely related someone else's history, not his own.

" 'Tis simple enough. Vincent's people hated mine with an undying passion. My family returned the favor. Our parents and the rest of their generation are all dead and gone, so it is left to my cousin and me to carry on the feud."

"But why?"

Hugh turned the cup in his big hands. " 'Tis a long tale."

"I should very much like to hear it, my lord."

"Very well. I shall tell you the main part of it. I owe you that much under the circumstances." Hugh paused again as though gathering thoughts from some deep, hidden place.

Alice did not move. It seemed to her that a strange spell settled on the interior of the tent. The candle burned low and the embers on the brazier dimmed. Outside, the sounds of laughter and song grew faint, as though they emanated from a vast distance.

Shadows coalesced within the tent. They seemed to swirl around Hugh.

"My father was named Sir Matthew of Rivenhall," he said. "They tell me that he was a respected knight. His liege lord made him a gift of several fine manors."

"Pray, continue, sir," Alice prompted gently.

"A marriage was arranged for him by his family. The lady was an heiress. It was considered a fine match and Sir Matthew was, by all accounts, much pleased. But that did not stop him from lusting after the young daughter of one of his neighbors. Her father held the fief of Scarcliffe. My grandfather tried to protect his only child but Sir Matthew convinced her to meet him in secret."

"The woman was your mother?"

"Aye. Her name was Margaret." Hugh turned the cup between his hands. "Matthew of Rivenhall seduced her. Got her with child. And then he went off to give service to his liege lord. I was born while he was in Normandy."

"What happened?"

"The usual." Hugh moved one hand in a negligent gesture. "My grandfather was furious. He went to Rivenhall and demanded that Matthew be forced to marry my mother when he returned from Normandy."

"He wished them to break Sir Matthew's betrothal?"

"Aye. Sir Matthew's family made it plain that they had no intention of allowing their heir to throw himself away on a young woman who could offer only one small, rather poor manor as a dowry."

"What of Sir Matthew's betrothed? How did she feel?"

"Her family wanted the marriage to take place as much as Sir Matthew's did. As I said, it was considered an excellent match."

Alice nodded in comprehension. "So no one wished to see the betrothal severed, is that it?"

"Aye." Hugh glanced at her and then he looked into the dying coals on the brazier. "Least of all Matthew of Rivenhall. He had no intention of abandoning his fine heiress for my mother. But he did come to see her once after he returned from Normandy."

"To tell her that he loved her and would love her always even though he must wed another?" Alice asked quickly.

Hugh's mouth quirked upward at the corner in a humorless smile. "You seek to salvage a romantic ending for this tale?"

Alice blushed. "I suppose I do. Is there one?"

"Nay."

"Well, then? What did Matthew of Rivenhall say to your mother when he met with her and learned that he had a son?"

"No one knows." Hugh took another swallow of wine. "But whatever it was, my mother apparently did not care for it. She murdered him and then took her own life. They were both found dead the following morning."

Alice's mouth fell open. It took her several tries before she could speak. When she did so, the words emerged as a squeak. "Your mother murdered your father?"

"So they say."

"But how? If he was a great knight, how could she possibly manage to kill him? Surely he would have been able to defend himself against a woman."

Hugh looked at her with grim eyes. "She used a woman's weapon."

"Poison?"

"She put it in the wine she served to him that night."

"Dear God." Alice stared down into the red wine in her cup. For some reason she no longer had a taste for it. "And then she drank the wine herself?"

"Aye. Vincent's father, Matthew's younger brother, became the heir to the Rivenhall estates. He was killed three years ago. Vincent is now the lord of Rivenhall."

"And he bears enmity toward you because he believes that your mother murdered his uncle?"

"He was taught to hate me from the cradle even though he became lord of Rivenhall because of my mother's action. In truth, I was taught to return the favor."

"Who had the rearing of you?"

"My grandfather for the first eight years of my life. When he died I was sent to live in the household of Erasmus of Thornewood. I was fortunate in that I did not become a foundling."

"But you were denied your birthright," Alice whispered.

" 'Tis true that I lost Rivenhall, but that part no longer matters so far as I'm concerned." Hugh's mouth twisted in cold satisfaction. "I have lands of my own now. My grandfather's manor is mine, thanks to Sir Erasmus."

She thought of how she had lost Benedict's inheritance and swallowed a small sigh. "I am pleased for you, sir."

Hugh seemed not to hear her. "Scarcliffe has suffered much since my grandfather's death twenty-two years ago. In truth, it had fallen into decline even before he died. But I intend to make it plump and profitable once more."

"A worthy goal."

"Above all, I shall hold on to it for my heirs." Hugh's hand tightened around his cup. "By the blood of the devil, I vow that Vincent will not be able to do the same with Rivenhall."

Alice tensed at the chilling tone of his voice. "Why is that?"

"Rivenhall Manor is in very poor condition these days. 'Tis not at all the fine, prosperous land it once was. Why do you think Vincent enters every joust and tournament he can find? He is attempting to make enough money to save his lands."

"What happened to them?"

"Vincent's father was devoid of all sense of responsibility. He squandered the income from the Rivenhall estates to finance a trip to the Holy Land."

"He went on Crusade?"

"Aye. And died in some distant desert as so many did, not from a Saracen's blade, but from a foul disease of the bowel."

Alice frowned. "I believe my mother wrote of the many illnesses that afflicted those who went on Crusade."

Hugh set aside the empty wine cup. He rested his elbows on his knees and loosely clasped his hands. "They say Vincent's father was born wild and reckless. He had no business sense and no notion of duty to his own family. There was a reason why his people were so devastated by the loss of my father, you see. Everyone knew that his brother would ruin the estates. And he very nearly succeeded. Unfortunately, he died before he could complete the task."

"And now Sir Vincent is desperately seeking to save them."

"Aye."

"What a sad tale," Alice said.

"I warned you it did not have a romantic ending."

"True, you did."

Hugh slanted her an odd glance. "In some ways 'tis no more sad than your own tale."

"What happened to me and my brother was my own fault," Alice said grimly.

Hugh's expression darkened. "Why do you say it was your fault? It was your uncle, Sir Ralf, who deprived Benedict of his inheritance."

"He was able to do so only because I was unable to defend my father's manor." Alice rose restlessly and moved to stand closer to the dying brazier. "I did my best, but it was not good enough."

"You are too hard on yourself."

"I shall always wonder if there was something more I could have done. Mayhap I could have phrased my arguments to Lord Fulbert more cleverly. Or found a way to convince him that I could manage the defense of my brother's lands until Benedict came of age."

"Alice, hush. Your uncle no doubt meant to take your brother's lands from you the moment he learned of your father's death. And Fulbert was likely pleased to see him do so. There was nothing you could have done."

"You don't understand. My mother trusted me to protect Benedict's inheritance. She said that in spite of what my father believed, Benedict would one day prove that he was a worthy heir." Alice twisted her fingers together in front of her. "But I failed to give my brother his opportunity. *I failed.*"

Hugh got to his feet and crossed the carpet to stand directly behind her. Alice shivered as his powerful hands settled on her shoulders. She experienced an almost overpowering urge to throw herself into his arms again as she had done earlier that afternoon. It was all she could do to resist.

"Alice, you are possessed of a brave and bold spirit, but even the bravest and the boldest cannot win every battle."

"I did everything I could but it was not enough. I felt so alone." With a small cry, Alice spun around and buried her face against Hugh's broad chest. Her tears flowed in silence, dampening the front of his black tunic. Her shoulders shuddered.

It was the first time she had cried since her mother had died.

Hugh said nothing. He simply held her. The candle burned lower and the shadows thickened within the tent.

The tears stopped eventually, leaving Alice drained. But to her surprise, she felt calmer, more at peace with herself than she had in some time.

"Forgive me, my lord," she mumbled into his tunic. "I do not usually indulge myself in tears. I fear it's been a long and somewhat trying day."

"Aye, that it has." Hugh tipped her chin up with the edge of his hand. He studied her face as though she were a mysterious volume he was determined to decipher. "And a most instructive one."

She looked into his shadowed gaze and saw the pain as well as the iron-willed determination that pain had inspired in him. Those amber eyes held darker, fiercer, infinitely more dangerous versions of the pain and determination that had been etched into her own soul. *Storm winds.*

She longed to reach inside him and still the savage tempests but she did not know how to go about it.

And then, quite suddenly, Alice knew that she wanted Hugh to kiss her. She wanted it more than she had ever wanted anything in her entire life. In that moment she suspected that she would have cheerfully sold her soul for his kiss.

As if he could read her thoughts, Hugh bent his head and covered her mouth with his own.

Alice nearly collapsed. Had Hugh not held her as securely as he did, she would have crumpled to the carpet.

The disturbing male energy in him poured into her, a force that was all the more awesome because of the control Hugh exerted over it. It revived Alice's spirits the way a shower of rain renews wilted grass.

The excitement that had flashed through her the first time Hugh had kissed her returned in a heated rush. The sensation seemed stronger, more vibrant this time, as though her body had been tuned for it by the first embrace. The desire she felt radiating from Hugh set a torch to Alice's senses.

She moaned softly and then something gave way inside her. The pain and defeat of the past were forgotten for the moment. The danger of the afternoon was a distant memory. The future was an unknown haze that did not seem to matter.

Nothing was of any import save this man who held her with a strength that simultaneously overwhelmed Alice and made her feel incredibly powerful.

Alice wrapped her arms around Hugh's neck and held on for dear life.

"I chose well," Hugh whispered.

Alice wanted to ask him what he meant by those odd words but she could not speak. The world shifted around her. She squeezed her eyes tightly closed as Hugh lifted her off her feet.

A moment later she felt the softness of the pallet blankets beneath her. She gasped as Hugh came down on top of her. His weight crushed her into the bedding. She felt his leg slide between her thighs and dimly realized that her skirts were hiked up above her knees. She knew she ought to have been horrified by that fact but for some reason she gloried in it.

Curiosity overcame good sense and modesty. The need to

know where this aching, surging, swelling feeling inside her would ultimately lead was simply too strong to ignore. Surely she had a right to explore these exhilarating sensations.

"I never dreamed that it could be like this between a man and a woman," she said against his throat.

"You have not yet experienced the half of it," Hugh promised.

His mouth moved on hers, demanding, coaxing, claiming. Alice could do nothing but respond. She felt his hands on the laces of her gown but she paid no attention. She was too busy savoring the heat and scent of him. Then he touched her bare breast with a hand that was callused from years of gripping the hilt of a sword.

For an instant Alice could not breathe. She opened her mouth on a small shriek of amazement. No man had ever touched her in such an intimate manner.

It was thrilling.

It was immodest.

It was the most exciting thing that had ever happened to her.

"Hush." Hugh quickly covered her mouth with his own, swallowing the startled cry she made. "We are surrounded by my men and the encampments of others. A lover's sweet cries will travel on the night air as though borne on wings."

A lover's sweet cries?

Alice opened her eyes abruptly. "By Saint Boniface's cloak, my lord, you speak the truth. We must stop."

"Nay." Hugh raised his head slightly to look down at her. He drew his rough fingertip along the edge of her cheek as though he touched rare silk. "There is no need to stop. We must simply be cautious."

"But, my lord—"

"And silent. Close your eyes, Alice. I will take care of everything."

She sighed and closed her eyes, surrendering control of the

moment in a way that she had never been able to do before in her life.

Suddenly she saw herself as apprenticed to an alchemist who knew the secret of transforming base metal into gold. She was on the brink of wondrous new discoveries.

She would study whole realms of natural philosophy that had heretofore been closed to her. She would learn strange truths that had been concealed so well that, until this moment, she had not even guessed at their existence.

Hugh gently took one nipple between thumb and forefinger. Alice shuddered with pleasure. He moved his palm downward until he found her bare leg. Alice flinched in reaction and then instinctively bent her knee.

Hugh slid his hand up along the inside of her thigh and Alice clutched at him so fiercely that she wondered she did not leave marks.

And all the while Hugh kept her mouth covered with his own, swallowing each telltale gasp as though it were a rare, honeyed wine.

When he touched the hot, wet place between her legs Alice thought she would go mad. She could barely breathe. Her whole body was inflamed as if with fever. There was a curious tightness within her that clamored to be eased.

"Silence," Hugh said in a velvety whisper that teased and tormented as surely as his hand. "Not a word. Not a sound, my sweet."

The knowledge that she could not even give voice to these astounding sensations only served to intensify them. Alice shivered again and again as Hugh stroked her.

He parted her carefully with his fingers. Alice sucked in her breath. A small, terribly urgent whimper escaped her.

"Have a care," Hugh murmured against her mouth. "Remember that silence is all tonight."

He eased one finger partway inside her and then withdrew it.

Alice wanted to scream. She grabbed his head and pulled his mouth more tightly against hers. She thought she heard him laugh softly in the darkness but she paid no heed.

He moved his hand one last time against her softness and the night exploded around her. Nothing mattered, not the knowledge that Hugh's men might overhear her or the fact that there were encampments scattered all around the black tent.

Alice was utterly lost to the sensation that seized her. At that moment the only other person in the whole world so far as she was concerned was Hugh.

She thought she screamed but she heard no sound. She dimly understood that Hugh must have swallowed the cry, just as he had all the others.

"Blood of the angels . . ." Hugh's arm tightened around her as she convulsed beneath him.

Alice barely heard him. She sighed deeply and floated gently down to earth. A lovely sense of contentment filled up all the empty places within her.

Dreamily she opened her eyes and looked up at Hugh. His face was set in startlingly rigid lines. His eyes glittered.

"My lord, that was—" Words failed her. "That was—"

"Aye?" He traced the outline of her mouth with one big, blunt finger. "What was it?"

"Most instructive," Alice breathed.

Hugh blinked. "Instructive?"

"Aye, sir." Alice stirred lazily. "An experience quite unlike anything else I have ever come across in my study of natural philosophy."

"I'm glad you found it instructive," he muttered. "Have you had other instruction of this sort?"

"Nay, my lord, this was quite unique."

"Instructive and unique," he repeated carefully. "Ah, well. I suspect that, given your unusual nature, I should be satisfied with that much."

It dawned on her that he did not appear entirely pleased. She threaded her fingers through his black mane. "Have I offended you, my lord?"

"Nay." He smiled faintly and shifted his position on top of her. " 'Tis just that I find making love to you instructive and unique also. I feel certain that we both have a great deal to learn."

"Making love?" Alice froze. Her fingers tightened abruptly in Hugh's hair. "Dear Saints. That is what we are doing, is it not?"

"Aye." Hugh winced and reached up to gently unknot her fingers. "There is no need to pull out my hair in the process."

"Oh, my apologies, my lord." Alice struggled to rise. "I did not mean to injure you."

"I appreciate that."

"But we must stop this now, at once." She shoved against his broad shoulders.

Hugh did not move. "Why?"

"Why?" She widened her eyes, astonished. "You ask me that?"

"It seems a reasonable question under the circumstances."

"Sir, I may not have had much personal experience with this sort of thing, but I am an educated woman. I am well aware of what must happen if we continue on as we are."

"What of it?"

"You would be furious with yourself and with me if I allowed you to finish what you have started."

"I would?"

"Of course you would." She tried to wriggle out from under his heavy frame. "And knowing the sort of man you are, I am well aware that if you seduce me under such circumstances, you would feel honor-bound to go through with the marriage."

"Alice—"

"I cannot allow it, sir. Indeed, I will not allow it."

"You won't?"

"We made a bargain, sir. I owe it to you to keep you from breaking it."

Hugh braced himself on his elbows. "I promise you, I am in full control of my passion."

"You may believe that to be true, sir, but 'tis obvious you are not at all in control. Just look at yourself, my lord. If you were exerting your usual degree of self-mastery, you would have stopped several minutes ago."

"Why?" he asked flatly.

"Because you would not wish to find yourself caught in a trap," she snapped, thoroughly exasperated.

"Alice," he said with ill-concealed impatience, "what if I told you that I am quite willing to go through with the marriage?"

"That's impossible."

"Give me one good reason why it's impossible," he growled.

She glared up at him. "I can think of a hundred but the most obvious is that I would make you a dreadful wife."

Hugh stilled. Then, very slowly, he sat up beside her. "What in the name of the devil makes you say that?"

"I am not at all what you require in a wife, my lord." Alice fumbled with her clothing. "We both know that."

"Do we? I disagree. I do not think we both know that." Hugh loomed over her. "In truth, I believe one of us is confused."

"I know, my lord, but try not to become overanxious about it. You will soon come to your senses."

"I am not the one who is confused, Alice."

She eyed him warily. "You're not?"

"Nay." He watched her coldly. "What makes you think that you would not make me a good wife?"

She was taken aback by the outrageous question. " 'Tis obvious, my lord."

"Not to me."

A strange sense of desperation descended on her. "I can bring you nothing. As the lord of a manor, you are in a position to wed an heiress."

He shrugged. "I do not require an heiress."

"Is this some sort of nasty game you are playing with me, sir?"

"I do not play games. I believe that you would make me a good wife and I am willing to turn our bargain into a true betrothal. Where is the problem?"

Realization hit her. She narrowed her eyes. "Have you come to this decision simply because I am convenient, sir?"

"That is only one of several reasons," he assured her.

Alice had an overwhelming urge to kick him in the shin. She restrained herself with an effort and because, given their present positions, such an action was not practical.

"What are the other reasons, pray tell?" she asked through her teeth.

He seemed to find nothing odd about her tone of voice. Instead, he took the question quite literally. "From what I have observed of you during the past three days, Alice, 'tis apparent that you have a sound understanding of loyalty, duty, and honor."

"Whatever gave you that idea?"

"The manner in which you have fought to defend your brother's future," he explained.

"I see. Anything else?"

"You are intelligent and practical by nature. I admire that in a woman. Or anyone else, for that matter."

"Pray continue, sir."

"You appear to be well versed in the arts of household management." Hugh was clearly warming to his subject. "I place a high value on professional abilities of any kind. I believe in employing only the most skilled craftsmen and the most talented stewards, for example."

"Do go on, sir." Alice could barely speak. "This is fascinating."

"You are obviously healthy and strong. That is important, of course."

"Aye." She would throttle him, Alice decided. "Is there more?"

He shrugged. "That is all, I think. Except for the obvious fact that you are free to wed, as am I. And we are already betrothed. That makes everything quite simple and straightforward."

"Efficiency and convenience."

"Aye." Hugh looked pleased at her intelligent grasp of the matter.

"My lord, I would have you know that I do not consider it any great thing to be wed simply because I can manage a household and I happen to be conveniently at hand."

Hugh frowned. "Why not?"

Because if I am to marry, I wish it to be for love, her heart whispered silently. Alice beat back the illogical response. Hugh would never comprehend it. "It seems somewhat cold-blooded."

"Cold-blooded?" Hugh looked startled. "Nonsense. 'Tis a most reasonable approach."

"Reasonable?"

"Aye. It seems to me that you and I are in the unusual position of being able to make our own decision on the matter. That decision will be based upon a practical knowledge of each other's temperaments and skills. Think of it as a continuation of our bargain, Alice."

Alice felt herself turn warm. "But I had plans to enter a convent. I had intended to devote myself to investigations of natural philosophy."

"You can study natural philosophy as my wife," Hugh said in a soft, deeply seductive tone. "You shall have both the time and the income with which to finance your investigations if you wed me."

"Hmm."

"Think of it, Alice," Hugh said as though offering her a treasure chest of gems. "Unlimited opportunities to purchase books, astrolabes, and alchemical apparatus shall be yours. You will be able to collect all the odd stones that catch your attention. You may have any number of dried insects. Pile them all the way to the ceiling of your study chamber, if you like."

"My lord, I do not know what to say. Everything is spinning about in my head. I do not believe that I have recovered from your kisses. I think you had best leave."

He hesitated for a tension-filled moment. Alice held her breath, sensing the struggle going on within him. He was a passionate man, she thought. But he was completely in control of that passion.

"If that is your wish." He rose from the pallet with predatory grace. "Think upon what I have said, Alice. You and I will suit each other well. I can offer you everything the convent can offer and more."

"My lord, I pray that you will give me ample time to contemplate this proposal." Alice fumbled with her gown as she got to her feet. She felt tousled and disheveled and more than a little disgruntled. "This is all happening much too quickly."

Hugh narrowed his eyes. He looked as if he wanted to argue. Instead, he brushed his mouth lightly across hers. In the instant of fleeting contact, Alice could feel the powerful force of the control he was exerting over himself. She shivered.

"Very well." Hugh lifted his head. "There is no need to give me your answer tonight. You may think upon it."

"Thank you, sir." She wondered if he noticed the tart sarcasm in her words.

"But do not take too long," Hugh advised. "I do not have

a great deal of time to waste on such a simple matter. There is much to be done at Scarcliffe. I need a wife who is also a reliable business partner."

He was gone before Alice thought to dump the contents of the flagon of wine over his head.

She consoled herself with the realization that there would doubtless be other opportunities.

Chapter 9

Hugh had not realized how dreary the village of Scarcliffe was until he rode into it three days later with Alice at his side. This was the place where he had been born. It was where he now intended to carve out a future for himself and his descendants. It had not appeared nearly so drab to him when he had set out from it in search of the green crystal a short while ago.

The image of Scarcliffe that had burned in his imagination for weeks now was of how it would appear in the future.

He had plans for this manor. Great plans.

In a year or two Scarcliffe would begin to sparkle as brightly as a fine jewel. The fields would burst with an abundance of crops. The wool on the sheep would be thick and soft. The cottages would be clean and in good repair. The villagers would be content, prosperous, and well-fed.

But today he was forced to view it through Alice's eyes. He had to admit that one could say the village bore more resemblance to a lump of coal than a polished gem.

Hugh, who normally paid little attention to such minor

inconveniences as the weather, was irritated to see that it had recently rained. The ominous, leaden sky did not add to the questionable charms of Scarcliffe. The stone keep itself, which loomed beyond the village, was hidden in a shroud of gray fog.

Hugh cast an uneasy glance at Alice to gauge her reaction to his new lands. She did not notice his wary scrutiny.

She was slender and graceful in the saddle. Her red hair blazed, a bright, cheerful flame set to ward off the encroaching gray mist. She appeared intent on her surroundings, her intelligent features serious and studious as she examined the village.

Her curiosity, as always, was aroused, Hugh realized, but he could not tell what she thought about that which she viewed. He wondered if she was dismayed, disgusted, or disdainful.

Given the bleak picture of Scarcliffe, it was very possible that she was experiencing all three emotions. She was, after all, a lady who was too fastidious to eat in a man's great hall. She ordered her food specially cooked and her clothes seemed to be always fresh and sweet-scented.

She no doubt found the barren fields and dismal little village distasteful.

Hugh was forced to admit that the untidy collection of thatched cottages, most of which were in need of repair, together with their accompanying goat pens and pigsties, did not present an inspiring sight. The afternoon air was heavy. It bore the unmistakably rank odor of the village ditch where the refuse of years lay moldering.

The tumbledown stone wall that surrounded the small convent and the church spoke of long neglect. The recent rain had done nothing to cleanse Scarcliffe. It had merely deepened the mud in the single rutted street.

Hugh clenched his teeth. If Alice was not particularly impressed with this view of the village and nearby fields, she was going to be appalled by the sight of Scarcliffe Keep.

He told himself he would worry about that problem later. In the meantime he had an announcement to make, one he intended should carry across his lands and into the halls of his neighbors. All would know that Hugh the Relentless had returned with proof that he was the rightful lord of Scarcliffe.

He had pushed his company hard, determined to arrive in Scarcliffe on market day. As he had anticipated, virtually everyone who belonged on the manor and its surrounding farms was gathered in the narrow street to witness the triumphant return of their new lord.

This should have been a moment of enormous satisfaction, Hugh thought. He had it all now. He had retrieved the green crystal and he had betrothed himself to a suitable lady. He was ready to settle down as lord of Scarcliffe.

But things were not going as smoothly as he had planned and that made him uneasy. He was said to have a talent for stratagems. Some claimed he had a mage's skill at such. But something had gone badly awry the other night when he had tried to convince Alice to make their betrothal genuine.

He was still stinging from the blow she had unwittingly landed. *She acted as though she preferred the convent to sharing a marriage bed with him.*

That news did not set well, especially now that he suspected that he would very likely walk through hell if it meant an opportunity to finish what he had begun between her soft thighs.

His body grew taut and hard whenever he recalled the way she had shivered in his arms. As he had spent much of the journey with just such thoughts plaguing him, he had passed the time in an uncomfortable condition.

Leaving Alice alone in the tent the other night and the two nights since had taken more heroic effort than a dozen forays on the jousting field. What annoyed Hugh the most was the realization that in her innocence, she had no appreciation of how much self-mastery he had been forced to wield. In truth, the stunningly volatile nature of his own need made him deeply wary but it did nothing to lessen his desire.

Acknowledging his own ravenous appetite for Alice's sweet, warm body had been one of the most difficult things Hugh had ever done.

He had spent the past three nights staring at the stars while he concocted excuses for his fierce urge to claim her. There were logical reasons for his thundering blood and deep hunger and he had enumerated all of them as though he were doing sums on his abacus.

He had been too long without a woman.

He had always been attracted to the unusual and Alice was nothing if not unique.

The promise of passion in her green eyes was enough to compel any man with the wit to perceive it.

And touching her had been akin to touching the heart of a storm.

Aye, there were reasons enough to explain why he had just finished a hard ride in a state of near arousal.

But unlike his abacus, which always gave him a satisfactory answer, none of the explanations had done much to lighten Hugh's grim mood. If anything, they darkened it.

No matter how he examined the situation he was forced to come to the same conclusion. He wanted Alice with a degree of desire that was dangerous. He would have to exert more care in the future.

He would also have to find a way to convince her to make the betrothal real.

"A lady. He brings a fine lady with him."

"Mayhap a wife."

"I did not think to see him again. Thought he'd get himself killed as the others have all done."

The excited murmur of the gathering crowd interrupted Hugh's reverie. Several people turned to one another to exclaim in amazement, as though they witnessed a great wonder rather than merely the return of their lord.

Prioress Joan and a handful of nuns came to stand at the convent gatehouse. Their eyes went straight to Alice. One of the women leaned forward to whisper in the ear of the tall nun who stood next to Prioress Joan. The tall woman nodded in response. She alone did not appear pleased by the sight of the returning company.

Hugh glanced at her fleetingly and recognized the healer, a woman named Katherine. She was a lady of somber, melancholy mien who appeared to be in her late forties. He had met her the night that Prioress Joan had sent for him to inform him of the loss of the green stone.

Hugh prayed that he would never need her professional services. The notion of being treated by a healer whose expression indicated she expected a poor outcome was not particularly appealing.

He raised a hand to bring his men to a halt. When the clatter of hooves and wagon wheels had stilled, he urged his horse slowly toward the prioress.

Joan waited with a smile that was composed of equal parts of relief and welcome.

Hugh was only a few paces from the convent gate when a scrawny, hulking figure in a brown monk's cowl surged out of the crowd. The hood of the man's robes concealed his face, but Hugh swallowed a silent oath when he recognized Calvert of Oxwick.

Hugh had hoped that the wandering monk would have wandered on to another village by the time he and his company returned.

"My lord, I bid you welcome to Scarcliffe," Calvert intoned in a rasping voice that grated on the ears. "I give thanks to God that you have returned alive."

"I had no intention of returning in any other fashion, monk." Hugh drew his horse to a halt and waited until he had everyone's attention. "Bring forth the stone, Sir Dunstan, so that all may see that it is safely returned to Scarcliffe."

"The stone," someone muttered. "He has found the stone."

An expectant hush fell over the crowd.

"Aye, m'lord." Dunstan rode forward. There was a small wooden chest balanced on the pommel of his saddle.

A gasp of anticipation rippled through the throng of on-lookers. All eyes were fastened on the chest. With a suitably grand flourish, Dunstan unlocked the chest, raised the lid, and revealed the contents.

The ugly green crystal gleamed dully in the gray light.

The sharp silence was broken by a great cheer. Caps soared into the air.

"I knew this was our rightful lord." The blacksmith swung his anvil against the forge. The crash of sound mingled with the clang of a church bell.

" 'Tis the crystal, right enough." John the miller grinned at his wife. "Lord Hugh has brought it back, just as the legend says."

His youngest son, a child of four called Young John, bounced up and down and clapped his small hands. "He found it. Lord Hugh found it."

"Lord Hugh has recovered the stone," another boy called gleefully to a friend. "All will be well now, just as my father said."

Amid the uproar, Prioress Joan stepped out from the shadow of the gate. She was a woman of middle years with strong, well-defined features and warm, cheerful blue eyes.

"My lord, I am delighted to see that you have been suc-cessful in your quest to recover the stone."

"Hear me, good people of Scarcliffe," Hugh called out in a voice that was loud enough to carry to the brewer's cottage at the end of the street. "The legend has been fulfilled. I have recovered the green crystal and I vow to keep it safe in my hands. Just as I shall keep Scarcliffe and its people safe."

Another shout went up.

" 'Tis not only the stone I have brought back with me," Hugh continued, "but also my betrothed, Lady Alice. I ask you to welcome her. My future and yours is now bound up with hers."

Alice flinched and then shot Hugh a sharp glance but she said nothing. Any words she might have spoken would have been lost beneath the villagers' roar of approval.

Calvert's hot eyes glittered in the shadow of his cowl. Hugh ignored the monk. He was more concerned with Alice's reaction to this clamoring welcome.

She recovered quickly and swept the crowd with a genuinely gracious smile.

"I thank you for your kindness," she said with grand composure.

Calvert threw back his hood, exposing his cadaverously thin face and feverish dark eyes. He raised his staff to command attention.

"Hear me, daughter of Eve." He fixed Alice with a burning gaze. "I shall pray that you will be a meek and proper wife to Lord Hugh. As there is no priest in this village, I, myself, will undertake to instruct and guide you in your duties as a bride."

"That will not be necessary," Alice said coolly.

Calvert paid her no heed. He aimed a skeletal finger at her. "Under my direction you shall become the most estimable of wives, one who is neither quarrelsome nor difficult. One who is modest in her dress and restrained in her speech. One who embraces her position at her husband's feet. One who will find glory in humbling herself before her lord and master."

Hugh was about to silence the irritating monk when another, far more interesting stratagem occurred to him. He would allow Alice to deal with Calvert.

A woman of Alice's temperament needed to be able to exercise her many skills and talents else she would be discontented and unhappy. Furthermore, as with all those who took a professional approach to their business, she required respect and appreciation for those skills and talents.

Hugh strongly suspected that one of the reasons Alice had caused her uncle so much trouble at Lingwood was that Ralf had never comprehended the true extent of her intelligence and capabilities, nor had he given her the opportunity to wield them. Instead of respecting her abilities, he had attempted to treat her as though she were a servant.

Hugh had no intention of making the same mistake. He made it a rule to employ the most adept individuals and then he gave those individuals the authority to carry out their duties. The stratagem had always worked well for him in the past. He saw no reason not to apply it to a wife.

Hugh readied himself for Alice's response with a sense of relish.

"I thank you for your generous offer, monk," Alice said in an icy, polite voice, "but I fear I am too old and too set in my ways to learn such things. Lord Hugh must take me as I am."

"Red-haired, green-eyed women always have sharp tongues," Calvert snapped. "They must be taught to control them."

"Only a coward fears a woman's tongue," Alice said, far too sweetly. "I assure you, monk, that Lord Hugh is no coward. Do you dare to say otherwise?"

An audible gasp greeted the soft taunt. The onlookers edged closer.

Calvert blanched. He cast a hurried glance at Hugh and then quickly returned to his tirade. "Do not twist my words, my lady. 'Tis a fact that flame-haired women are known to possess shrewish tempers."

"I have heard it said that although Hugh's temper is difficult to arouse, 'tis akin to the darkest of storms once it is raised," Alice murmured. "Surely a man who possesses such a temper of his own need not flee a lady's ill humors."

Calvert sputtered furiously. He seemed to be having great difficulty finding words.

Hugh decided the combat had continued long enough. The monk stood no chance against Alice.

"You have the right of it, madam," Hugh said easily. "Furthermore, I would have you know that there are other parts of me that can be aroused and raised up with far less effort than it takes to coax forth my temper. I trust that you will discover those parts to be far more entertaining."

Laughter flowed through the crowd.

Alice scowled with confusion. Clearly she did not immediately comprehend his meaning. Then she turned a pretty shade of pink.

"Really, my lord," she muttered repressively.

Calvert, meanwhile, turned an interesting shade of purple. For a moment Hugh wondered if the man's bulging eyes would literally pop out of his head.

The monk glowered at Alice in outrage and then whirled toward Hugh. "Beware a woman who will not submit herself to the guidance of men, my lord. Such a woman will cause naught but trouble in your household."

Hugh grinned. "Do not concern yourself, monk. I do not fear my betrothed's tongue. Indeed, I find her speech . . . *interesting*."

More chuckles sounded from the villagers.

Calvert was not amused. He shook his staff at Hugh. "My lord, attend me. I speak as your religious counselor. If you would marry this woman, you must first learn to govern her. I tell you, your life will become a hellish existence if this lady is not taught to conduct herself in a proper and fit manner."

Alice rolled her eyes toward heaven.

Hugh looked at her and raised his voice so that all could hear him. "Be assured that I am willing to take my betrothed lady exactly as she is. Indeed, I look forward to doing so at the earliest opportunity."

There was another round of laughter, mostly male this time. Hugh thought he saw Prioress Joan suppress a grin. Most of the nuns gathered behind her were smiling broadly. The exception was Katherine. Hugh doubted if anything could alter Katherine's eternally solemn countenance.

It was Joan who moved to divert everyone's attention. She raised a palm. Silence descended on the villagers.

"Welcome, my lady," she said to Alice in a clear, calm voice. "I am the prioress of this convent. The well-being of this religious house is linked to the well-being of this manor. I am pleased to know that the new lord of Scarcliffe has taken steps to ensure the future of these lands."

Alice slid off her palfrey without any warning. She was on the ground, walking toward Joan, before Hugh realized her intention. He dismounted slowly, wondering what she was going to do next. Alice would never be predictable, he thought.

She went straight past Calvert as though the monk were invisible. Then to Hugh's and everyone else's surprise, Alice knelt gracefully in the mud in front of Joan.

"Thank you for your gracious welcome, my lady," Alice said. "I ask your blessing on Sir Hugh and myself and on all the inhabitants of these lands."

Hugh heard the murmur of appreciation from those around him.

Joan made the sign of the cross. "You have my blessing and my promise to assist you in your new duties to this manor, Lady Alice."

"Thank you, madam." Alice rose with complete disregard for the mud that now stained her traveling cloak.

As he went forward to take Alice's arm, Hugh saw Calvert's face contort into a mask of fury. The monk had been unmistakably rebuffed in front of one and all by the new lady of the manor.

Alice's triumph was complete. She had made it clear that so far as she was concerned the person who held true religious authority here on Scarcliffe was Prioress Joan. That fact would not be lost on anyone present.

Joan looked at Hugh with a measure of concern in her gentle eyes. "Will you return the green stone to its vault in the convent, my lord?"

"Nay," Hugh said. "The task of protecting the stone is mine. I shall take it to Scarcliffe Keep, where I can make certain that it is secure."

"An excellent notion, my lord." Joan did not trouble to hide her relief. "I am delighted to see the green crystal given into the care of its rightful guardian."

Hugh took a firm grip on Alice's arm. "It has been a long journey. I must take my lady to her new home."

"Aye, my lord." Joan moved back to the shelter of the gatehouse.

Hugh handed Alice back up into the saddle and then he remounted his own horse. He raised his hand to signal the company to set off toward the keep.

"That was very nicely handled," Hugh said for Alice's ears alone. "The prioress is the one person on these lands in whom the villagers place some degree of confidence. She and her women have seen to many of the basic necessities around here while the previous lords have come and gone."

"I believe that I shall like her very much," Alice said. "But I cannot say the same for the monk. He may be a man of God, but I find him extremely annoying."

"You are not alone. I don't believe Prioress Joan cares much for him either, although in her position she must tolerate him. Calvert does possess a certain zeal for lecturing women on their duties and frailties, does he not?"

"Bah. I have met his kind before. He is not concerned for the salvation of women's souls. He is merely frightened of females and seeks to weaken them by suppressing their spirits with remonstrations and sour speeches."

Hugh smiled. "Aye, no doubt."

Alice frowned in thought. "You seem to have satisfied your people with the manner in which you carried out the terms of the legend, sir."

"Aye, a nuisance, but 'tis finished." Hugh was cheered by that fact. "Now I can get on with more important matters."

"A nuisance, my lord?" Alice's brows rose. "I am crushed to learn that. I would remind you that had you not been obliged to search for the green stone, you would not have encountered me. I was under the impression that you were quite pleased to find yourself such an efficient and convenient betrothed."

Hugh winced. "I did not mean that the way it sounded. I was referring to the business with that damned crystal, not you."

"Then I am convenient and efficient, after all?" Mischief flashed in her eyes. "I am vastly relieved to know that. I would not want to think that I had failed to uphold my end of our bargain."

"Alice, I do believe you are trying to bait me the way a small hound teases a bear. I warn you, 'tis a dangerous game."

She cleared her throat discreetly. "Aye, well, be that as it may, there is a question concerning the local legend that I have been meaning to ask you."

"What is that?"

"You said that in addition to protecting the green stone, the true lord of Scarcliffe must discover the rest of the treasure."

"Aye, what of it?"

"You obviously satisfied your people that you were able to guard the green stone. But how will you go about locating the missing Stones of Scarcliffe? Do you have any notion of where they are?"

"I doubt that they even exist."

Alice stared at him. "Then how will you find them?"

"I am not concerned with that part of the legend," Hugh said carelessly. " 'Twas the recovery of the green stone that was most important. Now that I have brought it back to Scarcliffe, the villagers will assume that eventually I shall fulfill the rest of the prophecy. There is no great rush to do so."

"Eventually someone will notice that you have not succeeded in finding the stones, my lord."

"Once this manor is plump and prosperous, no one will care about those damned stones. If I am ever required to produce a small chest of costly baubles, I shall do so."

"But how?"

Hugh raised his brows at her naivete. "I shall simply purchase them, of course. I can afford to do so if necessary. 'Twould be no more costly than a few chests of spices."

"Aye, mayhap, but they will not be the true Stones of Scarcliffe."

"Think upon it, Alice," he said patiently. "No one living today has ever seen any of the so-called Stones of Scarcliffe except the green crystal. Who will know the difference between a bunch of gems purchased from a London merchant and the stones of the legend?"

Alice regarded him with an odd expression, a mix of awe and admiration. Hugh discovered to his surprise that he rather liked it. He basked in the warmth of it for a moment.

"My lord, only a man who is himself a legend could be so casually arrogant about fulfilling the terms of one."

Hugh grinned. "You think me arrogant? Only a woman who is unafraid of the power of legends herself would dare to strike a bargain with a man believed to be one."

"I told you that I do not have much faith in legends, sir. I am, however, much impressed by a man who is clever enough to invent whatever he needs to fill in the missing bits and pieces of his own."

"Thank you. Always pleasant to be admired for one's wits."

"There is nothing I admire more than keen wits, my lord." Alice broke off abruptly to stare straight ahead into the mists. Her eyes widened. "By the wounds of the Saints, is that Scarcliffe Keep?"

Hugh steeled himself. He gazed at the great stone edifice that was emerging from the gloom. "Aye. 'Tis Scarcliffe." He paused to give weight to his words. "Your new home, madam."

"For a while," she said absently.

"One becomes accustomed to it," he assured her.

"Indeed?" She studied the keep with curious eyes.

Hugh tried to view it objectively. He had been born in Scarcliffe Keep but he had no memories of the place.

After his beloved daughter had swallowed poison, Hugh's grandfather had taken his infant grandson to live with a widowed aunt in the north. The old man had lost all heart for the task of managing Scarcliffe. His thoughts had been focused only on revenge. Upon his death, Scarcliffe had fallen into other hands. A great many of them.

Scarcliffe had continued to decline under the succession of greedy, negligent lords.

The keep itself was a dark stone fortress that projected outward from the cliffs that loomed over and around it. It was said that the original owner had intended the structure to last until the crack of doom and it showed every possibility of doing just that.

The walled keep had been fashioned of an unusual black stone. No one whom Hugh had questioned had known where the ashlar had been quarried. Some said the great blocks of onyx-colored stone had been hewn from deep inside the maze of caverns that were etched in the cliffs. Some said it had been brought from a distant land.

"Who built this keep?" Alice asked in a voice that was soft with wonder.

"I am told he was called Rondale."

"An ancestor of yours?"

"Aye. My mother's grandfather. It was he who is said to have lost the Stones of Scarcliffe. The legend claims that he hid them in the caves and then was unable to find them."

"What happened to him?"

"According to the tale he went into the caverns many times in search of the treasure." Hugh shrugged. "On the last such occasion, he never came back out."

" 'Tis a most unusual keep," Alice said politely.

Hugh gazed at it proudly. "A fine, stout fortress that can withstand any siege."

"It reminds me of the magical castles one hears about in the troubadours' poems. The sort of place that the knights of the great Round Table were always happening upon in the middle of enchanted forests. It certainly has the aspect of a keep that has been under a sorcerer's spell."

She hates it, Hugh thought. The knowledge weighed heavily on him.

Chapter 10

The following morning Alice dusted off her new desk and seated herself behind it. She gazed around her with a sense of satisfaction.

The chamber she had chosen to use as a study was located on the highest floor of the keep. It was spacious and filled with a surprising amount of light. There was even a certain grace to the proportions of the room. It was a chamber that would lend itself well to investigations of natural philosophy.

Her books and chests of stones, the tray of dead insects, and her alchemical apparatus had been unpacked and carefully arranged on the nearby shelves and worktables. The astrolabe was on the windowsill. The green crystal sat on the corner of her desk.

Alice felt curiously at home. In all the months she had lived at Lingwood Hall she had never once known this feeling. She could be happy here, she realized. All she had to do was accept Hugh's offer to make their betrothal genuine.

All she had to do was marry the man they called *Relentless*.

All she had to do was wed a man who clearly valued efficiency and convenience far more than he valued love.

She was not at all certain that Hugh even believed in love.

Memories of her mother drifted through her head in silent warning. Helen had once believed she could teach a man to love, Alice thought sadly. She had been wrong.

Alice knew her mother had once been a warm and vibrant woman, a woman passionately in love with her husband. But Bernard had managed to kill that love by treating it callously and by refusing to return it.

Helen had married a man who had never learned to love her. She had paid a steep price. And so had her children.

Alice glanced at the handbook her mother had written. Sometimes she almost hated the thing. It contained much knowledge and the results of painstaking study and correspondence with learned people all over Europe. But Alice and Benedict had suffered a great deal because of it.

Toward the end of her life the handbook had absorbed more and more of Helen's devotion and attention. There had been very little left for Alice and her brother.

Alice got to her feet and went to the window. The stony cliffs of Scarcliffe brooded over the keep in what could be perceived as either a threatening or a protective fashion.

Yesterday she had been startled by her first view of the forbidding black fortress. There was a bleak strength in it that certainly offered the promise of protection but there was no evidence of warmth or softness in the stark edifice. It suited its new master well, Alice thought. Hugh and his keep had a great deal in common.

But what of Hugh's heart? Was it as hard and cold as the stone walls of this great fortress? Or was there some hope that she could find some gentleness in him?

Such insidious, seductive thoughts were dangerous to her peace of mind.

She turned away from the window, aware that her own heart was in grave jeopardy. The fact that she was even contemplating the notion of making the betrothal real should have sent a shaft of grave alarm through her.

Aye, she could be happy here, Alice told herself. But the odds were against it.

Best to maintain a certain distance. Best to hold herself apart. Best to keep her emotions safely locked inside.

She must not make the same mistake her mother had made.

*T*hree days later Hugh looked up from his desk to see his new household steward hovering in the doorway. "Aye?"

"Sorry to dis-disturb you, m'lord." Elbert, a lean, awkward young man possessed of what Hugh perceived to be a very anxious disposition, swallowed several times in an obvious attempt to gather his courage. And to find his tongue. Elbert had an unfortunate tendency to stutter whenever he was in Hugh's presence.

"What is it, steward?" Hugh put aside his abacus and waited impatiently.

Privately he admitted that he knew little of the qualifications that were desirable in a household steward. But whatever those qualifications were, Hugh was convinced that Elbert lacked them all. The man was clearly terrified of his new master and was inclined to stumble over his own feet whenever Hugh was in the vicinity.

On top of his other faults, Elbert's skill at managing the household was not impressive. Although he had seen to it that the chambers were cleaned, the midday meals had been harrowing experiences. Food had arrived from the kitchens cold and poorly spiced. There had been an insufficient number of bread trenchers to serve everyone. The crash of falling ale mugs and overloaded platters had created an unpleasant din.

Hugh was not looking forward to his next meal.

Alice, he noted grimly, had been spared the ordeal. She and Benedict had taken their meals in the chambers that she had claimed for their personal use. Special instructions had been given to the cooks. Hugh had a strong suspicion that she was eating far better than he.

The only reason Hugh had not dismissed Elbert from his new post within an hour after he had been appointed was that Alice had been the one who had chosen the new steward. She had agreed to do so only after Hugh had specifically asked her to assume the task.

He had thought that she would take charge of the entire household. Instead, she had simply selected Elbert, as requested, and then she had returned to her own chambers.

Things were not going according to the stratagem Hugh had so carefully worked out. He was more than willing to give Alice all the responsibility and authority she wished but she did not seem eager to claim it. He was baffled and irritated by the failure of his plan.

"Well?" Hugh prompted when Elbert simply stared at him, openmouthed.

Elbert hastily closed his mouth. "A messenger, m'lord."

"A messenger?"

"Aye, m'lord." Elbert straightened his red cap with an awkward gesture. "He arrived a few minutes ago with a letter for you. He says he's to stay the night."

"Send him to me, steward."

"Aye, m'lord." Elbert backed hurriedly out into the corridor and managed to trip in the process. He caught himself, whirled, and ran down the hall.

Hugh sighed and went back to work on the abacus. A few minutes later Elbert conducted into the chamber a lean, jaunty man who somehow managed to appear fashionable in a travel-stained cloak and muddy boots.

"Greetings, Julian," Hugh said. "A good journey, I trust?"

"Aye, sir." Julian swept Hugh an elegant bow and handed him the letter. "A good horse and no rain. A bit of trouble with a pack of robbers on the Windlesea road but I showed them your seal and that was the end of the matter."

"I am pleased to hear that." Hugh glanced at the letter.

Julian coughed discreetly. "Your pardon, sir, but I feel obliged to point out that there likely wouldn't have been any trouble at all if I had been wearing a proper livery. I think something in blue and yellow trimmed with a bit of gold braid would be nice."

"Later, Julian."

"My post requires something quite eye-catching. Robbers would notice it straight off. They would recognize your man and never bother him at all."

Hugh glanced up warily. "We've discussed this matter before, messenger. You are supplied every year with a serviceable robe, cloak, boots, and a new leather pouch."

"Aye, m'lord, and 'tis most generous of you," Julian murmured. "But everything you supply comes in only one color."

"What of it?"

"Black is not a fashionable color, m'lord," Julian said with a hint of exasperation. "I look like a wandering monk on the road."

"Would that you would travel as frugally as one. Your quarterly expenses were outrageous. I meant to speak to you about them."

"I can explain them all," Julian said smoothly.

"I trust you can."

"Sir, about the new livery."

"What new livery?" Hugh growled. "I just told you there will not be any new livery."

Julian plucked at his sleeve with an expression of disgust. "Very well, let us assume that we stick with the basic black."

"An excellent assumption."

"It would be somewhat more attractive if you would at least allow some gold braid."

"Gold braid? For a messenger to wear in the mud and snow? Madness. You'd likely be murdered on the highway for the trim on your robe."

"Not three months past John of Larkenby gave his personal messenger a fine new robe of emerald green," Julian said persuasively. "Trimmed in orange. And a matching cap. Very nice."

"Enough of this nonsense. Any word of my liege lord's health?"

Julian's handsome face sobered. "I gave him your regards, as you requested."

"You saw Sir Erasmus?"

"Aye. He received me only because I am your man. I hear that he sees very few visitors these days. His wife handles most of his affairs now."

"How did he appear?" Hugh asked.

" 'Tis obvious he is very ill, my lord. He will not speak of it, but his wife is red-eyed from weeping. The doctors believe his heart is failing him. He is very thin. He starts at every small sound. He looks exhausted and yet he says he cannot sleep."

"I was hoping the news would be better."

Julian shook his head. "I am sorry, my lord. He sent you his best wishes."

"Aye, well, what will be, will be." Hugh slit the seal on the letter. "Go to the kitchen and get yourself something to eat."

"Aye, m'lord." Julian hesitated. "About the livery. I know how you feel about the expense. But it strikes me that now that you've got lands of your own and a fine keep, you'll want the members of your household dressed in a fitting manner. After all, m'lord, the world judges a man by the clothing his people are given to wear."

"When I find myself concerned with the opinion of the world, I'll let you know. Begone, messenger."

"Aye, m'lord." Julian had served Hugh long enough to know when he had pushed his master's patience far enough. He bowed himself out of the chamber with his elegant, slightly supercilious manners and went off down the hall, whistling.

Hugh gazed unseeingly at the letter in his hand. *Erasmus of Thornewood was dying.* There could no longer be much doubt. Hugh knew that he was soon going to lose the man who had been in many ways a father to him.

He swallowed heavily to relieve a sudden fullness in his throat, blinked once or twice to clear his eyes, and then he concentrated on the letter.

The missive was from his London steward. It reported on the successful arrival of a shipload of spice. The steward had, in his usual punctilious fashion, listed each chest, its contents and estimated value, together with notes concerning the expenses. Hugh reached for the abacus.

"Excuse me, my lord," Benedict said from the doorway.

Hugh glanced up from his work. "Aye?"

"Sir Dunstan sent me to tell you that the stables have been cleaned and made ready. He wants to know if you wish to speak with the blacksmith." Benedict caught sight of the abacus and paused. "What is that, my lord?"

" 'Tis called an abacus. It is used for making calculations."

"I have heard of such." Benedict came forward with an intent expression. His staff thumped on the floor. "How does it work?"

Hugh smiled slowly. "I'll show you, if you like. One can do sums, multiply, or divide. Most useful for keeping one's accounts."

"I would like to learn how to use it." Benedict glanced up shyly. "I have always been interested in such matters."

"Have you?"

"Aye. Alice taught me as much as she knows about calculations but, in truth, 'tis not an area of great interest to her. She prefers matters of natural philosophy."

"I know." Hugh studied Benedict's rapt expression. "Benedict, I think it's time that you dined in the great hall together with your lord and the rest of the men of this manor. You will present yourself downstairs today at the midday meal."

Benedict looked up sharply. "Dine with you, my lord? But Alice thinks it best if we eat in our own chambers."

"Alice may do as she pleases. But you are one of my men and you will dine with the rest of us."

"One of your men?" Benedict looked startled at that notion.

"Your sister is betrothed to me and you live here at Scarcliffe," Hugh said casually. "That makes you a member of my household, does it not?"

"I had not thought of it in such terms." A shy eagerness appeared in his eyes. "You are right. I will do as you command, my lord."

"Excellent. Speaking of Alice, where is your sister?"

"She went into the village to speak with Prioress Joan." Benedict picked up the abacus with reverent hands.

"Did she go alone?"

"Aye."

"Did she say when she would return?"

"Not for some time." Benedict carefully moved one of the red counters along a thin wooden rod. "I believe she mentioned something about searching out some new stones for her collection."

Hugh frowned. "Stones?"

"Aye. She expects to find some interesting ones in the cliff caves."

"Hellfire and Saints' bones." Hugh surged to his feet and

started around the edge of his desk. "Your sister is going to turn me into a madman."

"That's what Uncle Ralf always used to say, too."

Hugh paid no attention. He was already halfway down the hall, heading for the staircase.

Chapter 11

"As you will see, Lady Alice, there is much to be done here." Joan lifted a hand to indicate not only the convent garden in which she and Alice stood, but the whole of the village. "I have accomplished what I could during the three years I have been prioress of this house, but it has been difficult without a proper lord to govern these lands."

"I understand, madam." Alice surveyed the neat gardens. Several nuns were working industriously to weed and water the plants and prepare the ground for winter.

The walk into the village had been a curious one. Alice had been greeted by a wide variety of people. Farmers had paused in their work to nod respectfully. Small children at play had smiled shyly at her as she went past. The brewer had come to the door of her cottage to offer a mug of new ale. The blacksmith had beamed from the other side of his glowing forge. The miller's wife had given her a loaf of bread, which her son, Young John, had proudly handed to her.

Alice was aware that an air of expectancy hovered over Scarcliffe today. Its people believed that the legend had come true, or at least that it was well on its way to being fulfilled. Their rightful lord was among them. The curse had been lifted and all would be well.

A pang of regret went through Alice at the realization that even the earnest and good-hearted Joan was speaking to her as though she really would be the next lady of the manor.

The prioress was right. There was much to be done here, Alice thought. And Hugh would see to it that things would be accomplished. He would take care of these lands because his own future was tied to them.

But she was not at all certain that she could take the risk of binding her own future to Hugh's and to Scarcliffe. *I did not believe that I was a coward,* she thought. *Ah, but never before has my own heart been at stake.*

Life would be simpler and calmer in a large, cloistered convent. Far more conducive to the study of natural philosophy.

"That ridiculous legend did not help matters." Joan led the way along one of the garden paths. " 'Twas a great nuisance to have it hanging over our heads all these years. I would like to have a few words with the idiot who invented it."

Alice glanced at her in surprise. "Surely you do not believe in the legend yourself?"

"Nay, but the people of Scarcliffe certainly do. I must admit that the longer these lands went without a strong lord, the more evidence seemed to indicate that the curse was real."

"Legends seem to take on a life of their own."

"Aye." Joan grimaced as she halted near the herb garden where a tall nun labored alone. "Lately, we have even begun to suffer from the predations of outlaws and robbers because there was no lord with a household of strong knights to protect us."

"Outlaws will no longer be a problem now that Lord Hugh is master of Scarcliffe," Alice assured her with great confidence.

The tall nun paused in her work. She leaned on her hoe. Beneath her wimple, her eyes were dark and somber. "There are other calamities every bit as bad as a plague of robbers. The curse is real, Lady Alice. Lord Hugh will learn that soon enough."

Joan rolled her eyes indulgently. "Pay no heed to Sister Katherine, my lady. She is a skilled healer but she often sees only the most dismal possibilities."

Alice smiled at Katherine. "If you believe in the curse, then surely you are satisfied that all is well here once more. The legend has been fulfilled."

"Bah. I care nothing for the legend of the green crystal and the Stones of Scarcliffe," Katherine muttered. " 'Tis but a tale for children."

"Then what concerns you?" Alice asked.

"The true curse on this land is the bad blood between Rivenhall and Scarcliffe. Betrayal and murder fester in the manner of an infection that cannot be cured."

"You refer to the old enmity between the two manors, I presume," Alice said.

Katherine hesitated in obvious surprise. "You know of it?"

"Aye, Lord Hugh told me the sad tale. But if you fear that there will be war between Rivenhall and Scarcliffe because of it, you may set your mind at ease. There will be no violence between the two manors."

Katherine shook her head with a doleful air. "The seeds of revenge were planted in the past. They have sent forth a dark herb that poisons this land."

"Nay." Alice was beginning to grow angry with the healer's grim view of the situation. "Calm yourself, Sister. Lord Hugh explained to me that there will be no violence. He said that both he and Sir Vincent have sworn oaths to the same liege lord, Erasmus of Thornewood. Sir Erasmus has expressly forbidden them from engaging in anything more bloodthirsty than the occasional joust."

" 'Tis said that Erasmus of Thornewood is dying." Katherine's hand tightened around the hoe. "When he is gone, who will control Sir Vincent and Sir Hugh? Scarcliffe and Rivenhall are a long way from the centers of power. The lords of these lands will be free as unleashed hounds. They will go straight for each other's throats."

"Sister Katherine has a point." Joan frowned. "I have always considered our remote location to be one of the few good things about these lands. It is safer to live far from men who command armies and worry about who is on the throne. But it does mean that we are dependent upon Lord Hugh to maintain peace."

"He will do so," Alice insisted.

She was not quite certain why she felt so compelled to defend Hugh's good intentions. Mayhap it was because she knew him far better than these women did and she wanted them to have confidence in him.

"There will never be peace for Scarcliffe and Rivenhall," Katherine whispered.

Alice decided it was time to change the subject. "Is this your herb garden, Sister?"

"Aye."

"Sister Katherine joined this house many years ago," Joan said. "She is expert with herbs. At one time or another we have all been grateful for her tonics and potions."

"My mother was a healer," Alice offered. "She was a great student of herbal lore. She had many unusual plants in her gardens."

Katherine ignored the comment. She gazed steadily at Alice. "How long have you been betrothed to Hugh the Relentless?"

"Not long. And his name is not Hugh the Relentless anymore. He is Hugh of Scarcliffe now."

"When will you be wed?"

"Sometime in the spring," Alice said vaguely.

"Why do you choose to wait so long?"

Joan gave her a reproving look. "Lady Alice's wedding plans are no concern of yours, Sister."

Katherine's thin mouth tightened. "A betrothal may be broken easily enough."

"Nonsense." Joan was clearly annoyed. "A betrothal is a solemn and most binding commitment."

"But it is not a vow of marriage," Katherine said.

"That is enough, Sister," Joan said sternly.

Katherine fell silent but she continued to stare at Alice.

Alice flushed beneath the scrutiny. "Lord Hugh wished to wait until spring to wed because he has so many other important matters that must be seen to immediately."

"Quite understandable," Joan said crisply. "Pray, return to your labors, Sister. Lady Alice and I will continue our tour of the convent grounds." She started off down another path, drawing Alice in her wake. "Come, let me show you our wine-making workrooms. Then, mayhap you would care to see the library?"

Alice brightened. "Oh, yes, I should very much like to see it."

"I hope you will make use of it." Joan waited until they were out of earshot of Katherine before adding softly, "You must forgive the healer. She is very good at her work but she suffers greatly from melancholia."

"I understand. 'Tis a pity she cannot heal herself."

"She takes a tonic made from poppies when her spirits are especially low, but other than that, she says there is little that can be done for her condition."

Alice frowned. "Potions made from poppies must be used sparingly."

"Aye." Joan slanted her an interested look. "You sound knowledgeable on the subject. Did you follow in your mother's footsteps, my lady?"

"I have studied herbal lore and I have kept my mother's handbook on the subject, but after she died I turned to other interests."

"I see."

"I consider myself a student of natural philosophy." Alice came to a halt and looked toward the forbidding cliffs that rose behind the village. "As it happens, I had planned to further my investigations in such matters later this morning."

Joan followed her gaze. "You intend to explore the cliffs?"

"Aye. I have never seen a cave. It should prove most interesting."

"Forgive me, my lady, but I'm not certain that is a sound notion. Does Lord Hugh know of your intention?"

"Nay." Alice smiled brightly. "He was occupied with weighty affairs of business this morning. I chose not to intrude."

"I see." Joan hesitated as though she felt she ought to say more on the subject but she changed her mind. "You told Sister Katherine that you did not think there would be war between the manors of Rivenhall and Scarcliffe."

"Aye. What of it?"

"Are you certain? This land has suffered much, my lady. I do not know if it could survive such a disaster."

Alice chuckled. "Have no fear, Lord Hugh will protect Scarcliffe."

"I trust you are right." Joan broke off abruptly as she glanced at a spot directly behind Alice.

A jolt of awareness went through Alice at that instant. She knew without turning around that Hugh was in the garden.

"I am well pleased to learn that you have such great faith in my abilities, lady," he said in his emotionless voice. "I would wish that I could have a similar degree of faith in your good sense. What is this I hear about your plans to explore the caverns of Scarcliffe?"

Alice whirled about to find him looming as large and solid as Scarcliffe Keep itself on the path behind her. His black hair was windblown. His amber eyes gleamed with a dangerous intelligence. She had seen very little of Hugh during the past three days but on each occasion she'd had a similar reaction.

Whenever she happened upon him, even for a fleeting moment, the impact on her senses was startling. Her pulse quickened and something curled deep in her stomach. Memories of the night in Ipstoke when he had touched her so intimately warmed every part of her body.

She had not been able to sleep well for thinking of that passionate interlude. Last night she had prepared a hot drink of chamomile tea to settle her senses. She had got herself to sleep but she had dreamed. *How* she had dreamed.

"You startled me, my lord." She fought her unsettled reaction to him by glowering ferociously. "I did not hear you come into the garden. I thought you were occupied with your accounts this morning."

"I was very busy with them until I learned that you planned a venture into the caverns." Hugh inclined his head slightly toward Joan. "Good day to you, madam."

"Good day, my lord." Joan glanced from Hugh's grim face to Alice's scowling features and back again. She cleared her throat discreetly. "Mayhap 'tis just as well you have come, my lord. I was a trifle concerned myself about Lady Alice's plans. She is new to this land and does not yet know all its dangers."

"Aye," Hugh said. "And at the moment the most serious danger she faces is me." He braced his fists on his hips. "What in the name of the devil do you think you are about, lady?"

She refused to be intimidated. "I merely wish to search for some interesting stones."

"You are not to go into the caverns alone. Ever. Is that understood?"

Alice patted his sleeve in a soothing manner. "Calm yourself, my lord. I am quite skilled in the science of natural philosophy. I have been collecting interesting specimens for years. I will come to no harm."

Hugh hooked his thumbs into his leather belt. "Heed me well, Alice. You are not to go beyond the bounds of this village alone. I forbid it."

"Would you care to come with me? I could use a stout man to help me carry whatever interesting objects I may discover."

For a second or two, Hugh looked completely taken aback by the invitation. He recovered immediately and cast a disparaging glance at the leaden sky. "There will be rain soon."

"Unlikely, I think." Alice looked up. " 'Tis just somewhat overcast."

A speculative gleam appeared in Hugh's eyes. "Very well, madam, as you are the expert on matters of natural philosophy around here, I shall bow to your judgment. I'll escort you on your expedition."

"As you wish." Elation welled up inside Alice. She tried to appear unconcerned, as though Hugh's decision was of no great moment.

Joan looked relieved. "Take care not to stumble upon our wandering monk while you're traipsing about in the vicinity of the cliffs. I am told that he is encamped in one of the caves."

Hugh frowned as he took Alice's arm. "Why is Calvert of Oxwick sleeping in the caves?"

Joan's features remained serenely composed but her eyes sparkled with humor. "No doubt because I refused to give him a cell here in the convent. There really is nowhere else for him to spread a pallet except Scarcliffe Keep itself. Apparently he did not dare to impose on your hospitality, my lord."

"Just as well," Alice grumbled. "I would not have Scarcliffe Keep supply any accommodations to that obnoxious man."

Hugh raised his brows but made no comment. Belatedly it occurred to Alice that decisions regarding the extension of the keep's hospitality were rightfully his. She was not even his true betrothed. And she had made herself a promise that she would not get overly involved in household matters.

"Well, then," she said briskly. "We had best be off, my lord. The day is getting along, is it not?"

*T*he first drops of rain struck as they started up the rocky hillside beneath the caverns.

"By the Saints." Alice fumbled with the hood of her mantle. "We will get soaked to the skin if we do not get into the shelter of the caves."

"I told you it was going to rain." Hugh grabbed her hand and pulled her swiftly toward the first of the dark openings etched in the cliffs.

"Do you make it a habit to point out your infallibility on each of those occasions when you happen to be correct in your estimation of a situation?" Alice broke into a run to keep up with him.

"Nay." Laughter warmed Hugh's eyes as he pulled her beneath the overhang of a large cavern. "As I am almost always correct, 'twould be too much of a bother to mention that fact every time it is proven."

She glowered at him for a moment and then her attention was captured by his rain-dampened hair. For some reason the sight of it, tousled and plastered against his well-shaped head, made him look somehow different. Gentler, even a trifle vulnerable.

She caught her breath on a wild rush of hope. If Hugh really did have some gentleness in him, some degree of softness and vulnerability, mayhap he could learn to love her.

The rain began to fall in earnest. Thunder rolled in the distance.

As though he meant to squash any false illusion of underlying softness, Hugh ran careless fingers through his wet mane. He brushed it ruthlessly behind his ears, exposing his high forehead and the severe, predatory lines of his cheekbones. In the blink of an eye he was transformed back into a man who could easily shoulder the weight of a legend.

Alice smiled wistfully. "You are impossible, my lord."

A hint of amusement edged his mouth. He glanced curiously around at their surroundings. "Behold your cave, madam."

Alice followed his gaze and shivered a little. " 'Tis somewhat dark, is it not?"

"Caves tend to be gloomy places," he said dryly.

The cavern was large. Its depths were lost in the shadows that shrouded the far end. The gray light of the rain-drenched day did not reach more than a short distance into the interior. There was an air of perpetual dampness about the place. Somewhere water dripped on stone.

"Next time I must remember to bring a torch," Alice said.

"Aye. Without one we cannot see much, can we?"

"Nay." She refused to admit that she was glad that they had a good excuse not to go deeper into the cavern. " 'Tis unfortunate that we must limit our investigations today, but it cannot be helped."

Hugh rested one hand against the rocky wall and looked out over the village and fields of Scarcliffe. "There is a fine prospect from up here, even when rain is falling."

Alice saw the pride of possession in his golden eyes. "On a clear day one would be able to see a great distance."

"All the way to Rivenhall."

The dangerous softness of his tone made Alice uneasy. She recalled the healer's words. *The seeds of revenge were planted in the past. They have sent forth a dark herb that poisons this land.*

Alice told herself that she did not believe in legends. She gazed out into the rain and wondered why the healer's words had held the ring of truth.

"Well, Alice?" Hugh said after a moment. He did not turn to look at her. His attention was still on the landscape spread out before him.

"Well what, my lord?" Alice leaned down to examine a chunk of dark stone.

"It seems to me that you have had ample time for contemplation. What is your decision?"

She froze over the dark stone as his meaning became plain. She stifled a groan of dismay and sought refuge in a pretense of misunderstanding. " 'Tis an interesting bit of rock but I do not believe that it is all that unusual. I would like to find a sample of the stone that was used to build the keep. Now that is a most interesting sort. I have never seen its like."

"I was not talking about that damned stone and well you know it." His gaze flickered briefly with cold impatience. "Have you made up your mind to wed me?"

"Bones of the Saints, my lord, it has been a mere three days since you requested my decision. I would point out that both of us have been extremely busy during that time."

"Busy? You have done little except choose a clumsy oaf of a steward."

"Elbert will make you an excellent steward," she countered. "And how dare you accuse me of idleness? I have hardly had a chance to think, let alone to weigh the merits of such an important matter as marriage."

Hugh said nothing for a moment. Then he lowered himself onto a rocky outcropping and rested his elbows on his knees. His gaze remained fixed on the distant lands of Rivenhall, which were shrouded in a rainy mist.

"Do you hate this land, Alice?"

She was startled by the question. "Scarcliffe? Nay, my lord. I do not hate it."

"You find it ugly."

"Nay, that is not true. I'll grant you that it is not a gentle landscape, but 'tis an interesting and varied place."

"Scarcliffe will soon flourish. I will see to it."

"I do not doubt that, my lord."

"What of the keep?" he persisted. "Do you dislike it?"

"Nay. As you noted, it appears strong. Easily defended." She paused, wondering where this line of inquiry was going. "And, in truth, 'tis more comfortable inside than it first appeared."

"So you do not object to making your home in it?"

"Uh, well, as I just said, there is nothing in particular to object to in the keep."

"I am pleased to learn this." Hugh picked up a small pebble and tossed it carelessly down the sloping hillside. It was a surprisingly playful gesture, a gesture at odds with his decidedly stern nature. "If in future you do discover that there is a problem with the keep you will tell me about it and I will see that it is remedied at once."

"Aye, my lord. Thank you." Alice watched him skip another pebble down the wet hillside. She wondered what sort of childhood Hugh had experienced. A short one, no doubt, just as her own had been. A bastard would have been forced to assume the mantle of manhood early in his life.

"So, you do not find the manor to be unpleasant and you are content with the keep," Hugh concluded.

"Aye, my lord," Alice said warily. "I am content."

"Then there is no reason to put off the marriage, is there?"

Alice threw up her hands in exasperation. "My lord, I begin to perceive why it is that they call you Hugh the Relentless."

"I do not care to waste unnecessary time."

"I assure you, we are not wasting time. I need every bit of it that I can get." She sat down on a large rock near the mouth of the cave and opened the sack the miller's son had given her. "Would you care for a bit of fresh-baked bread?"

Hugh frowned at the loaf as she withdrew it from the sack. "You are attempting to change the subject."

"Very observant of you."

"Alice, I am not a man who is much given to hesitation or delay."

"I am learning that truth all too well, my lord." Alice tore off a chunk of the bread and handed it to him. "But in this matter, I fear you must learn patience."

Hugh pinned her with his hunter's eyes as he reached out for the bread. "How long will it take you to make up your mind?"

"I have no notion." She nibbled determinedly at her portion of the loaf.

Hugh tore a large chunk out of his bread and chewed grimly.

Silence fell. So did the rain, heavily and steadily.

After a moment Alice cautiously relaxed. Hugh was apparently willing to let the subject of marriage drop, at least for the moment.

She took another bite of the crusty bread and indulged herself in the fleeting pleasure of Hugh's company. It was good to sit here alone with him, to pretend that they were friends and partners and that they would share the future together. Surely such a fantasy did no harm.

"Elbert is creating havoc in the keep," Hugh said after a long interval. "Do you think you should choose another to carry out his duties?"

Alice pulled herself out of her warm reverie. "Elbert will learn quickly. I spoke to several possible candidates for the position and he was by far the most intelligent and eager. Give him time, my lord."

"That is easy for you to say. As you choose to dine alone

in your chambers, you have not yet experienced the adventure of taking a meal in the great hall with the rest of us. I assure you, Elbert's supervision makes it an unforgettable event."

Alice glanced at him. "If you find it unpleasant to dine in the great hall, why do you not do as I do? Have your meal sent to your private chambers." She hesitated and then added, very daringly, "Or you could join me, my lord."

"That is not possible."

Alice felt her face grow hot at the unequivocal rejection of her offer. "Forgive me for suggesting it. I did not mean to overstep my bounds."

He shot her an irritated look. "Do you not realize that a lord must take his main meals in the company of his men?"

Alice shuddered delicately. "I cannot imagine why. The rude conversation and the crude jests are enough to ruin any meal. I have no interest in the obnoxious chatter about weapons and jousts, nor in all that talk of the glories of past battles or the hunt."

"You do not comprehend. One of the ways in which a lord secures the bonds between himself and those who serve him is by dining with them." Hugh munched bread. "A strong lord is as tied to those who depend upon him as they are to him. He must let them see that he respects them and appreciates their loyalty."

"And he does that by dining with them?"

"Aye. 'Tis one of the ways he accomplishes it."

"Ah, that explains it." Alice smiled in sudden comprehension. "I wondered why a man as intelligent as you was willing to tolerate the coarse manners that are so common in great halls."

"One grows accustomed to it."

"I do not think that I could ever grow accustomed to having every meal ruined by such conversation and activities. It must be very difficult for you to face the future knowing that you will have to make such a great sacrifice every day of your life."

Annoyance flashed briefly in Hugh's eyes. "I do not consider it such a great sacrifice. We do not all share your fine sensibilities. The talk of arms and armor is not dull to a knight, madam. 'Tis business."

"And the rude jests and the laughter and the lamentable manners of your companions? Do you enjoy those, too?"

"They are normal enough when men gather over food and drink."

"True." Alice bit off another bite of bread.

"As I said, dining in one's great hall is a matter of respect and loyalty." Hugh paused. "In most households, the lord's lady joins him at table."

"So I have been told, but I cannot imagine any lady wanting to do so."

"She does so for reasons similar to those that oblige her lord to dine with his people." Hugh sounded as though he were speaking through clenched teeth.

Alice ceased chewing. "For reasons of respect and loyalty?"

"Aye. She sits beside him in the presence of their people so that all will see that she respects her lord and is loyal to him."

Alice sucked in her breath and tried to swallow her bread at the same instant. She promptly sputtered, gasped for air, and began to cough.

Hugh frowned in concern. He reached out and slapped her forcefully between her shoulders. "Are you all right?"

"Aye," she managed. She caught her breath and swallowed several times to get rid of the wayward bite. "I'm fine."

"I'm pleased to hear that."

Silence fell again. This time Alice was not relieved. She felt oddly discomfited.

Mayhap Hugh believed that her refusal to eat in the great hall was a sign of her lack of respect for him. She wondered if his men and the others in Scarcliffe Keep thought her unloyal.

"Alice, I would have you tell me precisely why you cannot make up your mind to marry me," Hugh said. " 'Tis the reasonable, practical, logical thing to do."

Alice shut her eyes. "I thought we had finished with that topic for today."

"If you tell me why you hesitate, I will be able to do something to correct the matter."

It was too much. Alice lost her patience. "Very well, my lord, I shall be blunt. If I am to wed, I would prefer that it be for reasons of true affection, not efficiency and convenience."

Hugh went very still. His eyes locked with hers. "Affection?"

"Aye. Affection. My mother married a man who wanted nothing more from her than an heir and someone to manage his household. She was doomed to great loneliness with only her studies to comfort her."

"She had you and your brother."

"We were not enough," Alice said bitterly. "They say my mother died from poison, but in truth, I think she died of a broken heart. I will not make the same mistake that she made."

"Alice—"

"I prefer the peace and tranquillity of the convent to a marriage that is barren of affection. Now do you understand my hesitation, my lord?"

He watched her warily. "You wish to be wooed? Very well, madam, I shall attempt a proper wooing, but I must warn you that I have no great skill in such matters."

Alice leaped to her feet, her temper in full blaze. "My lord, you are missing the point here. I do not want a false wooing. You may save your flowers and poems. I speak of love. That is what I require. *Love.*"

Comprehension lit his eyes. He got to his feet and reached for her. "So 'tis passion you want, after all. Rest assured that you shall have all you wish of that commodity."

He covered her mouth with his own before Alice could even begin to lecture him on his grave misunderstanding.

For a few seconds she raged in silence and then it struck her that passion might well be all that Hugh could give her at this time.

It might also be the one emotion that could lead him to love.

She threw her arms around his neck and kissed him back with all the love that had flowered in her heart since the first night she saw him.

Chapter 12

*E*lation crashed through Hugh with the force of a great sea wave when he felt Alice soften against him. He had been correct in his assessment of the situation. Passion was the key to unlocking this sweet, well-defended keep, he thought.

Alice wanted him. Her womanly desire was the richest, most intoxicating of rare spices.

He fitted his hands to the curves of her firm, rounded buttocks and lifted her up high against his chest. He felt her arms tighten around his neck and heard her whispered gasp. Deliberately he crushed her to him, letting her feel his fully aroused manhood.

"My lord, you have the most astounding effect on my senses." Alice kissed his throat. "I vow, I do not comprehend it."

"This is what the poets call love." Hugh tugged the woven mesh net from her hair, allowing the red tresses to spill over her shoulders. "Myself, I have always believed that passion is a more honest word for such emotion."

She raised her head from his shoulder. For a moment her eyes met his. He thought he would drown in their emerald depths. "You are wrong, my lord. My mother's experience taught me that passion by itself is not love. But I begin to believe that the two may be bound together."

Hugh smiled wryly. "I confess that I am beyond engaging in a reasoned argument about the subject at the moment, Alice."

"But, my lord, I think the distinction between the two is very important."

"Nay. 'Tis not at all important." Hugh silenced her with his mouth.

He did not release her until her lips had parted beneath his and she clung to him so tightly he knew she could not, of her own accord, let go. Only then did he ease himself away from her long enough to unbuckle his sword belt and remove his black outer tunic.

She watched with brilliant eyes as he set the scabbard down close by. He was wryly chagrined to see that his hand shook slightly. He took a deep, steadying breath and then he spread his tunic on the stone floor of the cave.

The simple task seemed to require an enormous degree of concentration. When he was finished he straightened and looked at Alice from the other side of the makeshift bed.

He saw the shadows in her eyes and a terrible fear clawed at his guts.

Then, with a tremulous smile, she gave him her hand.

Hugh breathed a silent sigh of satisfaction and overwhelming relief. He lowered himself onto the black tunic and gently pulled Alice down to join him. Her skirts frothed around his thighs as she sprawled, warm and inviting, across his chest.

Her eyes widened with concern as she settled into place. "My lord, you will surely be mashed against the hard stone."

He chuckled. "I have never had a softer quilt."

She touched his cheek with her fingertips and wriggled into a more comfortable position. Hugh groaned as her gently rounded thighs pressed more firmly against his rigid shaft. Without warning the desire that smoldered within him flared into a searing blaze. He felt the flames devour the last vestiges of his control.

Alice wanted him and she was his betrothed wife. Nothing stood in his way. Nothing else mattered.

Hugh surrendered to the firestorm that he had ignited. He caught Alice's face between his hands and kissed her with an urgency he could no longer conceal. To his soaring delight, she responded enthusiastically, if awkwardly, to the bruising kiss. He heard a muffled *mmmph* and then he almost laughed aloud as her teeth clinked against his own.

"Easy, my sweet," he said into her mouth. "There is no need to swallow me whole. You shall have all you want of me before we have finished."

She moaned and buried her fingers in his hair.

He cradled her head in place with one hand and reached down to raise the hem of her skirts. His palm slid along the length of her bare thigh all the way to the gentle curves above. He found the valley that divided the luscious hillocks and followed its course to the hot spring that awaited him.

"*Hugh.*"

He stroked her carefully, preparing her for his entry. He wanted her delirious with need so that she would not feel pain, if there was any, when he claimed her. He wanted everything to be perfect.

Thunder shook the skies. The rain was a gray curtain in front of the cavern mouth.

When Hugh fumbled with his undertunic and loosened his braies, Alice raised her head briefly to gaze down at him with passion-clouded eyes. For a few heart-stopping seconds he thought she was going to ask him to halt the lovemaking. He wondered, with an odd sense of detachment, if doing so would kill him on the spot.

"*Hugh.*"

The sound of his name on her lips made his blood pound. Excitement tore through him. She was thoroughly ensnared by their mutual passion, he told himself.

It would be a fine stratagem indeed, if Alice were to believe herself in love.

With a groan he crushed her mouth against his own and moved his hand between her thighs. Her murmurs of longing were sweeter than honeyed dates, more potent than an alchemist's elixir. The more he tasted of her, the more he hungered. Hugh was engulfed with a seemingly insatiable need.

He pulled Alice's skirts up to her waist and eased her legs apart so that she straddled him. The scent of her dewy body filled him with an overpowering eagerness.

He freed himself completely from his braies and probed until he found the plumped, moist petals that hid the entrance to the secret citadel. He entered her with a care that strained his self-mastery to the limit. Her body was impossibly tight around him. It was as though he tried to ease himself through the narrow entrance of a cave passage.

It was as he had thought. She was a virgin.

He must be careful, Hugh told himself. He must not take this keep too quickly.

His jaw clenched with the effort to control his own need.

He stormed the fragile gates slowly, steadily, until both of their bodies were damp with perspiration. Alice's nails bit through the fabric of his undertunic.

"You are well guarded," he whispered hoarsely. "Am I hurting you?"

"Aye, a little."

He closed his eyes, gathering himself, seeking restraint. "I would not have it so. Do you want me to stop?"

"Nay."

Hugh breathed a small sigh of relief. In truth, he had not been certain that he possessed the will to halt what had been begun. "I shall proceed slowly," he promised.

Alice eased aside the neck opening of his undertunic and nibbled gently at his shoulder. "I do not want you to proceed slowly. I would have done with this business quickly."

He groaned. "This is supposed to be a pleasurable task, not one that requires fortitude."

"Will you finish it when I give the command?"

He flexed his hands on her hips. "Mayhap you are right. It would be less painful if it were done swiftly."

"Do it now then." Without warning Alice sank her teeth into his shoulder.

"*Blood of the devil.*" Startled by the small, sharp, and wholly unexpected pain, Hugh instinctively tightened his hold on Alice, sucked in his breath, and surged upward.

Alice gave a muffled squeak but Hugh could not have retreated if he had wished. The last remnants of his self-mastery gave way as surely as the delicate barrier that had guarded Alice's chastity.

Loosed from the bonds that he had used to govern himself for most of his life, Hugh drove deep into Alice. She clenched fiercely around him, snug and hot.

Outside the cave the storm reached its peak. Lightning flashed in the distance. The rain roared on the stony cliffs. The world shrunk down to the cavern in which Hugh lay with Alice. Nothing else mattered, he thought. Nothing.

He heard Alice moan softly. He reached his hand down between his own body and hers, found the taut little nubbin of womanly flesh, and stroked.

She tensed and cried out. The delicate shivers rippled through her.

Hugh lifted himself again and again, thrusting deep into

the tight passage until the world spun around him. Thunder shook the cliffs as his release rolled through him. It was a release far different from any he had ever known. For the first time in the whole of his thirty years he knew what it was to be consumed by passion. He understood why the poets wanted to give this intense sensation another, more glorious name.

For a brief, fleeting instant, he thought he comprehended at last why they wanted to call it love.

*A*lice stirred a long while later. She was aware of a distinct soreness between her legs but she felt strangely content. A part of her looked into the future and knew a cautious hope.

She had traveled to a fascinating new land with Hugh this day. Surely the experience that they had just shared would bind them together.

She opened her eyes and found him watching her with an unblinking, shuttered gaze. Some of her joyous anticipation faded. She saw at once that the indications of softness and vulnerability she thought she had discovered in him had already vanished. The dark knight had resumed the mantle of his own legend.

A wistful regret dimmed her newly formed dreams for the future. She told herself she must have patience. Hugh was not the sort of man who would change overnight.

She tried to think of something truly brilliant and fascinating to say, something that a woman in her position, a woman who had just shared a passionate interlude with a legendary knight, might say. Something that would touch his heart. Something magical.

She cleared her throat delicately. "I believe that it has ceased raining, my lord."

"Are you all right?"

So much for finding memorable words. Alice scowled. "Of course. Why wouldn't I be perfectly all right? What a silly question."

His hard mouth kicked up a little at one corner. "It seemed the appropriate thing to ask under the circumstances."

It occurred to Alice that he might not be any more skilled at conversations of this sort than she. The thought warmed her. "Rather like my comment on the rain?"

His expression softened slightly. "Aye." He eased her to a sitting position beside him. He frowned when he saw her wince. "Alice?"

" 'Tis nothing, my lord." She fumbled with her gown.

Before she could get her skirts arranged he reached out to touch her inner thigh. She blushed with embarrassment when he withdrew fingers that were stained with a reddish moisture.

Hugh stared at his hand. "Alice, we must talk."

"About the rain or my health?"

"About marriage."

Alice paused in the act of adjusting her gown. "This is too much, sir. 'Tis one thing to be called *Relentless*. 'Tis quite another to feel compelled to live up to the title at every single opportunity."

"Alice—"

"How dare you spoil such a pleasant, intimate interlude by returning to our old argument before I have even righted my skirts?"

"A pleasant, intimate interlude? Is that all this was to you?"

She flushed. "Nay, my lord, but I assumed that was likely all it meant to you. Surely you do not intend to tell me that this is the first time you have made love to a woman?" She paused. The possibility that they had shared this experience for the first time together sent a bright shaft of happiness through her. "Or is it?"

His eyes narrowed. " 'Tis the first time I have made love to a woman to whom I am bound by a vow of betrothal."

"Oh." Of course he had been no true virgin, she thought. He was thirty years old. And a man. His honor was not bound up with his chastity. "Well, I do not see that it makes a great deal of difference."

He caught her chin on the edge of his fist. "Most women in your position, madam, would be pleased to discuss marriage at this moment."

"I would rather talk about the weather."

"That is unfortunate, because we are going to discuss marriage."

Not until you learn to love me, she vowed silently. "Sir, I would remind you that we made a bargain."

"That bargain has been altered by what just happened here, Alice. There is a question of honor at stake."

She caught her breath at the sight of the determination gleaming in his golden eyes. There was no tender emotion in him, no talk of love or even of passion. Hugh was, as always, simply proceeding along the most direct path to his goal. Nothing, least of all a woman's heart, would be allowed to get in the way. Her stomach clenched.

"Sir, if you thought to use lovemaking as a stratagem to force me to marry you, then you have made a grave error."

He appeared startled. Then anger flashed in his eyes. "You were a virgin."

"Aye, but that changes nothing. As I never intended to wed, I had no duty to save my virginity for my husband. I am as free as you yourself, sir, and I have chosen to exercise that freedom today."

"Damnation, you are the most stubborn female I have ever encountered," he exploded softly. "You may be free, but I am not. I am bound by my honor in this matter."

"What has honor to do with this?" she demanded.

"You are my betrothed." Hugh moved one big hand in a gesture of masculine outrage. "We have just consummated this marriage."

"Not to my mind. Canon law is not at all clear on this subject."

"Bones of the devil, woman," Hugh roared. "Do not talk to me as though you had studied the finer points of law in Paris and Bologna. We are speaking of my honor here. I shall make my own judgments in this thing."

Alice blinked. "Really, sir, you are behaving in a most distraught fashion. I'm certain that when you've had an opportunity to settle your nerves—"

"My nerves are just fine, thank you. 'Tis my temper with which you had best concern yourself. Hear me well, Alice. We have crossed the river that separates a betrothal from a marriage. There are no longer any grounds to distinguish between the two."

"Well, as to the legality of the thing," she countered primly, "I just told you, canon law is a bit vague."

"Nay, madam, it is not in the least vague. Furthermore, if you think to drag this matter through the Church courts, I promise you that there will be the devil to pay."

"My lord, you are clearly overwrought."

"What is more," Hugh added with an ominous gentleness, "the devil will receive his due long before the Church gets around to dealing with your case. Do I make myself plain?"

Alice's resolve wavered in the face of the blatant threat. She swallowed and tried to gather her courage. "Sir, I warn you, I will not be intimidated or coerced into marriage."

"'Tis too late to go back, Alice. We must go forward along this new course."

"Nay, our bargain holds. I have not yet made up my mind. What is more—" Something moved in the gloom at the far end of the cave. Alice stared past Hugh's broad shoulder.

Her spirited protest died in her throat. For a terrible instant stark fear froze her tongue. "*Hugh.*"

He was on his feet in the blink of an eye. Steel whispered against leather as he slid his sword from its scabbard and whirled to face whatever threat had materialized behind him. An invisible cloak of battle-ready tension flowed around him.

Alice scrambled to her knees and peered past Hugh. A cowled figure emerged from the darkness of a concealed tunnel. He held a nearly extinguished torch in his hand.

"Greetings, Lord Hugh," Calvert of Oxwick said in his rasping voice.

Hugh slammed his sword back into its scabbard. "What the devil are you doing here, monk?"

"I was at my prayers." Calvert's eyes burned in the shadows. "I heard voices and came to see who had invaded these caverns. I feared thieves or robbers."

"You were at your prayers?" Hugh pulled his tunic over his head and buckled his sword belt in place with a swift, practiced motion. "In a cave?"

Calvert seemed to retreat deeper into his cowl. "I have found a place deep within these caverns where a man may pray without distractions from the outside world. A humble chamber of stone that is well suited to the mortification of the flesh."

"Sounds an enjoyable enough place," Hugh said dryly. "Myself, I would prefer a garden but to each his own. Fear not, monk. My betrothed and I will not intrude further on your prayers."

He took Alice's arm and led her out of the cavern with the same arrogant grace he might have used to escort her out of a royal audience chamber.

Calvert said nothing as he watched them leave. He remained where he was in the shadows. Stern disapproval emanated from his skeletal body in an almost palpable vapor. Alice could feel his gaze, feverish with righteous indignation, as it seared her spine.

"Do you think he saw us making love, my lord?" she asked anxiously.

"It matters not." Hugh's attention was clearly focused on the task of choosing a safe path down the hillside. He appeared completely unconcerned about Calvert.

"But 'twould be most embarrassing if he were to spread gossip."

"If the monk has any wits, he will guard his tongue." Hugh led Alice around a clump of scrubby bushes. "But even if he were to speak of what happened between us, who would take note? We are betrothed. Difficulty would arise only if you refused to take the final wedding vows."

"You never lose an opportunity to pursue your goal, do you?"

"I learned long ago that determination and will are the only true means of securing my ends." He steadied her with a sure grip as her soft boots skidded on a patch of loose pebbles. "By the bye, I must journey to London on matters of business. I shall be gone for a few days, no more than a sennight at most."

"London?" Alice stopped short. "When do you leave?"

"Tomorrow morning."

"Oh." Alice experienced an unexpected pang of disappointment. A whole sennight without Hugh stretched out ahead of her and it promised to be quite dull. There would be no fiery quarrels, no stolen moments of passion, no excitement.

"As my betrothed, you shall be in charge of affairs here at Scarcliffe while I am gone."

"Me?" She stared at him in amazement.

"Aye." Hugh smiled at her expression. "I leave everything in your hands. You will be safe enough. I shall leave Dunstan and all but two of my men here to guard the keep and the lands. Julian, my messenger, will also stay here. You may send him to me in London if you need to convey a message."

"Aye, my lord." Alice's head was reeling with the sudden, unexpected weight of her new responsibilities. *Hugh trusted her to look after his precious Scarcliffe.*

"As we shall be married upon my return," Hugh added casually, "you may as well spend the time preparing for the celebration of our wedding."

"By the Saints' eyes, sir, how many times must I tell you that I will not be wed simply because you find such a marriage efficient and convenient?"

"Believe me, madam, efficiency and convenience are not proving to be your strongest points. Oh, there is one more thing."

"What is that, my lord?"

Hugh came to a halt. He removed the heavy black onyx ring from his finger. "You will take this. 'Tis an emblem of my authority. In giving it to you, I would have you comprehend that I trust you and rely on you as I would a true wife—"

"But Hugh—"

"Or a sound business partner," he finished wryly. "Take it, Alice." He placed the ring in her hand and folded her fingers firmly around it. He held her small fist for a moment. "I would have you remember something else equally important."

Her heart leaped. "Aye, my lord?"

"You are never to go into those caves alone. Do you understand?"

Alice wrinkled her nose. "Aye, sir. Allow me to tell you that 'tis just as well you chose a career as a knight. You would not have been a success as a poet or troubadour. You have no talent for graceful words."

Hugh shrugged. "If I ever need such words, I shall employ a skilled poet or troubadour."

"Always employ the most expert craftsman, eh, my lord? Is that not your favorite rule?"

"Alice, there is one thing I wish to ask you."

She glanced at him. "Aye?"

"A short time ago you said that as you had never intended to wed, you did not feel obliged to save your virginity for a husband."

Alice studied the landscape of Scarcliffe. "What of it?"

Hugh's harsh face was fixed in an intent frown. "If you saw no reason to avoid such intimate embraces, why did you do so until now?"

"For the obvious reason, of course," she said gruffly.

He looked blank. "What is the obvious reason?"

"I had not encountered a man who appealed to me until now." She strode off down the hillside, leaving Hugh to follow in her wake.

*A*lice turned the heavy green crystal over and over in her hands. For the hundredth time she watched the way the light from her study-chamber window moved across the heavily faceted surface. As always, she sensed that there was something she did not comprehend about the stone. It was as if it harbored a secret, one that awaited her discovery.

She had the same feeling about Hugh.

She told herself she should be glad that she would be free of his overwhelming presence for a few days. She would be able to consider her situation in peace and tranquillity. Mayhap she would be able to come to an intelligent decision.

A brusque knock on the door of her study chamber roused her from her thoughts. "Enter."

"Alice?" Benedict stuck his head around the door. His face was alight with excitement. "You will never guess what has happened."

"What is it?"

"I am to travel to London with Lord Hugh." Benedict's staff tapped eagerly on the floor as he came into the chamber. He had Hugh's abacus tucked into his belt pouch. "*London,* Alice."

"I envy you." It occurred to Alice that she had not seen such glowing pleasure on Benedict's face for several months. Hugh was responsible for this sudden change in her brother, she thought. "You are most fortunate. 'Twill be a wonderful experience."

"Aye." Benedict balanced on his staff and rubbed his hands together with satisfaction. "I am to assist Lord Hugh with his business dealings."

Alice was astonished. "In what way? You know nothing of business."

"He has said he will teach me the ways of the spice trade. I am to be his assistant." He tapped the abacus. "He has already begun to instruct me in the use of this amazing instrument. One can add and subtract and even multiply and divide on it."

"When did Lord Hugh tell you that he would take you with him to London?" she asked slowly.

"A short while ago while we were dining in the hall."

"I see." A thought made Alice pause. "Benedict, I would like to ask you a question. You must give me an honest answer."

"Aye."

"Has anything been said about the fact that I do not dine in the great hall?"

Benedict started to speak and then appeared to change his mind. "Nay."

"Are you certain? No one has suggested that my failure to eat with the others is a mark of disrespect to Lord Hugh?"

Benedict shifted uncomfortably. "Sir Dunstan told me

that one man made such a comment yesterday. Lord Hugh heard it and ordered him out of the hall. Sir Dunstan says no one else will dare to speak of it again."

Alice tightened her mouth. "But they are all no doubt thinking such thoughts. Hugh was right."

"About what?"

"Never mind." Alice got to her feet. "Where is he?"

"Who? Lord Hugh? I believe he is in his chambers. He said something about dismissing the new steward, Elbert, from his post."

"He said that?" Alice forgot about her intention to apologize to Hugh for any humiliation she might have caused him. "He cannot do that. I will not allow it. Elbert will make a perfectly good steward."

Benedict grimaced. "Today he himself served Lord Hugh and managed to drop an entire flagon of ale in his lap."

" 'Twas surely an accident." Alice rounded the edge of the desk and went to the door. "I must set matters straight."

"Uh, Alice, mayhap you should leave well enough alone. Lord Hugh is master here, after all."

Alice ignored her brother's warning. She picked up her skirts and hurried down the hall to the staircase. When she reached the level below, she turned quickly and went straight along the corridor to the chamber where Hugh conducted his business affairs.

Alice came to a halt in the doorway and looked into the chamber. Elbert stood in front of Hugh's desk. The young man was trembling. His head was bowed in utter dejection.

"I pr-pray your forgiveness, my lord," Elbert whispered. "I have tried very hard to per-perform my duties as Lady Alice instructed. But something seems to happen whenever I find myself in your presence."

"Elbert, I do not wish to dismiss you from your post," Hugh said steadily. "I know that Lady Alice selected you personally for the position. But I cannot tolerate your clumsiness any longer."

"My lord, if you would gi-give me one more chance," Elbert began.

"I think that would be a waste of time."

"But, sir, I want very much to be a steward. I am alone in the world and must make a career for myself."

"I understand. Nevertheless—"

"This keep is the only home I have. My mother came here to Scarcliffe to live after my father died. She wished to enter the convent, you see. I found a place in this household with the last lord, Sir Charles. But then he was killed and you came here and—"

Hugh broke into the rambling explanation. "Your mother is in the local convent?"

"She was, but she died last winter. I have nowhere else to go."

"You will not be forced to leave Scarcliffe," Hugh assured him. "I shall find another position for you. Mayhap in the stables."

"The st-stables?" Elbert was clearly appalled. "But I am af-afraid of horses, my lord."

"You had best overcome your anxiousness quickly," Hugh said with no sign of sympathy. "Horses sense fear."

"A-aye, my lord." Elbert's shoulders sagged. "I shall try."

"Nay, you will do no such thing, steward." Alice picked up her skirts and stalked into the chamber. "You have all the requirements to fulfill your present post and you shall do just that. You merely need some practice and experience."

Elbert turned to her, a desperate plea in his eyes. "Lady Alice."

Hugh eyed Alice. "I shall deal with this matter, madam."

She walked to the desk and curtsied so low that her gown puddled on the stone floor. She bowed her head in graceful supplication. "My lord, I ask that you give Elbert time to adjust to his present duties before you dismiss him."

Hugh picked up a pen and absently tapped the tip of the quill against the desktop. "I don't know why it is, lady, but for some reason I am most cautious around you when you are displaying your most graceful manners. The last time you did this, I found myself making a bargain that has brought me nothing but trouble."

Alice felt her cheeks burn. She refused to be disconcerted. "Elbert merely needs time, my lord."

"He has had several days to adjust to his post and there has been little improvement. At the rate things are proceeding, I shall need to order several new tunics to last the winter."

"I shall see to the new tunics, if necessary, sir," Alice said. " 'Tis Elbert's desire to please you that makes him awkward, my lord." She rose from the deep curtsy. "I feel certain that all he needs is some instruction and a bit more practice."

"Alice," Hugh said wearily, "I do not have time for this. There is too much to be done around here. I cannot afford an ill-trained steward."

"Sir, I ask that you allow him to become comfortable with his responsibilities while you are in London. I myself shall instruct him in those duties. When you return, you may judge him again. If you still find him lacking, you may dismiss him then."

Hugh leaned back slowly in his chair and studied her from beneath half-lowered lashes. "Another bargain, madam?"

She flushed. "Aye, if you wish."

"What have you to trade this time?"

She caught her breath at the sight of his gleaming eyes. Outrage swamped her fine manners. "I am offering to produce a good steward for you, sir. I should think that would be enough."

"Ah." Hugh's mouth curved. "That sounds more like the

lady I have come to know. Very well. You shall have the next few days to turn Elbert into a master of his craft. When I return, I shall expect to have this household supervised by an expert. Understood?"

"Aye, my lord." Alice smiled confidently.

"Elbert?" Hugh prompted.

"A-aye, my lord." Elbert bowed several times. "I shall practice very hard, sir."

"Let us hope so," Hugh said.

Elbert fell on his knees in front of Alice, grabbed the hem of her skirt, and kissed it with fervor. "Thank you, my lady. I cannot describe to you how grateful I am for your confidence in me. I shall exert every effort to succeed in my quest to become a great steward."

"You will make a fine steward," Alice assured him.

"Enough," Hugh said. "Take yourself off, steward. I wish to be private with my betrothed."

"Aye, my lord." Elbert shot to his feet and bowed himself toward the door.

Alice winced when he accidentally backed into the wall. She saw Hugh raise his eyes toward the heavens but he did not say anything.

Elbert straightened abruptly and fled.

Alice turned back to Hugh. "Thank you, my lord."

"Try to keep him from demolishing the entire keep while I am gone."

"I'm certain that Scarcliffe Keep will still be standing when you return, sir." Alice hesitated. "I am told that you intend to take my brother with you."

"Aye. Benedict appears to have a talent for numbers. I can use an assistant with such skills."

"I had intended that he study the law," Alice said slowly.

"Do you object to his interest in accounts and business matters?"

"Nay. In truth, I have not seen him as happy as he is this afternoon for a long while." Alice smiled. " 'Tis your doing, my lord."

" 'Tis no great thing. As I said, it suits me to encourage his skills. They will prove useful." Hugh ran the quill through his fingers, aligning the feathers. "Will you miss me while I am in London, Alice?"

Sensing a trap, Alice took a quick step backward. She summoned a brilliant smile. "That reminds me, I must send word to Prioress Joan. I wish special prayers to be said at mass tomorrow morning before you leave."

"Special prayers?"

"Aye, my lord. For your safe journey."

Alice turned and hurried out of the chamber.

*T*hat evening, Alice paused in the act of moving one of the heavy black chalcedony chess figures and frowned at Hugh. "You do not appear to be paying attention to the game, sir. I am about to claim your bishop."

Hugh gazed down at the inlaid black crystal board with a brooding eye. "So it would seem. A clever move, madam."

"It was child's play." Alice studied him with growing concern.

Hugh was acting oddly in her estimation. He had invited her to join him for a game of chess in front of the hearth and she had accepted with enthusiasm. But it had been evident from the opening move that his thoughts were elsewhere.

"Let us see if I can recover." Hugh rested his chin on his hand and studied the board.

"Your preparations for the journey are all in order. You will be able to leave directly after mass tomorrow. What troubles you, sir?"

He flicked her a startled glance and then shrugged faintly. "I am thinking about my liege lord."

"Sir Erasmus?"

"I intend to visit him while I am in London. Julian tells me that he went there to consult some more doctors."

"I am sorry," Alice whispered.

Hugh's hand curved into a fist. "There is nothing to be done, but God's teeth, he seemed so strong and healthy only a few months ago."

Alice nodded sympathetically. "I know how much you will miss him."

Hugh sat back and picked up his cup of spiced wine. He gazed into the flames. "All that I have today is owed to him. My knighthood, my learning, my lands. How does a man repay such a favor?"

"With loyalty. And the whole world knows you have given Erasmus that, sir."

" 'Tis little enough." Hugh sipped from the cup. His face was shadowed in the firelight.

Alice hesitated. "What are his symptoms, my lord?"

"What?"

"The symptoms of his grave illness. What, precisely, are they?"

Hugh frowned. "I'm not altogether certain. Some are vague. He startles easily, as though he were a wary hart rather than a trained warrior. That is the thing I noticed most when I was last in his presence. He is always anxious now. He cannot sleep. He has grown thin. He told me that at times his heart pounds as though he were running."

Alice grew thoughtful. "A man of Sir Erasmus's renown must have known a great many battles."

"He has seen his share, beginning with the Crusade he undertook when he was barely eighteen. He once told me that his journey to the Holy Lands was the worst event of his entire life even though it brought him glory and wealth. He said he saw sights there, terrible sights that no decent man should see."

·   ·   ·

*H*ugh's words stayed with Alice until late that night. Unable to sleep, she got out of bed and slipped into her night robe.

She lit a candle and let herself quietly out of her bedchamber. Then she padded down the cold hall to her study chamber and went inside. Setting the candle on her desk next to the green crystal, she reached up and plucked her mother's handbook from the shelf.

She pored over it for an hour before she found what she wanted.

Chapter 13

"'Tis a woman's natural weakness that leads her into temptation," Calvert roared from the pulpit of the small village church early the next morning. "In her silly arrogance she seeks to raise herself above man at every opportunity and thereby puts her very soul in jeopardy."

The crowd that filled the church stirred unhappily. Alice sat seething at the center of the uneasy waves. She had not been this angry since the day Sir Ralf had installed his eldest son in her family's manor hall.

This stupid lecture from Calvert was not what she had ordered for this morning's service. Yesterday she had sent word to Prioress Joan that she wanted special prayers said for Hugh's journey to London.

The news that the new lord and his betrothed would attend morning mass in the village church rather than in the keep's private chapel had spread swiftly. Virtually the entire population of the tiny hamlet of Scarcliffe and all of the nuns from the convent had turned out to enjoy the exciting event. It was not every day that they were invited to pray in the company of the lord of the manor.

Alice, seated beside Hugh in the front row, had been pleased with the turnout until disaster, in the form of Calvert of Oxwick, had struck.

Joan had just finished the opening prayers and was launching into a very nice homily on the dangers of the road when the monk strode into the church.

Calvert banged his staff on the stone floor as he forged his way to the front of the crowd. His brown robes billowed around his scrawny, sandaled feet. When he reached the pulpit he ordered Joan to sit with her nuns. The prioress hesitated and then, tight-lipped, obeyed. The Church insisted on a man in the pulpit when one was available.

Calvert had promptly seized the wooden lectern and launched into a tirade against the evils of women. It was a tried-and-true theme, one familiar to everyone present. Visiting priests and wandering monks were excessively fond of sermons that chastised women and warned men of their temptations.

"Ye frail, sinful daughters of Eve, know ye well that your only hope of salvation lies in submitting yourself to the will of your husbands. You must accept his power over you for it is ordained by the Divine Creator."

Alice fumed. She glanced at Hugh out of the corner of her eye. He looked bored. She crossed her arms and began to tap the toe of her soft boot.

"The fires of hell burn hottest for those weak women who dare to raise themselves above men."

The women endured the monk's tirade with barely concealed disgust. They had heard it all before, many times over.

Joan shifted slightly in her seat and leaned forward to whisper to Alice. "My apologies, my lady. I know this was not the sort of preaching you wanted this morning."

"They dare speak aloud in church," Calvert thundered,

"uncaring that men of virtue do not wish to hear the noise of their prattling tongues. They govern religious houses, taking authority upon themselves as though they had the rights and privileges of men."

Alice narrowed her eyes at Calvert. He continued to hold forth, either oblivious to her growing annoyance or unconcerned with it. His piercing gaze sizzled into her.

"Some practice their lustful ways on even the strongest and most noble of knights. Woe be to the man who listens to the whispers of such a female. He shall find his strength weakened. He will discover himself to be at her mercy and that mercy is the work of the devil."

Alice froze. This was becoming personal, she realized.

"She shall use the treacherous tricks of her sinful body to lure her victim into hidden places. There she will fall upon him as a succubus in the night."

"By the Saints," Alice muttered. One question was answered. Calvert had seen her lying on top of Hugh in the cavern. Embarrassment dissolved in a torrent of anger.

"Be warned." Calvert's gaze swerved toward Hugh. "Every man is at risk. He who would keep his rightful place in the natural order of the world must be forever alert. He must don armor against the ways of women, even as he clads himself in steel before he goes to war."

"*Enough.*" Alice leaped to her feet. "I will hear no more of this foolish harangue, monk. I requested prayers for my betrothed husband's safe journey, not this nonsense."

There was a collective gasp from the crowd. Every head turned toward Alice. Out of the corner of her eye Alice saw Hugh smile.

"The woman who is not properly governed by a man is an affront to all righteous men everywhere." Calvert glanced quickly at Hugh, as though expecting assistance from that quarter. " 'Tis the duty of a husband to control his wife's tongue."

Hugh did not move. He watched Alice with great interest and more than a hint of his familiar, cool amusement.

"Come down from that pulpit, Calvert of Oxwick," Alice ordered. "You are not welcome to preach here. You slander and berate all the good women of this village and those of the convent with the bitter poison of your words."

Calvert leveled an accusing finger at her. "Hear me." His voice shook with passionate rage. "This poison you speak of is but an antidote for the evils of your female nature. You would do well to swallow it as the sound medicine it is and thereby save your immortal soul."

"I shall entrust my soul to those who comprehend the true meaning of divine compassion, monk, not to you. I want you gone from this church and from this village today. I will not tolerate these insults."

Calvert's face contorted with fury. "Your red hair and green eyes bear witness to your wild nature, lady. I can only pray that your future lord and master may crush your unruly will with his own before you cause grave harm to his house and his soul."

"Lord Hugh can take care of himself," Alice retorted. "Begone, monk."

"*I do not do the bidding of a mere woman.*"

Hugh stirred. It was a very slight move, the barest shift of his powerful shoulders, accompanied by a gathering coldness in his eyes, but it instantly riveted the attention of everyone present.

"You'll do the bidding of this particular woman," he said very calmly. "She is my betrothed. The ring she wears on her finger is evidence of her authority. A command from her is the same as a command from me."

A soft *aaaah* of whispered satisfaction echoed through the tiny church. The people of Scarcliffe grasped their lord's meaning immediately. Alice's power had been firmly established.

"But . . . but, my lord," Calvert sputtered, "surely you do not intend to turn this pulpit over to a woman."

"You heard my betrothed," Hugh said. "Take yourself off, monk. My lady prefers to hear other prayers than yours."

For a moment, Alice feared that Calvert was about to suffer a fit. His mouth worked, his eyes bulged, and his whole body contorted as though every muscle convulsed.

Anticipation rose from the crowd in a wave.

And then, without a word, Calvert grabbed his staff and stormed out of the church.

A hushed silence fell. The assembled throng stared in wonder at Alice, who was on her feet. Hugh gazed at her politely as though curious to see what she would do next.

Alice was dazed, not by what she had just done, but by the fact that Hugh had supported her with the full weight of his authority.

His action had been no small gesture of indulgence, she realized. It went much deeper than that. He had made it clear to one and all that she wielded true power on these lands.

This was the second time that he had demonstrated respect for her decisions. The first occasion had occurred yesterday afternoon when he had allowed her to reinstate Elbert as steward. And now he had defied a representative of the Church itself to uphold her choice of preachers.

He had shown her great respect, she thought, elated. Such respect from Hugh the Relentless was surely a hard-won prize. He would award it only to those he truly trusted.

"Thank you, my lord," she managed to whisper.

Hugh inclined his head very slightly. The morning light streaming through the windows heated the amber in his eyes. "Mayhap we should proceed with the prayers, madam. I would like to start on my journey sometime before sunset."

Alice blushed furiously. "Of course, my lord." She looked at Joan. "Pray continue, Prioress. My lord and his companions have a long ride ahead of them."

"Aye, my lady." Joan rose with a grace that bespoke her own noble heritage. "I would be delighted to pray for Lord Hugh's safe journey. And for his speedy return. I am certain that everyone present feels the same."

Several of the nuns smiled broadly at Alice as she sank back down onto the bench. The only one whose countenance remained somber was Katherine. Alice wondered briefly if she was suffering one of her bouts of melancholia.

Joan returned sedately to the front of the church. She concluded her small, cheerful sermon regarding caution on the roads and then closed with prayers for the travelers' safe journey.

The final prayers were spoken in a very fine Latin. It was highly doubtful that anyone other than Alice, Hugh, Benedict, and the nuns understood the actual words but that didn't stop the villagers from enjoying them.

Alice closed her eyes and offered up a small, silent prayer of her own. *Dearest Lord, take care of these two people whom I love so much and guard well those who travel with them.*

After a few minutes she slid her palm a short distance along the wooden bench until she touched Hugh's hand. He did not look down but his fingers reached out to close very tightly around her own.

A few minutes later the worshipers spilled out the door of the church to watch the leave-taking. Alice stood on the steps and watched as Hugh, Benedict, and the two men-at-arms who accompanied them mounted.

Distracted by the commotion Calvert had caused, Alice very nearly forgot her parting gift for Hugh. At the last moment she remembered the bundle of herbs and the instructions she had written out.

"One moment, my lord." She plunged her hand into the pouch that hung on her belt as she hurried toward Hugh's horse. "I almost forgot. I have something for you to give to your liege lord."

Hugh looked down at her from the saddle. "What is this?"

"When you described Sir Erasmus's symptoms to me last night I thought that they sounded somewhat familiar." Alice held out the herbs and the letter of instructions. "My mother made a note of such symptoms in her handbook."

"She did?" Hugh took the small bundle from her and stowed it in his own belt pouch.

"Aye. She once treated a man with similar symptoms. He had been through great hardships in battle. I cannot say for certain that Sir Erasmus is suffering from the same illness as that man, but these herbs may help."

"Thank you, Alice."

"Tell him that he must have his healer follow the directions in that letter quite carefully. Oh, and he is not to allow the doctors to bleed him. Do you comprehend that?"

"Aye, madam."

Alice stepped back. She smiled tremulously. "I wish you a safe journey, my lord."

"I shall return in a sennight," Hugh promised. "With a priest to perform our wedding."

"I vow, my lord, I do not know who appeared more astonished, Alice or the monk." Benedict, astride a sturdy palfrey, flashed a grin. "Alice is not easily surprised, you know."

Hugh smiled faintly. They had gotten a late start due to Alice's insistence on the elaborate morning prayers, but he did not regret the delay. It had been worth it to know that Alice cared enough to summon the entire village to call on heaven's protection for the travelers. He knew that her chief concern was undoubtedly for Benedict, but he had determined not to let that bother him.

It had been the sort of farewell that made a man want to return as swiftly as possible to his own hearth. Hugh savored the knowledge that he had a hall of his own. And he very nearly had a wife to complete the satisfying image. *Soon,* he promised himself. Very soon. The thing was as good as done.

The two men-at-arms who accompanied Hugh and Benedict rode a short distance behind their lord, bows at the ready in the event they encountered outlaws. It was an unlikely possibility. Even the boldest of robbers would hesitate to take on a band of four armed and well-mounted men, one of whom was clearly a trained knight. If the sight of the weapons did not discourage them, the fact that all four wore Hugh's distinctive black tunics would most certainly do so.

Outlaws were not only cowards by nature, choosing the easiest prey, they were also cautious. Early in his career, Hugh had made it clear that he would hunt down any who dared to rob those who rode under his banner or that of Erasmus of Thornewood. It had taken only one or two short, decisive forays to prove he could be relied upon to uphold his oath.

"I wondered how long your sister would tolerate Calvert's rantings before she took action," Hugh said to Benedict. "Indeed, I was surprised she did not speak up sooner."

Benedict gave him a strange look. "In the old days she would not have put up with his preaching for a moment. I believe that Calvert lasted as long as he did this morning only because Alice was uncertain, sir."

"Uncertain?"

"Of her prerogative." Benedict sounded as though he were choosing his words carefully. "Of just how much power she commands as your betrothed."

"Your sister is a woman who is accustomed to wielding authority," Hugh observed.

"That is no less than the truth." Benedict grimaced as only a younger brother will. "To be fair, she did not have much choice in the matter. She saw to the business of my father's manor for years, you know."

"I am aware that your father did not spend much of his time on his estates. What of your mother?"

"Our mother was content to pursue her studies. Over the years, her work with herbs became the only thing of importance to her. She shut herself away in her chambers and left everything to Alice."

"And Alice excelled at the tasks she assumed."

"Aye, although I think she was lonely at times." Benedict frowned. "She first felt the weight of responsibility when she was still too young, I believe."

"And she was left to shoulder the added burden of hanging on to your father's manor."

"It was the first time Alice had ever failed to fulfill what she saw as her duty." Benedict's hand tightened on the reins. "It was not her fault. She lacked the power to stand her ground against our uncle. But she blamed herself nevertheless."

" 'Tis the way of her kind." *Our kind,* Hugh corrected himself silently. *Such a failure would have gnawed at me also, even as my failure to avenge my mother's death does.*

"It is not in her to surrender to fate."

"Nay, your sister has great courage," Hugh said with satisfaction.

"Aye, but there are times when I worry greatly about her." Benedict flashed an uneasy glance at Hugh. "Occasionally I happen upon her standing at the window of her chamber, gazing out at nothing. If I ask her to tell me what is wrong, she will say only that 'tis nothing or that she's had a bad dream during the night."

"She should not be shamed by the loss of your father's manor. Sir Ralf told me that she wagèd a very spirited battle to hold on to it."

"Aye." Benedict smiled reminiscently. "She wrote letter after letter pleading her case. When she had to accept failure, she called it a disaster. But she immediately went to work on her scheme to send me off to study law and to get herself into a convent. Alice always has a plan, you see."

" 'Tis her nature."

"You appear to comprehend her well, sir."

"He who would command others must understand the nature of those he seeks to lead," Hugh said.

Benedict gave him an assessing glance. "I believe Alice would agree with that statement. I do not think that she expected you to back up her authority as you did today, sir."

"Your sister is the kind who cannot be content without responsibility and the authority that must accompany it," Hugh said. "She requires that as much as she requires the air she breathes."

Benedict nodded.

"She and I have more in common than she realizes. Mayhap by the time we return she will have begun to comprehend that."

Understanding dawned in Benedict's eyes. "This journey to London is one of your clever stratagems, is it not, my lord?"

Hugh smiled slightly but said nothing.

"It all becomes clear now." Benedict's tone held a hint of awe. "You wish to demonstrate to Alice that you trust her to supervise not only Scarcliffe Keep but the manor as well. You wish to show her that you respect her abilities."

"Aye," Hugh said simply.

"You hope to lure her into marriage with a taste of the authority and responsibility that she will assume as your wife."

Hugh grinned. "I perceive that you will make me a very clever assistant, Benedict. You have the right of it. I would have Alice conclude that she will discover as much satisfaction and contentment in her duties as my wife as she will in a convent." *And far more in my bed.*

"A bold scheme, sir." Benedict's eyes were lit with admiration. "But you had best pray that Alice does not reason out your true motives for herself. She would be furious if she thought you had deliberately ensnared her with yet another stratagem."

Hugh was unconcerned. "I trust she will be far too busy managing affairs on the manor to give overmuch time to thinking about why I suddenly decided to travel to London."

"Aye," Benedict said thoughtfully. "She will relish the opportunity to take command once more. Mayhap it will even take her thoughts off her failure to hold my inheritance."

"Your sister thrives on challenge, Benedict. I believe that the task of helping me turn Scarcliffe into a prosperous manor will entice her into marriage far more effectively than a casket full of jewels."

*T*hree mornings later Alice stood alongside Joan and watched as a thatcher clambered up onto another roof to begin repairs.

"Only three more cottages to go and then they will all be finished," Alice observed with satisfaction. "If we are fortunate, they will be done by the time Lord Hugh returns from London. He will be pleased."

Joan chuckled. "To say nothing of the people who live in those cottages. Winter will soon be upon us. If Lord Hugh had not provided for the repairs, I fear some of these good folk would have faced the snow with holes in their roofs."

"My lord would not have allowed that to happen. He takes care of his own." Alice started off down the street to inspect the progress on the new refuse ditch. The reek of the old one decreased daily as the men worked to bury the contents beneath a thick layer of dirt.

Joan looked at her as she fell into step beside her. "You have great faith in Lord Hugh's intentions for this manor, do you not?"

"Aye. 'Tis most important to him. He is a man who does not turn aside from a goal or a responsibility." Alice gazed about at the tiny village. Already it appeared less dreary. The air of hope that clung to it gave it a healthy sheen.

The past three days had passed in a whirlwind of activity for Alice. She had leaped into the task of supervising Scarcliffe affairs the minute Hugh and his party had vanished in a cloud of dust. It had been invigorating to assume such responsibilities once more. She was good at this sort of thing.

It occurred to her that she had not experienced such a degree of cheerful enthusiasm for any project since Ralf had forced her from her home.

Hugh had given her this gift, she thought. She wondered if he had any notion of how much she valued it.

A loud knock on her bedchamber door roused Alice from her sleep two nights later.

"Lady Alice," a muffled voice called. "Lady Alice."

Alice sat up slowly. She tried to collect her wits. They had been scattered by a strange and disturbing dream involving dark corridors and an unseen menace.

"Lady Alice."

"One moment," Alice called.

She pushed aside the heavy curtains that hung around the bed and reached for her night robe. She slid off the high bed and went, barefoot, across the carpet to answer the door.

She opened it a crack and saw a young maid with a candle waiting in the hall. "What is it, Lara?"

"I pray your pardon for waking you at this hour, m'lady, but there are two nuns from the village convent in the hall. They said that Prioress Joan sent them."

Alarm swept through Alice. Something must be terribly wrong. "I'll dress and go downstairs at once."

"Aye, m'lady." Lara frowned. "Best bring a cloak. I believe they mean for you to return to the village with them."

Alice opened the door wider. "Use your candle to light my own."

"Aye, m'lady." Lara moved quickly into the bedchamber.

Alice dressed swiftly. When she was ready she grabbed her heavy woolen cloak and hurried downstairs.

The two nuns waited near the cold hearth. Dunstan and his men, roused from their pallets by their arrival, stood quietly in the shadows.

The women looked toward Alice with anxious expressions.

"Prioress Joan sent us to ask if you will come to the miller's house, my lady," one of the women said. "Their youngest son is dreadfully ill. The healer has exhausted her remedies and does not know what else to try. The prioress hoped you might have some advice."

Alice recalled the laughing, dark-haired little boy she had seen playing outside the miller's door. "Of course I will come with you but I do not know what I can do. If Sister Katherine has no answers, then I doubt that I will have any."

"Prioress Joan thought that you might have learned of some special medicine from your mother's work."

Alice stilled. "My mother was a very learned woman but some of her recipes are dangerous." *Some can kill.*

"Prioress Joan and the healer believe that Young John is dying, my lady," the second woman said quietly. "They say there is nothing left to lose."

"I understand." Alice picked up her skirts and turned to climb the tower stairs. "I will fetch my mother's handbook of recipes and bring it with me."

When she returned a few minutes later, Dunstan moved out of the shadows.

"I will escort you to the miller's cottage," he said brusquely.

"There is no need," Alice said.

"There is every need," Dunstan muttered. "Sir Hugh would likely hang me from the keep's battlements if I allowed you to go out alone at night."

.   .   .

A short time later Alice rushed into the miller's small cottage just as Katherine placed a cool cloth on Young John's fevered brow.

Alice was horrified by the changes the illness had wrought in the lively boy she had seen scampering about only that morning. His eyes were closed. He lay wan and limp on top of the bedding, his small body hot to the touch. His breathing was labored and desperate. He whimpered fretfully once or twice but he seemed unaware of those who hovered anxiously around him.

"There is nothing more I can do." Katherine rose to her feet. "He's in God's hands now."

Her face was more somber than usual but there was no other sign of emotion in her features. She seemed distant, Alice thought, almost detached, a healer who knew and accepted the limits of her medicines. How different her own mother had been. Helen had never surrendered until death had claimed its victim.

Joan crossed herself.

The miller's wife cried out with a mother's anguish and burst into fresh tears. Her husband, a barrel-chested, kind-faced man, gathered her close and awkwardly patted her shoulder.

"There, there," he whispered over and over again. He looked helplessly at Alice over his wife's shoulder. His own eyes were damp. "Thank you for coming, my lady."

"Of course," Alice said absently. Her attention was on the small patient. She went to stand beside his pallet. Her mother's words came back to her as she gazed down at Young John. *Determine all the symptoms before you apply the remedy.*

Joan spoke softly from the other side of the pallet. "I realize there is likely little to be done but I could not abandon all hope entirely until we had consulted with you."

"I know the usual remedies for fevers of the lungs," Alice

said quietly. "As does Sister Katherine. I assume you've applied the appropriate ones?"

"Aye," Katherine said stiffly. "All that I know. But this fever does not respond to medicines."

Young John's mother sobbed louder. The miller closed his eyes in pain.

Joan's eyes met Alice's. "You told me that your mother was a learned healer and that she had developed many unique potions and tonics. Do you know of anything that we can try?"

Alice tightened her grip on the leather-bound handbook she carried. "There are one or two infusions that my mother created for strange fevers that are accompanied by lung infections. But she advised great caution in their use. They may be very dangerous."

"Can anything be more lethal than what this child faces?" Joan asked simply.

"Nay." Alice looked down at the youngster and knew that death was even now reaching out with icy hands to claim him. "That rash on his chest—"

"What of it?" Katherine asked quickly. "Have you seen its like before?"

"Nay, but mayhap my mother did." Alice knelt beside the pallet and felt for Young John's pulse. It was weak and much too fast. She looked at the miller. "Tell me everything you can about this sickness. When did it come upon him, John?"

"This afternoon, m'lady," the miller whispered. "One minute he was dashing about chasing the chickens and the next he did not even want to eat a bit of the pudding his mother had made."

Alice opened the handbook and quickly turned the pages until she found the section on strange fevers of the lungs. She studied it for a time. *A redness of the chest. Harsh breathing. Great warmth.*

"My mother notes that she tended a small child with such symptoms once." Alice turned the page, frowning.

The miller's wife moved slightly in the circle of her husband's arm. She wiped tears from her eyes. "Did the other child live?"

Alice looked at the woman. *You must give hope as well as medicine,* her mother had once said. *Hope is as crucial to the cure as the right herbs.* "Aye," she said gently. "He lived."

"Then we must try this remedy," the woman begged. "Please, my lady."

"We will," Alice assured her. She turned to Katherine. "I shall give you a list of the herbs I will need. Please bring them as quickly as possible."

The healer's mouth tightened. "Aye, my lady."

Alice wondered if she had offended Katherine by taking command of the situation. If so, there was nothing to be done about it. She looked at Joan. "I will need a pot and some fresh water."

"I shall get them," Joan said quickly.

"Set them on the fire."

*Y*oung John's fever broke shortly before dawn. His breathing quickly grew less labored. By the time the first light of the new day had appeared it was obvious that the child would live to chase chickens again.

The miller and his wife wept unashamedly with relief.

Alice, exhausted from the lengthy vigil, crouched beside the pallet one last time to check Young John's pulse. She found it steady and strong.

"I think he will soon be wanting a bit of pudding," she said quietly.

"Thank you, Lady Alice," Joan said softly.

"Do not thank me." Alice looked down at Young John.

The boy's color was good. His sleep appeared normal. " 'Tis my mother's work."

Katherine gazed at her for a long while. "Your mother must have been a very learned woman."

"Aye. She corresponded with the wisest and most skilled herbalists in Europe. She collected their wisdom and added it to her own discoveries. And she put all that she learned into this book."

Joan's eyes were warm as they met Alice's. "Such a book has no value unless it be used by one who has a talent for identifying diseases through an analysis of symptoms. Such a talent, I have discovered, is uncommon."

Alice did not know what to say.

"Your mother would be proud of you, my lady," Joan continued softly. "You have learned how to make use of the knowledge she provided in that book. And tonight you used that knowledge to save this boy. 'Tis a great gift you have received from your mother."

Alice looked at the handbook Helen had written during the long, lonely years of her marriage.

Alice thought of how she had sometimes resented her mother's passion for her work. There had been so many times when it had seemed to bring the melancholy Helen far more solace than her children could ever provide.

But tonight the contents of Helen's handbook had saved a child's life.

There was a price to be paid for such a valuable gift. Alice knew that, in her own way, she had paid part of that price. So had Benedict. Helen had paid the highest price of all.

Yet tonight a little boy lived because of it. He was not the first one to be saved because of Helen's work, Alice reminded herself. He would not be the last.

Somewhere deep inside Alice a gentle warmth blossomed in a place that had known only resentment and sadness.

"Aye, Prioress. You are right. For some reason, I did not realize what a great inheritance my mother had left to me until now."

Young John stirred on his pallet and opened his eyes. He looked up at his mother. "Mama? Why are there so many people here?"

His parents answered with shaky laughter and went down on their knees beside the pallet.

Alice held her mother's handbook close to her heart. *Thank you*, she said silently.

Chapter 14

 lice stood in the center of the great hall and
concentrated intensely. There was a fire on
the hearth but the chamber was cold. "There is something
missing from this hall, Julian."

"Stolen, do you mean?" Julian put down the harp he had
been plucking in a negligent manner. "Not likely. No one
would dare steal anything from Hugh the Relentless. The devil
knows that there would be no peace for the poor thief."

"Not stolen. Just . . . missing." Alice waved a hand to
indicate the barren walls and rush-covered floor. "This is
where Lord Hugh dines every day with his men. It is where he
sits to judge matters of law on Scarcliffe. 'Tis where he will
entertain his guests. And it lacks a certain aspect. It needs
something."

"Ah, now I comprehend you, my lady." Julian grinned.
"The word you are groping for is *elegance.*"

"Elegance?"

"Aye. This hall lacks elegance, grace, charm, and fashion."

"All of that?" Alice bit her lip as she studied the chamber.

"All of that and more. Lord Hugh is skilled at many things, my lady, but he has no interest in matters of fashion and elegance and, no offense, it shows."

"I do believe you are correct."

"The problem, as I see it," Julian continued, "is that Lord Hugh orders everything from his boots and tunics to his messenger's travel cloak made up in only one color. Black."

"Hmm. He does seem to have a strong preference for it. I do not believe that he would care to return and discover that everything had been done over in sky blue or pumpkin orange, however."

"I would not dream of suggesting that you get rid of the black." Julian began to stroll around the hall, examining it in some detail. "Black suits Lord Hugh in some way. But what if we were to enliven it with another color?"

"What color do you suggest?"

"Green or red, mayhap. The contrast would be most effective, I believe. White would be interesting, too."

Inspiration struck Alice. "Amber."

"My lady?"

Alice smiled with satisfaction. "Amber is the color of Lord Hugh's eyes. 'Tis a lovely hue. Almost gold. We shall use amber in contrast to the black."

Julian nodded thoughtfully. "A rich amber would suit this room rather well."

"I shall order a canopy made of those colors to go over the head table." Alice's enthusiasm grew swiftly as images formed in her mind. "And I shall have a new tunic made up for him in amber and black."

" 'Tis almost time for Sir Hugh to order new garments for his men," Julian said smoothly. "He does so every year. 'Twould be an excellent occasion to change the colors of their robes also."

"Of course." She was not particularly skilled at this sort of thing but it was clear that Julian had a talent for it. "See to it, will you, Julian?"

Julian swept her a deep bow. "With great pleasure, my lady. Shall I order a new gown for you also?"

Alice had a vision of herself greeting Hugh in a gown sewn in his new colors. "Aye. That would be most appropriate."

In London Hugh steeled himself against the gloom and despair that seemed to emanate from the very walls of Erasmus's private chamber.

"Ah, Hugh." Erasmus looked up from his chair near the fire. His smile of welcome was weak but it conveyed his pleasure. " 'Tis good to see you. Who is this with you?"

"This is Benedict, my lord." Hugh motioned for Benedict to step forward. "He is the brother of my betrothed."

"Welcome, young Benedict."

"Thank you, my lord." Benedict made a proper bow.

"Come here so that I may become acquainted with you," Erasmus said. "Tell me what you and Hugh did down at the docks this morning."

Hugh exchanged a glance with Erasmus's wife as Benedict obediently went toward the hearth. Eleanor was a fine-looking woman who was not much older than Hugh. She gave him a brave little smile as Erasmus spoke quietly with Benedict, but nothing could hide the shadows in her eyes. Hugh knew that Eleanor was very fond of her lord. The couple had two children, a boy and a girl.

"There has been no improvement?" Hugh asked her quietly.

"The attacks grow worse. I dismissed the doctors."

"Always a sound notion," Hugh muttered.

"Aye. I am convinced that they were doing him more harm than good with their vile instruments. I vow, they were going to bleed him dry. And those terrible purges." Eleanor shook her head in disgust. "They did no good at all. He has reached the point where all he wishes to do is die in peace."

Hugh looked at Erasmus. His liege lord had aged ten years in the last few months, he thought. The strong, compelling figure who had been the center of Hugh's life during his youth and the man to whom he had given his loyalty and sword as an adult was now pale and thin beyond belief.

"I cannot believe we are losing him," Hugh said softly. "He is only in his forty-second year and he has always enjoyed good health."

"He barely sleeps at all at night," Eleanor whispered. "And when he does manage to fall asleep he awakes with a terrible start. He rises, shaking, and paces until dawn. His greatest fear is not that he will die, but that he may be going mad."

"My betrothed sent these herbs and this letter of instructions." Hugh reached into his black leather pouch and took out the contents. "I do not know if they will be effective but it cannot hurt to try. She has a certain skill with medicines."

Eleanor frowned slightly. "I do not wish him to suffer any more from harsh remedies."

"My liege lord is a warrior at heart," Hugh said. "Whatever this sickness is, it will not have altered that fact. Let him fight one last battle before you abandon all hope."

"Aye, you are correct, Sir Hugh." Eleanor closed her hand very tightly around the herbs and the letter.

Erasmus raised a hand. "Hugh, come here. I would speak with you for a few minutes."

Hugh walked toward the fireside, his heart heavy with impending grief.

*A*lice surveyed the warm, bustling kitchen with a critical eye. Two massive iron caldrons, each packed with various stews, stuffed chickens, and savory puddings, simmered over the large cook fire. Sweat beaded the brows of the scullions who turned the handles of the roasting spits. Meat pies browned on a hot plate set at the edge of the flames.

"See that the caldrons are completely emptied, cleaned, and scoured every sennight, Elbert," Alice said briskly. "I do not favor the common practice of using them continuously for months on end without scrubbing them well."

"Aye, m'lady." Elbert's face was set in an earnest, intent frown.

In the five days that Hugh had been gone, Scarcliffe Keep had been cleaned from top to bottom. Every linen chest and wardrobe had been emptied, dusted, and fitted out with fresh herbal scent bags. Each chamber, from the one where Hugh slept to the smallest storeroom, had been opened and assessed. Elbert had been at her side during the entire process. He had made careful notes on his wax tablet as she rattled off an endless list of instructions.

Alice had saved the kitchens for last.

"Make certain that the scullions are given other tasks on a regular basis. I do not want any of them to spend too long near the fire. 'Tis hot, uncomfortable work."

"Other tasks." Elbert made another note with his stylus. "Aye, m'lady."

The sweat-streaked scullions grinned.

Alice walked through the busy kitchen, pausing at various points to observe certain things more closely. She smiled at the cooks, who were clearly awed and excited by her presence. Alice knew that they were also quite anxious. It was the first visit she had paid them. Their only other contact with her had been via Elbert, who had brought them the precise instructions and menus she had made up for her personal meals.

Alice studied a worktable where a cook was chopping onions. "I want the special green pottage that you make for me served once a day to Lord Hugh and everyone else in the keep."

"Special green pottage," Elbert repeated. "Served to everyone. Aye, m'lady."

" 'Tis very healthful," Alice explained. "Also, I want at least three vegetable dishes served at the midday meal."

"Three vegetable dishes. Aye, m'lady."

"Do not allow the cabbages to be boiled for too long."

Elbert made another note. "Aye, m'lady."

Alice peered down at the wheat and milk concoction cooking in an earthenware bowl. "Have the frumenty sweetened with honey. 'Tis rather plain without it."

"Honey in the frumenty." Elbert's stylus skimmed across the tablet.

"I shall provide you with a list of ingredients for a sauce made with cloves and cardamom and another made with ginger and saffron. Quite tasty. They should be used on dishes of boiled fish or on the roast meats."

"Aye, m'lady." Elbert glanced at her with sudden anxiety. "As to the spices, m'lady, how should we go about obtaining them?"

Alice looked at him in surprise. "What do you mean? Sir Hugh has a vast quantity of excellent spices stored in chests here in the keep."

Elbert cleared his throat cautiously. "His lordship keeps the keys to the storerooms. He has given strict instructions that I am to come to him whenever spices are needed in the kitchens. But on the two occasions that I went to him to request the spices the cooks wanted, he was most annoyed."

"Why?"

"He, uh, complained of the quantity that was requested," Elbert said unhappily. "He said that I had no notion of economy and that I was encouraging the cooks to be wasteful."

"I see." Alice chuckled. "Lord Hugh enjoys dining well, but he has never been obliged to actually prepare his own meals, let alone plan dishes for a household this size. These cooks must feed forty people daily. More on special occasions."

"Aye," Elbert said glumly.

"Sir Hugh may be very good at figuring his accounts, but he has no notion of proper quantities of ingredients for dishes."

"Nay, m'lady, he does not," Elbert agreed fervently.

"Do not concern yourself, Elbert. Sir Hugh gave me the keys to the storerooms before he departed. I shall keep them permanently in my possession after he returns. From now on, see to it that a list of the spices needed each day is given to me in the mornings. I will measure them out for the cooks."

Hope lit Elbert's eyes. "I will not have to go to Lord Hugh for the spices?"

"Nay. I will deal with it."

Elbert relaxed visibly. "My thanks, m'lady."

"Now, then, as to the menus. I shall prepare several. You may alternate among them as you choose." Alice smiled at two women who were stirring a pudding. "Be certain to bring me any suggestions that the cooks make. I'll no doubt find them useful for adding variety to the list of dishes."

The two women glowed.

Alice moved on toward a table laden with eggs. "Egg dishes are quite strengthening. I want at least one served at every midday meal."

"Aye, m'lady." Elbert studied the vast pile of eggs. "How do you wish them to be prepared?"

"They are most healthful when cooked with—"

"My lady," a servant called from the doorway. "Pray, pardon me, madam."

Alice turned from the eggs. "What is it, Egan?"

"I am sorry to disturb you but there's a lad here," Egan said. "He says he must speak with you at once. He claims 'tis a matter of life and death."

"A boy?" One of the cooks scowled. "Tell 'im to be off. Lady Alice is occupied with more important matters."

Alice looked at the small figure who hovered behind Egan. She saw a lad with dark hair and yellow-brown eyes standing in the kitchen doorway.

He appeared to be about eight years of age. She did not recognize him as one of the village children. His clothing was smudged with dirt and grime but it was of excellent quality.

"I must speak with the lady." The boy sounded as though he were out of breath. " 'Tis most important. I will not leave until I've talked with her."

"That's what ye think." One of the kitchen workers hoisted a bread paddle in a mildly threatening manner. "Begone, boy. Ye smell like a garderobe."

The breeze through the open doorway proved the servant correct. There was no denying that the distinctive odor of a privy clung to the lad.

"Put that paddle down," Alice said firmly. She smiled at the newcomer. "I am Lady Alice. Who are you?"

The boy straightened his shoulders and elevated his chin. The simple gesture conveyed a pride so innate that it easily transcended his grubby attire and unpleasant odor. "I am Reginald, my lady. My father is Sir Vincent of Rivenhall."

Elbert sucked in his breath. "Rivenhall."

The kitchen suddenly became very quiet. Reginald's small jaw tightened but he stood his ground. His gaze did not waver from Alice's face.

"You're from Rivenhall Manor?" Alice asked carefully as she walked toward Reginald. "Sir Vincent's son?"

"Aye." Reginald gave her a crisply executed bow and then raised eyes that held equal measures of desperation and determination. "I have come to plead with you to help me save my father's manor and my mother's honor."

"By the Saints. What in heaven's name are you talking about?"

"My mother said that it was no use appealing to Scarcliffe, but there is no place else I can go. You are the only ones close enough to help. I have heard my father say that he and Hugh the Relentless are cousins. So I came here today."

"Calm yourself, Reginald," Alice said soothingly.

"They tell me Sir Hugh is away in London but you are here and many of his men-at-arms are here, too. You can help us. Please, madam—"

"You must tell me this tale from the beginning," Alice said firmly.

But something seemed to have snapped inside Reginald. It was as though he had held himself together by sheer willpower for too long. Now it was all coming undone. Tears shimmered in his eyes.

"We are lost if you do not come to our aid." The words poured out of him in a torrent. "My father is far away in the south attending a joust. He says we need the money. Most of the household knights and men-at-arms are with him."

"Reginald—"

"Sir Eduard arrived yesterday and forced his way into our hall. My mother is terrified. I do not know how to get a message to my father in time to save her."

"Hush. I will deal with this." Alice put a hand on his shoulder and guided him to a pail of water that sat by the hearth. "First, we must get rid of that dreadful odor." She glanced at the steward. "Elbert, send someone for a change of clothing."

"Aye, m'lady." Elbert signaled to one of the kitchen scullions.

It took only a few minutes to get Reginald washed and changed into fresh clothing. When he was clean once more Alice sat him down at one of the kitchen tables.

"Will someone please bring our guest a mug of my special green pottage?" she said.

One of the cooks ladled the thin vegetable broth into a

mug and brought it to the table. The comforting aroma of the parsley root with which the pottage had been flavored wafted gently upward.

"Take a sip," Alice instructed as she sat down across from him. "It will have a strengthening effect."

Reginald gulped the pottage as though he had been starving. He stopped abruptly after the first swallow, however, and grimaced when he put down the mug. "Thank you, my lady," he said with a politeness that sounded forced. "I was very hungry." He started to wipe his mouth on the back of his sleeve and then stopped, obviously embarrassed by the display of ill manners. He flushed and took a deep breath.

"Now tell me who Sir Eduard is and how he forced his way into your father's hall."

"Eduard of Lockton is a landless knight," Reginald said. "He is a mercenary who sells his sword where he can. My mother says he is no better than an outlaw."

"Why did Eduard come to Rivenhall?"

"My mother said it was because he knew that my father was far away and that he had taken most of his men with him. She says Sir Eduard believes that Hugh the Relentless will not come to the aid of Rivenhall because of the bad blood between the two manors."

"Eduard of Lockton just strode into your father's hall and took command?"

"Aye. When he arrived yesterday he claimed he came in friendship. He demanded lodging for the night for himself and his men. Mother did not dare refuse. There was no way we could mount a defense with the few men my father left behind."

"So she let him into the hall hoping he would leave in the morning?"

"Aye. But he stayed." Reginald looked miserable. "He has put his own men on the walls. He acts as though he were lord of Rivenhall. He has taken our keep without even laying siege to it."

"Surely your father's liege lord, Erasmus of Thornewood, will take action against Sir Eduard when he learns of this."

"My mother says that Sir Erasmus is dying. He will likely be dead before we can get word to him."

"A *fait accompli*," Alice murmured.

"That is what Mother called it."

Alice recalled how her uncle had installed his son in her father's hall. It was all well and good for clerics to argue the fine points of royal law, canon law, and the law of custom, but the truth was that possession was everything. A man or a woman who could not defend what he or she held soon lost it to someone more powerful. It was the way of the world.

"I know how you feel, Reginald."

Reginald looked at her with worried eyes. "Last night, after the meal, Sir Eduard tried to force my mother to go to his chamber with him. She was terrified. I believe that he intended to hurt her."

A cold chill went through Alice. "Dear God. Is your mother . . . ? Is she all right? What happened?"

"She broke free of him, grabbed my hand, and told me that we must flee to the tower room. We managed to get inside and lock the door."

"Thank the Saints," Alice breathed.

"Eduard was furious. He pounded on the door and made all sorts of threats. Eventually he left but not before he vowed to starve us out of the tower room. Mother is still there. She has had nothing to eat or drink since last night." He looked down at his empty mug. "This is all I've had since yesterday."

Alice glanced at a cook. "Bring our guest a meat pie, please."

"Aye, m'lady." The fascinated cook plucked a pie from a hot plate and set it down in front of Reginald.

Alice studied the boy. "How did you free yourself?"

"There is an old garderobe in the tower room." Reginald fell on the pie with a good deal more enthusiasm than he had displayed for the nourishing pottage. "The shaft is somewhat wider than most."

"Just wide enough for a boy your size?"

Reginald nodded. "It was difficult in places. And the smell was terrible."

"I can imagine. How did you descend?"

"Mother and I fashioned a rope out of an old bed curtain. I used it to lower myself down the shaft."

That explained the unpleasant stench that hung about Reginald's clothing, Alice thought wryly. The poor boy had exited the keep through a privy drain. Odor aside, it must have been a frightening experience.

"You are very brave, Reginald."

He ignored that. "Will you help us, Lady Alice? If we do not do something, I fear that Sir Eduard will hurt Mother."

Dunstan stormed into the kitchens at that moment. His whiskers twitched with outrage. He glowered at everyone and then his gaze settled on Alice.

"What the devil is going on here?" he demanded. "What's this about a boy from Rivenhall?"

"This is Reginald, Sir Vincent's son." Alice got to her feet. "Rivenhall Keep has been taken by a mercenary knight named Eduard of Lockton. We must save the keep and Reginald's mother, who is being held captive there."

Dunstan's jaw dropped in astonishment. "Save Rivenhall? Are you mad, m'lady? If that keep has truly fallen into the hands of another, Sir Hugh will order a great feast to celebrate the occasion."

"Don't be ridiculous, Dunstan. 'Tis one thing to carry on a feud within the family. 'Tis quite another to allow an outsider to take control of a cousin's holdings."

"But m'lady—"

"Please command the men to arm themselves and mount their horses. Have a palfrey saddled for me. We leave for Rivenhall within the hour."

Dunstan's eyes blazed. "I cannot allow it. Sir Hugh will likely hang me as a traitor if we go to the aid of Rivenhall."

"If you fear him so much, you may remain behind here at Scarcliffe. We shall go without you," Alice said calmly.

"God's teeth, madam, if Hugh hangs me, I shall be the more fortunate of the two of us. There is no telling what he will do to you. *You are his betrothed.* He will never forgive you for betraying him in this manner."

"I do not intend to betray him." Alice steeled herself against the cold unease that unfurled in her stomach. "I am going to the aid of his blood kin."

"He despises his blood kin."

"Surely he does not despise young Reginald or Reginald's mother."

"You speak of Vincent's heir and his wife." Dunstan looked at her in disbelief. "Sir Hugh cannot feel any more charity toward them than he does toward Vincent."

"Sir Hugh left me in command of this manor, did he not?"

"Aye, but—"

"I must do what I feel is right. You have your instructions, Sir Dunstan."

Dunstan's features twisted into a mask of frustrated rage. He picked up an earthenware pot and hurled it against the kitchen wall. It shattered into a dozen shards.

"I told him you would be trouble. Nothing but trouble." He swung around on his heel and stalked out of the kitchen.

*T*wo hours later Alice, garbed in a vivid green gown, her hair bound in a silken net anchored with a silver circlet, rode through the gates of Rivenhall Keep. Young Reginald, mounted on a small gray palfrey, was at her side. No one tried to stop them from entering the bailey. Alice realized that Eduard did not dare challenge Hugh the Relentless.

Tension flowed through her. She could feel the wary eyes of the men who stood guard on the wall. They were no doubt assessing the force she had brought with her.

She took comfort in the knowledge that her company made an impressive, thoroughly intimidating sight. Sir Dunstan and the contingent of household knights and men-at-arms Hugh had left at Scarcliffe rode at her back. Even Julian had ridden with them. He had explained to Alice that any man who was employed by Sir Hugh was obliged to learn how to handle a sword or a bow, regardless of whether or not it complemented his attire.

The gray light of the misty day glinted on polished helms and touched the points and blades of bristling weapons. Black banners snapped in the breeze.

"Greetings, my lady." A huge, burly man with wild, unkempt brown hair, a bushy beard, and glittering eyes hailed her from the front steps of the keep. "I am pleased to make the acquaintance of any who ride under the banner of Hugh the Relentless."

"That is Sir Eduard," Reginald hissed to Alice. "Look at him. He acts as though he were lord here."

Alice studied Eduard's features as she reined her palfrey to a halt. The mercenary reminded her of a boar. He had a thick neck, wide jaws, and small, flat eyes. He no doubt possessed a brain to match.

She looked down the length of her nose at him as Dunstan and his men arrayed themselves behind her. "Please inform the lady of this manor that her new neighbor has come to call."

Eduard grinned, displaying several gaps in his dirty yellow teeth. "And who might you be?"

"I am Alice, betrothed wife to Hugh the Relentless."

"Betrothed wife, eh?" Eduard surveyed the armed men

behind her. "The one who caused him to miss the joust against Sir Vincent at Ipstoke fair, I'll wager. He was not well pleased with you that day."

"I assure you that Sir Hugh is quite content with his choice of a bride," Alice said. "So content, in fact, that he does not hesitate to leave me in command of his lands and his men."

"So it would seem. And where is Sir Hugh?"

"On his way back to Scarcliffe from London," Alice said coolly. "He will return soon. I intend to visit with Lady Emma until he arrives."

Eduard gave her a crafty look. "Does Sir Hugh know you're here?"

"Rest assured he will discover that fact soon enough," Alice said. "If I were you, I would be gone from Rivenhall by then."

"Do ye threaten me, lady?"

"Consider it a warning."

"You are the one who should take heed, madam," Eduard drawled in an unpleasant voice. "You obviously do not comprehend how it is between Rivenhall and Scarcliffe. Mayhap your future lord did not see fit to explain his personal affairs to you."

"Lord Hugh has explained everything to me, sir. I enjoy his full trust and confidence."

Eduard's face tightened with anger. "That will soon change. Sir Hugh will thank me for occupying this keep. 'Tis true that his liege lord has forbidden him to take vengeance against Rivenhall. But I promise you that he will not interfere when he learns that another has achieved his goal for him."

"It is you who do not comprehend the situation," Alice said softly. "You have interfered in family affairs. Sir Hugh will not thank you for it."

"We shall see about that," Eduard retorted.

"So we shall." Alice smiled coldly. "In the meantime I

would pass the time with Lady Emma. Is she still in the tower chamber?"

Eduard narrowed his tiny eyes. "So the boy told you about that, did he? Aye. She's locked herself inside and will not come out."

Alice turned to Reginald. "Go and fetch your mother from the tower. Tell her that I look forward to making her acquaintance. Tell her that Sir Hugh's men-at-arms are here to guarantee her safety and yours."

"Aye, my lady." Reginald slid down off the gray palfrey. He shot Eduard an angry glance as he dashed up the steps and disappeared into the hall.

Eduard planted hamlike fists on his hips and confronted Alice. "You're risking more than you know by dabbling in this business, Lady Alice. Aye, far more."

"That is my concern, not yours."

"When Sir Hugh returns he will be furious with you for this betrayal. 'Tis no secret that loyalty is all to him. The very least he'll do is end the betrothal. And then where will you be, you foolish woman?"

" 'Tis you who are the fool, Eduard." Alice looked at Dunstan. "Will you assist me in dismounting, sir?"

"Aye, m'lady," Dunstan growled. He kept his eye on Eduard as he got down off his horse. He walked to where Alice's palfrey stood and reached up to help her from the saddle.

She saw the tightness about his mouth and smiled reassuringly. "All will be well, Sir Dunstan. Trust me."

"Sir Hugh will likely have my head for this day's work," he muttered for her ears alone. "But before he does, I will tell him that his betrothed has enough courage to match his own."

"Why, thank you, sir." Alice was startled and warmed by the grudging praise. "Try not to be too anxious. I will not allow Lord Hugh to blame you for any of this."

"Sir Hugh will assign the blame as he chooses." Dunstan's expression was one of grim fatalism.

"Lady Alice, Lady Alice," Reginald called from the doorway. "I would like you to make the acquaintance of my lady mother, Emma."

Alice turned to see a lovely, fair-haired woman with soft eyes and a gentle mien standing beside Reginald. She appeared exhausted by worry and what had no doubt been a sleepless night but there was an unbending pride in her stance and a hint of hope in her gaze.

"Greetings, Lady Alice." Emma darted a quick, disgusted glance at Eduard. "I regret the poor welcome you have received. As you see, we are obliged to endure the nuisance of an unwanted guest."

" 'Tis only a temporary problem." Secure in the knowledge that she was protected by Scarcliffe men-at-arms, Alice went up the steps. "Rest assured my betrothed husband will soon rid you of this vermin."

*H*ugh wondered if Elbert had gone mad. He'd had his doubts about the young man from the start. "Lady Alice did *what?*"

Elbert trembled but he did not step back. "She took Sir Dunstan and all the men-at-arms and went to rescue Rivenhall Keep from the clutches of someone called Eduard of Lockton. That's all I know, my lord."

"I do not believe this."

Behind Hugh the tired horses stamped their feet and blew noisily, eager to get to the stables. Benedict and the two men-at-arms were equally weary. They had already dismounted and were waiting to see what was wrong.

Hugh had pushed his small party hard today in order to reach Scarcliffe a day sooner than would otherwise have been the case. He'd entertained a pleasant vision of arriving home to find Alice waiting for him on the front steps.

He should have known that something would be amiss. His stratagems rarely went according to plan when he was dealing with Alice. Nevertheless, he could not bring himself to believe that she had gone to Rivenhall.

" 'Tis true, sir," Elbert said. "Ask anyone. Young Reginald arrived here this morning and begged her to help him and his lady mother."

"Reginald?"

"Sir Vincent's son and heir, my lord. He was quite desperate to protect his mother as well as his father's keep. Lady Alice told him that she knew you would want her to ride to Rivenhall's aid."

"She would not dare go to Rivenhall," Hugh said softly. "Not even Alice would dream of challenging me in such a fashion."

Elbert swallowed. "She felt it was necessary, my lord."

"By the fires of hell." Hugh glanced at the groom who had come to take his horse. "Bring me a fresh mount."

"Aye, m'lord." The groom rushed off toward the stables.

"Sir?" Benedict handed the reins of his own horse to another groom. "What's wrong? Has something happened to Alice?"

"Not yet," Hugh said. "But it will quite soon. I shall see to it personally."

*A*lice could feel the tension in the great hall of Rivenhall Keep but she pretended not to notice. She sat with Emma near the fire and talked quietly. Reginald was perched on a stool near the hearth.

From time to time Alice saw Emma's angry gaze go to Eduard, who lounged insolently in Sir Vincent's chair. The intruder munched gingered currants from a bowl as though he had every right to them. Three of his scruffy-looking men-at-arms occupied a nearby bench. Their eyes were fixed on Dunstan and the two knights he had stationed in the hall next to Alice. The rest of the Scarcliffe men-at-arms had replaced Eduard's men on the bailey wall.

"I mean no offense, Alice," Emma murmured, "but it is as if this keep has been taken twice in the past two days. Once by Eduard's men and now by Sir Hugh's."

"You shall have your keep back as soon as Hugh returns from London." Alice plucked a handful of nuts from a dish. "My lord will deal with Eduard."

"I pray you are correct." Emma sighed. "But from what my husband has told me of the history of this family, I am not certain it will be as simple as all that. What if Sir Hugh decides to acquiesce to Eduard's occupation of this keep?"

"He won't."

"And I am concerned for you, Alice. What will Sir Hugh say when he learns of what you have done here today? He is very likely to regard it as a betrayal."

"Nay, he will understand once I have explained it all to him." Alice popped three of the nuts into her mouth and munched. "Sir Hugh is a man of great intelligence. He will listen."

Reginald bit his lip anxiously. "What if Sir Hugh is too angry to heed your explanations, madam?"

"My lord's intelligence is exceeded only by his powers of self-mastery," Alice said proudly. "He will not take action until he has first assessed the situation."

A muffled shout echoed from the courtyard. Steel-shod hooves rang on the stones. Dunstan stirred, straightened, and glanced at his men.

"Ah, about time." Eduard heaved himself to his feet. He shot Alice a triumphant look. "It sounds as though Sir Hugh has at long last arrived. We shall soon see what he has to say about his betrothed wife's presence here in his enemy's keep."

Alice ignored him.

Outside, thunder crashed, announcing the arrival of the storm that had been threatening all afternoon. A moment later the hall door was thrown open.

Dunstan met Alice's eyes. "They say that 'tis easier to raise the devil than to banish him, m'lady. You certainly have a talent for the former. Let us all pray that you have some skill with the latter task as well."

Chapter 15

Hugh swept into the great hall of his sworn enemy with deadly grace and intent. He brought with him the gathering fury of the storm and the dark promise of oncoming night. His black cloak was a whirlwind that swirled around his black leather boots. His onyx hair was windblown. His eyes were molten amber.

He was not wearing his armor but the folds of his cloak were thrown back to reveal the black leather sword belt buckled low on his hips. One big hand rested on the hilt.

No one moved. Everyone in the hall stared at the apparition that had coalesced out of the impending tempest.

Hugh took in the frozen chamber with a single searing glance. Alice realized that he had assessed the whole situation in that instant. Assessed it and made the lightning-swift calculations that would determine his actions and the fate of everyone in the hall.

The manner in which he immediately dominated the hall was breathtaking. He commanded the wary respect of all within the chamber in the same fashion in which a great storm commands the skies.

Eduard of Lockton suddenly appeared a good deal smaller and much less intimidating than he had a short while earlier. Unfortunately, he looked just as mean and vicious.

Hugh's eyes came to rest on Alice.

"I have come for my betrothed." His voice was a whisper that carried to the farthest corner of the hushed hall.

"Dear heaven." Emma's hand went to her throat.

Reginald gazed at Hugh with rapt curiosity. "He is very big, is he not?"

Eduard jolted to his feet as though freed of the invisible spell that had temporarily imprisoned him. "Sir Hugh. Welcome to this hall. The Lady Alice is my honored guest."

Hugh paid him no heed. "Alice. Come here."

"*Hugh.*" Alice leaped to her feet, picked up her skirts, and rushed down the length of the hall to greet him properly. "My lord, I am so very glad to see you. I feared that you would be another day on the road. Now you will be able to put this matter right."

"What do you do here, Alice?" Hugh's eyes reflected the flames on the hearth.

"My lord, I pray you will but listen to me for a moment and all will be made quite clear." Alice came to an abrupt halt directly in front of him. She sank into a deep curtsy and bowed her head. "I can explain everything."

"Aye, no doubt. And you will do so later." Hugh did not extend his hand to assist her as she rose slowly. "Come. We are leaving."

He turned on his booted heel.

Behind Alice, Emma made a small, soft, despairing sound.

"All will be well, Mother," Reginald whispered. "You'll see."

"One moment, my lord," Alice said. "Sir, I fear that we cannot take our leave just yet."

Hugh paused and turned slowly around to face her. "Why not?"

Alice mustered her determination. It was not easy. She realized that she must tread warily if she would banish the devil in him. Her only ally at this moment was his own intelligence. "First you must tell Eduard of Lockton to take himself and his men out of this keep."

"Is that so?"

Eduard gave a harsh crack of gloating laughter as he came forward. "Your betrothed is a charming little creature, my lord, but obviously headstrong and willful." He leered at Alice. "I admit that I envy you the pleasure of taming her. 'Twill prove interesting, I'll wager."

Alice whirled on him. "That is enough out of you, you great, obnoxious oaf. Who do you think you are? You have no rights here in this hall. Sir Hugh will soon get rid of you."

Eduard's yellow teeth flashed in his beard. He slanted Hugh a knowing glance. "If you want my opinion, m'lord, you've been too indulgent with the lady. She seems to think that she can give you orders as she would a servant. A touch of the whip would likely teach her to control her tongue."

"One more insult to my betrothed," Hugh said very softly, "and I will cut you down where you stand. Do you comprehend me, Eduard?"

Alice glowed with satisfaction.

Eduard flinched but recovered instantly. "Sir, I meant no insult. 'Twas merely an observation. I myself occasionally enjoy the saucy types."

Alice shot Eduard a disgusted look and then turned back to Hugh. "Tell him to leave at once, sir. He has no business here."

"Bah. Women." Eduard shook his large head. "They do not comprehend the ways of the world, do they, m'lord?"

Hugh studied him with the sort of idle interest a well-fed falcon might exhibit toward a fresh meal. "Why are you here?"

A crafty gleam lit Eduard's malicious eyes. "Why, 'tis obvious, is it not, sir? 'Tis no secret that Rivenhall's lord no longer commands the money or the men to defend his lands."

"So you thought to take them while he was gone?" Hugh's voice held only cold curiosity.

" 'Tis well-known that you have sworn an oath to Erasmus of Thornewood not to take them." Eduard spread his hands. "Your reputation as a man who does not violate his oath is legendary, sir. But your oath to your liege lord does not apply to the rest of us poor knights who must make our own way in the world, does it?"

"Nay, it does not."

Eduard grinned. "Erasmus of Thornewood is dying, by all accounts. He will not ride to the defense of Rivenhall."

Emma gasped. "You will not take my son's inheritance, Sir Eduard."

Eduard's small eyes glittered. "Who will stop me, pray tell, Lady Emma?"

"Sir Hugh will stop you," Reginald said loudly. "Lady Alice promised."

Eduard snorted. "Don't play the fool, lad. Lady Alice does not command her lord, whatever she may believe. 'Tis the other way around. She will soon discover that for herself."

Reginald clenched his fists at his sides and faced Hugh. "Sir Eduard tried to hurt my mother. Lady Alice said you would not allow him to stay here at Rivenhall."

"Of course he will not allow it," Alice declared.

Emma took a single step forward. She lifted her hands in a beseeching gesture. "My lord, I know that you hold no love for this house, but I pray you will honor your betrothed's oath to defend it."

"He will," Alice assured her. "Lord Hugh left me in command. He granted me the authority to act in his stead and he will support me."

"She promised that you would help me save my father's keep." Reginald fixed Hugh with an expectant look.

Eduard slapped his thigh as though at a fine jest. "The boy's got a lot to learn, eh?" Two of his men chuckled uneasily.

"Enough." Hugh silenced the hall once more with the single word. He looked at Eduard. "Take your men and begone."

Eduard blinked two or three times. "What's this?"

"You heard me," Hugh said quietly. "Leave this hall at once or I will order my men to retake the keep." He glanced once more around the chamber, clearly taking note of the position of Dunstan and the Scarcliffe men-at-arms. "It should not take more than a few minutes to do so."

Eduard was outraged. "Have you lost your wits, man? You would save this hall on the orders of a woman?"

"Lady Alice spoke the truth. I left her in command in my stead. I will support her decision in this matter."

"This is madness," Eduard snarled. "You cannot mean to force me out of here."

Hugh shrugged. "I could not help but notice as I rode into the yard that my men outnumber yours on the wall. It would appear that Sir Dunstan has things under control in this chamber. Do you wish to put the matter to the test?"

Eduard turned red with fury. Then a shrewd look appeared on his face. "By the blood of the damned. Now I comprehend. You wish to possess this hall yourself, do you not? In spite of your oath to Erasmus, you mean to take advantage of the situation to grab these lands and have your revenge against Rivenhall. I respect that, sir, but mayhap you would consider an alliance with me?"

"My lord Hugh," Emma cried desperately. "I pray you will have mercy."

"By the Saints." Alice fitted her hands to her waist and

glowered at Eduard. "Don't be any more of an ass than you can help, Sir Eduard. Lord Hugh would not dream of violating his oath." She scowled at Hugh. "Would you, sir?"

Hugh watched Eduard. "A man's honor is only as good as his oath. Lady Alice acted in my stead when she ordered you from this hall, Eduard. The authority she wields flows from me. Do you comprehend?"

"You cannot mean this, m'lord," Eduard sputtered. "You would allow a mere woman to give orders in your name?"

"She is my betrothed," Hugh said coldly.

"Aye, but—"

"That makes me his partner," Alice informed Eduard.

"Leave at once," Hugh said. "Or prepare for battle."

"By the teeth of the demon," Eduard roared. "I do not believe this."

Hugh's hand tightened around the hilt of his sword.

Eduard took a hasty step back. "I do not want war with you, Sir Hugh."

"Then you will leave."

"Bah. Who would believe that Hugh the Relentless has fallen under the spell of a sharp-tongued, red-headed—"

"Enough," Hugh said.

Eduard spat into the rushes. "Mark my words, you'll regret the day you submitted yourself to a woman's whims."

"Mayhap, but that is my problem, not yours."

"I have had enough of this foolishness." Eduard turned and stalked toward the door. He signaled his men to follow.

Hugh looked at Dunstan. "See him through the gate."

Dunstan relaxed slightly. "Aye, m'lord." He motioned to the Scarcliffe men-at-arms.

Alice watched with satisfaction as Eduard and his men departed. "There, you see, Reginald? I told you all would be well."

"Aye, my lady." Reginald gazed at Hugh with awe.

Emma clasped her hands tightly together. Her anxious eyes

went from Alice to Hugh. "My lord, I pray you do not . . . I mean, I must ask if you intend to . . . to—" She broke off helplessly.

Alice knew what Emma was thinking. It would be all too easy for Hugh to take what Eduard of Lockton had just surrendered. "There, there, Emma. Rivenhall is safe from Lord Hugh."

"I am not going to take this keep, my lady," Hugh said without any emotion. "I gave my oath to Erasmus of Thornewood and in spite of what some would believe, he is still alive. While he lives, he has my loyalty."

Emma gave him a shaky smile. "Thank you, my lord. I know that your oath did not bind you to come to the defense of Rivenhall. It would have been most convenient for you to have let it fall to Eduard of Lockton."

"Aye." Hugh gave Alice an unreadable look. "Most convenient."

Reginald stepped forward and gave Hugh a courtly bow. "On behalf of my father, sir, I thank you for your assistance today."

"Do not thank me," Hugh said. " 'Twas the work of my betrothed."

"She was magnificent," Emma breathed. "We shall be forever grateful to her. We would have been lost without her."

Alice smiled happily. " 'Twas no great matter. I merely invoked the power of Lord Hugh's legendary reputation."

"So you did." Hugh's eyes burned. "And you will soon learn that all power commands a price."

"She meant well, my lord." Dunstan watched with morbid fascination as Hugh turned the wine cup slowly between his hands. "She is a woman, after all. With a woman's soft heart. When young Reginald pleaded with her to save his mother, she could not bring herself to deny him."

Hugh gazed into the flames on the hearth. He had come directly here to his study chamber as soon as he had returned from Rivenhall with Alice and his men. There had been no opportunity to speak to Alice during the wild ride through the storm.

Outside, the full fury of wind and rain lashed the black walls of Scarcliffe. The tempest mirrored his own mood. He had come so close. His hand tightened briefly on the wine cup. *So very close.* Vengeance had been all but within his grasp.

"Given your original opinion of my betrothed, I am amazed to hear you defend her, Dunstan."

Dunstan flushed. "She could not have known of your plans, sir."

"It was to have been so very convenient." Hugh looked into the heart of the fire. "Rivenhall was balanced on the brink of disaster. Vincent has stripped his own lands of what little his father left in order to pay for his endless jousts. He did not even leave enough men behind to guard his keep. It was ripe to fall into the hands of someone such as Eduard of Lockton."

Dunstan exhaled heavily. "I am aware that you have been waiting for Rivenhall to fall of its own accord."

" 'Twas such a simple stratagem, Dunstan."

"Aye."

"Yet she managed to tangle herself up in my net. She ruined it all."

Dunstan cleared his throat. "You did leave her in command of Scarcliffe, sir."

"Scarcliffe. Not Rivenhall."

"You did not make the limits of her authority clear to her," Dunstan insisted.

"A mistake that I will not repeat in the future." Hugh sipped wine from the cup. "I always learn from my mistakes, Dunstan."

"Sir, I must tell you that she acted with great daring. Never have I seen the like. She rode through the gates of

Rivenhall with armed men at her back as though she were a queen in command of an army."

"Did she?"

"You should have seen the expression on Eduard of Lockton's face when he saw that it was a woman who rode beneath your banners. He was most anxious. He did not know what to think. He fell back on the hope that you would not support her when you discovered what she had done."

"I had no choice but to support her. She left me no other option. She acted in my name." Hugh's mouth twisted. "Nay, it went beyond that, you know. She thinks herself my partner. A *business* associate."

"Whatever else you may say about her, you must know that she possesses a courage that is the equal to that of any man." Dunstan paused meaningfully. "Indeed, a courage equal to your own, my lord."

"Do you think I am not aware of that?" Hugh asked very softly. " 'Tis one of the reasons I decided to wed her, if you will but recall. I wanted to breed such courage into my heirs."

"Sir, I heard you tell her that power commands a price. Mayhap courage does also."

"Aye. So it would seem. She has certainly seen to it that I paid a very high price for that commodity, has she not? And to think that I believed myself skilled at matters of business and bargaining."

Dunstan drew a deep breath. "My lord, I ask that you consider that Lady Alice could not have known of the depth of your feelings toward all things Rivenhall."

Hugh looked up from the flames at last, straight into his old friend's eyes. "Ah, now that is where you are wrong, Dunstan. She knew how I felt about Rivenhall. She knew full well."

·   ·   ·

"I vow, it was the most astonishing sight, Alice." Benedict struck his staff against the floor to emphasize his enthusiasm. He turned from the window, his face alight with excitement. "Chests of spices were stacked to the roof. Cinnamon, ginger, cloves, pepper, and saffron. Lord Hugh is obliged to hire guards at all times to keep watch on the storerooms."

"I am not surprised." Alice folded her hands together on top of her desk and tried to listen with proper attention as Benedict described his trip to London. It was not easy. Her mind kept returning to the events of the previous day.

The storm had vanished with the morning sun. The warm light pouring through the window lit her collection of crystals, giving even the ugly green stone on her desk an inner glow.

Alice hoped the rare fine weather would find a reflection in Hugh's temper, but she was not counting too heavily on that possibility. She had neither seen nor spoken to him since they had arrived home last night. She was not at all certain that she wished to do so.

She knew that she had roused the fires of the past within him. It only remained to see how long they would blaze before they died down once more. In the meantime she sensed it would be prudent to avoid the source of the conflagration.

"He employs many men, Alice. He has scribes and clerics and stewards. They deal with members of the Guild of Pepperers and they forge contracts with the captains of sailing vessels. They barter with powerful merchants. One afternoon we went down to the docks and watched as a ship was unloaded. It brought the most amazing goods from the East."

"It must have been a fascinating sight."

"Aye. But the most interesting thing was the library where the records of the voyages and cargoes are maintained. The steward in charge of that chamber showed me how each item in a shipment is entered into a log. He uses an abacus, just as Lord Hugh does, but he works it far more swiftly. He can do great sums in a moment. Sir Hugh says he is expert at the business."

Benedict's enthusiasm caught Alice's full attention. She eyed her brother thoughtfully. "It sounds as if you would enjoy such work."

"If I could work for Sir Hugh, I would certainly enjoy it," Benedict agreed. "He says he hires only the most highly skilled people and then he gives them the authority to carry out their duties in whatever manner they see fit. He says that is the best way."

Alice grimaced. "What does he do if someone in his employ exceeds his authority?"

"He dismisses the person, I suppose," Benedict said carelessly.

"I wonder if he will dismiss a betrothed wife as easily," Alice muttered under her breath.

A small sound out in the hall caught her attention. She glanced anxiously toward the door, hoping that the faint footsteps she heard heralded the arrival of Elbert or one of the servants. An hour ago she had sent the steward to Hugh with a request to speak privately. Thus far there had been no response.

The footsteps passed her study chamber door without pausing. They receded down the hall. Alice heaved a tiny sigh.

Benedict glanced at her. "What did you say?"

"Nothing. Tell me more about your stay in London. Where did you stay?"

"At an inn that Sir Hugh favors. The food was plain but the cook did not attempt to disguise old meat in her stews and the bedding was clean. Sir Hugh says that is what one looks for in an inn."

"Were there any women at this inn?" Alice asked cautiously.

"Aye, some worked in the tavern. Why do you ask?"

Alice picked up the green stone and pretended to study it. "Did Sir Hugh talk to any of those women?"

"Certainly, when he commanded that food or ale be brought to our table."

"Did Sir Hugh go off with any of them?" Alice asked softly.

"Nay." Benedict looked puzzled. "Where would he go with a tavern wench?"

Something inside Alice eased. She set the stone down and smiled at her brother. "I have no notion. I was merely curious. Tell me more about London."

" 'Tis an astounding place, Alice. So many people and shops. So many buildings."

"It must have been fascinating."

"It was. But Sir Hugh says he prefers the comforts of his own hall." Benedict paused by a worktable to toy with the astrolabe. "Alice, I have been thinking about my future. I believe I know what I would like to do."

Alice frowned. "You have chosen a career?"

"I wish to become Sir Hugh's man."

Alice stared at her brother, astonished. "In what capacity?"

"I want to deal in the spice trade," Benedict said eagerly. "I want to learn to keep the accounts and make contracts with the ships' captains. I want to supervise the unloading of the vessels and the sale of the spices. 'Tis so exciting, Alice. You cannot imagine."

"You truly believe that you would enjoy that sort of career?"

" 'Twould be ever so much more interesting than a career in the law."

Alice smiled wistfully. "I see that Sir Hugh has accomplished what I failed to do."

Benedict glanced at her. "What is that?"

"He has given you a taste of the world and a hunger for your own future. 'Tis a fine gift."

And while Hugh had been graciously bestowing that gift on her brother, Alice thought sadly, she had been depriving him of his long-sought vengeance.

A startled hush fell over the great hall that afternoon when Alice descended the tower stairs for the midday meal.

The clatter of mugs and knives ceased momentarily. The bustling servants paused to stare. The men seated on the benches at the long trestle tables stopped talking. A burst of loud laughter was cut off abruptly.

Everyone gazed at her in astonishment. Alice knew they were held rapt not only by her presence but by the sight of her new black and amber gown. The significance of her apparel was not lost on anyone. Hugh's betrothed wore her future husband's new colors.

A soft murmur of wonder and curiosity swept through the chamber.

Alice smiled wryly. Her entrance had created a sensation second only to the sort that Hugh himself was fond of making.

She looked down the length of the chamber to where he sat beneath the new black and amber canopy.

In spite of the tension in the hall, Alice could not help but be pleased with the effect Julian had created. There were cloths on the tables. Tapestries hung on the walls. Fresh herbs scented the clean rushes. Many of the servants were already garbed in the new colors.

Hugh looked especially fine seated at the head table in his great black chair, Alice thought.

He also looked very cold and very remote. Her momentary flicker of pleasure evaporated. He had not forgiven her for going to the aid of Rivenhall.

"My lady." Elbert appeared at Alice's elbow. His expression was anxious. "Will you dine with us today?"

"Aye."

Elbert beamed with unmistakable pride. "Allow me to escort you to the head table."

"My thanks." It was obvious that Hugh was not going to perform the courtesy, she thought.

Hugh watched with chilling intensity as she walked toward the head table. He did not rise from his ebony chair until she was almost upon him. At the last moment he got to his feet, inclined his head in an icy gesture, and took her hand to seat her. His fingers were iron bonds around her own soft palm.

"How kind of you to honor us with your presence, Lady Alice," he murmured.

At his tone she shivered and knew that he must have felt her reaction. She tried to calm her racing pulse as she took her seat.

"I trust that you will enjoy the meal, sir." Alice hastily freed her hand from his grasp.

"Your presence will definitely add a certain seasoning to the dishes."

She knew that his laconic remark had not been intended as a compliment but she decided to pretend otherwise. "You are most gracious, sir."

Hugh took his seat once more. He relaxed against the inlaid back of the chair and rested one elbow on a massive arm. He studied Alice with dangerous eyes. "May I ask why a woman of such refined sensibilities has chosen to dine in such rude company?"

Alice felt herself turn pink with embarrassment. "I do not consider the company rude." She nodded toward Elbert, who sprang into action. "I look forward to dining with you, my lord."

"Do you, indeed?"

He had not even noticed her new gown.

This was not going to be easy, Alice acknowledged. But, then, things rarely were with Hugh. She cast about for a way to change the topic. Her gaze fell on an unfamiliar man seated at the far end of one table. He was dressed in religious robes.

"Who is our guest?" she asked politely.

"The priest I brought back with me." Hugh flicked a mildly curious glance at an elegant dish of poached fish as it was set in front of him. The fish had been garnished with a saffron-tinted sauce. "He will perform the wedding service to-morrow."

Alice swallowed. "Wedding service?"

"Our marriage ceremony, madam." Hugh's mouth curved in a wintry smile. "Or had you forgotten about it?"

"Nay, of course not." Alice picked up her spoon, gripping it so tightly that the blood left the tips of her fingers.

By the Saints, he is furious, she thought. Far more so than she had realized. She wondered what she should do next. She had no notion of how to handle Hugh when he was in this mood. Despair threatened to sweep over her. She fought it with sheer willpower.

"You have not answered my question." Hugh helped him-self to a slice of the hot cheese and leek tart that a servant brought to the table.

"What question was that, my lord?"

"Why have you condescended to dine with your future lord and his men?"

"It was not an act of condescension. I merely wished to enjoy the meal with you. Is that so odd?"

Hugh considered briefly as he sampled a bite of the tart. "Aye. Most odd."

He was toying with her, Alice thought. Baiting her. "Well, 'tis the truth, sir." She concentrated on a dish of almond-flavored vegetables. "I wanted to welcome you home from London."

"Welcome me or placate me?"

Alice's temper flared. She put down her spoon with a thump. "I am not here because I seek to placate you, sir."

"Are you certain?" A humorless smile played around the edges of Hugh's mouth. "I have often noticed that your manners improve greatly when you seek a boon. One could view your actions today as those of a woman who knows she has overstepped herself. Mayhap you think to make amends for what you did yesterday?"

Alice knew she could not eat a single morsel now. She stood up abruptly and turned to confront him. "I did what I thought was necessary."

"Sit down."

"Nay, I will not sit down, sir. I came to dine with you here today because I wished to see if you cared for the improvements that have been made in this keep." She waved a hand at the black and amber canopy overhead. "You have not said one word about the decorations."

"Sit down, Alice."

"Nor have you bothered to pay attention to the excellent food." She glowered at him. "I spent hours organizing this household while you were gone and you have not deigned to extend a single kind word. Tell me, do you find the tart tasty, my lord? Did you notice that it was warm, not cold?"

Hugh narrowed his eyes. "I am more interested in other matters at the moment."

"Have you tried the ale? It is newly brewed."

"I have not sampled it yet."

"Did you enjoy the pleasant scent of your linens? What about the fresh rushes on the floor? Did you note that the garderobe shafts have all been washed with a great quantity of water and now exude a pleasant fragrance?"

"Alice—"

"What of the new colors that Julian and I so carefully chose? I added amber to match your eyes."

"Madam, I vow, if you do not sit down immediately, I shall—"

She ignored him to shake out the folds of her skirts. "And

what about my new gown, sir? The maids worked late into the night to finish the embroidery. Do you like it?"

He raked the black and amber garment with a single glance. "Did you think that the sight of you wearing my colors would sweeten my temper?" His hand closed fiercely around the arm of his chair. "By the devil, do you believe that I care more about clean garderobes than I do about vengeance?"

Alice was incensed. "I did no more than you yourself would have done had you been here when young Reginald came to plead for aid."

Hugh's eyes gleamed with fury. "You think to excuse your actions with such poor logic?"

"Aye, my lord, I do. You will never convince me that you would have let Lady Emma, her young son, and her entire household fall into the clutches of that horrible Eduard of Lockton. Regardless of your feelings toward Rivenhall, you are far too noble to allow the innocent to suffer for the sake of your vengeance."

"You know nothing of my nature."

"In that you are wrong. I know a great deal about you, sir. And in my opinion, 'tis most unfortunate that your fine nobility of manner is exceeded only by your monumental stubbornness."

Alice whisked up her skirts, turned, and fled from the high table. Tears burned in her eyes by the time she reached the door. She rushed down the steps and out into the sunlight.

She did not pause or look back as she dashed through the keep's gate.

Chapter 16

She did not know what made her choose the cave as her destination. But for some obscure reason Alice found solace in the shadows of the large cavern where Hugh had made love to her.

It had been a long, witless flight. What had she thought to accomplish by fleeing the keep so ignominiously? she wondered.

She sat down on an outcropping of stone near the cavern entrance and breathed deeply to recover from her wild run. She was disheveled and exhausted. The circlet that bound her hair had slipped to the side. Wispy red tendrils blew lightly about her cheeks. Her soft black leather shoes were scuffed. The skirts of her new gown were stained with dirt.

She had been so certain that, once his temper had cooled, Hugh would comprehend why she had gone to the rescue of Rivenhall. So certain that he would forgive her. He was a man of keen intelligence, after all, not a brute of a man as was Eduard of Lockton.

On the other hand, Hugh was not known as *Relentless* for naught, she reminded herself. Those who knew him maintained that nothing could alter his course once he had determined upon it. And he had been determined upon revenge since the day of his birth.

There was a great heaviness in Alice's heart. Her normally optimistic outlook had turned to a painful and quite unfamiliar mood of deep gloom. She was so accustomed to planning for the future that it came as a shock to realize that that future might well be empty.

She gazed out over the landscape of Scarcliffe and wondered morosely how she could marry a man who had no heart.

Mayhap it was time to reconsider a life within the calm, cloistered walls of the convent.

Mayhap it was time to abandon her fledgling dreams of love.

It was strange to realize that until she had met Hugh, she had never even been tempted to dream such dreams.

Alice tried to force herself to think calmly and logically about the situation. She was not yet wed. There was still time to escape the betrothal.

She could force Hugh to honor his portion of the bargain they had made. When all was said and done, he was a man who could be counted upon to abide by his word of honor. She'd had ample evidence of that last night at Rivenhall. He had stood by his oath to her even though it had cost him his vengeance.

Of course there was always the possibility that he would be only too happy to dissolve the betrothal, she thought bleakly. She had proven to be a good deal more inconvenient than even Hugh had anticipated.

The thought brought the tears to her eyes again. She started to dash them away with the sleeve of her gown, hesitated, and then succumbed to the urge to cry. She lowered her head down onto her folded arms and gave herself up to the storm of emotion that swept over her.

She had never felt so alone in her life.

*I*t was a long time before the floodtide of feeling exhausted itself. Alice eventually ceased sobbing and sat quietly, her head pillowed on her arms, until she grew calm once more.

Then she embarked upon a series of short, silent, bracing lectures.

Nothing was ever resolved with tears, she reminded herself. One could not waste time regretting the past. In truth, even if she had it to do over again, she would not alter yesterday's events. She could not have turned her back on young Reginald and Emma.

She had been so certain that Hugh would understand, so sure that he would have done as she had done.

Clearly she had been mistaken in her judgment of the dark legend that was Hugh.

One had to put one's mistakes behind one. It was time to go forward. If she had learned naught else in her life, it was that a woman had to be strong if she wished to remain in control of her own destiny.

The difficulty she faced now lay in the fact that she was dealing with a man who had learned the same hard lesson.

She wiped her eyes with the folds of her skirts, drew a deep, steadying breath, and slowly raised her head.

The first thing she saw was Hugh.

He leaned casually against the wall of the cavern, his thumbs hooked in his leather sword belt. His expression was unreadable.

"You certainly contrived to shock the priest," he said blandly. "I do not believe that he has ever before witnessed such an entertainment at dinner."

Alice's stomach clenched. "How long have you been stand-ing there spying on me, sir? I did not hear you arrive."

"I know. You were well occupied with your tears."

Alice looked away from his hard, implacable face. "Have you come to taunt me further? If so, I must warn you that I am in no mood for more battle."

"What a strange notion. I have never known you to weary of combat, madam."

She glowered at him furiously. "By the Saints, Hugh, I have had enough."

"If the truth be known, so have I."

The wry tone of his voice disconcerted her. She instantly quashed the spark of hope that leaped within her. "Have you come to apologize, my lord?"

He smiled faintly. "Do not press your luck too far, Alice."

"Nay, of course you did not come here for such a logical, sensible reason. Well, my lord, why did you follow me then, if not to make amends?"

"I told you that you were not to come here to the caves alone."

He was avoiding the issue, she thought, surprised. That was most unlike Hugh.

"Aye, so you did. The day you gave me your ring." She glanced down at the broad onyx stone that weighed heavily on her thumb. Another wave of sadness washed over her. "But surely this transgression pales into insignificance compared with my astounding sins of yesterday," she muttered.

"Aye. It does."

She wished she could tell what he was thinking. His mood was indecipherable. He did not appear especially furious, how-ever. It struck her that Hugh himself may not have been cer-tain of his own feelings. The flicker of hope resurged.

"Have you come to tell me that you wish to break our betrothal contract?" she asked coolly.

"Will you pursue me through the courts if I do choose to sever it?"

She bristled. "Don't be ridiculous. We made a bargain, if you will recall."

"Aye." Hugh straightened and came away from the wall. He reached down, grasped her by the shoulders, and lifted her gently to her feet. "You would not sue me for breach of promise, would you?"

"Nay, my lord."

"In fact, you would be only too glad to escape into a convent. Is that not so?"

She stiffened. "My lord, I know that you are very angry about what I did, but I would have you know—"

"Hush." Hugh's eyes gleamed. "We will not speak again of what happened yesterday."

She blinked. "We won't?"

"After much contemplation I have been forced to conclude that what occurred yesterday at Rivenhall was not your fault."

"It wasn't?"

"Nay." He dropped his hands from her shoulders. "It was my fault and mine alone."

"It was?" Alice felt as though she had stepped through a magical window only to emerge into a strange land where the normal logic of the world was slightly askew.

"Aye." Hugh folded his arms across his broad chest. "I did not set clear limits on the authority I granted to you. I did not anticipate all possible situations. I did not make allowance for your soft heart."

"You could hardly have done that, sir." Alice began to feel quite waspish. "Given the fact that you do not seem to know what it is to possess a heart. And you may as well know that even if you had expressly forbidden me to ride to Rivenhall's defense, I would have disobeyed you."

Hugh smiled faintly. "You do not know when to stop, do

you, Alice? And to think the world calls me *Relentless*. You could give me lessons in the art."

"I still maintain, my lord, that if you had been here to see young Reginald plead for help, even the stone you use in place of a heart would have melted."

"Unlikely. I would have kept my eye on the ultimate goal."

"Sir, that boy is your blood kin, whether you like it or not. Furthermore, he and his mother had nothing to do with what happened in the past. None of you living today had anything to do with it. Let the sins of the past rest."

"Enough." Hugh cut off the flow of her words with a finger on her lips. "It may surprise you to know that I did not come here to quarrel with you."

"Nay?" Alice gave him a look of mock astonishment.

"Nay." Hugh's jaw tightened. "Not another word on the subject of yesterday's affairs at Rivenhall, Alice. What's done is done."

She gazed mutely up at him, intensely conscious of the exciting roughness of his callused finger against her soft mouth. For a moment he simply looked at her as though he sought some sign in her widened eyes.

"Alice, on the last occasion when we were in these caves you told me that the reason you had never before made love was that you had never before met a man who appealed to you."

" 'Twas the truth." *Not quite all of the truth. The real truth is that I had never before met a man whom I could love,* she added silently. "What of it?"

He did not answer. Instead he pulled her close, anchored her tousled head with one big hand, and kissed her.

The dark passion in his embrace was very close to the surface. Alice shivered beneath its onslaught.

Always she had been aware of the depths of his control

when he held her in his arms. But today she sensed that he was fighting the steel bonds that he had imposed on himself. She wondered what awesome force had brought him to the edge of his own limits of control.

She tasted the residue of his anger and frustration in his kiss. His mouth moved on hers, relentless in its demands. She thought that she could actually hear the storm winds that howled across his soul.

But he would not, could not hurt her, Alice realized suddenly. A wondrous joy leaped within her. Her arms stole softly around his neck.

Hugh raised his head just as she moaned and parted her lips for him. He gazed broodingly at her mouth. " 'Tis time we returned to the keep. There is much to be done before we are wed tomorrow."

Alice stifled a groan. She drew a deep breath and tried to steady herself. "My lord, mayhap we should wait a while longer before we take our vows."

"Nay, madam." His voice hardened. " 'Tis too late."

"If this is only a matter of knightly honor for you, my lord, rest assured, I will not—"

"*Only* a matter of honor?" His amber eyes were suddenly fierce. "My honor is everything to me, madam. *Everything.* Do you comprehend that? All that I am flows from it."

"Sir, I did not mean to imply that I thought your honor unimportant. On the contrary, I have always been most impressed—" Alice broke off as she caught sight of an object out of the corner of her eye. She turned her head to peer into the shadowed depths of the far end of the cavern.

Hugh frowned. "What is it?"

"By the Saints," Alice breathed. "Does that look like a sandal?"

Hugh glanced toward the opening. His eyes narrowed. "Aye, it does." He released Alice and strode toward the dark passage. "If that damned monk is still hanging about these parts, I vow, I shall personally throw him off Scarcliffe lands."

"But why would he wish to stay here if he could no longer preach?" Alice asked as she followed Hugh.

"An excellent question." Hugh came to a halt near the yawning tunnel. He paused and then crouched down as though to get a better look at the sandal.

"What is it?" Alice hurried toward him and looked over his broad shoulder. A deep unease filled her. The air emanating from the passageway suddenly seemed very cold. *"Eyes of the Saints."*

The sandal was still attached to Calvert's foot. The monk lay ominously still on the stone floor of the cave. His brown robes were tumbled about his scrawny frame as though they were so much dirty linen.

In the deep shadows it was possible to see that Calvert's body was oddly contorted. He looked as though he had been in great pain for a time but it was very clear that he was far beyond feeling anything at all now.

"He's dead," Hugh said quietly.

"Aye. Poor man." Alice crossed herself. "I could not like him but I am sorry that he died here alone. What do you think happened to him?"

"I don't know. Mayhap he fell and hit his head against a sharp stone." Hugh clamped a hand around the monk's ankle.

"What are you doing?"

"I want to get a closer look at him. There is something strange about this." Hugh dragged the monk's body out of the passage.

Alice backed hurriedly out of the way. Then she saw the odd blue color around Calvert's mouth. A shiver of dread gripped her.

She recalled something her mother had written about potions made from the juice of a rare herb. She glanced at Calvert's fingernails. His hands had stiffened into clawlike shapes but she could make out the blue tinge beneath his nails.

"My lord?"

"Aye?" Hugh asked absently. He was concentrating on the task of stretching the monk's body out in the light of the cavern entrance. When he had finished, he stood and gazed down at Calvert with a speculative expression.

"I do not believe that the monk died from a fall," Alice whispered.

Hugh gave her a sharp, assessing look. "What are you saying?"

"I believe that this is the work of poison."

Hugh studied her for a long moment. "You are certain?"

Alice nodded bleakly. "My mother's book contains several pages of notes on the subject."

"In that case," Hugh said very evenly, "you will say nothing concerning the manner of his death. Do you comprehend me, Alice?"

"Aye." She was bemused by the intensity of his voice. "But I do not understand. Why is it so important that I keep silent?"

"Because the entire village witnessed your anger toward him in church." Hugh went down on one knee beside the monk's body. "And because everyone knows that you are expert with herbal potions."

Alice went cold to the bone. Nausea assailed her. She swallowed rapidly, trying to control the churning in her stomach. "Dear God. People may believe that I had a motive to murder poor Calvert and that I know enough of poisons to do so."

"I will not have my wife touched by such gossip if it can be avoided." Hugh unfastened and removed the leather pouch that was suspended from Calvert's belt. "This land has seen enough of legends and curses. I do not want new ones added to the old."

Alice was dazed. She barely registered Hugh's actions. Her

legs were unsteady. She flattened her hand against the wall of the cave to brace herself. "And if such gossip cannot be avoided?"

Hugh shrugged as he got to his feet, Calvert's pouch in one hand. "Then I shall deal with it."

"Of course." Alice hugged herself against the chill that enveloped her. "It would seem that I am destined to cause you endless inconvenience, my lord."

"Aye, but there will no doubt be compensations." He opened the leather pouch and studied the contents. "Interesting."

His expression finally penetrated Alice's anxious mood. Her own natural curiosity reasserted itself. "What is it?"

Hugh drew out a sheet of rolled parchment. He unfurled it carefully. "A map."

She took a step toward him. "Of what?"

Hugh studied the drawing for a moment. When he looked up at last, his golden eyes gleamed. "I believe this may be a drawing of the passages of the caves of Scarcliffe. Or at least of those passages that Calvert had time to explore."

Alice hurried to where Hugh stood. She gazed down at the lines on the map. "Look, my lord, he marked several of the tunnels. See, here, he has indicated that these two passages are empty." She glanced at Hugh. "Empty of what, do you suppose?"

"I do not believe that our monk spent all of his time praying in these caverns. It appears that he was searching for something. There is only one treasure that would lure a man into these caves."

"The stones of Scarcliffe," Alice whispered, amazed.

"Aye. Mayhap he was murdered for them."

"*Y*ou sent for me, sir?" Julian paused in the doorway of Hugh's study chamber.

"Aye." Hugh put aside his journal of accounts. "Enter, Julian. I wish to speak with you."

"I trust you are not going to send me off to London with a message before the marriage feast this afternoon." Julian sauntered into the chamber and stood before Hugh's desk. "I have been looking forward to the banquet. The food has greatly improved around here in recent days. Have you noticed?"

Hugh narrowed his eyes. "I have noticed. But I did not send for you in order to discuss the well-spiced dishes that now grace my table."

"Of course not." Julian smiled blandly. "I trust that you know who to thank for the excellent meals we all enjoy."

"Nor do I need any more pointed observations on the well-organized manner in which this household is now functioning. I have had a surfeit of such comments. I am well aware that the improvements are the result of my betrothed's skills in the business of household management."

"Naturally," Julian murmured. "Then how may I serve you, my lord?"

Hugh drummed his fingers on the desk. "You have a certain facility with graceful compliments and flowery words, do you not, Julian?"

Julian affected an air of modesty. "I do dabble a bit in poetry and I have written several songs, sir."

"Excellent. I need a list of compliments."

Julian looked baffled. "A list?"

"Three or four should do nicely."

Julian cleared his throat. "Uh, what sort of compliments do you prefer, my lord? Would you like me to concentrate on your skills with a sword or your triumphs in battle? I can do a nice line or two about your loyalty and honor."

Hugh stared at him. "What in the name of the devil are you talking about?"

"You said you wanted compliments, my lord."

"Not for myself," Hugh snapped. "For my betrothed."

Laughter appeared in Julian's eyes. "Ah. I see."

Hugh clasped his hands on the desk and frowned in concentration. "I am skilled at many things, messenger, but not at inventing the sort of compliments that please ladies. I wish you to draw up a list of pretty phrases that I may memorize and speak to my bride. Do you comprehend me?"

"Aye, my lord." Julian smiled complacently. "And may I say, sir, that, as always, you have employed the most skilled artisan for the task. I promise that you will not be disappointed."

*T*he following night Alice paced the carpet of Hugh's large bedchamber and tried to still the fluttery sensation in her belly. She had never felt more unsettled in her life than she was at this moment. She and Hugh were no longer partners in a bargain, they were husband and wife.

She stalked past the fire and paused once more at the door, listening for the sound of footsteps in the hall. She had dismissed her women almost an hour ago. Hugh should have come to her by now.

She wondered if he was deliberately making her wait, thinking to arouse her passions to a fever pitch. If that was his purpose, she thought, he was due for a surprise.

She was not growing more lovesick by the moment. She was becoming quite irritated.

She had had enough of Hugh's clever stratagems, she thought resentfully. It had been a very long day.

It had begun with the burial of Calvert of Oxwick. He had been laid to rest in the small graveyard behind the village church. Alice, Benedict, Hugh, and Joan had been the only ones present. The priest, Geoffrey, who had accompanied Hugh and Benedict to Scarcliffe, said the prayers for the dead over the grave. No one had shed any tears.

A few hours later, shortly before noon, Geoffrey had conducted the wedding service in front of the church door.

The endless festivities and an elaborate banquet had followed. Alice was so exhausted from smiling and being gracious to everyone that she had thought to fall asleep the instant she got anywhere near a bed.

But the moment she had been left alone in the bedchamber to await Hugh a deep uncertainty had driven out her exhaustion. She stopped pacing and went to sit on a stool in front of the fire. She gazed into the flames and tried to envision her future.

It appeared shrouded in a fog that was not unlike the mist that clung to Scarcliffe that day. There was only one clear certainty.

She was Hugh's wife.

A small shiver went through her. Alice drew the folds of her night robe more closely around her. All her plans for the future had been irrevocably altered. There was no going back, no changing her mind. She was committed.

The door opened without warning behind her.

She turned her head quickly as Hugh entered the chamber. "Welcome, my lord."

She was relieved to note that he was alone. Apparently Hugh had decided to eschew the custom of a boisterous escort to the bridal bed.

"Good evening . . . wife." Hugh lingered over the last word, as though he found it of great interest.

His black leather boots made no sound on the carpet as he came toward her. He was truly a creature of the night, a dark sorcerer who absorbed the firelight and gave off shadows.

He wore one of the new black tunics embroidered with amber thread that Alice had had made for him. His black hair was brushed straight back from his high forehead. His eyes were brooding in the firelight.

Alice jumped to her feet. She glanced at the table where

two cups and a flagon had been set out. "Would you care for some wine?"

"Aye. Thank you." Hugh stopped in front of the fire. He held out his hands to the blaze and watched Alice as she poured the wine. He cleared his throat.

"Have I ever told you that your hair is the color of a brilliant sunset in that moment before it is enveloped by the night?" Hugh asked quite casually.

The flagon trembled in Alice's hand. She felt the blush rise in her cheeks. "Nay, my lord. You never mentioned it."

" 'Tis true."

"Thank you, my lord."

Hugh's brows rose as the wine splashed into a cup. "You are anxious."

"Is that so very strange under the circumstances, sir?"

He shrugged. "Mayhap not for most women, but you are not like most women, Alice."

"And you are not like most men, sir." She turned to him with the cup in her hand.

His fingers brushed lightly against hers as he took the wine. "In what way am I different from other men?"

This was not the sort of conversation she had planned to have on her wedding night, Alice thought. She wondered if he expected a serious answer to his question or if he was engaged in some new stratagem designed to disconcert her.

"You are more intelligent than the other men I have known," she said cautiously. "Deeper. More difficult to comprehend at times and yet, at other times, much clearer."

"Is that why you married me?" Hugh met her eyes over the rim of the wine cup. "Because I am more clever than other men? More interesting? Do I intrigue your curiosity? Arouse your questioning nature? Do you regard me as an unusual object, one worthy of adding to your collection, mayhap?"

A trickle of unease went through Alice. She was suddenly very wary. "Nay, not precisely."

Hugh began to prowl the chamber, wine cup in hand. "Did you marry me because I proved useful?"

She frowned. "Nay."

"I did rescue you and your brother from your uncle's hall," he reminded her.

"Aye, but I did not marry you because of that."

"Was it to gain permanent possession of the green stone, mayhap?" Hugh asked.

"Of course not." Alice scowled. "What a ridiculous notion, my lord. I would hardly marry merely to possess that strange bit of crystal."

"Are you certain?"

"Quite certain," Alice said through set teeth.

Hugh paused near one of the posts of the huge, black bed. He smiled his dangerous smile. "Was it because of the passion, then?"

Anger flared in Alice. "You are taunting me again, sir."

"I merely seek information."

"Bah. You believe that I would wed you simply for the pleasure of a few kisses?"

"Not for the kisses alone," he mused, "but for what follows upon them. You are possessed of a most passionate nature, madam."

"Sir, this has gone much too far."

"And there is your great curiosity." His voice roughened. "Your appetite for sensuality has been whetted and you wish to experience more of it. The only practical way of doing so is in the marriage bed, is that not true?"

Alice was stunned. "You did it deliberately, did you not? 'Twas all a stratagem. I had begun to suspect as much."

"What did you suspect?"

"That you kissed me and touched me and made love to me until I was breathless because you thought to ensnare me with passion."

"If you think that what you have experienced thus far is interesting, wait until you discover how much more there is to learn of the subject. Mayhap you should keep a pen and some parchment beside the bed so that you can record your observations."

"Oh, you are a demon, my lord." She slammed her cup down on the table. She clenched her hands into fists. "But you are wrong if you think I would have wed you simply to secure more of your lovemaking."

"Are you certain?"

"I do not comprehend your goal in this unpleasant conversation. Nor will I participate in it." She started determinedly toward the door.

"Where do you think you're going?"

"To my own chamber." She wrapped her fingers around the iron door handle. "When you have emerged from this odd mood, you may send word to me."

"What is odd about a man wishing to know why his wife married him?"

Alice whirled around, outraged. "You are far too intelligent to play the fool, sir. You know full well why I married you. I did so because I love you."

Hugh went utterly still. Something dark and desperate swirled in his eyes.

"Do you?" he finally whispered.

Alice saw the lonely hunger in him and forgot all about escaping to her own bedchamber. She knew the depths of his emotions because she had experienced them herself.

"My lord, you are not nearly so alone in this world as you seem to think," she said softly. She released the doorknob and ran to him.

"*Alice.*"

He caught her up in his arms, holding her so tightly that she could not breathe.

Then, without a word, he untied her night robe and let it fall to the floor. Alice trembled as he put her down on the white linen sheets.

He jerked off his own clothing, tossing them aside in a careless heap.

When he stood before her, Alice drew in her breath at the sight of his heavily aroused body. A torrent of emotion washed through her. She was disturbed, excited, and apprehensive, all at once. She reached out to catch hold of his hand.

"My wife." He sprawled on top of her, crushing her into the bedding.

She glimpsed the aching need and the raw passion in his golden eyes as he bent his head to take her mouth. She knew in that instant that the turbulent gales that howled at the core of his being had been freed at last.

She was lost in the storm of his embrace. It was unlike anything she had yet known with him. This was no slow, calculated seduction. This was a furious ride on the winds of a savage tempest. She was buffeted and tossed about until she could barely breathe.

She was aware of his callused hand on her breast. The instant her nipple firmed, Hugh took it into his mouth. His teeth grazed lightly across the sensitive bud. Alice shuddered.

A ragged groan surged through Hugh's chest. His hand went lower, flattening across her belly, searching out the soft, tangled thicket. She gasped and squeezed her eyes shut when she felt him moisten his fingers in the dampness that material-ized between her legs.

And then, before she could catch her breath, he was part-ing her thighs, settling himself between them. Big, he was so *big*. And warm. And hard. Alice felt as though she were being swallowed alive. The words of his beautiful compliment came back to her. *Sunset before it is enveloped by the night.*

Hugh levered himself up on his elbows to look down at

her. His features were starkly drawn, his eyes brilliant in the firelight. He captured her face between his strong hands.

"Tell me again that you love me."

"I love you." She smiled tremulously up at him, unafraid. In that moment she could see the secrets of his soul. *You need me,* she thought, *just as much as I need you. Someday I pray you will comprehend that truth.*

He surged into her with stunning force.

Chapter 17

She loved him.

A long time later Hugh lay back against the plump pillows and contemplated the embers on the hearth. He was aware of a curious sense of peace. It was as though the dark storm winds that had raged within him for so long had quieted at last.

She loved him.

Hugh savored the memory of Alice's passionate declaration. She was not the kind of woman who would say such words lightly, he assured himself. She would not say them at all unless she believed them to be true.

He stirred and stretched cautiously in the great bed, not wanting to awaken Alice. She was snuggled close against him, her hips fitted neatly into the curve of his body.

Her skin was so soft, he thought. He touched the curve of her thigh with a sense of deep wonder. So warm. And her fragrance was more compelling than the rarest of spices.

She shifted slightly, responding to his touch even in her sleep. He tightened his arm around her when she nestled closer. He had chosen well, he thought. Alice was everything she had appeared to be that night when she had bravely faced him in her uncle's hall and dared to bargain for the future of herself and her brother.

Everything and more. He was the most fortunate of men, Hugh told himself. He had hoped for a wife who possessed the qualities of courage, honor, and intelligence that were so important to him. In addition he had gotten one who loved him with a sweet, hot passion that took away his breath.

"You look pleased with yourself, my lord," Alice murmured in a drowsy voice. "What are you thinking?"

He looked down at her. "That, contrary to your early fears, I was in no danger of being cheated when I paid your bride price. You were definitely worth two full chests of spices."

Alice gave a muffled giggle. "Sir, you are a rogue and an unchivalrous scoundrel."

She scrambled to her knees, grabbed a pillow, and began to pummel him unmercifully.

Hugh gave a shout of laughter as he made a halfhearted attempt to defend himself. "I surrender."

"I want more than surrender." Alice whacked him again with the fluffy weapon. "I want an apology."

He grabbed the pillow from her hands and tossed it aside. "How about a compliment instead?"

She pursed her lips, considering the matter closely. "I will have to hear it before I can determine if it will satisfy me as much as an apology."

"Your breasts are as sweet and round as fresh summer peaches." Hugh cupped one gently.

"That is a very nice compliment," Alice conceded.

"There are more where that one came from," he promised.

"Hmm."

He tugged her down on top of him. She tumbled across his chest, warm and soft and so enticingly female. He stroked the edge of her fine-boned cheek. Memories of the day he had saved her from the robbers in Ipstoke came to mind. He recalled the way she had run to him. *As if she had known, even then, that she belonged in his arms.*

"Many more," he whispered.

Alice folded her arms on his chest. "Well, my lord, compliments are certainly very pleasant and I shall look forward to hearing more of them, but I think that in this case they will not do."

"You still want the apology?"

"Nay." She chuckled. "What I want is a boon."

"A boon?"

"Aye."

"What sort of boon?" he asked, suddenly cautious. He threaded his fingers through her tousled hair. She looked so lovely lying here in his bed. He shuddered to think how if it had not been for an old legend and the whim of fate, he might never have found her.

Then again, Hugh thought, mayhap he had been destined to find her from the day of his birth.

Alice smiled beatifically. "I don't know yet. I wish to hold this boon in reserve, so to speak, until such time as I decide to collect it."

"I shall no doubt regret this, but I am in no mood to bargain with you again tonight. You may have my promise of a future boon, madam."

She batted her lashes outrageously. "You are too kind, my lord."

"I know. 'Tis no doubt one of my greatest failings."

*T*he following morning Dunstan spat into the dirt with his usual gusto and eyed the sagging door of the storeroom. "A fine day, m'lord."

"Aye." Hugh surveyed the broken door with a sense of

deep satisfaction. "No rain in sight. That means we'll be able to finish the work here in the bailey without delay."

He was pleased with the progress that had been made in such a short time on the manor of Scarcliffe. The last of the villagers' cottages had been repaired. The new refuse ditch was finished and the bridge across the stream stood firm once more. The first items on his list of priorities were completed.

It was time to see to less critical matters here in the keep itself. Matters such as the drooping storeroom door. The clang and clash of tools rang out across the yard.

"No shortage of men," Dunstan observed.

Hugh had been surprised at first by the number of villagers who had arrived early that morning to assist with the repairs. He had not ordered the men to appear. He had simply sent word that there was work for those who could spare the time from their farms.

Virtually every able-bodied male in Scarcliffe had presented himself, tools in hand, within the hour. They had immediately set to work with an astoundingly cheerful mien.

"We can thank my wife for the number of laborers we have here today," Hugh said dryly. "She seems to have made a favorable impression on the villagers while I was in London."

"Lady Alice is swiftly becoming as much of a legend as yourself, m'lord. It did not go unnoticed that she saved Young John, the miller's son, when the healer had given up the effort."

"I heard about that," Hugh said quietly.

"Nor has anyone forgotten that scene in the church when she ordered Calvert of Oxwick out of the pulpit."

"Memorable, indeed."

"And she was most industrious in overseeing the repairs you ordered done while you were gone."

Hugh smiled wryly. "Alice is very good at managing things."

"Aye. But I think it safe to say that the incident that

warranted that she would become a true legend was the rescue of Rivenhall."

Hugh grunted, his indulgent mood dissolving in an instant. "You mean the villagers were awed by her bravery?"

"Aye, m'lord. *Awed* is certainly the word for it."

"I'll grant that my wife does not lack courage but she did not rescue Rivenhall alone. She had you and most of my men with her. Eduard of Lockton knew he was no match for such a force, nor would he have challenged me by taking up arms against my betrothed."

"It was not the lady's bold ride into Rivenhall that gained the admiration of one and all." Dunstan grinned. "It was the fact that she survived your temper afterward that has us awestruck."

"By the bones of the devil," Hugh grumbled.

Dunstan shot him a knowing look. "Some say that she wields a mystical power over you."

"Is that so?" Hot memories of the night just past burned in Hugh's mind. He smiled. "Mayhap those that whisper of her magical talents have the right of it."

Dunstan quirked a brow. "Marriage appears to have had an interesting effect on your temper, m'lord."

Hugh was saved from having to reply by a shout from one of the watchtowers.

"Three visitors approach, m'lord," one of the men called down from his perch.

"Visitors?" Hugh frowned. "Who would come to visit Scarcliffe?"

"You are not entirely without friends," Dunstan drawled.

"None would have come without sending a message first." Hugh looked up at the guard in the watchtower. "Armed men?"

"Nay, m'lord." The guard studied the road from Scarcliffe. "One man wearing only a sword. He is accompanied by a woman and a child."

"*Damnation.*" A sense of deep foreboding swept over Hugh. He swung around to face the open gate. "Surely he would not be so stupid as to pay a neighborly visit."

"Who?" Dunstan asked.

The question was answered a moment later as Vincent of Rivenhall rode through into the bailey. Lady Emma and young Reginald were at his side.

Hugh groaned in disgust. "Can a man not even be allowed to enjoy the morning after his wedding night in peace?"

"It would seem that things have changed in the history of Scarcliffe," Dunstan murmured.

Work came to a halt as everyone in the vicinity turned to stare at the newcomers. Grooms rushed up to take the heads of the visitors' horses.

Hugh watched morosely as Vincent dismounted and turned to assist Emma from her mare. Young Reginald hopped down from his saddle and grinned at Hugh.

Vincent, his face set in lines of grim determination, took his wife's arm and walked forward as though he went to the gallows.

"Sir Hugh." He came to a halt in front of his reluctant host and nodded stiffly.

"I see you finally left off your jousting long enough to pay your estates a visit," Hugh said laconically. "What a pity you did not do so earlier. You would have saved my wife a deal of trouble."

Vincent flushed deeply and set his jaw. "I comprehend that I am in your debt, Sir Hugh."

"If you are in anyone's debt, it is my wife's. I do not want you laboring under the assumption that you owe me a damn thing."

"Believe me, I have no desire to be beholden to you, my lord." Vincent spoke through gritted teeth. "Nevertheless, I must thank you for what you did for my wife and son."

"Save your thanks. I do not want them."

"Then I will give them to your lady," Vincent snarled.

"That won't be necessary. Lady Alice is at work in her study chamber this morning." It occurred to Hugh that he had better rid the yard of the Rivenhall crowd before Alice realized they had visitors. "She does not care to be interrupted."

Emma spoke up quickly. "We understand that you were wed yesterday, my lord. We have come to offer you our congratulations." She gave him a tremulous but gracious smile.

Hugh barely inclined his head in acknowledgment. "You will forgive me if I do not declare a banquet to celebrate your unexpected presence in my bailey, madam. In truth we are not able to entertain at the moment. We are concerned with more pressing matters."

Emma's face fell.

Vincent glowered furiously. "Damn your eyes, cousin, I will discharge this debt if it is the last thing I do."

"You may do so by seeing to the welfare of your own keep so that Scarcliffe never again finds itself obliged to defend Rivenhall lands." Hugh smiled thinly. "I'm certain you understand my feelings on the matter. Rescuing Rivenhall goes much against the grain."

"No more so than having to be the recipient of Scarcliffe's assistance goes against mine," Vincent retorted.

"*Lady Emma. Lady Emma.*" Alice's cheery voice got the attention of everyone in the bailey. "Welcome. How wonderful that you have come."

"God's teeth," Hugh muttered. So much for getting Vincent and his family out of the bailey before Alice learned of their presence.

He and the others raised their eyes to the tower window. Alice leaned partway out of the narrow opening, madly waving a kerchief in greeting. Even from this distance, Hugh could see that her face was alight with excitement.

"You are just in time to join us for the midday meal," Alice shouted down to Emma.

"Thank you, my lady," Emma called back. "We are delighted to be able to dine with you."

"I'll be right down." Alice disappeared from the window.

"Blood of Satan," Vincent said sourly. "I was afraid of this."

"Aye," Hugh muttered. It was clear that Alice and Emma had established a fast friendship.

" 'Tis a wise man who knows when to retreat," Dunstan offered helpfully.

Hugh and Vincent both turned on him with ferocious scowls.

Dunstan spread his hands in a placating gesture. "I'll see to the horses."

*T*wo hours later Alice stood with Emma at the window of the study chamber and watched anxiously as Hugh and Vincent crossed the yard together. The two men were headed for the stables.

"Well, at least they did not go at each other's throats with their eating knives during the meal," Alice commented.

They had dined in an atmosphere of tension that could not have been good for anyone's digestion, but there had been no outbreak of violence, much to Alice's relief. She and Emma had kept the conversation moving along at a brisk pace while Hugh and Vincent had downed their food in grim silence. The one or two remarks exchanged between the men had been in the nature of sharp, taunting barbs.

"Aye." Emma's brows drew together in an uneasy expression as she watched the men enter the stables. "They are both innocent victims of that old feud between their families. Neither of them had anything to do with what happened all those years ago, but their elders burdened them both with the anger and the demand for vengeance."

Alice glanced at her. "What do you know of the history of the feud?"

"Merely what everyone else knows. Matthew of Rivenhall was betrothed to another when he seduced Lady Margaret, your husband's mother. He went off to France for nearly a year, during which time Hugh was born. When Sir Matthew returned he apparently went to see Margaret."

"And died?"

"The men of Rivenhall are convinced that she fed him poison that night and then drank the evil potion herself."

Alice sighed. "So 'tis unlikely that Sir Matthew went to see her to tell her that he intended to wed her, then."

Emma smiled sadly. "Lord Vincent assures me that there was no possibility of his uncle breaking his betrothal to the heiress. The match was a rich one and both families wanted it. But mayhap Sir Matthew intended to keep Lady Margaret as his leman."

"And she was too proud to continue as his lover while he wed another." Alice shook her head. "I can comprehend her feelings on the matter."

"Aye." Emma met her eyes. "But I doubt that one of your gentle nature would have resorted to poison in order to obtain your vengeance. And you surely would not have taken the potion yourself, thereby leaving your infant son motherless."

"Nay, I would not have done that, no matter how angry I was." She touched her belly with fleeting fingers. She might even now be carrying Hugh's babe. The thought sent a wave of fierce protectiveness through her.

"Neither of us would have done such a thing," Emma whispered.

Alice thought of Calvert of Oxwick, dead by poison. She shivered as though an icy wind had touched her. "What if Lady Margaret did not do it, either?"

Emma gave her a bemused look. "What do you mean? There is no other explanation for what happened that night."

"You are wrong, Emma," Alice said slowly. "There is one other possibility. What if someone else fed Sir Matthew and Margaret the poison?"

"For what reason? It makes no sense. No one else had a motive."

"I suppose you are right and in any event we cannot know the truth at this late date." *Unless, after all these years, the poisoner had returned to Scarcliffe,* she thought. *But why choose the monk as a victim?*

Thoughts churned in Alice's brain, making her suddenly restless. She turned away from the window, crossed the chamber to her desk, and picked up the green crystal. "Would you care to see my collection of stones, Lady Emma?"

"Stones? I did not know that anyone collected stones."

"I intend to write a book describing the various kinds."

"Really?" Emma glanced down into the bailey and froze. "Dear heaven, what are they doing?"

"Who?"

"Our husbands." Emma's eyes widened. She clapped her hands to her mouth in horror. "They have drawn their swords against each other."

"They would not dare." Alice sprang for the window and leaned out to get a clear view.

She saw at once that Emma was right. In the center of the bailey, Hugh and Vincent faced each other. Their bare swords gleamed in the sun. Neither man had donned helm or hauberk, but each carried a small shield. The villagers who had been doing repairs and several of the men-at-arms had put down their tools. A crowd quickly gathered to watch.

"Stop that nonsense at once," Alice yelled from the window. "I will not have it, do you hear me?"

The crowd in the bailey looked up at her. Several of the men hid wide grins. Alice saw a number of them turn to one another and mutter behind their hands. She knew they were placing wagers.

Hugh glanced at the window with a quelling glare. "Go back to your stones and beetles, madam. This is men's sport."

"I do not want any swordplay between you and our guest, my lord." Alice gripped the windowsill very tightly. "Find some other way to entertain Sir Vincent."

Vincent looked up. Even from this distance it was possible to see the feral quality of his smile. "I assure you, my lady, I am well content with this entertainment. Indeed, I cannot think of anything I would enjoy more than a bit of sword practice with your lord."

Emma glowered down at her husband. "Sir, we are guests in this house. I bid you respect Lady Alice's request."

"But her lord has suggested this sport," Vincent called. "How can I refuse?"

Alice leaned farther out the window. "Sir Hugh, kindly inform your guest that you wish to pursue other sport with him."

"What other sport would you suggest, madam?" Hugh asked innocently. "Shall we engage in some practice with the lance, mayhap?"

Alice lost her temper. "Show Sir Vincent the new refuse ditch, if you cannot think of anything more entertaining. I do not care what you do, but I will not allow the two of you to stage a joust in this keep. Do I make myself clear, sir?"

A breathless silence emanated from the bailey. All eyes were on the tower window.

Hugh studied her very intently for a moment. "You will not allow it?" he finally repeated carefully.

Alice took a deep breath. Her fingers dug into the sill. "You heard me. 'Tis not a seemly way in which to amuse a guest."

"Madam, it may have escaped your notice, but I am lord of this keep. I will entertain my guest as I see fit."

"Do you recall the boon you promised me last night, sir?"

"*Alice.*"

"I am claiming it now, my lord."

Hugh's expression was more dangerous than it had been at any time during the meal. He held himself quite still for a few taut seconds and then, with a lethal *whoosh,* he rammed his blade back into its scabbard.

"Very well, madam," he said without inflection. "You have claimed the boon and it has been granted." He smiled coldly. "I shall show Sir Vincent the village ditch."

Vincent gave a roar of laughter, sheathed his sword, and clapped Hugh roughly on the shoulder. "Do not concern yourself, sir," he said, not without sympathy. "I have every confidence that you will soon adjust to married life."

A short while later Hugh rode past the convent in the company of the man he had been taught to hate since birth. Neither he nor Vincent had spoken since they had ridden out of Scarcliffe Keep.

"Are you actually going to show me the village ditch?" Vincent asked dryly.

Hugh grimaced. "Nay. In truth there is a matter we should no doubt discuss." He had been debating how much to tell Vincent concerning the murder of Calvert and he had finally come to a conclusion.

"If you intend to lecture me further on my duties to Rivenhall, you may save your breath. I have finally acquired enough money from the jousts to enable me to see to my estates. I do not intend to leave them again."

Hugh shrugged. "That is your affair. But as we are neighbors whether we like it or not, you should know that murder has been done very recently on these lands."

"Murder?" Vincent shot him a startled glance. "Who was killed?"

"I discovered the body of a wandering monk named Calvert of Oxwick in one of the cliff caves. I believe he may have been killed by robbers."

"Why would anyone kill a monk?"

Hugh hesitated briefly. "Because he was searching for the Stones of Scarcliffe."

Vincent snorted in disbelief. "That is nothing but an old tale. If there ever were any Stones of Scarcliffe, they have long since disappeared."

"Aye, but there are always those who believe in legends. The monk may have been one."

"And the murderer?"

"He may have also believed in the legend," Hugh said softly.

Vincent frowned. "If a thief killed the monk for the sake of a nonexistent treasure, he has no doubt realized his mistake by now. Likely he has already departed these lands."

"Aye. But in light of the fact that you've decided to return to your manor and assume your responsibilities, I thought you might want to take note of the incident. Neither of us needs a murderer in the neighborhood."

"You wield sarcasm as well as you do a sword, Sir Hugh."

" 'Tis the only weapon my wife has seen fit to leave me today," Hugh muttered.

Vincent was quiet for a moment. The hooves of the horses thudded softly in the dirt. Several of the nuns at work in the convent gardens glanced at the pair. The miller's son waved energetically from the shelter of his parents' cottage.

"Sir Hugh, Sir Hugh," the boy cried happily.

Hugh lifted a hand in greeting. Young John laughed with delight.

Vincent watched the boy disappear into the cottage. Then he looked at Hugh. "They say that Erasmus of Thornewood is near death."

"Aye."

"I shall miss him," Vincent said sincerely. "Other than his demand that you and I not go to war with each other, he has been a good liege."

"Very good."

Vincent glanced around at the repaired cottages. "You have accomplished much here in the past few months, Sir Hugh."

"Aye. With the aid of my wife." Hugh knew a deep sense of pride and satisfaction. Order and stability had been brought to Scarcliffe. In the spring, it would begin to know prosperity as well.

"Tell me," Vincent said, "do you still hunger for Rivenhall, or are you content with these lands?"

Hugh raised his brows. "You are asking if I will take Rivenhall when my oath to Erasmus is severed by his death?"

"I am asking if you will *attempt* to take it," Vincent corrected dryly.

"Attempt?" Laughter welled up out of nowhere within Hugh. It roared forth from the depths of his being. It rang in the street, drawing the attention of the nuns on the other side of the convent wall.

"I'm glad you find the question amusing." Vincent watched him with wary eyes. "I'm still waiting for your answer."

Hugh managed to control his mirth. "I suspect that Rivenhall is safe so long as my wife calls your wife friend. I do not care to contemplate the endless scolding I would be obliged to endure were I to lay siege to Rivenhall."

Vincent blinked owlishly and then he started to grin. "Something tells me that you have already begun to settle in nicely to the life of a married man."

"There are worse fates."

"Aye. There are."

.   .   .

The following morning dawned dark with ominous clouds. Hugh was forced to light a candle on his desk so that he and Benedict could work.

Hugh was midway through an examination of a list of spices when he noticed that the flame of the taper was shimmering in an odd manner. He put down his quill and rubbed his eyes with thumb and forefinger. When he opened them again he saw that the flame had grown very large. Too large.

"Is something wrong, sir?" Benedict leaned across the desk, his expression one of concern.

"Nay." Hugh shook his head to clear it of the cobwebs that seemed to have enveloped his wits.

Benedict's features started to run together. His eyes and nose flowed into his mouth.

"Lord Hugh?"

Hugh forced himself to concentrate. Benedict's face returned to normal. "Have you finished those sums?"

"Aye." Benedict pushed aside the cups of green pottage that had been brought to the chamber a short while ago. "I will have the amounts ready for Julian to take to London on the morrow. Sir, are you certain you are well?"

"Why in the name of the devil is that candle dancing about? There is no draft in here."

Benedict glanced at the candle. "The flame appears steady, sir."

Hugh stared at it. The flame was leaping wildly. It was also turning a strange shade of pink. Pink flames?

He tore his gaze from the candle and focused on the tapestry that hung on the wall. The unicorn woven into the center came alive even as he watched. It turned its graceful head and regarded him with a politely curious expression.

"The pottage," Hugh whispered.

"My lord?"

Hugh looked at the half-empty cup of pottage in front of

him. A terrible premonition pierced his fogged brain. "Did you drink any?" His voice was a harsh whisper of sound.

"Of the green pottage?" Benedict's features wavered, just as the flame did. "Nay. I do not care for the stuff. I know Alice believes it to be very beneficial to the humors, but I dislike it. I usually throw it down the nearest garderobe shaft."

"*Alice.*" Hugh grabbed the edge of his desk as the chamber began to spin slowly around him. "The pottage."

"What is wrong, my lord?"

"Get her. Get Alice. Tell her . . . tell her . . . *poison.*"

Benedict leaped to his feet. "Sir, that is impossible. How dare you accuse her of being a poisoner?"

"Not Alice." Hugh could barely manage the words. "This is Rivenhall work. My own fault. Should never have let them into the keep—"

As he crumpled heavily to the floor Hugh was dimly aware of Benedict's footsteps pounding out the door and down the hall. And then the unicorn walked out of the tapestry and came across the chamber to gaze solemnly down at him.

"This is how it was for your father and your mother," the unicorn said gently.

Chapter 18

"My lord, I am going to stick my fingers down your throat. I pray you will not bite them off." Alice crouched beside Hugh, turned his head, and pried open his mouth.

A moment later Hugh groaned and obligingly discharged the contents of his stomach into the chamber pot that Benedict held for him.

Alice waited until the first spasms began to ease and then she inserted her fingers down his throat a second time.

Hugh convulsed violently. The little that remained in his belly spewed forth.

Benedict looked at her, fear in his eyes. "Will he die?"

"Nay," Alice vowed fiercely. "He will not die if I can help it. Get me water, Benedict. A large flagon of it. And milk. Hurry."

"Aye." Benedict grabbed his staff, lurched to his feet, and rushed from the chamber.

"And Benedict?"

He paused, one hand on the door frame. "Aye?"

"Tell no one about this, do you comprehend me? Say that I have requested the water and milk so that I may wash my face."

"But what if the pottage is poisoned? Everyone will have taken their morning cup."

"The pottage was not poisoned," Alice said quietly. "I drank a full cup of it myself only a short while ago. So did my maid."

"But—"

"Hurry, Benedict."

He hurried from the chamber.

Hugh opened his eyes briefly. His amber eyes burned. "Alice."

"You are a very large man and you did not even drink all of the pottage, my lord. I have got most of what you did consume back out of you. You will live."

"I will kill him," Hugh vowed. He closed his eyes again. "My oath to Erasmus will not protect him after this."

"Who are you talking about?"

"Vincent. He tried to poison me."

"Hugh, you cannot know that for certain."

"Who else?" Another spasm overtook Hugh. His powerful body shuddered but there was nothing left in him. "It must have been him."

Benedict pounded around the edge of the door, breathless from the dash downstairs to the kitchens. He carried two flagons in one hand. "I have both milk and water."

"Excellent." Alice reached for the first flagon. "Help me get this down him."

Hugh slitted his eyes. "No offense, madam, but I do not have much of an appetite at the moment."

"My mother wrote that it is wise to give great quantities of liquids to a victim of poison. It rebalances the bodily humors." Alice cradled Hugh's head in her lap. "Please, my lord. I pray you will drink this."

There was still a sheen of sweat on Hugh's brow but humor glinted briefly in his gaze as he looked up at the curve of her breasts. "You know I am lost when you employ your fine manners. Very well, madam, I shall drink anything you please unless it be green in color."

Alice looked up at Benedict. "I do believe he is already feeling much better. Fetch Sir Dunstan. We will need his help to get my lord to his bedchamber."

"Aye." Benedict made for the door again.

"Devil's teeth," Hugh muttered. "I will not be carried like a child."

In the end he managed the length of the hall on his own two feet but it took Alice, Benedict, and Dunstan to support his weight. When he finally tumbled into his massive ebony bed, Hugh fell asleep instantly.

"*P*oison?" Dunstan stood at the foot of the bed, his hands bunched into huge fists at his sides. "Sir Hugh was given poison? Are you certain?"

"Aye." Alice frowned at him. "But you must say nothing of this for the moment, Sir Dunstan. Thus far only we four know the truth. I would have it stay that way for a time."

"Say nothing?" Dunstan stared at her as though she were mad. "I shall turn this damned keep upside down. I shall hang every servant in the kitchen one by one until I discover the person who put the brew into Sir Hugh's cup."

"Sir Dunstan—"

"Likely it came from Rivenhall." Dunstan's brow furrowed as he worked the problem out to his satisfaction. "Aye, that would explain it. Before he took his leave yesterday, Sir Vincent no doubt bribed a servant here in Scarcliffe Keep to put the foul herbs in the pottage."

"Sir Dunstan, that is quite enough." Alice rose from the stool beside the bed. "I shall handle this."

"Nay, madam. Sir Hugh would not want you involved in a bloody business such as this."

"I am already involved." Alice gritted her teeth to keep her voice to a whisper. "And I know far more about poison than you do, sir. I shall discover the means by which this deed was done. Then, mayhap, we shall know who to blame."

"Sir Vincent of Rivenhall is to blame," Dunstan stated.

"We cannot be certain of that." Alice began to pace the chamber. "Now, then, we know that only Sir Hugh's pottage was poisoned. That means that the herbs were either placed in his cup while it was carried to his study chamber or—"

"I'll find that traitorous servant," Dunstan interrupted furiously. "I'll have him hung by noon."

"Or," Alice added quickly, "the poison was already in the cup when the pottage was poured into it."

Dunstan's face went blank with incomprehension. "Already in the cup?"

"Aye, sir. The kitchens are a busy place. A few drops of a very strong poison placed in the bottom of the cup would likely go unnoticed when the pottage was poured into the vessel."

"Would a few drops be sufficient to kill a man?"

"There are some brews made from certain herbs that are so virulent that they retain their lethal properties even when distilled. The hot pottage could have activated such a brew."

Some brews, not many, Alice added silently. And the herbs used in such bitter potions were rare, according to her mother's treatise.

Benedict looked at Alice across Hugh's sleeping body. " 'Tis no secret which dishes Sir Hugh uses. 'Twould be easy enough for a poisoner to choose his cup from among the others."

"Aye." Alice continued to stride back and forth, hands clasped behind her back. "Sir Dunstan, I will conduct this investigation, do you comprehend me? Much rides on the outcome. War with Rivenhall will cost many lives. I will not have those deaths on my hands if there is an alternative."

"Rest assured, madam, there will be no alternative when Sir Hugh awakes." Dunstan's expression was savage. "He will have his vengeance as soon as he can sit a horse."

Alice glanced at Hugh. Even in sleep there was an unrelenting implacability about him. No one knew better than she that once Hugh set out upon a course of action, nothing could halt him.

She swung around to face Dunstan and Benedict. "Then I must act quickly."

*A*lice closed her mother's book, folded her hands on her desk, and regarded the young kitchen lad who stood before her.

"You took the green pottage to Sir Hugh this morning, Luke?"

"Aye, m'lady." Luke grinned proudly. "I have been assigned the duty of taking his pottage to him every morning."

"Who instructed you in that duty?"

Luke gave her a quizzical look. "Master Elbert, of course."

"Tell me, Luke, did you stop to talk to anyone on your way to Lord Hugh's study chamber today?"

"Nay, m'lady." Alarm appeared in Luke's eyes. "I did not pause at all, I swear it. I went directly to his chamber, just as I was bid. I vow, the pottage was still warm when I got there. If it was cold when his lordship drank it, it was not my fault, m'lady."

"Calm yourself, Luke. The pottage was warm enough," Alice assured him gently.

Luke brightened. "Lord Hugh is pleased with my service?"

"I would say that he was quite astonished by it this morning."

"In that case, mayhap Master Elbert will soon allow me to serve in the great hall," Luke said happily. " 'Tis my greatest ambition. 'Twill make my mother proud."

"I'm certain that you will realize your goal one of these days, Luke. You seem a determined lad."

"I am, my lady," Luke assured her with great fervor. "Lord Hugh told me that the secret of every man's true strength, regardless of his station in life, lies in his determination and will. If they be powerful, he can achieve his ends."

In spite of her anxious mood, Alice smiled fleetingly at the thought of Hugh dispensing advice to a kitchen boy. "That certainly has the ring of something Lord Hugh would say. When did he give you this bit of wisdom?"

"Yesterday morning when I asked him how he could stomach the green pottage every day. I never touch the stuff myself."

Alice sighed. "You may go back to your duties now, Luke."

"Aye, m'lady."

Alice waited until Luke had bustled out of her study chamber before she opened the handbook again. One question had been answered, she thought. Luke was an honest boy. She believed him when he claimed that he had not met anyone en route to Hugh's study chamber.

That meant the poison had not been added to the cup after the pottage had been poured into it.

Which, in turn, told her that she was searching for a poison that could have been deposited, unnoticed, in the bottom of the clean cup. It would need to be a brew so powerful that only a few drops were required to achieve illness or death.

She squeezed her eyes shut at the thought that she could so easily have lost Hugh. A terrible shiver of dread went through her.

She had to discover the would-be murderer before he or

she could strike again. She had to find the poisoner before Hugh laid siege to his blood kin and destroyed forever any hope of peace between Rivenhall and Scarcliffe.

Alice forced herself to concentrate on the notes her mother had made concerning the herb banewort.

When prepared according to this recipe, a small amount can ease severe pain in the bowel. Too much, however, will kill . . .

A discreet knock on the door announced another visitor.

"Enter," Alice called, not taking her eyes from the page.

Elbert stuck his head around the door. "You sent for me, my lady?"

"Aye, Elbert." Alice glanced up. "I want you to see to it that every dish and cup in this household is scrubbed today before another meal is served."

"But all of the dishes and cups are always washed after every meal, my lady, just as you specified," Elbert stammered, clearly confused by the instruction.

"I know, Elbert, but I want them washed again today before the midday meal. Is that clear?"

"Aye, m'lady. Before the meal. I shall give the orders at once. Will there be anything else?"

Alice hesitated. "Lord Hugh will not dine with the household today. He is in his bedchamber and does not wish to be disturbed."

Elbert was immediately alarmed. "Is something wrong, my lady?"

"Nay. He has taken a slight chill. I have given him a tonic. He should be well on the morrow."

Elbert's face cleared. "Shall I send some more green pottage to his chamber?"

"I do not think that will be necessary. Thank you, Elbert.

You may go. Do not forget to have the dishes, mugs, and cups washed immediately."

"Aye, my lady. It will be done at once." Elbert bowed and left to carry out his orders.

Alice shook off the morbid fears that threatened to overwhelm her. She turned another page of the handbook and studied her mother's neat script.

The water clock on her desk dripped slowly. Another hour passed.

A long while later, Alice closed her mother's journal and sat quietly for a long time. She considered what she had learned.

As she had suspected, the secrets of concocting a poison strong enough to be administered in the manner in which this one had been given were shrouded in mystery.

The fear of poison was common enough but in truth there was little real danger from it. The fact was, most poisons simply did not work well.

Contrary to what many people believed, the concocting of lethal potions was not a simple task. Only a skilled gardener knew the proper plants. Much study and experimentation were required to prepare the brews. Only an unusual herbalist, one who studied poisons and their antidotes in order to discover cures, for instance, or an alchemist seeking knowledge of the black arts, would bother to invest much time in the study of potions that could kill.

There were a number of practical problems involved in the creation of poisonous potions. It was exceedingly difficult to determine the proper dose. It was also extremely hard to refine the poison to the point where only a small amount was required to achieve results. And it was even more difficult to achieve a degree of reliability. Most poisons were notoriously unpredictable in their effects.

As her mother had written in the handbook, a person was

far more likely to fall ill and die from rancid food than true poison.

Alice mentally outlined her conclusions. There were not many people in the vicinity of Scarcliffe who could have created a deadly poison and then found a way to ensure that it was administered to its intended victim.

Nay, make that victims.

For there had been two, Alice reminded herself. Calvert of Oxwick had also been poisoned.

But who would want to kill both an irritating monk and a legendary knight? What was the link between them?

Alice pondered the matter for a long time.

The only thing that connected the victims so far as she could discern was an interest in the Stones of Scarcliffe. But once Hugh had gotten his hands on the green crystal, he had ceased to search for the rest of the treasure. He did not even believe in the existence of the rest of the fabled gems.

Calvert, on the other hand, had apparently believed the old tale. So much so that he had risked the treacherous caves of Scarcliffe to hunt for the treasure.

The two men shared no obvious bond that Alice could discern.

She wondered if the truth lay elsewhere in the past. There had, after all, in this region once been another case of poison.

A short, cheerful young novice ushered Alice into the prioress's study late that afternoon.

Joan rose, smiling, from the other side of her desk. "Lady Alice. I pray you will be seated. What brings you here at this hour?"

"I am sorry to disturb you, madam." Alice waited until the novice had closed the door. Then she sank down onto a wooden stool.

"Have you come alone?" Joan reseated herself.

"Aye. The servants believe that I have gone out for a late afternoon walk. I must return to the keep as soon as possible." She wanted to get back before Hugh awoke. "I will not take up much of your time."

"I am always pleased to see you, Alice, you know that." Joan folded her hands and studied her with gentle concern. "Is aught troubling you?"

"Aye, madam." Alice braced herself. "I must ask you some questions."

"About what?"

"About Sister Katherine, your healer."

Joan frowned. "You shall ask your questions of her directly. I shall send for her at once."

"*T*his is impossible." The skirts of Joan's habit rustled as she went swiftly along the stone corridor. "Sister Katherine is a trained healer. She would not poison anyone."

"Do you not find it odd that she has disappeared?" Alice asked.

"She must be somewhere here on the grounds of the convent."

"We have checked the chapel, the garden, and the still room. Where else could she be?"

"Mayhap she is meditating in her chamber and did not hear the novice I sent to knock on her door. Or she may be suffering from one of her bouts of melancholia. The medicine she takes for it sometimes puts her into a deep sleep."

"This is very troubling."

"Your suspicions are even more so," Joan said brusquely. "Sister Katherine has been with this convent for nearly thirty years."

"Aye, that is one of the facts that caused me to wonder if

she was somehow involved in all this." Alice glanced at the rows of wooden doors that lined the hall. Each was set with a grated window and opened onto a small, spare cell.

The hall was very still and silent. Most of the cells were empty at this time of the day. The nuns were busy at their various tasks in the gardens, the kitchens, the scriptorium, and the music chamber.

Joan glanced over her shoulder. "You said Lord Hugh's parents were poisoned nearly thirty years ago?"

"Aye. Everyone assumed his mother was the poisoner. She was said to be a woman scorned. But today I began to question that assumption."

"What makes you think that Sister Katherine would know anything about the incident other than whatever rumors came to her at the time?"

"Do you recall the day that I met her in the convent garden?"

"Of course."

"She said something at the time about how easily a man could sever a vow of betrothal. She seemed oddly bitter."

"I told you, Katherine suffers from melancholia. She frequently appears sad or bitter."

"Aye, but I believe that in this instance there was something personal about her reaction. She warned me not to put off my own wedding lest I be left abandoned."

"What of it?" Joan came to a halt in front of the last grated door. " 'Twas a practical bit of advice."

"She spoke as one who had been through the humiliation of a broken betrothal," Alice insisted. "I have begun to wonder if she herself took the veil because of a severed betrothal."

" 'Tis hardly an uncommon occurrence." Joan rapped briskly on the heavy oak paneling. "Many women have entered a convent for that reason."

"I realize that. But I wish to ask the sister if that was her reason."

Joan's eyes met hers. "And if it was?"

"Then I wish to know if the man who broke his vow of betrothal to her was Hugh's father, Sir Matthew of Scarcliffe."

Joan frowned. "But according to the tale, Sir Matthew never did break his vows. From all I have ever heard, he fully intended to marry the lady his family had chosen for him. Everyone believes that he wished to keep Hugh's poor mother as his leman. They say that was why she flew into a heartbroken rage and gave her lover a poisoned cup."

"So the story goes," Alice admitted. "But what if that was not what occurred? What if Matthew came back from France, discovered he had a son, and determined to marry the woman he had seduced?"

"You're saying that the lady to whom he was betrothed may have sought vengeance?"

" 'Tis possible, is it not?"

" 'Tis somewhat extreme," Joan said crisply.

"You said yourself that Sister Katherine is a woman who suffers from extreme humors," Alice reminded her.

Joan stood on tiptoe and peered through the grate. "Her cell is empty. She is not inside. There is something very strange about all this."

"It would appear that she has left the convent."

"But where could she have gone? Surely someone would have noticed if she had taken one of the horses from the convent stable."

Alice went to peer through the grate. "There is a sheet of parchment on her bed."

"Sister Katherine is excessively neat. She would not leave personal items scattered about."

Alice glanced at her. "Unless she meant for someone to discover it."

Joan's gaze grew more troubled. Without a word she lifted the heavy ring that was attached to her belt. She selected one of the iron keys from it and inserted it into the lock of Katherine's door.

A moment later Alice walked into the tiny chamber. There was little to be seen other than the narrow bed, a small, wooden chest, and the rolled sheet of parchment that lay on the straw mattress.

Alice started to reach for the parchment. She paused and glanced at Joan. Joan mutely nodded her permission.

Alice picked up the parchment sheet and carefully unrolled it. A heavy gold ring set with a green gem fell onto the bed. Alice examined it closely. "Does this belong to Sister Katherine?"

"If it does, she has kept it hidden all these years. I have never before seen it."

"It looks familiar." Alice glanced up. "I believe that Lady Emma wears one very similar to it. She said that Sir Vincent gave it to her when they exchanged their vows."

"Worse and worse," Joan muttered. "What does the letter say?"

" 'Tis only a short note."

"Read it."

Alice frowned intently over the painstakingly precise script.

The bastard son has paid for the sins of his father and mother. It is finished.

"Dear heaven, what does she mean?" Joan whispered.

"Katherine no doubt believes that she has had her vengeance." Alice rerolled the parchment. "She cannot know yet that she failed."

Joan's keys rattled on the iron ring as she turned toward the door. "I shall ask one of the nuns to talk to the villagers. Mayhap someone has seen Katherine."

Alice glanced through the narrow window of the cell. Outside the gray mist had grown darker. "It grows late. I must return to the keep before someone becomes anxious about my absence." *Namely Hugh, who might even now have awakened and begun to plan his vengeance against Rivenhall.*

Joan led the way out of Katherine's cell. "I will send word to you if I locate the healer."

"Thank you," Alice said quietly. "I think it best if poison is not mentioned, Prioress. You know how people fear it."

"Aye. I shall not speak of it," Joan promised. "God knows we do not need any rumors of poison spread about on this manor."

"Agreed. I will speak with you tomorrow, madam. Now, I must hurry home if I am to resolve this situation before a new storm is loosed upon these lands."

*B*enedict was waiting for Alice in the great hall. He greeted her with an urgency that spoke volumes.

"Thank the Saints you have returned," he said. "Lord Hugh awoke less than an hour ago and immediately asked for you. When I told him you had gone out, he was most displeased."

Alice unfastened her cloak. "Where is he?"

"In his study chamber. He said you are to go to him at once."

"I intend to do precisely that." Alice started for the stairs.

"Alice?"

She paused, one toe on the bottom step. "Aye, what is it?"

"There is something I have wanted to tell you." Benedict glanced around quickly to make certain that none of the servants was within hearing distance. He took a step closer to Alice and lowered his voice. "I was with Sir Hugh when he fell ill."

"I know. What of it?"

"The first word he spoke when he realized that he had drunk from a poisoned cup was your name."

Alice flinched as though she had been struck. A great weight settled on her. "He thought I tried to murder him?"

"Nay." Benedict smiled wryly. "At first I believed that was his meaning. I told him it was not possible. Then he made it clear that he was asking for you because he knew you were the only one who could save him. He blamed Vincent of Rivenhall from the beginning. He never once suspected you."

The intolerable burden lifted from Alice's soul. She gave Benedict a shaky smile. "Thank you for telling me that, brother. It eases my heart more than you can possibly know."

Benedict flushed. "I know how much you care for him. Sir Dunstan says that a man of Lord Hugh's nature does not allow himself to indulge in soft emotions. Sir Dunstan told me that Lord Hugh scoffs at love and would never give his heart to a woman. But I thought you should know that he at least trusts you. Sir Dunstan says that it is most unusual for my lord to trust anyone."

" 'Tis a start, is it not?" Alice whirled and hurried up the stairs.

She clutched Katherine's note and the ring very tightly as she swept down the corridor at the top of the staircase. She came to a halt in front of Hugh's door and knocked sharply.

"Enter." Hugh's voice held a bone-chilling edge.

Alice drew a breath and opened the door.

Hugh was seated at his desk. There was a map spread out in front of him. He looked up when Alice entered the chamber. When he saw her he surged to his feet. His palms flattened on the desk. His eyes were savage.

"Where in the name of the devil have you been, madam?"

"The convent." Alice studied him closely. "You appear to have recovered from your ordeal, sir. How do you feel?"

"I have regained my appetite," Hugh said. "And I seem to have acquired a taste for vengeance."

"You are not the only one who craves that particular dish, my lord." Alice tossed the parchment and ring onto the desk. "Today it appears as though you were the victim of a woman whose hunger for vengeance is even greater than your own."

Chapter 19

"The healer was the poisoner?" Hugh looked up from the short letter Katherine had left on her bed. He was stunned by what Alice had told him. But he could not deny the evidence she had brought back from the convent.

"Judging by that ring and the words of the note, I suspect she was the woman who was betrothed to your father." Alice sank down onto a stool. "I would hazard a guess that when Sir Matthew returned from France he sent word to her that he intended to break the betrothal."

"So that he could marry my mother, do you think?" Hugh forced himself to keep his voice utterly calm and detached. But an unfamiliar surge of emotion flooded his veins. *Mayhap his father had intended to claim him.*

"Aye." Alice's eyes were warm and gentle. "I believe that is very likely the case, my lord."

Hugh looked at her and knew that she understood everything. He did not have to try to explain what her news meant to him. As usual, Alice comprehended his meaning without his having to find the words.

"And Katherine retaliated by poisoning my parents." Hugh released the edges of the parchment and watched as it slowly rerolled itself. "She murdered them."

"So it would seem."

"It is as though the history of my life was just rewritten," he whispered.

" 'Tis a great sin that the truth was hidden all these years."

"When I think of how I was taught from the cradle to hate all things Rivenhall—" Hugh broke off, unable to finish the sentence.

I will not forget, Grandfather.

Hugh felt as though the mighty stone pillars upon which his entire existence was founded had suddenly shifted beneath him.

His father had returned from France with the intention of wedding the mother of his babe. He had not seduced and then abandoned young Margaret of Scarcliffe.

"Just as Sir Vincent was taught to hate you," Alice said quietly, breaking into Hugh's reverie.

"Aye. It would seem that both families and these lands have paid a heavy price because of her crime." Hugh met Alice's eyes and forced himself to contemplate the present situation with some degree of logic. "But why did Katherine wait until today to try to poison me? Why did she not use her foul brew when I first arrived to claim Scarcliffe?"

Alice's brows came together in a frown of concentration. "I am not entirely certain. There are many questions that remain unanswered in this matter."

" 'Twould have been much easier to murder me weeks ago." Hugh tapped the rolled-up parchment against the desktop. "The household was very disorganized. There would have been numerous opportunities for a poisoner and no one about who possessed the skill to save me. *Why wait?*"

Alice pursed her lips. "Mayhap she took some satisfaction in the feud itself. As long as it persisted she could sip from the cup of discord and strife that she had created."

"Aye."

"Katherine may have been angered by the visit of Sir Vincent and his family yesterday. Everyone saw you and Vincent ride together through the village."

"Of course." Hugh wondered why that had not occurred to him immediately. He did not seem to be thinking clearly at all at the moment. The news of his past was having an unsettling effect on his powers of reason. "She would likely have viewed it as the first step toward ending the hostility between Scarcliffe and Rivenhall."

"Aye." Alice drummed her fingers on her knee.

"What troubles you?"

"I still cannot comprehend why she fed poison to the monk. It makes no sense."

"We shall likely never know unless we find her." Hugh got to his feet with sudden decision. "And I intend to do just that." He started around the edge of his desk.

"Where are you going, my lord?"

"To speak with Dunstan. I want Scarcliffe searched from border to border. The poisoner cannot have gotten far on foot. If we move quickly she will be found before the storm breaks."

A crack of thunder and a flash of lightning put an end to that plan even before Hugh had finished speaking.

"Too late, my lord."

"Damn it to the pit." Hugh went to the window.

The wind and rain struck with great force, whipping the black walls of Scarcliffe Keep and the cliffs behind it with blinding intensity. The torches would be useless in such a gale. Hugh seethed with a savage frustration as he closed the shutters.

"Never fear," Alice said. "You will find her in the morning."

"Aye," Hugh vowed. "I will find her."

He turned to see Alice watching him closely. Her gaze was shadowed with grave concern. *Concern for him.* This was the way she looked when she was anxious about someone who was important to her, he thought. Someone whom she loved.

His wife.

He was briefly enthralled by the simple fact that she was sitting right here in his study. Her skirts pooled gracefully around her feet. The glow of the brazier heightened the dark flames in her hair. *Hair the color of a sunset just before it is enveloped by the night.*

His wife.

Today she had saved his life and provided him with the truth about his own past.

She had given him so much.

Another rush of emotion cascaded through Hugh. The force of it was more powerful than the wild winds that scoured Scarcliffe this night.

He could not name the feeling that welled up inside him but it filled him with a deep longing. He suddenly wished with all his soul that he had a new list of fine compliments handy. He needed Julian's elegant words. He wanted to say something memorable, something a poet would say. Something as beautiful as Alice herself.

"Thank you," he said.

*H*ours later in the warmth of his great bed, Hugh leaned over Alice and drove himself into her softness one last time. He felt the delicate shivers first. Her soft, clinging warmth tightened around him. Then he heard her breathless cry of release.

For an instant he knew a dazed feeling of awe and gratitude. He was not alone in the storm. Alice was with him. He could touch her, feel her, hold on to her. She was a part of him.

The shatteringly intense awareness passed as quickly as it had come upon him. Once again he was lost in the sweet, radiant glow of Alice's passion. It swept him up and carried him aloft. He surrendered to the wild winds with a hoarse, muffled shout of satisfaction and wonder.

Here in the darkness with Alice he did not have to control the storm. Instead, he rode it with the freedom of a great hawk to a place where the past no longer cast shadows.

When it was over he lay quietly for a long time, luxuriating in the pleasure of having Alice next to him.

"Hugh?"

"Aye?"

"You are not asleep."

He smiled into the darkness. "Neither are you, it would seem."

"What deep thoughts keep you awake at this late hour?"

"I was not thinking. I was listening."

"To what?"

"To the night."

Alice was silent for a few seconds. "I hear nothing."

"I know. The winds have quieted and the rain has stopped. The storm is finished."

"'*T*is a strange day." Joan halted at the convent gatehouse. She folded her hands into the sleeves of her habit and gazed pensively into the thick shroud of fog that clung to Scarcliffe. "I shall be glad when it is done."

"You are not the only one who will welcome the end of this matter." Alice tucked her mother's handbook under her arm and adjusted the hood of her mantle. "I confess some small part of me prays that Lord Hugh will not find the healer."

Hugh had left at dawn to hunt for Katherine. He had

taken Benedict and virtually every able-bodied man in the keep with him. There had been no word from him since he had departed.

Restless, anxious, and filled with a deep unease, Alice had prowled the halls of Scarcliffe Keep until she could no longer abide her own company. With a view toward occupying herself in a useful endeavor, she had taken her mother's herb handbook and walked into the village.

There had been work enough in the convent infirmary. When she had finished dispensing cough remedies and tonics to ease joint pains, Alice had joined the nuns for midday prayers and a meal.

"I understand," Joan murmured. " 'Twould be easier if Katherine simply vanished but that is not likely."

"True enough. My lord will search for her to the very gates of hell if necessary." Alice eyed the mist. "I can only hope that when he finds her, he will also find peace."

Joan gave her a gentle, knowing look. "None of us can find true peace in the past, Alice. We must all search for it in the present."

Alice tightened her grasp on her mother's handbook. "You are very wise, madam."

Joan smiled wistfully. " 'Tis a lesson I had to learn the hard way, just as everyone must do."

For the first time Alice wondered what had led Joan to enter the religious life. Someday she would inquire, she told herself. Not today, of course. It was too soon for such intimacies. But there would be ample opportunity for such conversations in the future. Something told her that her growing friendship with the prioress would be important to both of them. In spite of the bleak day, Alice felt a genuine warmth flower inside her. Her future was here at Scarcliffe. It would be a good life.

"Good day, madam." Alice started toward the gate.

"Good day, my lady."

Alice lifted a hand in farewell and walked through the stone gates.

The fog had grown so thick that she could barely make out the wagon ruts in the street. She knew the mist must have seriously frustrated Hugh's search. She also knew that he would not readily abandon his quest. He would comb Scarcliffe and the surrounding lands with the relentless determination that was so much a part of him.

She could not blame him, Alice thought. He was, after all, hunting for the person who had, in all likelihood, murdered his parents. Alice knew that so far as Hugh was concerned, the fact that Katherine had apparently tried to poison him also paled into insignificance compared to her crimes of thirty years earlier.

Katherine had taken both mother and father from him. She had deprived him of the lands that should have been his rightful inheritance. She had consigned him to the care of an embittered old man who had viewed him as little more than an instrument of vengeance.

Alice shuddered to think what would have happened to Hugh had fate not led him to the household of Erasmus of Thornewood. Someday, she told herself, she would very much like to thank that shadowy figure who had single-handedly kept Hugh from being consumed by the fierce storms that forged so much of his nature.

Alice could not blame Hugh for his determination to find his quarry, but now that she was alone again, her sense of unease returned. There was something that did not feel right about the situation. Too many things remained unexplained. Too many questions were still unanswered.

Why murder the monk?

She pondered the question for the hundredth time that day as she went past the last of the village cottages. The fog had silenced everything. The men were not at work in the fields. The women were not in their gardens. The children were warming themselves by the hearth fires. Alice had the road to Scarcliffe Keep to herself.

The monk. Somehow there had to be a link between Calvert and the poisoning of Hugh's parents.

A dark, hooded figure materialized out of the fog directly in Alice's path. She froze. Fear washed over her in a thundering wave.

"About time you showed up." The man reached out to seize her. "We was beginning to wonder if you intended to dawdle in the convent until Vespers."

Alice opened her mouth to scream but it was too late. A rough hand was instantly clamped over her mouth.

She dropped her mother's book and kicked out frantically. Her legs tangled in the folds of her gown but she managed to strike her attacker's shin with the toe of her soft boot.

"Damn you," the man muttered. "I knew this wouldn't be so easy. Not a word out o' ye." He jerked the hood of her cloak lower over her face, effectively blinding her.

Alice struggled fiercely in his grasp. She flailed blindly, seeking a target, any target, as her assailant hoisted her off her feet. Then she heard muffled footfalls on the road and knew that the man who held her prisoner was not alone.

"Don't let her yell, Fulton, whatever ye do," the other man snarled. "We're not far from the village. Someone will surely hear her if she gets to screeching."

Alice redoubled her efforts to yell for help. She managed to sink her teeth into Fulton's palm.

"Damnation." Fulton gasped. "The vixen bit me."

"Stop her mouth with some cloth."

Alice fought back in wild panic as a length of foul cloth was drawn taut across her mouth and tied behind her head.

"Be quick about it, Fulton. We must get off this road. If Sir Hugh and his men blunder into us in this fog, we'll be dead before we know what happened."

"Sir Hugh would not dare touch us so long as we hold his wife prisoner," Fulton protested. But there was an anxious ring of uncertainty in his voice.

"I would not count on surviving such a meeting, if I were you," the other man muttered.

"But Sir Eduard says that Hugh the Relentless is uncommonly fond of his new bride."

Sir Eduard. Alice was so startled that she went still for a moment. Were these men speaking of Eduard of Lockton? Impossible. Eduard would not risk Hugh's wrath in this fashion. Hugh himself had been arrogantly certain of his own dominance over the unpleasant Eduard.

"Sir Hugh may be fond of the wench," the other man said, "but Erasmus of Thornewood did not cause the words *Bringer of Storms* to be inscribed on the dark knight's sword for naught. Hurry. We must move quickly or all is lost."

Alice knew that she had walked straight into a trap.

*A*lice blinked several times when the hood was finally pulled back from her face. She saw at once that she was inside one of the caves of Scarcliffe. Torch light cast unnerving shadows on the damp stone walls. Water dripped somewhere in the distance.

Fulton untied the cloth that had stopped her mouth. Alice grimaced and wiped her lips with the sleeve of her cloak.

Katherine walked slowly out of the darkness to stand in front of her. The healer's face was lined with a timeless melancholy. Her eyes were somber shrouds on her soul.

"You will not believe this, but I regret all that has happened, Lady Alice. 'Twas inevitable, I suppose. I warned you once that the sins of the past produced bitter herbs."

" 'Tis not the past that produced the poison, Katherine. It was you. Your latest effort failed, you know. You will not get another opportunity. Even now Sir Hugh is searching these lands. Sooner or later he will find you."

Eduard of Lockton loomed in the passageway. In the light of the torch, his features were akin to those of an evil troll. His small, cunning eyes gleamed with malevolence. "He has already searched the outer cavern. Little good it did him. But, then, he did not know where to look, did he, Katherine?"

Katherine did not turn her head toward him. Her gaze remained fixed on Alice as if she willed her to understand. "Eduard is my cousin, Lady Alice."

"Your cousin?" Alice stared at Eduard. "I do not comprehend this."

"That much is obvious." Eduard's yellow teeth flashed in his beard. "But you will, madam. Rest assured, you soon will comprehend all. And so will that bastard husband of yours just before I cut him down with my blade."

Alice was sickened by the sour anger that seemed to radiate from Eduard. "Why do you hate my husband so?"

"Because his birth ruined everything. *Everything.*" Eduard motioned irritably to Fulton and the other man. They both stepped back into the shadows of a dark passageway. Eduard moved closer to Alice. "Katherine was supposed to marry Matthew of Rivenhall, you see. I myself negotiated the betrothal."

"My parents died when I was but thirteen years," Katherine whispered. "Eduard was my only male relative. My fate was in his hands."

"She had a large dowry bequeathed to her from her mother's people and I had plans for her," Eduard growled. "Matthew of Rivenhall was heir to several manors. His family wanted Katherine's dowry. They were willing to trade one of their manors for her. It was a fine match."

"You hoped to profit from your cousin's marriage," Alice accused.

"Of course." Eduard lifted one burly shoulder in a mocking shrug. "Marriage is a business. Women are good for only two purposes, bedding and wedding. Any tavern wench can be used to satisfy the first purpose. Only an heiress can satisfy the second."

"So you set out to get your hands on lands of your own," Alice said angrily.

Katherine's mouth curved with great bitterness. "He wanted much more than a manor of his own."

Eduard scowled. "My plan was to get rid of Sir Matthew after the wedding. As his widow, Katherine would have been an even more valuable prize. I could have demanded even more land and a fine fortune in exchange for her hand."

"What did you intend to do?" Alice demanded. "Did you think to go on poisoning her future husbands so that you could continue to sell her in marriage over and over again?"

"I swear to you that I did not know what he intended," Katherine said forlornly. "I was only an innocent girl. I knew nothing of the plots of men."

"Bah." Eduard regarded her with vicious scorn. "It all came to naught. Matthew returned from France determined to wed that whore, Margaret. He knew his family would object so he thought to do the deed in secret. But I learned of his plans on the eve of the wedding."

"So you murdered both Matthew and Margaret?"

"Sir Matthew was not supposed to die," Eduard raged. "He was to marry Katherine, as I had planned. But the fool drank from the same cup as Margaret. He probably thought to offer up a lover's toast. And it killed him."

Alice stared at him. "Where did you learn so much of poison?"

Eduard's face contorted briefly into an expression of fierce satisfaction. "I learned to make the brew years ago when I lived for a time in Toledo. I have used it more than once over the years. 'Tis an excellent weapon because even if it is discovered, everyone assumes that the murderess is a woman."

"Just as they did thirty years ago," Alice said.

Eduard's smile was horrible to behold. "Aye. They all assumed that Margaret had poisoned her lover and then taken her own life. No one thought to look for the true murderer."

"Men are always so certain that poison is a woman's weapon," Katherine muttered.

Alice clutched her cloak more tightly about her to ward off the dreadful chill that permeated the cavern. "Why have you kidnapped me? What do you intend?"

" 'Tis simple, madam," Eduard said softly. "I intend to hold you for ransom."

Alice frowned. "What do you expect Sir Hugh to do? Hand over a chest of spices in exchange for me?"

"Nay, madam. I want something far more satisfying than a chest of ginger or saffron."

Alice gazed at him in dread. "What, then?"

"Revenge," Eduard whispered.

"But why?"

"Hugh the Relentless got what was to have been mine even though he was born a bastard." Eduard's voice was choked with fury. "He got lands of his own. Lands where a rare treasure is hidden."

"But no one knows where the Stones of Scarcliffe are hidden," Alice said desperately. "Indeed, Lord Hugh considers them merely a legend."

"They are far more than a legend," Eduard assured her. "Calvert of Oxwick knew that. He learned the secret from an aged knight who took holy vows after he grew too old to wield a sword. The knight had once served a lord of Scarcliffe. That lord had discovered an old letter that contained part of the truth."

Alice took a step back. "What is this great truth?"

"That the green crystal is the key." Eduard's eyes glinted. "Why do you think I have killed twice for it already, madam?"

"The peddler and the poor monk?"

"Aye. 'Twas very nearly necessary to kill that fool of a troubadour, Gilbert, also. But then you helped Sir Hugh recover the stone and everything changed. I vow, this entire affair has been like a game of dice."

"*Murderer.*"

"Murdering is a pleasant enough sport," Eduard conceded. "And this time 'twill be a particular pleasure. Hugh the Relentless cost me everything by his birth."

"It was not his fault that his father chose to break his vow of betrothal to Katherine."

"Ah, but it was, you see." Eduard's mouth tightened. "I'm certain that the reason Sir Matthew was so determined to wed his Lady Margaret was because the wench had borne him a son. He wanted to claim a lusty heir. I cannot conceive of any other reason why he would have wanted to marry a woman he had already bedded."

"Mayhap he truly loved her," Alice snapped.

"Bah. Love is for poets and ladies, not knights of Sir Matthew's reputation." Eduard's hand closed into a meaty fist. "I lost much thirty years ago but I shall have my due now. I shall finally gain great wealth and have my revenge while I am about it."

Alice drew a deep breath to steady herself. "What are you going to do?"

" 'Tis simple enough. I shall send a message to Sir Hugh instructing him that if he wants you safely returned to him, he must give me the green stone."

Alice tried to keep her voice even. " 'Tis well known that Lord Hugh trusts very few, Sir Eduard. But he is rather fond of me."

"I am well aware of that, madam. Indeed, that is the basis of my scheme."

"If you would convince him to pay the ransom, you must first make him believe that I am still alive. If he thinks me dead, he will pay nothing. He is too much the man of business to get himself fleeced in such a fashion."

Eduard glowered at her. "Why would he doubt my message? Soon he will know that you have disappeared."

Alice shrugged. "He may believe that I have merely lost my way in the fog and that some outlaw, having learned of my disappearance, has taken advantage of the fact to pretend that I am being held captive."

Eduard contemplated that closely for a time. Then his expression turned crafty. "I shall send him something of yours to prove that I hold you."

"An excellent notion, Sir Eduard."

"*When* this is finished, Elbert," Hugh vowed, "you will be banished from this hall forever."

"Aye, m'lord." Elbert hung his head. "I can only say once more that I am most desperately sorry. But in truth Lady Alice walks into the village every day. I saw no reason to send a guard with her today."

"Damn." Elbert was right and Hugh knew it. He stopped pacing and came to a halt in front of the hearth in the great hall. Berating the steward was pointless. No one knew better than Hugh that what had happened was not the young man's fault. If anyone was to blame, Hugh thought, it was himself. He had failed to protect his wife.

"Blood of the devil." Hugh stared down at the volume in his hand. It was the book of herbal lore that Alice had dropped on the road. He had found it on the way home from his fruitless search for Katherine.

"Mayhap she is merely lost in the fog," Benedict suggested in a worried tone.

Hugh tightened his jaw. "Unlikely. The fog is thick, but

'tis not so dense as to conceal familiar landmarks to one who knows the road. Nay, she has been taken by force."

Benedict's eyes widened. "You believe that she was kidnapped?"

"Aye." He had known the truth in that first terrible instant when he had seen the book lying on the road.

Hugh shut his eyes briefly. He willed himself to stay calm. He had to think clearly and logically. He had to master the storm of rage and fear that threatened to sweep aside his control or all was lost.

"But who would kidnap Lady Alice?" Elbert looked utterly bewildered. "Everyone loves her."

Alarm filled Benedict's eyes. "We must ride out again at once. We must search for her."

"Nay," Hugh said. "We could not even find the poisoner in this fog. We have no chance of discovering Alice until the kidnapper sends a message."

"But what if he does not do so?" Benedict asked angrily. "What will you do if there is no word?"

"There will be a message." Hugh moved his hand to the hilt of his sword. He wrapped his fingers around the worn black leather grip. "The only point of a kidnapping is ransom."

*T*he message was brought to the gate just as the cloak of night settled on the mist-shrouded lands of Scarcliffe. A worried-looking guard carried the demands directly to Hugh.

"A man came to the gate, m'lord. He said to tell you that if you would have Lady Alice returned, you must bring the green crystal to the north end of the old village ditch. You must leave it there and come back to this keep to wait. In the morning the stone will be gone and Lady Alice will be sent home."

"The green stone?" Hugh, seated in his massive ebony

chair, leaned forward. He rested one elbow on his thigh and contemplated the guard. "That is the ransom?"

"Aye, m'lord." The guard swallowed uneasily. "I pray you will remember that I merely convey the message, sir."

"Who sent this message?"

"The man says that his master is Eduard of Lockton."

"Eduard." Hugh gazed into the flames on the central hearth. "So he would challenge me, after all. Did the messenger say anything else? Anything at all? Think, Garan."

Garan nodded quickly. "He said that his master bid him give you a special message from Lady Alice to prove to you that he truly held her captive."

"What is it?"

Garan took a step back although Hugh had not risen from the chair. He held out his hand and opened his fingers to reveal a familiar ring set with a stone of black onyx. "Lady Alice sends you her betrothal ring and begs that you will remember well the words you spoke the day you gave it to her."

Hugh gazed at the ring. He was no poet. He had not spoken words of love to Alice that day.

He forced himself to recall every word that he had said to her.

You are not to go into these caves alone.

"Of course," Hugh whispered.

Benedict moved into the light. "What is it, sir?"

"Eduard holds Alice somewhere in the caves of Scarcliffe."

Chapter 20

Benedict was outraged when he learned of the stratagem. "What do you mean, you are not going to pay the ransom? For the love of God, my lord, you cannot leave my sister at the mercy of Eduard of Lockton. You heard his message. He will murder her."

Dunstan clamped a hand on his shoulder. "Ease your mind, Benedict. Sir Hugh has dealt with men of Eduard's nature many times before this. He knows what he is doing."

Benedict banged his staff on the floor. "But he says he will not give that crystal to Sir Eduard."

"Aye."

Benedict turned on Hugh. "You've said yourself, the green stone has little value. 'Tis only a symbol. Part of an old legend, you said. Surely my sister's life is worth more than that devilish stone."

Hugh did not look up from Calvert's plan of the caves. "Calm yourself, Benedict."

"I thought you had some tender feelings for Alice. You said you would care for her. You said you would protect her."

Tender feelings, Hugh thought. Those words did not begin to touch the emotion that he was struggling to control at this moment. He raised his eyes slowly to Benedict's taut, anxious face.

"The stone is worthless, as I told you," he said quietly. "That is not the point."

"Sir, you must pay the ransom," Benedict pleaded. "He will kill her if you do not."

Hugh studied Benedict in silence, wondering how much to tell him. He glanced at Dunstan, who shrugged. Nothing would be gained by lying to the youth, Dunstan's expression said.

"You do not comprehend the situation," Hugh said quietly. How did one explain to a woman's brother that his sister's life hung by the merest thread? For that matter, how did a man deal with the fact that his wife was at the mercy of a murderer?

Hugh forced himself to set aside his own fears. He would not be able to do anything for Alice if he indulged himself in horrible imaginings and bleak visions of a future without her.

"That's not true," Benedict raged. "I understand exactly what is happening. My sister has been kidnapped by Eduard of Lockton, who has demanded a ransom for her return. Knights demand ransoms of one another all the time. Pay it, my lord. You must pay it."

" 'Twill do no good," Hugh said. "If I leave the green stone at the old village ditch, as instructed, 'tis certain Eduard will murder Alice."

Dunstan nodded soberly. "Sir Hugh is right, Benedict."

Benedict stared, bewildered, first at Dunstan and then at Hugh. "But . . . but he has asked for a ransom. He says he will free her if it is paid."

"This is no joust or friendly tournament where ransoms are part of the sport." Hugh went back to his study of the cave map. "Do not make the mistake of believing that Eduard of Lockton will play this game by the rules of honor."

"But he is a knight," Benedict protested. "He took part in the jousts at Ipstoke. I saw him."

"With this act Eduard has proven that he is no true knight," Dunstan muttered.

"Until now he has played the part of a cunning fox who hides in the brush until he spies an opportunity to seize what he wants." Hugh traced a passageway with the blunt tip of his finger. "On the jousting field he is tame enough. There are too many people watching him there. Too many true knights who would be outraged if he were to cheat or act dishonorably. But this is a different matter."

"What are you saying?" Benedict demanded.

"He has gone too far." Hugh propped an elbow on the table and rested his jaw on his fist. "Seizing Rivenhall was one thing. He knew that I did not care what happened to that manor. If circumstances had been different—" He let the sentence hang, unfinished, in the air.

Benedict's expression was one of grim comprehension. "You mean if Alice had not ridden to Rivenhall's defense you would not have done so yourself?"

"Aye. If she had not taken it upon herself to save that manor Eduard could have had it with my best wishes. He knew that. But this . . . this is quite another matter."

Some new element was at work in this business. Hugh grappled with the possibilities. What did Eduard know about the green stone that made him willing to risk the wrath of a man whom he had, until now, treated with wary caution?

What did Eduard know about the crystal that made him willing to risk death to obtain it?

For the instant Eduard had seized Alice, he had signed his own death warrant. He must surely be aware of that fact.

"This most certainly is quite another matter." Benedict

slammed a fist down onto the table. "What makes you so certain that Eduard will kill Alice if the ransom is paid?"

"In kidnapping Alice, he has challenged me directly." Hugh frowned as he studied another passageway. "That means that for some reason he no longer fears me enough to be governed by caution. If that is the case, then he is no longer a fox but a boar. And no creature is so dangerous and unpredictable as a boar."

Benedict froze. Everyone knew that a boar was the most savage of beasts. Only the most skilled of hunters pursued such quarry. Endowed with a massive, heavily muscled body, great tusks, and mindless ferocity, it was capable of killing both a horse and the man unlucky enough to be in the saddle. The most valiant hounds could not bring it down without the aid of an entire pack of strong dogs and the arrows of the hunters.

"What are you going to do?" Benedict finally asked in a voice subdued by shock.

Hugh rolled up the small sheet of vellum on which Calvert had drawn the map. "I shall do the only thing one can do with a wild boar. I shall hunt him down and kill him."

*K*atherine's somber eyes met Alice's. "After Sir Matthew's death, my cousin spent most of my inheritance and was unable to contract another suitable marriage for me. He allowed me to enter Scarcliffe Convent. I saw little of him over the years and I was very glad of that fact."

"You were happy in the convent?"

"As happy as a woman of my temperament may be."

In spite of her predicament, Alice felt a measure of sympathy. "Prioress Joan told me that you suffer from bouts of melancholia."

"Aye. The work in the gardens is good for those afflicted with such humors, however. And I take satisfaction in mixing my herbs. For the most part I have been content."

Alice shifted uncomfortably on the hard stone floor of the cavern. She had been sitting in the corner of the vast cave with Katherine for what seemed an age. Quiet conversation with the healer was the only thing that was keeping her from succumbing to the fear that threatened to envelop her.

She was vastly more anxious tonight than she had been the day she braved Eduard in Rivenhall Keep.

The difference lay in something other than the obvious fact that on the previous occasion she'd had Dunstan and a contingent of Hugh's men-at-arms at her back. It had to do with a change in Eduard himself. A terrifying change.

There was a frenzied quality about Eduard tonight, an air of violent desperation. Alice sensed that he was far more dangerous this time than he had been when he had attempted to take Rivenhall. Then, he had been wary of Hugh. Tonight his eagerness to obtain the green stone seemed to have driven out all sense of caution.

To Alice's relief, Eduard had left the cavern a short while earlier. He had taken a torch and moved off down a dark passage with the confidence of a man who knew his way about the maze of tunnels.

This was the third time that Eduard had left the caves to spy on the old village ditch.

It seemed to Alice that the walls of the cavern were pressing closer. A torch propped against one wall burned low. Soot from the flames darkened the stone above it. The flickering shadows grew steadily darker and more dense.

A series of clicks on the stone floor caused Alice to glance across the chamber. Fulton and the other man, whose name, she had learned, was Royce, sat cross-legged, playing at dice. Their weapons were close at hand.

"My game," Fulton growled, not for the first time. He had enjoyed a series of wins.

"Bah. Give me the dice." Royce grabbed the small bone cubes and tossed them onto the stone. He glowered at the results. "By the entrails of the Saints. How do you come by all the luck?"

"Let me show you how to play this game." Fulton reached for the dice.

"Sir Eduard should have returned by now. I wonder what keeps him?"

"Who can tell?" Fulton rolled the dice. "He is in a strange mood tonight."

"Aye. He cannot think of anything except that damned green stone. 'Tis unnatural, if you ask me. Everyone knows the crystal has no great value."

"Sir Eduard believes that it does."

Alice hugged herself as she looked at Katherine. "It grows late."

Here in the bowels of the caves it was impossible to determine the position of the sun, but the passage of the day was apparent in other ways.

"Aye." Katherine clasped her hands together. " 'Twill no doubt be finished soon. We shall both be dead and Eduard will have the green crystal."

"My husband will rescue us," Alice promised softly.

She recalled that she had once made the same vow to Emma. Poor Hugh, she thought with a wry and extremely fleeting amusement. He was always having to make good on her promises.

Katherine shook her head sadly. "No one can rescue us, Lady Alice. The roots of the herb that poisoned the past have borne evil flowers."

"No offense, Katherine, but occasionally you do have a way of depressing one's spirits."

Katherine's expression grew more morose. "I prefer to deal in truth and fact. If you wish to comfort yourself with false hope, that is your affair."

"My mother was a great believer in the power of hope. She considered it as important as medicine. And I have every hope that my lord will deal quite satisfactorily with Eduard. You will see."

"You certainly seem to have great faith in the power of your husband," Katherine muttered.

"You must admit, he has not failed me yet." Alice straightened her shoulders. "And if you think that Eduard is any match for Sir Hugh, you are wrong."

"I myself have never had any reason to put my trust in men." Katherine was clearly resigned to a sad end.

Alice concluded she would have no luck attempting to change Katherine's bleak attitude, so she decided to change the topic instead. "Do you know who stole the green crystal from the convent a few weeks ago?"

Katherine twisted her hands together in her lap. "I did."

"*You?*"

Katherine sighed. "When Eduard learned that the crystal was the key to discovering the Stones of Scarcliffe, he sent word that I must take it from its vault. He . . . made certain threats."

"What sort of threats?"

"He promised to poison someone from the village or one of the other nuns if I did not obey him."

"Dear heaven," Alice whispered.

"I dared not take the risk. I did as he instructed. Late one night I took the stone and gave it to a man whom Eduard sent to the convent gate to collect it."

"Why did Eduard wait all these years before he tried to steal the stone?"

Katherine lifted one shoulder in a small, dismissive gesture. "He only learned of its true value a few months ago."

"When he discovered that Calvert of Oxwick had concluded that the Stones of Scarcliffe actually existed?"

"Aye."

Alice frowned. "That incident occurred at about the same time that Sir Hugh received the fief of Scarcliffe."

"Eduard was pleased to know that the loss of the green stone would cause Hugh much trouble, but that was not the reason he bid me steal it. The simple truth was that after learning that the Stones were more than a mere legend, he quickly become obsessed with discovering the treasure."

"What happened after you gave the green stone to Eduard's man?"

"The fool betrayed Eduard." Katherine's lips thinned. "He made off with it, determined to discover its value for himself. But when he could not learn its secret, he sold it to a peddler. From thence it came into your hands and finally it was restored to its rightful owner."

"In the meantime, Calvert was here, using his guise as a monk to search these caves at his leisure."

"Aye. Eduard realized that the monk had learned much about the caves and would prove useful. He struck a bargain with Calvert. He made the monk his partner. Eduard promised to find the green stone while Calvert searched the caves."

"But Eduard murdered Calvert."

Katherine nodded. "Aye. I'm certain that he intended to do so from the start, once he had what he wanted. But when Sir Hugh recovered the green stone and locked it away in Scarcliffe Keep, Eduard and Calvert quarreled."

"Why did they quarrel?"

"Calvert accused Eduard of failing to fulfill his part of the bargain. Eduard went into a rage and concluded that the monk was no longer of any use. After Calvert was dead, Eduard realized that he would have to try a different stratagem."

"So he kidnapped me," Alice whispered.

"Aye."

"He is a fool."

"Nay, he is a vicious, dangerous man," Katherine whispered. "Indeed, he has always been evil. But tonight I see something else in him. Something that terrifies me."

"A hint of madness?" Alice cast an uneasy glance at Fulton and Royce.

"Aye." Katherine looked down at her hands. "I hate him, you know."

"Your cousin?"

Katherine gazed unseeingly at the wall of the cave. "He took me to live with him after my parents died. He wished to control my inheritance."

Alice grimaced. "Not an unusual state of affairs. Few men can resist the opportunity to control an heiress's fortune and the law encourages them to do so."

"True enough, but my cousin's treatment of me was most unusual and . . . and unnatural." Katherine looked down at her tightly clasped hands. "He . . . he forced himself upon me."

Alice stared at her in shock. "Oh, Katherine." She touched the healer's arm with grave gentleness. "I am so very sorry."

"And then he tried to marry me off to Sir Matthew in order to obtain lands of his own." Katherine's face was rigid with pain. "God forgive me, but I hate Eduard with a degree of passion that other women reserve for love."

The scrape of a boot on stone made Alice stiffen. She turned her head to peer into the shadowed passageway. Torch light flared in the opening. A moment later Eduard loomed into view. His face was a mask of fury.

Fulton scrambled to his feet. His eyes went to Eduard's empty hand. "Sir Hugh has not yet paid the ransom?"

"The bastard taunts me." Eduard slammed the torch into Fulton's hand. " 'Tis now dawn and he has not left the green stone at the north end of the stinking ditch. The damned fog grows worse by the minute."

"Mayhap he does not believe the lady is worth the price." Fulton cast an aggrieved look at Alice. " 'Tis not hard to comprehend that he might prefer to be rid of her." He rubbed the palm of the hand that Alice had bitten. "The wench is tiresome."

Eduard rounded on him furiously. "You fool. You know nothing of this matter."

"Mayhap," Fulton muttered. "But I know that I do not like it much."

"Sir Hugh values his wife right enough." Eduard combed his beard with restless fingers. "He indulges her to the point of idiocy. You saw how he was that night in Rivenhall Keep. Because he had given his word to her on a whim, he allowed the lady to deprive him of his long-sought vengeance."

"Aye, but—"

"Only a man besotted would allow a woman to manipulate him in such a manner. Aye, the fool places great value upon her. He will bring me the stone, thinking to exchange it for her life."

Royce scowled. "I agree with Fulton. I do not like this business. Surely the stone is not worth the risk of being cornered like trapped rats by Hugh the Relentless."

"Cease your whining." Eduard began to pace the floor of the chamber. "We are safe enough in these caves. Now that Calvert is dead, no one else except me knows these passageways. Not even Sir Hugh would dare enter this maze."

"Aye. So you said." Royce dropped the dice into his belt pouch. "But that changes nothing. This cavern may be a clever place to hide for the moment, but it could just as easily become a snare."

Eduard stopped pacing and turned, eyes slit with menace. "Do you think to defy me, Royce?"

Royce did not cower. Instead he regarded his master with a considering expression for a moment. Then he appeared to come to a decision. "I believe I have had enough of this futile endeavor."

"What? You are my man," Eduard roared. His hand went

to his sword hilt. "I'll kill you where you stand if you think to desert me now."

"You are welcome to try." Royce reached for his own sword.

Fulton stepped back out of the way. "Blood of the demon, this is truly madness."

"*Traitor.*" Eduard jerked his blade from its scabbard and leaped forward.

"Stay back," Royce warned. He raised his heavy blade.

"Stop this nonsense," Fulton shouted. "Or all is lost."

Alice reached for Katherine's hand. "Come," she whispered. "This may be our only chance."

Katherine sat frozen on the stone. Her eyes were lit with horror. "We cannot flee into the caves. We will be lost."

Alice tugged impatiently on Katherine's wrist. "Nay, we shall follow Eduard's trail."

"What trail?"

"He has been through these passages often enough to mark them well with the soot from his torch." Alice prayed that would prove true. One thing was certain, the quarrel that had broken out between Eduard and Royce was an opportunity she and Katherine could not ignore.

"Do you really think we can escape?" Katherine looked confused. She had obviously set her mind on death. Hope was a difficult concept for her to grasp at the best of times. At this moment it clearly left her bewildered and befuddled.

"Come."

Alice kept a wary eye on Eduard and Royce, who were shouting and circling each other. Fulton paid no attention to the women. He was laboring in vain to calm the other two men.

Alice kept her grasp on Katherine's wrist as she edged cautiously toward the nearest torch. The hair stirred on the back of her neck just as she reached out to grab the torch. A shiver of awareness went through her.

There was no sound to herald Hugh's arrival, but Alice knew he was close by. She whirled to gaze at the passageway that Eduard had used a moment earlier.

A cold, ghostly wind wafted from the dark corridor. It carried before it the promise of doom. The torches in the large cavern flickered and sputtered wildly.

"Hugh," Alice whispered.

A faint amber glow appeared in the black tunnel. A few seconds later it revealed the shadowed outline of a man.

The quarreling men behind Alice did not hear the sound of their enemy's name on her lips, but there was no mistaking his voice. It cut through the tense atmosphere with the impact of lightning slicing through a night sky.

"*Enough*." The single word thundered off the cavern walls. "Lay down your arms or die where you stand."

Everyone in the vast chamber went still for an instant. They all stared at Hugh, who stood framed in the opening of the stone corridor.

Alice was as stunned as the others, even though she had been expecting him to appear. She knew without being told that tonight Hugh was a thousandfold more dangerous than she had ever seen him.

Katherine made the sign of the cross. "The *Bringer of Storms*."

Hugh was vengeance incarnate, a dark wind that would sweep all before it. His eyes were cold and utterly without mercy. His black cloak enveloped him from his shoulders to the tops of his black leather boots. He wore no helm but light glinted on the steel of his drawn sword.

Dunstan and Aleyn, one of the household guards, quickly emerged behind Hugh. They flanked him with gleaming blades. Benedict came up behind them. He held a torch aloft. His eyes anxiously searched the cavern until they settled on Alice. When he saw her, his face glowed with relief.

Eduard was the first to recover from the paralysis that had gripped everyone in the stone chamber.

"Bastard," he cried. "You have ruined everything. From the very day of your birth, you have tried to deny me what was rightfully mine. You shall pay."

He lunged, but not toward Hugh. He turned and bore down on Alice. She realized with horrified amazement that he intended to kill her. For an instant she was literally frozen with fear.

"Alice, *move.*" Hugh surged forward, but he was several paces away from Eduard.

Hugh's command broke the spell of terror that had trapped Alice. She sprang to the side just as the heavy weight of Eduard's sword crashed downward. It struck the floor where she had been standing a second earlier. The dreadful clash of metal on stone rang out across the cavern.

Alice's stomach churned. She felt a cold, clammy sensation on her skin. If she had not gotten out of the way, she would have been cut in half by the force of Eduard's blow.

Even now he was spinning toward her once more. He raised his sword with both hands.

Alice stumbled backward. Her foot tangled in the hem of her skirts. "Blood of the Martyrs." She struggled desperately with the folds of her new black and amber gown.

"Devil's own whore. This is all your fault." Eduard's small eyes were those of a savage beast as he crowded Alice back against the cavern wall.

Fury swamped Alice's fear. "Get away from me. Do not come near me."

"Die, whore."

Out of the corner of her eye Alice saw that Hugh was halfway across the cavern but still too far off to cut Eduard down.

She gathered herself and prepared to try to duck the next blow.

But reason finally intervened to temper Eduard's rage. "Stay back or I'll kill her," he warned Hugh.

Hugh reached into the swirling folds of his cloak and removed an object. The green stone gleamed in his hand. "This is what you wanted, is it not, Eduard?"

"The stone." Eduard wet his lips. "Give it to me and I'll let your wife live."

"Take it, if you can." Hugh hurled the stone at a point on the cavern wall just to the right of where Eduard stood.

Eduard's eyes widened. He screamed, "*Nay.*" He lurched toward the stone but could not catch it.

The green crystal smashed against the wall. It shattered instantly. A glowing rainbow of gems cascaded onto the floor. Rubies, golden beryl, pearls, emeralds, sapphires, and diamonds shimmered and sparkled amid the shards of the dull green casket that had once concealed them.

"The Stones of Scarcliffe," Alice whispered.

She suddenly realized that the green crystal had been fashioned of heavy glass. She told herself that she should have suspected as much all along. Instead she had assumed that it was a natural object, just as everyone else had done. Now she understood that it had been created by a superbly skilled craftsman who had found a way to simulate the look and feel of a great chunk of crystal.

Eduard shrieked, "The Stones." He stared for a second, fascinated, at the glittering heap. Too late he recalled Hugh's presence.

He whirled about to confront the cold and deadly storm of Hugh's blade. But his obsession with the stones had cost him dearly.

Steel clanged dissonantly on steel.

Eduard was driven to his knees by the force of Hugh's blows. Hugh raised his blade again and again, beating against Eduard's steel.

When Hugh raised his sword for the death stroke, his

eyes burned the same color as the flames that flared in the torches.

Alice turned away quickly, unable to witness what she knew must occur next. She saw Katherine staring past her, transfixed by the dreadful scene. On the other side of the cavern Dunstan and Aleyn held Eduard's two men at swords' points. Benedict watched it all from the shadowed passageway.

Alice held her breath but there was no death scream behind her.

Seconds ticked past, two, three, four, five. She looked up and saw that everyone was still staring at the spot where Hugh had driven Eduard to his knees.

Slowly she turned back to see what had happened.

Eduard lay on his back, still very much alive. He stared mutely up along the length of the blade that rested on his throat.

"Why do you hesitate?" Dunstan asked. "Have done with it. This night has been long enough for all of us."

"There are some questions I want answered," Hugh said. "Bind him and take him back to the keep, Aleyn. Put him in the dungeon. I shall speak with him on the morrow."

"Aye, m'lord." Aleyn hurried forward to take charge of the prisoner.

Hugh finally turned his attention to Alice. His eyes still burned but otherwise he appeared as calm as though he had just risen from his bath. "Well, madam, you do have a way of livening up my evenings."

"And you, my lord, have a way with legends." Alice looked at the brilliant gems that lay scattered on the stone floor. "You are certainly never at a loss when it comes to adding to your own."

"Alice?"

"Oh, Hugh." She felt tears of joyous relief clog her throat. "I knew you would save me. Indeed, you always do, my lord."

She ran to him. He crushed her close against his chest. The folds of his great black cloak swirled around her.

A long time later, Alice sat with Hugh in front of the hall fire and tried to get warm. She could not seem to ward off the cold. Whenever she thought of the hours spent in the cavern, a chill went through her. Mayhap she should take a dose of the medicine she had sent to Erasmus of Thornewood, she thought.

She pestered Hugh with yet another question. It was one of a multitude she had asked since their return to the keep two hours earlier.

"When did you discover that the Stones of Scarcliffe were inside the green crystal?" she asked.

"When it shattered against the wall of the cave." Hugh stretched out his legs and contemplated the flames with a brooding gaze.

Startled, Alice glanced at his hard profile. "You mean you did not suspect before that the crystal was merely a casket designed to hold the gems?"

"Nay. I have never particularly cared about the Stones of Scarcliffe, so I never took a close look at the green crystal. So long as I had it in my possession, I was content."

"I see." Alice fell silent again for a moment. "I think there is something wrong with me, Hugh."

He looked at her in sharp concern. "What's this? Are you ill?"

"Nay, at least not with a fever. But I cannot seem to calm myself. My nerves are unsettled."

"Ah. I see. 'Tis the natural aftermath of a violent event, my sweet. The feeling will fade with time." He put his arm around her shoulders and pulled her close.

"You do not appear to be affected by it," she muttered as she snuggled into his warmth.

"Rest assured, my nerves were badly unsettled when I learned that you had been kidnapped. 'Twas all I could do not to take to my bed in a swoon."

"Hah. I do not believe that you ever suffer from unsettled nerves, sir."

"Every man suffers from unsettled nerves at one time or another, Alice," he said with startling seriousness.

She was not certain what to say to that, so she changed the subject. "Thank you for not killing Eduard in front of Katherine tonight. She does not care for him, but he is her cousin, after all."

" 'Tis not seemly to execute a man in front of women, especially healers, if it can be avoided. In any event, there are some questions I want answered."

"Katherine answered one for me while we whiled away the hours waiting for you to make your grand appearance."

"Which question was that?"

"I wondered who had actually placed the poison in your cup. Katherine said Eduard told her how it was done. He sent one of his men into the bailey disguised as a farmer the day all the villagers showed up to assist with repairs to the keep."

Hugh studied the flames. "That was the same day that Vincent of Rivenhall came to dine. There was much confusion in the household that afternoon. It would have been a simple matter for someone to sneak into the kitchens."

"And equally simple to identify your cup after the midday meal. 'Tis the most grand of all the drinking vessels in this household."

"Aye."

"Hugh?"

"Hmm?"

"What questions do you intend to ask Eduard?"

Hugh stared into the flames. "I'm not yet certain. I'll think of some."

But Alice understood. Hugh wanted to know exactly what

had happened that night some thirty years ago when Eduard had poisoned another cup of wine.

Hugh wanted to hear Eduard tell him with his own lips that Sir Matthew had intended to wed Margaret and claim his infant son.

Chapter 21

*H*ugh's soft black boots made no sound as he strode swiftly along the shadowed stone corridor but his ebony cloak snapped in the air. He was furious. "Damn it to the pit. Are you certain he is dead?"

"Aye, m'lord." Dunstan angled his torch as he turned a corner in the passageway. "One of the guards found him so a short while ago."

"Why was he not searched?" Hugh followed Dunstan around the bend in the corridor.

The underground passages of Scarcliffe Keep were not very different from the tunnels and caverns of the hillside caves. They were dark, cramped, and forbidding. No natural light reached this section of the keep where spices, grains, goods, and the occasional prisoner were stored.

"He was searched," Dunstan said. "But the guards looked for blades and other such weapons." He came to a halt in front of a dank chamber sealed with an iron grate.

Hugh looked at the contorted body of Eduard of Lockton,

which lay sprawled on the floor of the chamber. Frustration rose like bile within him. There had been so many questions he had intended to put to Eduard, so much he had wanted to say to this man who had murdered his parents.

Most of all there had been the prospect of savoring both justice and revenge. Hugh had anticipated the satisfaction of those rich spices for so long that it took him some time to accept that they had been yanked from his grasp.

"No one found the poison he had secreted on his person, I see," Hugh muttered.

"Nay, m'lord. Mayhap 'tis just as well." Dunstan looked at Hugh. " 'Tis truly over now."

*H*ugh climbed the stone steps that led upward out of the bowels of the keep. He did not pause to think about where he was headed. He crossed the great hall, where preparations for the midday meal were underway. When he reached the tower stairs, he went up two more long flights of stone steps.

He reached the upper level of the tower, turned, and went down the corridor to Alice's study chamber. He opened the door without bothering to knock.

Alice looked up in surprise when he entered the chamber. She frowned in concern when she saw the expression on his face. "My lord." She closed the book that had been open on the desk. "What is it?"

"Eduard of Lockton took poison sometime during the night. He is dead."

Alice got up from her stool and came out from behind her desk. Without a word she went to Hugh and wrapped her arms around him. She leaned her head against his shoulder and said nothing.

Alice always comprehended him so well, Hugh thought. He did not have to put things into words for her.

He held her very tightly for a long time. After a while the bleak frustration that had seized him when he had learned that Eduard had escaped into death began to retreat.

A few more minutes passed in silence. Alice felt very soft and warm and good in his arms.

Eventually a sense of quiet peace stole over Hugh. The door to the past through which the cold storm winds had so often blown had finally been closed.

One month later on a crisp, fall morning, the watch-tower guard cupped a hand around his mouth and shouted his news down into the busy bailey.

"Riders approach, m'lord. A knight and five men-at-arms. Also servants and a baggage wagon."

Hugh silenced the clamor of weapons practice with a swift signal. He looked up at the guard. "What colors does the knight carry?"

"Green and yellow, m'lord."

Hugh glanced at Dunstan. "Those are the colors of Erasmus of Thornewood."

"Aye." Dunstan frowned. " 'Twill likely be one of his men come to inform us of his lord's death."

Sadness washed through Hugh. He had been expecting the news; nevertheless, it still came as an unwelcome surprise. He knew then that he had dared to hope that Alice's recipe would help Erasmus.

Hugh shaded his eyes against the morning sun and looked up at the guard again. "Are you certain of the knight's colors?"

"Aye, m'lord." The guard studied the road. "A very rich lord, from the looks of his party. And well armed. There is a lady with them."

"A lady?" Hugh wondered if Erasmus's widow, Eleanor, had come in person to bring the news of her lord's death. He motioned to Benedict. "Fetch Alice. Quickly. Tell her we will have several guests, including a lady, for the midday meal."

"Aye, my lord." Benedict handed to Dunstan the bow with which he had been practicing, grabbed his staff, and hurried toward the hall steps.

A few minutes later the party of riders halted in front of the gates of Scarcliffe Keep and politely requested permission to enter. The guard waved them into the bailey.

Alice appeared in the doorway of the keep. She glanced inquiringly at Hugh.

"Who comes, my lord?"

"Someone who no doubt brings word of the death of my liege lord," Hugh said quietly.

"What makes you think he has died?" She scowled at him. "Did you forget to give him that recipe for a soothing potion that I sent with you to London?"

"Nay."

"You did tell his wife to make certain the doctors did not continue to bleed him, did you not?"

"Aye, Alice, I gave her your instructions, but everyone, including Erasmus, felt that the end was near. A man can often feel his own impending death."

"Ridiculous. From what you told me, he suffered only from extreme excitement of the nerves."

The visitors rode through the gate before Alice could continue her lecture. Hugh looked at the knight who led the small company. He stared first in disbelief and then in growing wonder at the familiar face.

"My lord," Hugh whispered.

"Well?" Alice asked impatiently. "Who is he?"

"Erasmus of Thornewood."

"Eyes of the Saints," Alice muttered. "I was afraid of this. Julian arrived only this morning. Why did he not bring us word that Sir Erasmus intended a visit? What good is a messenger who does not bring important messages?"

Hugh started to grin. "Do not be too hard on Julian. He has his uses." He went forward to greet his liege lord.

Erasmus brought his muscled stallion to a halt in the center of the bailey. Sunlight sparkled on rich robes and polished steel.

"Welcome, my lord." Hugh reached out to catch hold of the horse's bridle. "From the look of you, I would wager that you are no longer amusing yourself with arrangements for your own funeral."

"I have discovered that funerals are not nearly so entertaining as christenings." Erasmus smiled at Eleanor, who had halted her palfrey beside him. "And I am pleased to tell you that we intend to plan one or two new ones for the future."

Eleanor's face glowed with happiness as she looked down at Hugh. "I have come to thank your lady wife for making it possible."

"Alice will be delighted to know that her potion worked so well." Hugh could not seem to stop grinning. "As am I. I have always said that my liege lord has a talent for rearing children. Allow me to introduce you to my lady wife."

Alice came down the steps with a welcoming smile. "I am pleased to see that someone followed my instructions."

*L*ater that evening when Erasmus looked up from the chessboard, his perceptive gray eyes were alight with appreciation. "Your move, I believe, madam."

"Aye."

"Hugh was correct. You are a very clever opponent."

"Thank you, my lord." Alice picked up a heavy black onyx bishop. She frowned intently as she concentrated on shifting it into position on the large board. "I enjoy the game."

"That much is obvious. I believe I may actually be in danger of losing this skirmish."

"Do not take offense, sir. My lord husband is the only

person who can win against me. He has a great talent for stratagems."

"I am well aware of that."

Eleanor's laughter made Erasmus turn his head. He smiled at the sight of his wife seated next to Hugh. The two were sharing a bowl of honeyed figs as they conversed together in front of the hearth. Nearby, Julian strummed a tune on a harp.

"Your move, my lord," Alice prompted.

"Aye." Erasmus brought his attention back to the board. He touched a rook and then hesitated. "I congratulate you, madam. Not many women could have quieted the storms that seethed within my friend Hugh."

"Me?" Alice looked up, astonished. She glanced at Hugh. He met her eyes and smiled before he turned back to his conversation with Eleanor.

"You have brought him contentment," Erasmus said. "It could not have been an easy or a simple task."

"Sir Hugh enjoys being lord of his own manor," Alice said. "I have often observed that a person is most content when he finds pleasure in his work. My husband is very good at managing these lands. But then, you, of all people, are well aware of his skill in business matters."

"Hugh's intelligence was evident from the first day he came to live in my household."

"It was good of you to educate him well and to allow him the opportunity to develop his spice business." Alice gave Erasmus a direct look. "Many lords in your position would have taken advantage of his natural talent for knightly skills and ignored his keen wits."

" 'Tis just as well that I did not ignore those wits," Erasmus said dryly. "I have needed both Hugh's clever stratagems and his skill with a sword many times over the years."

"You have rewarded him well."

"I did not give him Scarcliffe because of his intelligence or his knightly skills," Erasmus said. "I gave him these lands because he gave me something infinitely more valuable. Something I could not purchase at any price."

"What was that, sir?"

"His unswerving loyalty."

Alice smiled. "I understand."

"There have been many times when I have wished that I could give Hugh a gift as fine as the one he gave me."

"Rest assured, he is satisfied with his own manor."

"I do not believe that it is the lands of Scarcliffe alone that have brought him satisfaction, madam." Erasmus regarded her with shrewd consideration. "You are the true healer in this matter."

Alice was acutely embarrassed. "I doubt that, sir."

"He told me much about you when he came to see me in London. He said that you had great courage and daring. He claimed you approached him with a bold bargain."

"Aye." Alice contemplated her next move with knitted brows. "We have forged an excellent partnership."

" 'Tis more than a business arrangement, surely."

Alice blushed. "Well, as to that, we are married, after all, my lord."

"And you love him with all your heart, do you not?"

Alice clutched one of the chess pieces very tightly. "How do you know such things, sir?"

"I myself am not without some wits. When one spends as many weeks as I did believing that one is on the brink of death, one becomes more aware of certain things. More perceptive, shall we say?"

"Only a very intelligent man becomes more aware and more perceptive under such circumstances." Alice sighed. "You are quite right, as it happens. I am very fond of my husband. Even though he can be amazingly stubborn at times."

"Aye, well, he is a man. Some things are immutable. Speaking of my recent brush with death, madam, I wish to thank you for your potion."

"No thanks are necessary. 'Twas my mother's recipe. She bequeathed to me a book in which she wrote descriptions of many types of illnesses. I merely applied the remedy she prescribed for your particular symptoms. I am pleased that you tried it and found it effective."

"Most effective." Erasmus smiled. "You have my deepest gratitude. I owe you more than I can ever repay, madam."

"Nonsense, my lord. I assure you, the scales are evenly balanced."

"How is that?"

"You saved my husband's life when he was but a young boy of eight."

Erasmus furrowed his brow. "I do not recall that Hugh was ever in danger of dying at the age of eight. He did take one or two nasty falls while practicing at the quintain and there was an unfortunate incident involving a bridge and a rather deep stream one day, but other than that he was quite healthy."

"Now that is where you are wrong, sir." Alice smiled gently. "He may have been in fine health as regards his bodily humors, but there are things that can die within a boy even though he continues to live."

"Ah. I see what you mean." Erasmus regarded her with knowing eyes. "You are alarmingly perceptive yourself, madam."

"Nay, my lord, I merely make an observation," Alice said matter-of-factly. "It is clear to me that had it not been for you, Hugh would most assuredly have been torn asunder by the storms that threatened his heart and his soul."

"I may have taught him how to contain and control those dark winds, Lady Alice. But you accomplished far more. You have stilled them with the alchemy of a loving heart."

.   .   .

*H*ugh strode into Alice's study chamber one morning a few weeks after Erasmus and Eleanor had departed. He had ordered a new list of compliments from Julian. He was eager to try them out.

But at the sight of Alice standing at the window, he came to a halt, briefly transfixed. The graceful words he had so carefully memorized a short while earlier were momentarily forgotten. He wondered if he would ever grow accustomed to the realization that Alice was his wife.

Her lively features were composed in an expression of intense concentration as she studied the chunk of rock crystal in her hand. Her hair glowed in the morning sun. The gentle lines of her body aroused a familiar, aching need within Hugh.

She did not turn to greet him. He realized she had not heard him come into the chamber.

Hugh cleared his throat and searched his mind for the first compliment on his list. "Madam, the glorious fire in your hair burns so brightly that I need naught else but your silken tresses to warm my hands on the coldest morn."

"Thank you, my lord." Alice did not look at him. She tilted the stone she held so that it caught more light.

Hugh frowned. Mayhap he had paid too many compliments to her hair, he thought. She was likely bored with them. He made a note to instruct Julian to be more creative.

"Your neck is as graceful as that of a swan."

"Thank you, sir." Alice pursed her lips and studied the crystal more closely.

Hugh tapped the sheet of rolled parchment against his thigh. Julian's compliments were not having their usual effect. "Your skin is as soft as the feathers of a dove dipped in cream."

"How kind of you to notice." Alice put the rock crystal down on the table. She picked up a large, gray stone and bent over it intently.

Hugh surreptitiously unrolled the parchment in his hand

and quickly scanned the list of compliments. "It strikes me that your feet are as small and delicate as the unfurled fronds of small frogs."

Alice hesitated. "Frogs, my lord?"

Hugh scowled at the phrase. Damn Julian and his poor script. "Uh, ferns. As small and delicate as the unfurled fronds of small ferns." He hastily rerolled the parchment. That last had not been the easiest phrase to utter.

"Aye, of course. Ferns. Pray continue, my lord."

"Uh, well, that is about all that occurs to me at the moment." What was wrong with Alice today? She was not responding in her usual manner. Hugh wondered if Julian's skills were deteriorating.

"What of my eyes, sir? Do you think they are as green as emeralds or are they more in the nature of malachite?"

Hugh shifted restlessly. What if it was not Julian's skills that were slipping, but his own? What if he was not repeating the compliments in the proper fashion? "Emeralds, I believe. Although malachite is a very nice shade of green also."

"Thank you. Now, then, what of my breasts?"

Hugh swallowed. "Your breasts?" He generally saved that sort of compliment for the bedchamber.

"Would you say that they are still as delicately curved as ripe peaches?"

"Most assuredly."

"And what of my waist?"

Hugh narrowed his eyes. "Your waist?"

"Aye." Alice put aside the gray stone and picked up a darker one. She still kept her face averted. "Would you say that my waist is as dainty as the stem of a flower?"

There had been something about flower stems and small waists on Julian's last list. Hugh was about to repeat the old compliment when it struck him that Alice was a bit more rounded in some places today than she had been a few weeks ago.

He very much liked her this way, he decided, but he was not certain that she would be pleased to hear that she was a bit more plump.

"I, uh, had not given the matter of your waist much thought," he said cautiously. "But now that you mention it—" He broke off to study her form more closely.

It was not his imagination, he concluded. Silhouetted against the sunlight, Alice was not quite as slender as she had been when he took her from her uncle's hall. He remembered the pleasant shape of her beneath his hands last night and sighed.

"Well, my lord?"

"In truth, madam, I would not say that your waist is as narrow as the stem of a flower, but I find the new shape very appealing. Indeed, you look quite healthy and fit with a bit more meat on your bones." He paused, appalled, when he saw that her shoulders were trembling. "Alice, you must not cry. Your waist is exactly the width of a flower stem. I vow, I will challenge anyone who claims otherwise to a battle to the death."

"Very gallant of you, my lord." She swung around to face him. Her eyes were aglow with laughter, not tears. "But I much prefer you to be absolutely honest in such matters."

"Alice?"

"You're quite right. My waist is no longer as small as the stem of a flower. And, to be truthful, my breasts are a bit larger than summer peaches these days. And for a very sound reason. I am with child, my lord."

For an instant Hugh could not move. She was pregnant. With his babe.

"*Alice.*" Joy surged through him with the force of bright sunlight after a storm.

Hugh freed himself from the fragile spell that Alice's simple words had placed upon him. He swooped down on her and scooped her carefully, gently off her feet.

She put her arms around his neck. "Do you know, my lord, I never placed much credence in legends until I met you."

Hugh looked into her eyes and caught a glimpse of their future together. It was filled with the promise of love and happiness. "We are even, then. I never believed in the alchemy of love until I met you."

Alice's smile was glorious. "Love, sir?"

"Aye." Hugh grinned, happier than he had ever been in his life. "Love."

Chapter 22

On a warm day in late fall, Hugh took his infant son up onto the walls of Scarcliffe Keep and showed him the lands that would one day be his.

Hugh cradled the babe in one arm and gazed out at his prosperous fief with a sense of deep pleasure. The harvest had been good. The wool was of excellent quality this year. And there was always the income from his spice business.

"There is much for you to learn," he said to the babe, "but your mother and I shall be here to teach you everything you need to know."

Little Erasmus drooled happily and gripped his father's large thumb.

"Do you see those lands over there to the east? They belong to Rivenhall. Sir Vincent's son is learning to manage them. Young Reginald is your blood kin. Never forget that."

"Your father is correct, Erasmus." Alice emerged from the top of the watchtower steps. "Family is very important."

Hugh frowned at her. "Are you certain that you should be out here?"

"I am quite fit, as you can see. Indeed, I have been nicely recovered from childbed for several weeks. You are overconcerned, my lord."

She did appear healthy, even radiant, Hugh decided. The birth of his son had driven him close to madness, but Alice had gone through it with the aplomb of a skilled warrior going into a joust.

"Have you told Erasmus about the Stones of Scarcliffe?" Alice smiled down at her son.

"Not yet. There are more important matters he must learn first," Hugh said.

The infant gazed up at him with boundless interest. Hugh was convinced that he could already detect a keen intelligence in his son's eyes.

"Well, then," Alice continued, "have you told him about the legend of Hugh the Relentless?"

Hugh groaned. "Nay. That is a very dull subject. I would sooner instruct him on the spice trade."

Alice laughed. "Very well, sir, I shall make a bargain with you. You shall instruct him on matters of business. I shall teach him what he needs to know of family legends. Agreed?"

Hugh looked into her loving eyes. He thought back to that dark night in her uncle's hall when Alice had offered him the bargain that had bound them together for a lifetime.

"You know that there is no one with whom I would rather strike a bargain than you, my love," he said.